'ALL IT TAKES IS ONE BOMB TO CHANGE THE COURSE OF HISTORY'

SAVING PICASSO

Mark Skeet

Matador
9 Priory Business Park,
Wistow Road, Kibworth Beauchamp,
Leicestershire. LE8 0RX
Tel: (+44) 116 279 2299
Fax: (+44) 116 279 2277
Email: books@troubador.co.uk
Web: www.troubador.co.uk/matador

ISBN 978 1780881 966

British Library Cataloguing in Publication Data.
A catalogue record for this book is available from the British Library.

Typeset in 10.5pt ITC Giovanni Std Book by Troubador Publishing Ltd, Leicester, UK

Matador is an imprint of Troubador Publishing Ltd

Printed and bound in Great Britain by Clays Ltd, St Ives plc.

For
Sophy, Ava, Lara and Romy

BARCELONA, 1940

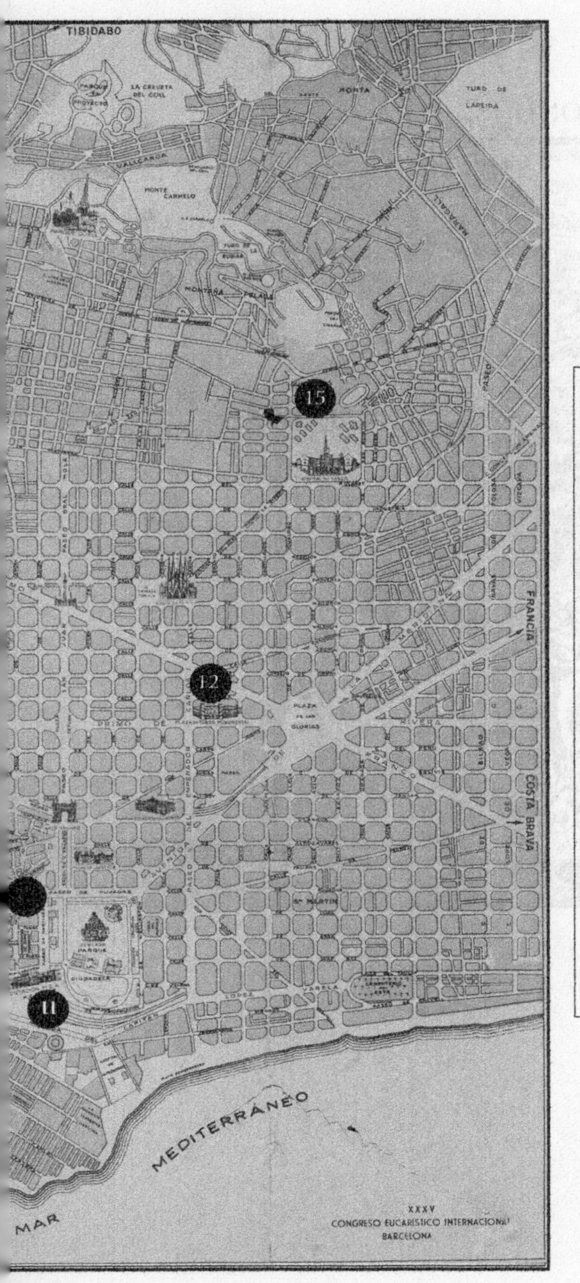

1 – Olympic Stadium
2 – Hotel Oriente
3 – Colom
4 – Hotel Comercio
5 – Tennis Club
6 – Montse's flat
7 – Jordan's office
8 – SIM torture cells
9 – Passport Office
10 – Carrer Fusina
11 – França Station
12 – Bullring
13 – Football stadium
14 – Miramar
15 – Hospital Sant Pau
16 – Montjuic Cemetery

POBLE OLIMPIC, MONTJUIC

1 – Olympic Stadium
2 – Casa de Prensa
3 – Palau Nacional
4 – Palau esport
5 – Velodrome
6 – Sal esport
7 – Administration
8 – Broadcasting
9 – Plaça España
10 – Font del Gat
11 – Poble Espanyol

* * * * *

On 6th July 1940, Adolf Hitler called off his threatened boycott of the Barcelona Olympic Games. Hours later, Benito Mussolini issued a communiqué confirming that Italy too would now be sending a team to Spain.

In Washington, President Roosevelt welcomed the news as evidence of a first thawing in relations between Nazi Germany and Soviet Russia since the end of the Spanish Civil War. Across Europe, Hitler's climb down was greeted with widespread relief. For the time being at least, the continent had stepped back from the brink of a second world war.

* * * * *

* * * * *

On 13 July 1940, Adolf Hitler called off his threatened boycott of the Barcelona Olympic Games. Hours later, Benito Mussolini issued a communiqué confirming that Italy too would now be sending a team to Spain.

In Washington, President Roosevelt welcomed the news as evidence of a first thawing of relations between Nazi Germany and Soviet Russia since the end of the Spanish Civil War. Across Europe, Hitler's climb-down was greeted with widespread relief. For the time being at least, the continent had stepped back from the brink of a second world war.

* * * * *

CHAPTER 1

Wednesday 24th July, 1940

A thin veil of black cloud hung low over the Pyrenees, like a cape abandoned by the Gods after a night of revelry. Slowly, as if infected by the lethargy of the morning, the Paris Express passed through the long tunnel linking Cerbère to Portbou, somewhere in the dark crossing over the line that divided France from Spain.

The train ground to a halt, the shadow of the hillside behind cutting a sharp pattern across the platform. Looking out of the carriage – at the militiaman sucking the last from his cigarette, an old woman hawking slices of watermelon, a man in a tatty brown suit wiping his shoes on a loose sheet of newspaper – Richard Clare could see that little had changed since he'd first passed through this frontier station, except of course the face staring back at him from the reflection in the window. A face that four years ago had belonged to a naïve twenty-one year old heading for the Spanish Civil War. And now? It seemed to him more like a mask. His sharp blue eyes, uncombed hair, and casual air giving little hint of the tensions churning his stomach.

Clare turned away from the window. To the five other men in the compartment, he was the special correspondent for *The London Evening News* on his way to Barcelona to cover the Olympic Games. Peter Wilson from *The Mirror*, Trevor Wignall of *The Express*, David Selwyn *The Times*, Peter Stewart *The Herald*, and Henry Forsyth *The Daily Mail* – all in their twenties and already old hands on the sports desk, friendly enough but what they really made of him, Clare couldn't quite tell. They were journalists and he wasn't, not really, the few articles he'd written for the paper hardly warranted such a prestigious assignment. The truth was he'd persuaded the editor to give him the job, shamelessly trading on his celebrity, the splash created by his memoirs of the war.

'I know the place. I speak the language. I can get you interviews,' he'd told the old man, then somewhat stretching the truth, 'I can get you Picasso.' Picasso was big news. The world's most famous artist and too tempting a prospect for the editor to ignore.

'Okay.' The old man had agreed to give it a shot. 'Rundell stays. You go.' Guy Rundell was the paper's chief sports correspondent and a veteran of the last two Olympics. Clare liked the man and was sorry to have taken his "ticket". He wished he could have been honest with him from the start – about Montse and why he had to get back to Spain – but in the end he'd just left it to the editor to say, 'I'm sorry, Guy. It's in the paper's best interests.'

'Everybody out!' The train spewed forth its passengers – most of them journalists, already the odd muttering as to how much more efficient it had been last time round, how at least in Berlin they hadn't had to contend with this heat. *'Sandia! Sandia! Hay Sandia!'* The old woman had a ready answer in her mound of watermelon. On the wall, awkwardly plastered over an old advertisement for El Niño condensed milk, a large poster by Picasso leapt out in greeting; vibrant and colourful. A contorted dove rising up out of the city, the legend bold against the sky – XIIth Olympiad. Barcelona, 1940.

'You speak Spanish. What the hell's he saying?' Wignall, who only two minutes earlier had declared Spain about as appealing as a rainy afternoon in Wigan, pointed Clare towards a young man in a loose fitting uniform, officiously herding them towards the main terminal.

Clare translated. 'He says we've got to get our passports checked.' Since the end of the Civil War, entry into Spain had been restricted to a smattering of journalists and diplomats. The sudden influx of visitors had clearly put the border guards on edge.

'Well, it wouldn't hurt for him to show some manners,' Wignall huffed.

Another day Clare might have laughed. The red star on the man's epaulettes marked him as an officer of the Servicio de Investigacion Militar, better known as the SIM. A secret police force set up by Orlov during the war, modelled on the Russian NKVD and just as ruthless.

Inside the terminal, there were three queues. At the head of each, more SIM. Plain clothes. Discreetly alert. There only if you knew how to spot them. Nothing to worry about Clare told himself, but still they left him with an uneasy feeling. A sharp reminder of why he'd been forced to stay away from Spain these last two years.

A tannoy informed that the onward train to Barcelona was running forty minutes late. While the conversation disintegrated into predictable Fleet Street banter, names and references that meant nothing to him, Clare found refuge in a two day old copy of *The Times*. The headlines bleak and depressing. Further violence in Paris – Communist and Fascist gangs fighting pitched battles in the streets around Montmartre. The unrest now spreading to Britain – two dead, eighty-seven injured in a clash between Mosley's blackshirts and striking dock workers; politicians in both countries beginning to suspect that the violence was being subtly orchestrated from Berlin and Moscow; the Prime Minister, Neville Chamberlain, arguing that the Barcelona Games represented Europe's best chance of reversing the slide towards a conflict more widespread and devastating than the Great War of 1914-18.

It took another hour to have their visas checked – valid for twenty-one days and restricted to a thirty mile zone around Barcelona – and another hour after that to reboard the train.

An endless series of petty delays. Clare leaned back against the hard wooden seat and closed his eyes, if only to avoid having to speak to the others. He knew it wouldn't be long, now that they were across the border. The questions about the war. Clare, you were here then – what was it like? He could see it in their eyes; the unspoken fascination. He had been under fire, they hadn't, and they wanted to know what it was like. What it was really like – the stuff he hadn't put in his book, the stuff that even his friends didn't know about, the stuff he'd only ever told Montse.

By the time they reached Figueres, Clare was asleep, dead to the spots of sunlight dancing on his eyelids, the sticky warmth of the morning and the countryside flashing past, so that it wasn't until the bridge over the River Besòs loomed into sight and Wilson gave him a sharp nudge in the ribs – 'Wake up, man. We're here' – that he was alert to the fact they'd finally arrived, the train limping into França with a last wheezing cough of steam.

The authorities had done their best to impress on the visitor a picture of pre-war normality. The platforms had been cleaned of years of accumulated pigeon shit, the broken panes of glass replaced in the vast steel roof, and the revolutionary slogans that had once adorned the walls all painted over. Below the station clock, a bullet riddled red and yellow banner hung in silent tribute to the Republican war dead. A reminder of the cost of victory over Franco and his allies. But of those other victims who'd survived the war, the limbless veterans who'd once thronged the concourse with their hard luck stories and their begging bowls, Clare could see no trace, supposing only that they must have been moved on into the suburbs or some out of town camp; an embarrassment now that the eyes of the world were again upon Spain.

Outside the station, the queue for a taxi stretched half way round the block. Clare elected to walk, Wilson, always up for an adventure, choosing to come with him. 'We'll catch you up in the bar,' Wignall called after them.

The route from the station took them along Passeig de Colom, a wide palm lined avenue that separated the city from the docks. On the seaward side, workers were loading a goods train from a large brick warehouse. Opposite, behind the imposing waterfront façade, lay a maze of narrow sunless streets and crumbling alleyways – the Barri Gotic. Crossing the road close to where he and Montse had once shared a flat, Clare could see that here too nothing had changed. The one-eyed shoe shine boy still working his patch. The frail Cuban with his walking stick and waxed moustache clasping a length of lottery tickets. A ginger cat licking its paws in the shadow of a newspaper kiosk.

The lobby of the Hotel Oriente was as busy as Clare had ever seen it; the marble floor a jumble of suitcases, weary travellers crouched in whatever space they could find, filling in registration cards, a phone ringing unanswered on the main desk. Clare took a form, filled it in, then went upstairs to find his room, declining Wilson's offer of lunch. 'There's a few things I have to do,' he said. *Someone I have to see*, he might have added. Was Montse still living in Barcelona? Was she with another man? Was she even alive? Two years of silence had played havoc with his imagination.

Clare found his room on the second floor of the hotel, complete with private bathroom, small balcony and a view over the Ramblas. He opened the windows to encourage a through flow of air, dug out a clean change of clothes, shaved, and then took a shower. A quarter of an hour later, he was in a taxi heading up to Montjuic, the large rock in whose shadow the city had been built.

'Your first time in Barcelona?' the taxi driver enquired in a thick Andalucian accent.

Clare shook his head. 'No. I was here during the war.'

'A brigadista?'

'Yes.'

'Then I don't charge you.' The taxi driver leaned over and shook him by the hand. 'You are my guest.' Clare tried to insist, but the driver – 'My name is Roberto' – was having none of it. 'It's I who owe you, compadre,' he said, raising his fist in salute, and not for the first time Clare felt himself strangely moved by the warmth and gratitude of a complete stranger. Campesinos. Factory workers. The man in the street. Always it was those who could least afford it, their humanity forged in the heat of battle, the blast of exploding bombs, and the memory of fallen friends.

The decision to locate the Olympics in Barcelona had been taken only at the last minute (originally they were to have been held in Tokyo but all invitations had been withdrawn after the outbreak of the Sino-Japanese War). There'd been the usual objections from the political right but in the end the IOC had had no real choice. Barcelona had the infrastructure in place. They had a plan – based on their bid to host the '36 Games, and most importantly they had Stalin's backing. After Berlin, he argued, it was the turn of the left; Russia's chance to impress on the world that they had nothing to fear from the Communist backed victory of the Spanish Republic.

The taxi dropped Clare off at the Olympic Press Office – the Casa de Prensa – like the rest of the Poble Olimpic purpose built for the 1929 Exhibition. The building was arranged over three floors, cool and elegant, the intricate brickwork patterned with tiles. Clare took the main staircase up to a room on the second floor where he'd been instructed to pick up his accreditation. '*Buenas dias* – welcome to Barcelona,' a pretty girl of about twenty – bright lipstick, curled hair and an over-compensation of make-up to offset the poor condition of her skin – greeted him with a bright smile, ticked his name off on a list, and handed him a press card, a programme of venues and events, and an information pack telling him all he needed to know about how to get an international line, where to pick up messages, order photographs, catch a bus to the Olympic Stadium …

'And if I want an interview with Picasso?' Clare asked, curious to see how difficult it was going to be to secure the old man his promised exclusive.

'For this you must speak to the Ministry of Information,' she said; a polite brush off that told Clare all he needed to know.

Coffee. Lunch. A short stroll around the stadium – Clare ate up a few hours then took a funicular ride back into town. Like a dog returning home, he followed his nose through the old city, visually marking his territory, making the ancient crumbling streets his own again, a patchwork of cane blinds drawn down over the doorways, windows and balconies; from within, the acrid smell of frying, and the round, staring eyes of young children.

In Carrer Avinyó, a strong smoke billowed from a brazier roasting horse chestnuts. A lively crowd thronged the pavement, men and women returning home from work, children spinning a rusted hoop over the cobbles, an old man bending to feed a scrap of food to a young dog lying under his chair. Clare stopped outside a scuffed brown door and knocked twice – for the second floor – then stepped back into the street. The windows were closed. The shutters drawn. No sign of life. He knocked again – more for form's sake than with any hope – then crossed the street to a small hole in the wall where he knew Montse liked to buy her fruit. The old woman and her twin sister who ran the stall were busy sorting through a box of mushrooms, cleaning the dirt from the stalks. 'Excuse me Señora, I'm looking for Montserrat Rafols,' Clare interrupted them. 'Do you know if she still lives here?' He pointed across the road to Montse's flat.

The two women regarded him suspiciously. 'Why do you want to know?'

'I'm a friend. I knew her during the war.'

'You're the Englishman?' Now they remembered.

'Yes.'

'We haven't seen her for a while.'

'But she still lives here?'

'Yes …'

'Carmen.' The more reticent of the two women shot her sister a sharp glance. 'The kettle.'

Clare tried them with a few more questions: When had they last seen Montse? Where did she work? What time did she get back home? But each time he hit a brick wall. He looked around for a familiar face, someone who might be able to help. The girl from the bakery. The mother of a young child whom Montse had once worked with. But here too, he encountered only a hurried shake of the head and a quickening of feet.

The man with the dog caught Clare's eye. 'You want to know why they're so scared?' he said, dropping his voice to a level where Clare could only just hear him. 'They arrested a man this morning, that's why they don't want to talk to you.'

What man? Why? Clare couldn't quite see the relevance. Either to himself or Montse. The old man gave a shrug. To the first question, he had no answer, and to the second only a warning. The man had been seen talking to a foreigner. These days, he explained, that was enough. Always the Party will assume the worst.

'You want my advice,' he said. 'Do your friend a favour – go home. You'll only bring her trouble.'

In the bar Cervantes, a radio was playing. A tune by Maria Yanez – *La Vaselina.* A one time favourite that called to mind a weekend spent with Montse in the Serra de Montseny, going to bed after a lunch of duck and pears, waking up naked in each other's arms, shivering, looking out of the window to see that it had started snowing, Montse pulling a sweater over her breasts, switching on the radio, Maria Yanez's teasing voice clear above the crackle '... *en la braza de mi amor*' against a riff that had them both singing 'Here comes the bride', falling back onto the bed, laughing, kissing, '... *mi amor bravo.*'

The bar was packed, the battered ceiling fan working overtime, its uneven labours feebly stirring the close summer stench of male sweat and tobacco. Clare stood for a while by the doorway, one eye on Montse's flat. A couple of hours passed, darkness fell, and the men in the bar returned home to their families and the promise of an evening meal. Clare drained his beer, threw a last look towards Montse's closed window, then set off back to his hotel, certain of only one thing.

Wherever else Montse might be spending the night – it wasn't in her own bed.

CHAPTER 2

Thursday 25th July, 1940

24th February 1938. The day Richard Clare's life changed forever. Not the day he first met Montse – that had already happened. Nor the day he first met Picasso – that was still to come. But the day that marked the beginning of the end of the war.

Clare could still recall the moment as if it were yesterday, sitting in bar Canaletes listening to the radio, a live broadcast from the Reichstag, the German Chancellor, Adolf Hitler, promising to pull his troops out of Spain so long as Stalin also agreed to withdraw the International Brigade.

The whole of Barcelona had poured out onto the streets in celebration. The war was now as good as won. Without Axis help the Fascists were doomed; Hitler's demand that the International Brigade leave too felt like nothing more than an attempt to save face. Across the city, men fired rifles into the air, women stood at their windows with lighted candles, music blared from every bar and street corner, yet Clare had felt only a deep gloom, just months after meeting Montse, after falling hopelessly in love with her, he was going to be forcibly repatriated.

Then miraculously, three days before he was due to pull out, Montse told him she'd found a way for him to stay; they'd been sitting on the roof of her parents' hotel by the dovecote that had been empty of birds since her grandfather died. 'I have a friend – Esteban Llull,' she told him. 'He works for the Ministry of Culture.'

The following day, Clare had taken Llull out to lunch and by the evening it was all arranged, Clare was to join the Ministry as a press liaison officer, his job to accompany Picasso's *Guernica* on a tour of the country (the government had decided to bring the picture back from France in order to raise morale and publicity). To get round what became known as the Berlin Accord, it was agreed that Clare should be officially employed by the Spanish Embassy in Paris, so on 6th March 1938, he'd taken a train to Paris, met Picasso, crated up the picture, and helped bring it back to Spain.

The following four months, he and Montse (Llull had also fixed her up with a job as his assistant) had travelled the length and breadth of the front line, stopping wherever they liked, setting up the picture in whatever space they could find, much like a travelling cinema. People were hungry for entertainment and news, and *Guernica* scored on both counts, the audience absorbing the images as they might a newsreel.

La Coronada de la Serena, Anaya de Alba, Mansilla de las Mula – Clare could still recall the names of many of the towns they'd passed through, then after dark, bedding down with Montse in the back of the truck, dreaming, talking, making love, night after night, week after week, wishing the war would never end.

* * * * *

Clare woke to the sound of thunder. A torrential downpour that hit the city in the early hours of the morning. For what seemed like an eternity, he lay in bed, listening to the rain pinging against the windows, unable to sleep, until finally he managed to doze off just as his alarm clock told him it was time to get up.

Reluctantly, Clare hauled himself out of bed, showered, shaved, and went down to breakfast. The sports desk had asked him to pen an introductory piece on the Poble Olimpic but already he'd decided it would have to wait. For now, he had other, more pressing matters, on his mind.

The last time Clare had set foot in the Generalitat, the 14th century palace from which Catalunya was governed, Spain had still been at war with itself. The corridors had been bristling with militia, Communist banners decorated the walls, and people addressed one another as "comrade", all a far cry from the ordered calm that greeted him this time around. The carefully contrived air of pre-war normality. Men in suits. Ladies elegantly fashionable. No whiff of egalitarianism about the corridors, just the heady scent of perfume and cigars.

'Richard Clare – *London Evening News*,' Clare introduced himself to a silver haired man in uniform seated behind the front desk. 'I'd like to speak to Esteban Llull.'

There was an uneasy pause. 'Señor Llull is no longer with us,' the man answered him.

'What do you mean?' Clare had been hoping not only for a back door route to Picasso but also for some news on Montse. How was she? Where was she? Who was she with? Of all her friends, Llull was the most likely to know.

'Just a minute, Sir.' The man picked up a telephone and mumbled a few words down the line. Minutes later, a second man emerged from behind a closed door, younger, dressed in a suit with close cropped hair and a face that reminded Clare of the comic German actor, Viktor de Kowa. 'What is your business with Llull?' The man, whose real name was Juan Sort, demanded to know.

'I'm a friend.'

Sort looked unimpressed. 'Your papers, please.'

Clare handed over his passport. 'Do you know where I can find him?'

'No.'

'Can you at least tell me when he left?'

'No.'

'But it can't have been that long ago.'

'All I can tell you there's no longer anyone here of that name.' Sort spoke with an impatience that told Clare he would be wise to cut his losses and try elsewhere.

But something about Llull had touched a nerve. 'Could I speak to one of his colleagues?' Clare persisted. 'Someone who knew him?'

'If you wish to interview a member of staff,' Sort handed him back his passport, his jacket falling loose enough for Clare to notice the pistol tucked into his belt, 'you must submit a request in writing.'

Clare had got the message.

In the square outside, they were hanging banners in preparation for Saturday's opening ceremony. Along one side of the Generalitat, a fleet of government cars stood parked in two neat ranks, their drivers gathered around one of the vehicles, laughing and smoking. On an impulse, Clare strolled over to them and asked if anyone knew Llull, guessing perhaps that someone might have driven him at some point in the past. 'Sure – I heard of him,' a spotty twenty year old with a strong Catalan accent piped up before any of his colleagues could think to stop him. 'He was that guy they shot for being a spy.'

'I'm sorry?'

'Last Christmas …' The youth's voice trailed off as he realised he'd spoken out of turn. 'At least, I think so …' he muttered unconvincingly. 'But I don't really know … it was before my time.'

Clare didn't press the man any further. They were all staring at him now. 'Thank you,' he said, and walked on across the cobbles, his step echoed by the sharp rap of a workman's hammer.

By the side of the cathedral, there was a small open space with a stone bench. Clare took a seat amongst the pigeons and quietly digested the news of Llull's death. Personally, he'd never much liked the man. Llull had been Montse's friend. An admirer from before the war. 'My white knight' was how she'd liked to describe him, although Clare had always found Llull's unrequited feelings for her somewhat creepy. 'You're just jealous,' she'd teased him. 'You can't accept that there are still people out there prepared to act from the goodness of their heart.'

Clare kicked away a pigeon pecking at his shoe lace. Now Llull was dead. Had he been a spy? Clare somehow doubted it. More likely, he'd fallen victim to a SIM purge, his fate like so many of those executed during the war, a shallow grave on the side of the road to La Rabrasada.

Clare got to his feet and stretched his shoulders. It was time to go see Rafael Capdevila.

Outside the cathedral, they were dancing a Sardana. A large circle of men, women and children holding hands and shuffling their feet in some imperceptible yet significant manner that Clare had never quite got to grips with. Skirting a party of lost looking Egyptians who'd stopped to watch, Clare took a left turn and followed the road round to where it joined Carrer Banys Nous. Here, at the top end of the street, he found Capdevila's gallery, sandwiched between an antiquarian bookshop and a churreria. In the window, placed on an easel, there was a large portrait of a young woman dressed in black against a grey background. Inoffensive. Mildly intriguing. The type of picture, Clare imagined, that the Party would wholeheartedly approve of.

Rafael Capdevila had been Picasso's agent in Paris. A self-serving charmer with a love of well cut English suits, American cocktails and Cuban cigars. Easy to like, impossible to trust. The kind of man – Clare had always felt – that one turned to only when all other avenues were exhausted.

As it seemed they were now.

Clare pushed open the door to the gallery. A pale faced woman gazed up at him from her typewriter, her eyes dark, intense and uncompromising, a strip of sunlight catching the grey streaks in her hair. *What do you want?* she stared at him.

Despite the vase of fresh flowers on her desk, the room bore the faint smell of cheap cigarillos. 'I'm looking for Rafael Capdevila,' Clare said. 'He's a friend.'

'Have you an appointment?' The woman, whose name was Margarita Mirabel, again hit him with her eyes.

'No.'

'Then, I'm sorry. I can't help.'

'My name's Richard Clare.' He handed her a business card. 'I knew Rafael in Paris.'

'You'll still need an appointment.' Margarita unceremoniously dropped his card onto a pile of unopened mail.

'Is Rafael here?' Clare pressed her.

'No.'

'When will he be back?'

'I don't know.'

'Today?'

'I don't know.'

'Then will you please give him this?' Clare took out a pen and scrawled two quick notes. One to Picasso, and the other to Capdevila; sealing both within an envelope marked to Capdevila's attention. 'I'm staying at the Oriente,' he said. 'Tell Rafael – he can leave a message for me at the desk.'

'I'll see that he gets it.' Margarita took the envelope and placed it in the top drawer of her desk.

The hell you will. Clare had made such promises before himself. 'Thank you for your help,' he smiled, and took his leave. *Another blank drawn*.

Clare made his way back to the Ramblas and hailed a cab. It was time to stop chasing ghosts and do some work.

Outside the Café Royal, Angel Carreto started up the engine of his black Hispano-Suizo T48. As Clare's taxi pulled away from the kerb, Carreto waited for a truck to pass, then nosed into the traffic behind it. In the passenger seat, Vicenc Rife lit a cigarette, tugged his shirt free from where his sweat had caused it to become stuck to the small of his back, and roundly cursed whichever prick had come up with a duty roster that had seen them up since five in the morning. Carreto laughed. He and Rife had worked together since the early days of the war. Together, they formed the best SIM surveillance team in Barcelona. Rife's only complaint, as Carreto well knew, was that they hadn't been handed a more high profile target to shadow than the British journalist, Richard Clare.

9.35pm. Bar Cervantes. Clare sat on his own, staring up at Montse's darkened windows, thinking about what the man with the dog had told him yesterday – *Do your friend a favour. Go home. You'll only bring her trouble.* For a second night in a row, Montse had failed to show – Clare had been waiting for her since he'd finished work at six. He thought of Esteban Llull lying somewhere in a shallow grave with a bullet through his skull. Had Montse come under suspicion too? Was that why she was avoiding him? Or – he was beginning to go round in circles now – maybe she wasn't avoiding him? Maybe she was with her parents? Or out of town? Or at the home of a lover? Or maybe he was just deluding himself? Maybe the simple truth was that she didn't want to see him again, and maybe, just maybe, he didn't altogether blame her.

Across the street, Clare watched a lamp lighter touch his taper to the lamp outside Montse's window, remembering how she'd once leaned over the edge of the balcony to light her cigarette from his flame.

It was time to go home.

Gathering up his jacket, Clare gulped down his beer and made his way back outside, unaware of the black Hispano-Suizo T48 parked on the corner. The two men inside extinguishing their cigarettes.

'Hello stranger! Where have you been hiding?' As Clare returned to the Oriente, Wilson gaily hailed him from across the bar. 'Grab a pew! I'll get you a drink.'

For once, Clare was grateful for the company. It was too early to call it a night and too late to stop drinking. 'I'll have a whisky,' he said.

'Hey Clare – you might have told us before!' Forsyth, his cheeks flushed red with alcohol, playfully remonstrated.

'Told you what?'

'The women in this town. They're bloody gorgeous!'

Selwyn, who gave every appearance of having matched Forsyth drink for drink all evening, grinned. 'Thought you could keep them to yourself, did you?'

'I could spend the rest of my life here and die happy.' Forsyth moved his chair round to make room for Clare, as Hylton Cleaver, Clare's rival on *The Standard,* dryly pointed out, 'They're prostitutes. I heard someone say the top Parisian brothels have shipped in their girls for the duration.'

'Well, *vive La France!*' Forsyth raised his glass in a toast.

'*Parlez moi d'amour, redites moi des choses tendres ...*' Wilson crooned.

'*Votre beau discours, mon coeur n'est pas las de l'entendre ...*' The others took up the refrain of the popular song, Forsyth beating out the rhythm with a cocktail stick. High spirited and carefree.

Clare forced a weak smile and knocked back his whisky. '*Pourvu que toujours vous répétiez ces mots suprêmes,*' he mumbled along unconvincingly with the others. '*Je vous aime ...*'

On the far side of the room, Vicenc Rife made a last entry in his note book.

22.34 hrs – Subject returned to hotel.

CHAPTER 3

Friday 26th July, 1940

A sharp blade of sunlight cut into the room. Outside the window, a tannoy blasted music across the Ramblas exciting the sparrows from the trees; a trumpet fanfare presaging the announcement of yet another public message.

Clare woke with a start, head pounding, throat so parched he felt sure he was going to be sick. He reached out a hand and poured himself a glass of water, then peered at his watch. Ten o'clock. *Blank.* Then he remembered. A few too many whiskies with Wilson and the others in the hotel bar. Before that, a fistful of beers in the bar Cervantes alone.

Clare tumbled out of bed and into the bathroom, drank another glass of water, then remembered what he was supposed to be doing that morning. Ten minutes later, he was ready to leave. He felt terrible but a glance in the mirror told him he'd pass muster. He gathered up his notebook and pen. The press conference was due to start in fifteen minutes. If he caught a taxi, he could still make it to Passeig de Gracia in time.

There were 1,183 correspondents accredited to the Games and it seemed to Clare that most of them were here with him now, crammed into the reception rooms of the Majestic Hotel Inglaterra awaiting the appearance of Jesse Owens – the four time gold medal winner from Berlin. The heat was unbearable. The feeling of dehydration worse. 'Morning, Clare,' Wilson flashed him an amused grin. Clare smiled weakly, fighting the urge to vomit. Once he'd been asked to name his worst moment of the war. 'Jarama,' he'd answered without hesitation,

'Valentine's day, 1937.' A moment recalled not for its carnage, nor his fear, but for the insufferable thirst he'd endured.

The battle had been well into its third day. Already two thirds of the British volunteers lay dead. He and a dozen others had become cut off from what was left of the Brigade, pinned down in a shallow, shadeless hollow, exposed to the full brutal force of the Castilian sun with not a drop of water between them, the metal plates of their ancient Maxim buckling in the heat, the gun useless without liquid to cool it.

Michael Brady had been the first to make a run for water. His body now lay grotesquely twisted on the ground, ringed by the splintered fragments of his skull, a collection of empty water bottles at his side. Four hours later, Clare had reached that same point of desperation. He no longer cared whether he drank or died. He just wanted an end to this terrible thirst.

Pat Tindell volunteered to make the run with him. They waited for a plane to fly overhead. Aussie Reilly spotted it, and Clare later thanked him for saving his life. It was a Junkers. Clare heard the cheers from the enemy lines as it flew closer. He sprang to his feet and started to run, head down, Pat Tindell at his side, the two of them almost tripping over each other as they stooped to pick up the loose water bottles from beside Brady's corpse, the Fascists still miraculously distracted by the plane above.

Their luck held for a few seconds more. Then the cheers died, dissolving into a rapid thud of machine gun fire. On they ran, stumbling down the hillside, the gunner mercifully slow to find their range, Clare strangely aware of a gorse bush being shredded of its bright yellow flowers as he threw himself into a gully, Pat Tindell landing on top of him.

For a while they'd both lain there, amazed by their good fortune, just a few cuts and bruises between them, then they'd continued on down the hill, following the course of the dried up stream towards a cluster of trees. Here the earth was a richer colour, less dry. Taking out their bayonets, they'd started to dig, feverishly clawing away the stones until they finally struck gold in the form of a dirty, foul smelling, brackish liquid.

A sudden popping of flashbulbs jerked Clare back to the Majestic Hotel Inglaterra. He craned his neck to see a face made familiar through countless papers and magazines – Jesse Owens. The four time Olympic hero made his way onto a raised platform, accompanied by the President of the Spanish IOC and the Mayor of Barcelona. The room quietened, and Clare flipped open his notebook. First, there were a few words of introduction, then Owens took the floor, as gracious as Clare had heard people say he was, courteously fielding questions from the press, diplomatic in his answers, sincere in his hope that these Games would help ease the tensions in international relations. Clare dutifully recorded Owens's words for the benefit of his London readers, all the while jealously eyeing the glass of water from which he sporadically sipped.

The battle of Jarama lasted seven days. Clare, like so many others, had been deeply shocked by the experience, his one thought on being pulled back from the front line being to desert. This wasn't his war, not his cause to die for. Antifascist, he may be. Communist, he was not. His journey from London to Spain had been more accident than pilgrimage, like so much in his life, a question of following after his elder brother, Gerald. All his life, Clare had lived in the shadow of his brother's brilliance; Clare minor in more than name. Scholar, poet, writer, Cambridge luminary, Gerald had been one of the brightest stars of their generation. When the Spanish Civil War had broken out, Clare had been lazing on the Amalfi coast with friends, just down from university with a third class degree. His response to the news had been to go for a swim. Gerald had jumped onto a train to Barcelona. Therein lay the difference between the two brothers.

Clare had returned to England in debt. He'd got a job writing short stories for a boy's adventure magazine, *The Captain*. For twelve pounds a week, he'd sat in a dingy office off Knightsbridge, churning out tales of daring-do, whilst Gerald was involved in the real thing. Every day, the papers were full of reports on the heroic defence of Madrid, how Franco's army had been halted in the outskirts of the city by an ill equipped collection of patriots and volunteers. After Christmas – a tedious affair spent with his parents in Kew – Clare had decided to throw it all in and join Gerald in Spain, 'Are you sure it's really you?' his mother's only comment.

On the 3rd January 1937, with a pitiful understanding of the issues involved, he'd boarded a train for Paris, intending to travel on to Barcelona, and from there to Albacete, headquarters of the International Brigade. There was at least one other making the same trip, Clare spotted him on the ferry quietly engrossed in a Spanish phrase book, an eighteen year old from Manchester by the name of Harold Collins. Unlike Clare, Collins seemed to know what he was doing. He had no suitcase, just a few possessions neatly packed into the pockets of his coat, a clean shirt, spare pair of socks, toothbrush, bar of soap, shaving kit and phrase book. 'There's no point in taking anything else,' he explained. 'They'll only make you leave it behind.'

'They?' Clare inadvertently betrayed his ignorance.

'The CPGB.'

Short for the Communist Party of Great Britain – Clare knew that much. They'd taken a lead role in recruiting volunteers to Spain.

'You're best off travelling with the CPGB,' Collins elaborated on the train journey from Calais to the Gard du Nord. Independent travellers ran a high risk of being turned away from Albacete; Clare would do better to come with him to an address he'd been told to present himself to in Paris – 12, Rue Sartine.

The address in question turned out to be a recently closed pharmacy; the glass door still bore an engraved advertisement for *Talc de Venise*. Collins explained Clare's predicament to a young man, then shook his hand and wished him good luck. Clare was led into an empty room and told to wait. The cup of tea he'd been offered never materialised but half an hour later he was joined by an energetic woman in her early forties, who introduced herself as Charlotte Haldane. 'Sorry to keep you waiting,' she said, feeding a form into a battered old typewriter. 'This won't take long. I just need to ask a few questions.' It was her job, she explained, to establish the political reliability of the British volunteers. Clare inwardly groaned, already imagining himself on the train back home, crawling into Knightsbridge on Monday morning, pleading for his job back.

'Name?' she asked.

He told her.

'Age?'

'Twenty-two.'

'Parents' occupation?'

'My father's a vicar. Retired. My mother doesn't work.'

'Do they know you've volunteered?' She gave him a materteral smile.

'Yes.' The idea of not telling them had never crossed his mind.

'Which political party do you belong to?'

'I don't.'

'Then why do you want to go to Spain?' Her fingers hovered over the typewriter waiting for an answer Clare didn't have. *To get away from London. For the adventure. To put off having to make a decision about my life.* 'To join my brother in the fight against Fascism,' he hazarded a guess as to what she might want to hear.

'You're Gerald's brother?'

'Yes.'

Charlotte held out her hand. 'Good to have you on board,' she smiled. A cup of tea arrived, followed by a lecture on sexual hygiene and temperance. Then, after a brief examination by a doctor, Clare was given a list of the things he was allowed to take. Collins had been right about the luggage. No suitcases or hand bags permitted. A clean shirt, spare pair of socks, toothbrush ... Clare already knew the list.

From Gare d'Austerlitz, they took the "red train" to Perpignan. At some point in the journey, Clare woke to notice a shadow lying across his shirt and drowsily he realised they'd struck sunshine, that they had left the north behind.

They crossed the border at Portbou, changing onto a slow train that took them through Barcelona, Valencia, and finally onto Albacete. As they trundled through small towns and villages, people waved and cheered, *'Viva los Internacionales!'*

The British were billeted just outside the town in the village of Madrigueras. After an introductory speech, Clare and the other new arrivals were marched to a disused warehouse, where they were told to help themselves to a uniform from various piles of clothes heaped around the room. The first shirt he picked out had three bullet holes through the front.

On the wall, there was a notice board, a few rules and regulations, the front page of the Brigade newspaper, *Volunteer for Liberty*, and a list of those killed in a recent action at Boadilla del Monte. Second from the top – it was in alphabetical order – Clare read the name of his brother, Gerald.

Madrigueras lay surrounded by olive groves and vineyards. Clare walked for hours along the rough tracks dissecting them, brooding on his brother's death. How quick had it been? How painful? Did his parents yet know? From the rise of a low hill, he could see the fractured skyline of Albacete, the path of the railway staked out by telegraph poles. There was a train back to Barcelona that night and he would be on it. There was nothing keeping him here now. He'd come looking for Gerald and he'd found him – on a list.

Approaching the station, he stopped by a bar, a crowded room fuggy with cigarette smoke. A babble of foreign voices, the clack of dominoes, it was somewhere to sit and grieve. After half an hour alone with a bottle of wine, he was joined by a Swiss German who'd been in Spain for six months but now had to get back to his law degree. *'No pasaran!'* The man, Ralf, raised his glass.

'No pasaran,' Clare wearily repeated the Republican battle cry.

No pasaran. They shall not pass. How many times had Clare heard these words over the previous week. Voices old and young, fists clenched, fire in their eyes. At the side of the railway track. At the stations. On the roadside. Seen them daubed on white sheets hung from windows, draped over the side of railway bridges. He'd felt their excitement, even begun to share their belief – that they could make a difference – and now he was going back home, leaving them to it.

'You'll need a travel pass,' Ralf warned him. 'You can't just buy a ticket.' Clare hadn't thought of this. 'You must get it signed by your commander,' he said. 'Or political commissar.' *Ralf was telling him he had to go back to Madrigueras.* 'See here.' Ralf showed him his own travel pass.

Clare saw.

The walk back to Madrigueras took him the best part of two hours. As the alcohol wore off and the cold night air began to bite, a blister formed on his heel, turning each step into discomfort, then pain. By the time he reached the warehouse, he was ready to drop.

A sentry challenged him. Clare told him to get lost and limped into the building, foraged himself a couple of blankets and fell asleep on the floor.

Reveille was at 5.30. Breakfast at 6.15. Fall in at 6.45. Before Clare knew it, he was standing on the parade ground in his ill fitting uniform being addressed by the Brigade commander, Wilfred Macartney. As Macartney droned on, Clare drifted off; drifted through the subsequent drill and rifle practice, drifted through the rest of the day until somewhere along the line he realised he'd lost the resolve to quit. He'd come this far, he might as well see it through.

Training was a joke. Amateurishly chaotic. He was appointed to a machine gun team – the guns 1914 vintage Maxims, heavy iron wheels, big, metal, water cooled jackets, thick steel shields, prone to jamming. After three weeks of instruction, he was pitched into the battle of Jarama – the nightmare from which he'd emerged miraculously unscathed vowing to desert.

The battalion had been withdrawn from the front. At first, he and the other survivors just concentrated on recovering, on the immediate necessities of life; food and sleep. Then they were told they were going back to Albacete. It was a lie. Or a fuck up. Whichever, it made no difference. They were disembarked from their trucks and marched straight back into the front line. This time at Guadarrama.

They dug themselves in and waited for an attack. When it came, they were ordered to retreat. Clare remembered thinking the odd thing about running away from shells was the way they seemed to follow you. He got lost. Very lost. The front line by now having become dangerously fluid. Twice he almost blundered into Fascist patrols. Only when he crawled into the heart of a dense tangle of brambles did he begin to feel at all safe. He had water, dry biscuits, and a determination to sit it out until the battle moved on.

That afternoon he counted sixteen soldiers, all of them Fascists; all seemingly as lost as he was, stumbling over the hillside in dribs and drabs. Then, as the sun cooled and the shadows grew long, he spied his first Republicans, a half dozen soldiers warily making their way up the dried river bed beside which he was hidden. They seemed to know where they were going. *'Rojo! Ingles! Comrade!'* he called from his thicket. *'Aqui! Ingles!* Don't shoot!' He pushed his rifle out first, scrabbling after it, cursing the thorns ripping at his face and arms, reassuring them over and over again, *'Ingles!'*

Five of them were Spanish, one Italian. None spoke any English. 'Which way?' Clare gesticulated up and down the valley. *'Donde?'* The soldiers laughed and slapped him on the back. They had no idea.

They cut up from the river bed as darkness fell, working their way round the side of a conical shaped hill to the distant sound of exploding shells and the odd burst of gunfire, then hit a road. No-one had a clue which way to go. They tossed a coin – Clare never did learn if it fell heads or tails – and turned southeast, towards the Fascist lines as fate would have it.

It was a dog that heard them first. A sudden, deep barking aimed at them from the dark. They hit the ground. The dog stood his – snarling fiercely until someone shot it. Not one of them. Somebody else. Clare grasped his rifle to his chest, hand shaking, trying to hold the imprint of the muzzle fire in his mind, marry it to the aim of his gun. Then came the sound of voices. Italian. Whoever had shot the dog was being sworn at, was answering back, was being passed by the rest of his company – Clare could see them now, a phantom army looming out of the night. He could hear the crunch of stone under their boots. Dozens of them. Too close to run from. Too many to fight. Their Italians. Fascists. A voice from the ground stopped them dead. 'Don't shoot!' Miraculously no-one did. 'Don't shoot!' Clare added his own frantic plea to the chorus of surrender, throwing his rifle to one side. 'Don't-'

He came to by the side of the road, the hair on the side of his head matted with blood from where the Italian rifle butt had made contact with his skull. It was impossible to tell how much time had passed. How much time then passed before the truck arrived. He remembered only blackness, and a fleeting vision of the Italian, their red Italian, being separated from the rest of them and a gun being put to his head; on the trip back to the Fascist headquarters, the Italian was no longer with them. Clare came round again in a military hospital. About the same time, he idly calculated, that Jesse Owens had been racing horses on the eastern seaboard.

'Did Mr Owens regret his decision to go professional?' a Spanish journalist from *Diari de Catalunya* asked from the floor.

'Not at all,' Owens grinned. 'I had my time. Now it's time for somebody else to have theirs.' Cue the end of the press conference and a rush of journalists stampeding for a phone to call through their copy. Clare walked over to the empty table and poured himself a glass of water. One day, he mused, he'd be able to tell his grandchildren he'd drunk from the same glass as Jesse Owens.

* * * * *

Major Antoni Jordan stubbed out his cigarette and lit another. It was not his usual custom to chain smoke but since it so annoyed Obersturmbannführer Krieger, head of the visiting Gestapo delegation, he found himself unable to resist. They'd been in the room all morning, himself, Colonel Boix and Captain Caraben, sitting round a table with their German counterparts reviewing the security arrangements for von Ribbentrop's imminent arrival in Barcelona.

A first step towards peace was how the press in London and Paris were describing Germany's last minute decision to send a team to the Barcelona Olympics. Personally, Jordan regarded Hitler's move as self interested and cynical, but these and other thoughts he wisely kept to himself. The political winds had changed direction too often in recent years for it to be prudent to nail one's colours too firmly to any one mast. Distasteful as it was, Jordan would do his best to ensure that the visit of the German Foreign Minister passed off without incident.

'My one concern,' Kreiger said after pronouncing himself otherwise satisfied with the arrangements outlined to him by Jordan, 'is that you have given insufficient thought to the possibility of a man working on his own.' He took out a file from his briefcase and from it, handed a document to Jordan. A typewritten list of names. A roll call of former German citizens now resident in Spain. All veterans of the International Brigade. Communists, Jews, homosexuals, revolutionaries, the type of troublemaker, Kreiger explained, who might be motivated to assassinate a leading Nazi politician.

'What are you saying?' Jordan ran a quick eye over the list. Several of the names were well known to him. Good party men. Hardly likely to go off half cock with a loaded pistol and a death wish.

Kreiger gave a smug smile. 'The Reichsführer requests that you confine these men for the duration of the Olympic Games.'

'I would need to clear it with Madrid.' *And Moscow too*, Jordan thought, although he didn't say it.

'Of course.' Kreiger retrieved a second document from his file. 'There is one other possibility.'

'What's that?'

Kreiger handed Jordan the document; a who's who of White Russians and Spanish Nationalists currently residing in Berlin. 'We too have many political refugees,' he explained. 'What we would propose is a simple exchange. Some mutual housekeeping. Of benefit to both our services, I think.'

Jordan didn't wish to say what he thought. The whole idea stank. But he could imagine the NKVD would leap at the opportunity to close its files on some of Stalin's more outspoken critics. 'I'll let you know,' he said, exhaling a lungful of cigarette smoke across the table.

Kreiger coughed. 'Thank you, Herr Jordan.'

The clock struck two. It was time for lunch. The men from the Gestapo rose, hungry for food and fresh air. 'Fascist scum,' Caraben muttered under his breath as they departed the room.

'So who wins from a bastard deal like this?' Boix contemplated the names on the two documents left them by Kreiger.

'That part of the meeting never happened.' Jordan took the documents off him and folded them into his jacket pocket, then ordered his assistant to fetch him a cheese sandwich and a bottle of sparkling water from a bar on Mallorca.

Boix inwardly bristled but said nothing. Much as he mistrusted Jordan's ambition and the encroachments into his own brief, he dared not give voice to his resentment. Jordan had powerful friends inside the NKVD. A reputation as a survivor, untouched by the purges that had seen so many of his colleagues sent to the camps, shot, or recalled to Moscow.

Those who knew Jordan best were all dead; his father and mother in Argentina, his high school teacher, a student doctor, Miguel, whom he'd befriended on the boat across. Those who knew him now, he kept at a distance. For their own good as much as his. In this business, friends were a weakness and lovers a liability. He was better off on his own. With his books, his music, and the ghosts of his past.

Boix and Caraben shuffled their papers away into their briefcases and took the lift down to the canteen. Jordan went upstairs to his office, where a neatly stacked pile of papers awaited him on his desk – the daily reports he demanded from his agents, plus those from his "people" in the hotels, the chamber maids, valets and clerks he'd charged to search the rooms of all visitors. As head of counter intelligence, it was his job to keep an eye on every foreigner attending the

Games. Mark the spies. Test the sympathies of the others. See if he couldn't recruit one or two along the way.

Outside, it was hot. The street almost empty of traffic. The pavements clearing to the clatter of shutters coming down over the shop windows; the sound of the city breaking for lunch. Jordan stood on the balcony for a moment and watched the three men from the Gestapo cross the road. It never ceased to amaze him how careless they were. Always the same restaurant. The same table. Every word picked up by a microphone he'd had concealed in the wall. It was how he'd learned Obersturmbannführer Kreiger couldn't stand the smell of cigarette smoke. It was why he had the patron keep the tables to either side of the Gestapo smoke free, to encourage them back into the restaurant.

Jordan stepped inside and hooked the shutters to the wall. It had been his one extravagance to have them repainted when he took possession of the office; the walls he'd left deliberately bare, finding the elegant mahogany finishings decoration enough.

The Hotel Oriente. Room 219. Richard Clare – Jordan pulled a report free from the pile on his desk. As a matter of routine, he'd ordered all 651 foreign correspondents to be randomly watched over a period of twenty-four hours. *Address: c/o The London Evening News, Northcliffe House, Tudor Street, London EC4.* Carreto had meticulously copied the details from Clare's registration form. *Thursday 25th July. 09.05hrs. Subject left hotel on foot. 09.12hrs. Subject arrived Generalitat* ... Jordan quietly digested Carreto's account of how Clare had spent the previous day. His various journeys across the city. His visit to Capdevila's gallery. To the house on Carrer Avinyó.

Why? Jordan wanted to know. What had any of this to do with Clare's work as a journalist covering the Olympic Games? Was there an innocent explanation? Or was Clare perhaps working to some other, covert agenda?

Then – a knock on the door. 'Yes?'

It was his assistant. In his hand, a wrapped cheese sandwich and a bottle of Vichy Catalan.

* * * * *

After a three course lunch at Roderigo's, an old favourite buried away in the narrow streets of the Raval, Clare felt ready to face the day. On leaving the press conference he'd taken an hour out and returned to his hotel for a lie down, an injection of coffee, and to try and make some sense of the notes he'd taken. He knew the sports desk would be going nuts for the copy – 'if the fucking *Standard* have got it, then why the fucking hell haven't we?' He'd blamed it on the phones. A breakdown at the exchange. 'Don't let it happen again,' he'd been bawled at. Then the line had gone dead.

For his next article, Clare had envisaged a piece about the facilities laid on for the British team. Unlike the '36 Games, there'd been neither the time nor the money to construct a purpose built Olympic village as the Germans had done in Berlin. The athletes and officials had instead been billeted in various towns outside Barcelona.

Clare wandered down to Paral·lel to look for a taxi to take him to Sant Feliu de Llobregat, home to the British Olympic team. He stood for a moment on the pavement gazing down the long, wide avenue of music halls and bordellos; a sleazy cacophony of popular music, street vendors and car horns. On the pavement ahead, a man in a shabby coat was hawking contraband cigarettes. A woman, dressed in black, had stopped to buy a packet of Chesterfields. Clare could see her waving a high denomination note at the man, who in turn was protesting that he had no change. As Clare walked past, the woman turned to him and asked if he could help. Clare obligingly dug a hand into his pocket and produced a fistful of coins from which he made up the amount.

'Thank you, Señor Clare.' This time the woman spoke in accented English. 'I must ask you now, please, to go to the Colom. He'll be waiting for you.' The woman hurriedly pressed a ticket into Clare's hand giving him entry to the monument. '*A las ocho*,' she reverted to Spanish.

'But ...'

'*A las ocho*,' she repeated firmly, turning her back on him, as if there could be nothing more to discuss. And then she was gone, disappeared into the crowd, leaving Clare with the vague feeling he'd seen her somewhere before.

Of course, the city was full of such women; pale faced, thin lipped widows in their fifties, all gathered in black. But the déjà vu lay in her eyes. Dark. Intense. Uncompromising. Somewhere he'd met that stare before. Clare put the ticket into his pocket and walked on. *He will be waiting for you*. Who? Why? She'd spoken as if he was supposed to know, as if there could be no doubt he'd do as she asked. Then he remembered. The eyes. The stare that had hit him at Capdevila's gallery.

The woman was his assistant. Margarita Mirabel.

Monday to Friday – 9.00am – 8.30pm. A weathered sign outside the entrance to the sixty metre high column warned visitors that closing time was imminent.

An evening crowd was already gathered round the *chiringuitos* bars across the road. Somewhere along the dockside, someone was playing an accordion. Clare waited until the tune died, then descended the stone steps into the base of the Colom, following the signs to the lift along a stark, brightly lit corridor. It was, he imagined, like entering an underground gun emplacement. The Maginot line, perhaps.

A member of the German Olympic party – in official white linen jacket, with swastika and Olympic emblem – stood waiting for the lift, stealing a kiss from his mistress. As the lift doors jerked open, the couple stood back to let a man out, then understanding that he was in fact the lift operator stepped inside, laughing at their mistake.

Clare squeezed in after them.

The operator wore a red, green and white striped lapel badge – the Bulgarian flag, Clare happened to know. Visitors to the Games were encouraged to wear the colours of their nation, Spaniards those of the languages they spoke. A Bulgarian speaking Spaniard or a Spanish speaking Bulgar? More likely the latter, Clare assumed, perhaps a former brigadista like himself. The man had a jagged scar running down the side of his head.

A clunk set the lift in motion. The Bulgar tore Clare's ticket, then those of the Germans with barely concealed disdain. The German took a silver cigarette case from his pocket. '*Nein. Verboten*.' The Bulgar wagged his finger vigourously even though the lift stank of cigarettes. The German shrugged and returned the cigarette case to his pocket, as if it meant nothing to him either way.

Clare was first out of the lift, stepping onto the observation platform concealed within the great orb at the top of the column, directly below the statue of Christopher Columbus.

Capdevila was already there waiting for him. Clare could smell him. The aroma of cheap cheroot on the sea breeze.

The German purposefully lit a cigarette.

Clare walked slowly round the column, anticlockwise, to find Capdevila standing at the rail, gazing out to sea. Picasso's former agent flicked the ash from his cheroot and turned to greet him. 'I got your message,' he grinned.

Clare could see that the last two years had left their mark on Capdevila. He recalled the elegant international art dealer with his well cut English clothes, fine cigars and pencil thin moustache. That was 1938. Now, the suit was from El Siglo – as ordinary as Capdevila's vanity allowed – the moustache rough and common, the cigar a cheroot, and the art, all Party approved. Only a chipped front tooth linked the two masks; for some reason, Capdevila had never seen fit to have it capped. 'It's good to see you,' Clare said, stepping up beside him.

'You too,' Capdevila smiled.

They stood for a moment staring out at the docks, neither saying a word, Capdevila waiting for the German couple to pass by, and Clare waiting for Capdevila to tell him why he'd dragged him all the way up to the top of the Colom rather than just drop by his hotel for a drink.

'I spoke to Picasso.' Capdevila at last broke the silence.

'You gave him my letter?'

'Yes.'

'Will he talk to me?'

Capdevila leaned in towards Clare, drawing on his cheroot. 'He wants to defect,' he whispered.

'What?'

Capdevila flicked Clare a glance. *Not so loud*. 'He wants you to help.'

'Me?'

'He trusts you.' Capdevila tucked an envelope into the pocket of Clare's jacket.

'What's this?'

'It's from him. So that you will know I am telling the truth. You are English, Richard. A friend. You will know who to contact.'

From the far side of the observation platform, they heard the lift doors open and a voice call out, 'Ten minutes!'

Capdevila could sense Clare's hesitation. 'All I'm asking is that you pass on the message. Richard, please. There's no-one else.' There was a desperation to Capdevila's voice that demanded Clare's attention. 'Pablo made a mistake coming back. Now they won't let him go. Everything he does. Everything he says. Everything he paints. He can't do anything without their permission. It's killing him ...'

Just a message?

'Please!' Capdevila made it clear there was no-one else to turn to. No-one he could trust. No-one Picasso could trust.

'Okay – I'll do it.' Clare knew he couldn't say no. The risk was obvious but so too the reward. 'I'll pass on the message. But that's all. And for that – you give me the story.' *He'd also want to renegotiate his deal with the old man.*

'You're a good friend, Richard. Thank you.' Capdevila made no attempt to hide his relief.

'How do I get in touch?'

'You don't. I'll be here next Friday. At six o'clock. You may tell me then what they say.'

'Okay.' *It sounded easy enough.*

Capdevila took a last drag on his cheroot and crushed the stub under his heel. 'It'll be best if we don't leave together.'

Clare could see the sense of that.

They shook hands and parted; Capdevila quick to fall in behind the German couple as they squeezed back into the lift.

The whole interchange had lasted less than three minutes.

Clare thrust a hand into his pocket and nervously felt for Picasso's envelope, as if to check that it was still there, that he hadn't just dreamed it. Above him, Columbus stood with his arm outstretched towards the sea; in promise of a new world.

A nice touch – Clare now realised; no accident surely that Capdevila had chosen the monument as a place to meet.

On leaving the Colom, Clare's first instinct was to head home for a drink but no sooner had he started up the Ramblas than he changed his mind, neither the solitude of his hotel room nor a bar full of journalists appealed. There were, of course, any number of other bars and cafés on the Ramblas in which to seek refuge, but tonight they all seemed somehow too crowded. Too full of tourists.

Clare headed off into the back streets, away from the distractions of the Ramblas into the dark heart of the Raval where the streets, ever narrower, merged into one, where even he got lost. Here, he could feel the cold hand of the Party. A closed bookshop. Slogans daubed on the wall. *Proletarios de Todos Paises! Unios!*

The faint sound of music – *Dias Felices* – drew him to a hole in the wall. A bar with no name.

Inside, two solitary men sat drinking, their suits as frayed as the upholstery. The barman stood by the radio, reading the paper, picking at a plate of tinned sardines. 'Whisky, please.' Clare spoke in English, not wishing to get drawn into conversation. The barman leaned down and retrieved a dusty bottle of Johnny Walker from the shelf, wiping it clean before pouring Clare a glass.

To Clare's surprise, it tasted genuine.

The barman returned to his newspaper. Clare took his drink over to a corner table at the back end of the room and tore open the envelope given him by Capdevila. Inside was a folded piece of paper. A pencil drawing by Picasso of himself, Dora Maar and Clare having lunch in Paris at a café just off Rue des Grands Augustins. On the wall, where Clare remembered a portrait of the owner's father, Picasso had purposefully placed a representation of his own picture – *Guernica*. The sketch was dated yesterday and signed, *A mon ami, RC*. It appeared genuine enough. On the table, by Dora's right hand, Picasso had drawn a gold cigarette lighter. A private joke that meant something only to the three of them.

Clare took a deep breath and reached for his glass. He now had his story. A beginning, at any rate, if not the end. Then – 'Richard?'

Clare froze. The accent was unmistakable. German. A voice he hadn't heard for two years.

'It is you. I thought so.' An intense, dark haired man with drawn cheeks and the worn look of an exile, limped towards him.

Clare slipped Picasso's drawing back into his jacket and rose to greet him. 'Werner!'

'I saw you outside in the street.' Werner's lips parted in what passed for a smile. 'I was on my way home.'

'Of course …' Clare remembered Werner once telling him that he had a room in the area. 'Sit down. Have a drink.'

'I am not interrupting you?'

'Hardly.' Clare asked the barman to bring them another glass and the bottle for good measure.

Werner eased himself into the corner seat. 'I didn't think you would return for the Games.'

'You didn't think they'd give me a visa?'

'I didn't think you'd want to come back.'

Clare laughed. Werner Bloch was as old as the century. That much, at least, the files of the German, Russian and Spanish intelligence services were agreed upon. *Born Berlin, 8th June 1900.* But thereafter the details blurred. There were gaps. Events impossible to substantiate. And some blatant untruths.

The version Werner had chosen to tell Clare – they'd been drinking one afternoon in a café on Plaça Catalunya – was ironically closest to that compiled by the Gestapo. For years Werner had been a thorn in their side as a Communist activist in Berlin, then Hamburg, and later, in exile in Paris and Spain, which was where Clare had met him during the war. Not on the battlefield – although they'd both fought at Jarama – but six months later at Radio Barcelona, broadcasting to the International Brigade. Clare in English, Werner in German.

'Prost!' Werner raised his glass into the light.

'Salud!' Clare joined in the toast. They drank; Werner clearly savouring the taste of the Scotch. Clare guessed he didn't get to drink it too often.

'How long have you been back?' Werner asked after a brief silence.

'Since Wednesday.'

'Where are you staying?'

'The Oriente.'

'Seen Montse yet?'

'No.'

'She's working in the Olympic Press Office. That's why I thought you might have seen her.' Werner looked at Clare askance. 'You are with the Press, aren't you?'

'Yes ...' *Montse was alive. Here in town. Working right under his nose. Clare couldn't believe his luck.* 'How is she?' he stuttered.

'Keeping her head down. Like the rest of us.' Werner stretched his leg, instinctively rubbing the wound he'd received at Jarama. It had happened on the fourth day of the battle. Werner had been at the head of a troop of stragglers making their way through an olive grove when he'd spotted enemy soldiers ahead. Turning to those following, Werner had gestured them to get down but the Spaniards amongst them had interpreted the simple up and down movement of his hand as a signal to come to him. The enemy had seen them and opened fire. Werner had been hit in the leg; several of the Spaniards had been less fortunate.

'Does she have a boyfriend?' Clare had to know.

'There was someone for a while.' Werner seemed oblivious to the tension in Clare's voice. 'A Russo. But that's all over now.'

'What happened?'

'He was "recalled to Moscow".'

'Was she upset?'

'No. It seemed he had another girlfriend in Madrid.'

'And now?'

'I heard a friend of hers from work – Esteban Llull – he offered to marry her. To help pay for the child. But she said no.'

'Esteban Llull is dead,' Clare chipped in.

'I didn't know.' Werner looked genuinely surprised.

'He was shot. By the SIM.'

Werner gave a wry smile. 'Then she made the right choice, didn't she?'

Clare smiled too. 'So what about you, Werner? What are you doing these days?'

Werner pulled a card from his pocket and handed it to him. Flimsy. Thumb soiled. A distinctive yellow logo that read Taxis David. 'I drive a taxi,' he said, then – '*Scheisse!*' – Werner dropped his glass of Scotch to the floor, nudging it behind the table leg, turning from Clare as if he didn't know him, as two militiamen came strolling in from the street, their uniforms a familiar mismatch of khaki.

Foot soldiers of the Catalan Communist Party – the PSUC.

In an instant the barman was on his feet, bringing over Werner a glass of wine, reinforcing the impression that he was drinking alone. But it was Clare the militiamen were interested in. Not Werner. 'Papers!' they demanded.

Clare offered up his passport and press card.

'English?'

'Yes.'

'Speak Spanish?'

'Yes.'

What was he doing here? they asked. Having a drink, he replied. On his own? Yes. Why not on the Ramblas? Too noisy. Why not in his hotel? Ditto. Why this bar? Why not? The militiamen looked unimpressed. Both were young, barely out of their teens. They took the barman to one side. Clare couldn't hear what was being said but he didn't like the way they kept looking at him, then something the barman said made the militiamen laugh and suddenly they were relaxed. All was explained. 'Enjoy your stay!' they grinned at Clare, as they completed their check and left.

'What did you tell them?' Werner's hand was still shaking as he retrieved his Scotch from the floor.

'That your friend was looking for a prostitute.' The barman coolly turned back to his newspaper and sardines. 'You should be more careful, *mon ami*.'

Clare caught Werner's eye. *More careful?*

Werner nodded. 'It's enough for them just to see us talking together. You know how their minds work. They'd think we had something to hide.'

'You're not the first person to say that ...' Clare was reminded of the old man with the dog on Carrer Avinyó.

Werner wasn't surprised. 'A lot's changed since you were last here.'

'How do you mean?'

'You haven't heard?'

'Heard what?'

'About the arrests.'

'I did hear something,' Clare admitted. 'Two years ago. From a guy I met in Paris. A colleague from the International Brigade. But since then ... it's not been easy to get any reliable news.'

'What did you hear?'

'That no-one was safe any more.'

'Then you heard right.'

'Tell me about it.'

Werner once more reached for his drink. 'There's not much to tell.'

'I need to know.'

'Why?'

'Because I still have friends here.'

'Montse?'

Clare nodded.

Werner shrugged.

'What's that supposed to mean?'

'Nothing.'

'So – tell me about it.'

Werner took a deep breath, glanced at his watch, refilled his glass – to the brim – then reluctantly wound back the clock. To August 1938 and the end of the Spanish Civil War.

Clare could picture the moment with absolute clarity. Himself and Montse – and thousands of others – in the streets of Granada, cheering the Republican victory.

Werner had been in Barcelona. He dryly recalled being summoned to a special meeting of the Communist Party in the upstairs room of what had once been the Asturias Club. The good guys had won. Hitler had been dealt a bloody nose. Democracy restored to Spain. 'We felt the time was ripe for revolution,' Werner spoke quietly, with half an eye on the two other men in the room. 'The left had only won because of us reds. Our discipline. Stalin's tanks and guns. But then come the moment of victory. The moment we had it in our hands to change the lives of every Spaniard – Moscow said no.' He shook his head at the memory. 'After all those years of war. All those deaths – I was so angry, Richard.'

Across the room, the radio coughed static. Werner leaned in towards Clare. 'You know what they told us? The reason Stalin cancelled the revolution?'

Clare didn't know.

'This'll make you laugh.' Werner took another drink. 'Stalin didn't want to give the rest of Europe a fright. He didn't want to scare Britain and France into making an alliance with the Nazis. The honest truth. That's what they told us.'

Clare could well believe it. After the war, it had seemed to many that the Fascists no longer posed quite the same threat as they had done before. The Nazis had been checked. The Communists had proved themselves a force to be reckoned with. Hitler could point to the Soviets in the east and the Spanish in the west and shout warning of a Bolshevik encirclement, knowing that there were many in Paris and London only too ready to listen.

Werner continued. 'Power before revolution. It was some such shit phrase they used. First we were to make the police force ours. Then the army. The unions. The politicians. Every half arsed back room committee. Revolution by stealth – that was the strategy. Think of Spain as a house. The revolution as a paint job.' Werner didn't even smile. 'Their exact words. We paint her red, comrades. But from the inside out. Maintain the fiction of democracy and then when the time is right – present the world with a *fait accompli.*' Werner momentarily faltered, as if swamped by the memory of it all. The bitterness. The regret. The choices made, the decisions forced on him, that had brought him to where he was now, to tonight even, to this bar with no name.

In the street outside, they could hear raised voices. A woman hauling her husband out of some drinking hole, shaking him down for the loose change she'd sent him off with to buy a loaf of bread. Werner recovered his thread. 'And that's when the arrests began. Soon after you left. A purge of the Party. Anyone who complained, who dared dissent, disappeared. A few here. A few there. To begin with. Then more openly. The same as in Russia – although we didn't know it at the time. Intellectuals. People who'd been abroad. Those they considered contaminated ...'

'Like Llull?'

'Yes. Like Llull.' Outside, the shouting had subsided. Werner let a gob of phlegm drop into his handkerchief and carefully folded it back into his pocket.

'And you?' Clare had heard enough.

'I keep to myself.' Werner took another slug of whisky. 'You remember Stani?' Clare nodded. Stani had been Werner's oldest and closest friend, dating back to the early days in Berlin. 'Two weeks ago they shot him,' Werner said matter-of-factly.

'I'm sorry ...'

'You don't have to be. You know why they killed him?'

'No.'

'For having a drink. With an American journalist.' Werner began to cough, then caught himself. 'Who knows what they were discussing. Likely as not it was the novels of F. Scott Fitzgerald. Whatever. It's not important.' Werner looked him in the eye. A wan smile. 'Like I said, it was enough for them to be seen talking. These days the Party will always assume the worst.'

'So why follow me in here?'

'What?'

'If it's so dangerous for you to be seen with me?' The thought only occurred to Clare as he was saying it but he knew that he wasn't mistaken; even in the low light he could read the signs on Werner's face. 'What do you want from me? What the hell are you doing here, Werner?' They'd never been that good friends, more work colleagues who'd got on.

'You're right.' Werner drew breath. 'I did have a favour to ask.'

'What?' Clare could feel an aggression creeping into his voice. First Capdevila. Now Werner. He was suddenly tired of it all.

Werner looked embarrassed. 'It's not important.'

'Just tell me what you want.'

'I was hoping you might get me a ticket. To the football. To the final.'

Clare stared at him in disbelief. *That was it?*

Werner looked away. 'Like I said, it's not important.'

Outside it was now dark. In the distance, Clare could hear fireworks popping. The rumble of music from the Ramblas. He'd left Werner inside with the remains of the Scotch and a promise to do what he could on the ticket front. That Werner was prepared to risk his life for a game of football seemed crazy. But then what did Clare know about football? Or Werner for that matter?

Across the road, an old letter writer sat hunched inside a cabin no larger than a telephone kiosk, a voluble young woman standing over him, frustrated at the old man's inability to keep up with her. Clare watched them for a while, conscious of Picasso's envelope sitting inside his jacket pocket like a hot gun, a part of him now beginning to wish that he could just forget about it, drop it into the gutter, let it sink out of sight and mind, or he fantasised, hand it to the letter writer – let him take care of the reply.

Wearily, Clare turned and set off back to the Ramblas, wondering where best to send a telegram from at this time of night.

* * * * *

The RAC club, Pall Mall, London. A cloud of cigar smoke hung over the three leather armchairs drawn around the fire. Two ex-Naval men in their mid-fifties and a linguist, twenty years their junior, sitting in the club room after dinner, talking politics, deliberating the overriding questions of the day. Could Europe peacefully accommodate the competing ambitions of the Nazis and the Soviets? Had the Spanish conflict made another world war inevitable? And if so, who did Britain have most to fear from? Hitler or Stalin?

'Mr Shaw, Sir.' The youngest of the three men turned his head to see the club footman standing at his shoulder, a folded note in his hand. 'A message for you.'

'Thank you, Donald.' Shaw took the note and read.

+ In Barcelona covering Olympic Games. Have dramatic and exclusive story. Please advise. Richard Clare +

It took Shaw a moment to remember – 1936. A naive twenty-two year old about to leave for Spain, intent on joining his brother in the International Brigade. One of the new boys in Section V (counter espionage) had tipped him off that Clare was going. A friend of a friend from university. Shaw had rung Clare and arranged to meet him in the Fitzroy Tavern off Charlotte Street. He'd been up front with him from the start: 'My name is Shaw. I work for the Secret Intelligence Service. SIS.' Honest: 'Our knowledge of events in Spain is somewhat scanty.' And to the point: 'What we'd like you to do is write to us from time to time. Keep us up to date. Fill in the gaps.'

'You mean spy?' Clare had seemed somewhat surprised.

'Yes. I mean spy.'

Clare had instinctively declined the offer. 'Think about it,' Shaw told him. 'You don't have to make up your mind now. You can let me know later. Just leave a message at my club.'

And now he had. Four years after the event.

Shaw screwed the piece of paper into a ball. 'Important?' one of his colleagues asked.

Shaw shook his head, throwing Clare's note into the fire – 'No.'

CHAPTER 4

Saturday 27th July, 1940

Programme of the XIIth Olympiad *Opening ceremony*

Santa Cruz de la mancha. A nowhere town, twenty odd miles north of Granada, but forever ingrained in Clare's memory as the place where it all started to turn sour between himself and Montse.

They'd been packing *Guernica* back into the truck, himself and a half dozen men of the local guard, Montse having gone in search of coffee and bread. An hour passed. Clare was ready to leave and still Montse hadn't returned. Irritated, he'd gone looking for her, searching the town twice over before thinking to look inside the church. He found her in tears in a side chapel, a telegram lying screwed up in a ball at her feet. Her sister Marta was dead. Marta's husband too. Killed in an air raid. Miraculously, their two year old son, Pep, had survived, his cot protected by a fallen beam. 'We'll have to look after him,' Montse told him through her tears. And what else could Clare do but agree? There was no-one else. Montse was right. It wouldn't be fair to land the child on her parents.

But he was twenty-three. Far too young to be trapped in a cramped, airless apartment with a screaming toddler; they were back in Barcelona now, the war over. That Montse was only twenty-one and uncomplaining just made it worse. They stopped talking. Or rather he stopped talking. He could tell she wanted him to explode, to vent his frustrations and resentments, but it wasn't his way. He was too English. Too immature, he later realised. And she too tired to provoke him.

Then one day, out of the blue, he received a summons ordering him to report to the SIM station on Via Laietana. That night, he and Montse talked for hours. What could they possibly want to see him about? Had somebody denounced him? Was it something he'd said, some throwaway remark? And then after they talked, they'd made love. For the first time in two months.

The last time they'd ever done so.

The SIM officer was far younger than Clare expected him to be. About Gerald's age, with close cropped dark hair, a silver streak above the right temple, deep brown eyes, smooth skin and a dimple on his cheek that brought out the boyishness in his face.

His name was Antoni Jordan.

Speaking with an Argentinian accent, Jordan asked Clare if he wanted a cup of tea. There was a teapot on the table and two cups; it was all very strange, not in the least what Clare had imagined. They talked about art, Jordan impressive in his range of reference and sharpness of opinion, Clare more reticent in his comment, not wishing to err too far from the Party line. The conversation progressed onto the subject of Picasso. What did Clare think of his work? What did he consider the role of the artist in modern society? At Madrigueras, the political commissar had once given them a lecture on the very same subject. Clare knew what he was supposed to say and said it. Jordan accepted his answer without comment, although Clare sensed he would have preferred a more honest conversation.

Jordan had then lit himself a cigarette – a Primeros – and cut straight to the chase. It was almost two and a half months since the war had been won and the most famous Spaniard alive, the creator of *Guernica*, a man who'd publicly championed the Republican cause, even donated money to it, had chosen to remain in Paris rather than return home to Spain. 'Doubtless Picasso has his reasons for staying,' Jordan conceded, but his reluctance to even visit Spain was beginning to give cause for concern. 'In some quarters, it is being read as a condemnation of the government'. By government, Jordan meant the Communist Party. 'We want you to go to Paris,' he told Clare. 'We want you to talk to him. Persuade him to come back.'

Clare felt a surge of relief – so they didn't want to lock him up after all.

'You've met him. He trusts you,' Jordan continued. 'You've toured the country with his work, seen how people respond to it. That's the kind of reassurance he needs.'

To Clare's shame, he'd leapt at the opportunity. He needed the break. Some time on his own. 'It'll only be for a few weeks,' he promised Montse later that night but he could read the disappointment in her eyes. 'I'll be back by Christmas.'

'No, you won't.' Montse was convinced that Clare meant to put an end to their relationship but was just too craven to say so. 'Leave now and you'll never come back.'

'Of course I'll come back.' Clare was indignant she should think otherwise. Why shouldn't he? He loved her. He wanted to be with her.

'Then don't go,' she pleaded.

But Clare's mind was made up.

Unreasonable. Selfish. Irrational. Dishonest. These were just some of the accusations they threw at each other. Clare promised. He swore on every memory they held sacred that he would be back by the end of the month until Montse was too tired to protest. 'Go then,' she told him. 'Go. Do what you want.'

And he had.

But as he'd picked up his bag and turned to leave, Montse had pulled him back, forcing him to look at her in that way she did when she knew he didn't want to listen. 'No-one will ever love you as I do,' she'd said. 'No-one.'

And then he'd walked out the door. Almost twenty-two months ago to the day.

* * * * *

3.22pm. The Casa de Prensa. Clare dictated the last of his copy over the phone, hung up on his sub-editor, then took the main staircase up to the second floor to attend to the following day's ticketing arrangements. The British football team had been drawn to play Sweden and he needed a press pass. A bright eyed, pretty young woman with curled blonde hair and thinly rouged lips issued it without question, advising him to be at the stadium at least half an hour before the game. Clare thanked her, then asked if she might also sort him out with an extra ticket to the final; he was thinking of Werner, speaking in Spanish in the hope that she might treat him with favour. 'I'm sorry I can't help,' she told him. 'You'll have to apply at the box office.'

'It's for a friend. A comrade from the war.'

'You were a brigadista?' She looked surprised.

Clare nodded. A little ashamed at playing the war card.

The woman hesitated, then told him to leave his number. She'd do what she could; somewhere on the outskirts of Madrid, there lay the grave of a brigadista who'd died saving her brother's life. 'My name is Lucia,' she added.

Clare smiled – in a way that made Lucia wonder if he was now going to ask her out for a drink. 'I have one more small favour to ask,' he said.

'Yes?'

'A friend of mine – Montse Rafols – she's working somewhere in the press office. Do you know her?'

Lucia shook her head. A pity, she thought. If he'd asked, I would have said yes. She pulled a typed list from the notice board behind her. 'What did you say her name was?'

'Rafols. Montse Rafols.'

Lucia flicked through the list until she found her. 'Rafols, Montserrat. She's up at the tennis club.' The tennis club was the venue for the fencing competition. Lucia gestured to the phone on her desk. 'You can call her if you want.'

'No. It's okay, thank you.' Clare made a note of the address. 'It's not important.'

Lucia smiled sweetly. *The hell it isn't.*

Exiting the Casa de Prensa, Clare made his way up past the magic fountains to the Palau Nacional. There was no time to visit Montse now – not before the opening ceremony – but he could at least take advantage of the few minutes he did have to drop by an old friend.

Entry into the national museum was free. Even so, there was nobody there save a security guard in his cabin and a cat sleeping in the shade. It felt more like a mausoleum than a gallery. Still, quiet and cool. Clare walked through the hall into an ornate, domed chamber, dominated by a large, white flat on which were suspended the twenty-seven square metres of painted canvas that had so changed his life.

Guernica. The most famous icon of the war. The painting that had turned Picasso into an international symbol of resistance to Fascism.

Alone in the room, Clare stood for a moment in silent contemplation, reacquainting himself with the brutal imagery of the canvas, thinking back to the first time he met Picasso, almost two and a half years ago.

Arriving in Paris: the short walk from the metro to La Rue des Grands Augustins, the concierge pointing him up to the attic, 'Take the stairs to your left at the top.'

He remembered the heavy oak door with an iron ring. The timid tinkling of the bell. A young girl with dark hair and a pretty smile leading him through a narrow room crammed full of clutter – negro masks, ceramics, twisted bits of glass, exotic hats, plaster casts and leather bound books, the dust so thick it had made him cough.

Then another room filled with yet more junk, discarded bottles of eau de cologne, crumpled cigarette packets, frayed shoes, a broken coffee grinder, and in the far corner, a circular stairway leading up to the studio proper. 'You'll have to wait until eleven,' the pretty smile said (she never did tell him her name), 'That's when he takes breakfast.'

Clare had parked himself on a green wooden bench and waited, a broken clock, one hand missing, the other stuck on three, staring up at him from the floor; from the window, a view across a jumble of slated rooftops and brick chimneys towards Notre Dame. Then, on the stroke of eleven, the soft trip of slippers descending the stairs. A short man, almost bald with wisps of white hair, dressed in a tan cashmere sweater; his first words to Clare, 'Have you eaten?'

'So this is what all the fuss is about!' A loud voice shattered the silence. Clare turned to see a party of Englishmen enter the gallery. 'Big isn't it?' 'Weird if you ask me.' 'What's with the light bulb?'

It was time to leave.

Clare bought a postcard of the painting from a kiosk outside the building, then joined the great flow making its way up the hill towards the Olympic stadium. Security, he could see, was tight. Militiamen on all the entrances. Plain clothes types pretending to mingle – SIM.

An official took his press card, checked his name against a list, and waved him through.

The area reserved for the press lay directly above the VIP box; the seats well spaced so that no-one would be disturbed by the comings and goings of the journalists. Clare found a seat between Wignall and Stewart, and took out his pen and notebook.

At about four o'clock, the VIPs began to arrive. A smattering of Royalty from Bulgaria, Italy, Greece and Sweden. Mussolini's sons. The Duke and Duchess of Windsor. And then a rustle of excitement as the Spanish President, Manuel Azana, made his entry. 'Clare, help me out here.' Wignall, looking defiantly English in his tweed suit, turned to him for help. 'I don't recognise a single one of these chaps.'

Clare obligingly labelled the grave, thickset man at Azana's side as the Prime Minister, Juan Negrin, and walking two steps behind him, the President of the Generalitat, Lluis Companys. And behind him ... Clare continued to reel off the names of Spain's leading politicians. First the window dressing, then the real power in the country – José Diaz, ailing chairman of the Communist Party, and the leading members of the Politburo, La Pasionara, Checa, Mije and Uribe.

'Now him – I do recognise.' Even with his face turned away from them, there was no mistaking Picasso. 'But who's he talking to?' Wignall pointed towards a short, severe looking man, uncomfortably dressed in a suit.

'That's André Marty. He was in charge of training the International Brigade.'

Wignall caught the distaste in Clare's voice. 'An old friend of yours?'

'We called him the Butcher of Albacete.' *He now ran the SIM – a thug.*

Clare watched as Picasso took his seat, sandwiched between Marty and the Soviet Foreign Minister, Molotov.

'You alright?' Wignall asked.

Clare nodded. 'Yeah. I'm fine.' *Although suddenly he felt anything but.*

'We swear that we will take part in the Olympic Games in loyal competition, respecting the regulations which govern them in the true spirit of sportsmanship ...' The flag bearers of the forty-three competing nations stood gathered in a semi-circle, solemnly reciting the Olympic oath.

The opening ceremony was drawing to a close, the colour of the preceding two hours already reduced in Clare's mind to the image of a lone protestor running onto the track, brandishing a Czechoslovakian flag in protest against Hitler's designs on the Sudetenland, the forced smiles of the politicians looking on from the reviewing stand, Blum, Truman, von Ribbentrop, Molotov and Lord Halifax, like shy school boys at a dance, wishing they weren't there.

The athletes stepped back from the podium. The flame was lit and 10,000 doves released into the sky. From the fort on top of Montjuic, there sounded a twenty-one gun salute. The ceremony was at an end. The Games declared open.

Clare stood up and stretched, in no hurry to file his copy. One of the few advantages of working for an evening paper was the lack of an evening deadline.

'Hey, Clare!' Peter Wilson was also in no mood to join the mad dash for the phones. 'Where can we get a drink around here?'

Cleaver too felt in need of a little light refreshment. 'What's the Miramar like?'

'Forget it,' Stewart advised. 'It'll be full of journalists.'

'The Font del Gat?' suggested Forsyth.

'Wherever you've been hiding these past few days will do,' Wilson joked.

Twenty minutes later they were swinging out over the harbour pressed into a cable car, below them the fishermen's nets laid out on the wharves, boats at anchor, the grim hulk of the prison ship, *Uruguay*, lying apart from the other vessels, above and beyond it the sky slowly draining of light, the horizon losing its definition.

The Café de Faros was a popular early evening spot at the end of the breakwater. Clare ordered beers all round and a plate of fried fish as the others admired the view back across the water towards the city.

'Good choice.' Stewart congratulated him.

The beers arrived and the conversation soon turned to the following day's events. Where the best story lay. 'What about the fencing?' Clare asked, thinking of Montse.

'Pointless.' Wilson dismissed the idea out of hand. 'The Italians and the central Europeans have got the whole show carved up between them. There's no chance of a medal there. You'd be wasting your time.'

The others agreed. There was nothing doing tomorrow except the athletics and the football – Great Britain's opening match against the Swedes.

Clare fell silent. Earlier, he'd checked his programme. Fencing was the one event scheduled for every day of the tournament. Montse would be up at the tennis club for the duration and now here was Wilson telling him he'd have no reason to be there.

Clare was sure of it now. Definitely – she was trying to avoid him.

CHAPTER 5

Sunday 28th July, 1940

Programme of the XIIth Olympiad
Athletics, Modern Pentathlon (cross country riding), Fencing, Wrestling, Hockey, Football, Weightlifting.

There were two buses. Every morning, they did the rounds of the main hotels, picking up the journalists and taking them on to the various venues scattered around town. Clare could see the first bus now, trundling across Plaça Catalunya towards the Hotel Colon, but which direction it was heading – one went to Montjuic, and the other to the Polo and Tennis Clubs – he couldn't yet tell.

Clare finished his coffee, left a couple of coins on the table and rose to his feet, joining the crowd of journalists shuffling towards the kerb; an inelegant free-for-all that drew a loud complaint from the man in front of him.

The bus pulled up outside the hotel, the direction board on the front now visible. 'Reial Club de Tennis only!' a woman called from the rear platform.

And Clare froze.

It was Montse. He couldn't believe it. Right there in front of him. The pretty press officer on the back of the bus, clipboard in hand, calling out to the waiting journalists – it was her.

'Those wishing to go to the Olympic stadium – please take the next bus,' she said, repeating the message in Spanish, French and German.

An American journalist pulled back from the queue, realising he was about to get on the wrong bus. Others started to board. Clare just stood and stared. She looked well. No – better than that, he decided, she looked great. No longer stressed from the strain of having to care for a traumatised two year old. And the uniform suited her too. Skirt tight around her waist. Unbuttoned jacket falling over her breasts. Hair tied back.

And then she saw him.

'Hi …' It was all he could think to say.

Montse met his gaze without sentiment and reached out a hand to pull the bell cord. Clare jumped up onto the bus – 'Montse …' – grabbing hold of the hand rail, steadying himself as the bus began to pull away into the traffic – 'Montse! Please …' But she just turned her back on him and made her way up to the top deck. *Don't even think about trying to follow me.*

The bus swung left into Passeig de Gracia, crossing into the right hand lane towards the last pick up point – the Majestic Inglaterra. *Get off now and he might never see her again. Is that what she wanted?*

Clare looked around for a seat.

A journalist – dark brown eyes, neat moustache and a suit to match – shuffled up to make room for him.

'Thank you.' Clare sat down beside him.

'You are welcome.' The journalist spoke in a Hungarian accent. 'English?' he asked. Clare nodded. The journalist smiled. 'I lived in London for two years.' Again Clare nodded, not wishing to encourage him into conversation. '10 Craven Hill Road. By Hyde Park.' The journalist held out his hand. 'How do you do? My name is Janos Balasc.'

'Richard Clare. *London Evening News*,' Clare muttered in surrender.

'Delighted to meet you,' Balasc beamed. 'I am a great

admirer of your newspaper. Of all things English. I am – how do you say – a true Anglophile.'

Clare smiled politely. *Just my luck.*

Balasc had initially been posted to London to cover the Abdication. In his opinion the King had been treated most shabbily. Clare learnt all this and much more besides as they drove up through the Eixample, the modernista grid pattern that made up much of the new part of the city. Balasc loved art; he liked to visit the National Gallery. He loved Hampstead Heath; he liked to walk there on weekends. He loved Jazz; had Clare ever been to The Minerva Club? Did it still exist? Etcetera, etcetera – until at last the bus turned right off Diagonal and drew up outside the Reial Club de Tennis.

Montse was first off the bus, pointing the journalists towards a door marked "Press". Balasc smoothed a crease from his jacket and wished Clare a good day. He was staying at the Hotel Victoria. Did Clare know it? Clare said that he did. 'Then perhaps we might meet up again one evening?' Balasc suggested. 'Continue our chat over a drink?'

Perhaps.

When at last the journalists had dispersed and the pavement was cleared, Montse finally acknowledged his presence. 'What are you doing here?' she asked tersely, grateful only that he hadn't tried to create a scene in front of the other journalists. 'What do you want?'

'To see you.' It wasn't exactly how Clare had imagined it would happen.

'So now you've seen me. There's nothing to say, Richard. It's over.'

'About Paris –' Clare started.

'– I don't want to talk about Paris.'

Neither did he. 'How's Pep?' He couldn't think of anything else to say.

'Fine.'

'I saw Werner.' He was floundering now. 'He told me he's driving a taxi.'

'Richard, it's over.' Behind them, a stray dog cocked its leg over a competitor's equipment bag. 'Go home. There's nothing for you here. We're finished.'

* * * * *

The Olympic stadium. Ninety minutes later. Clare finally made it to work. 'What happened to you?' Stewart moved his jacket to make room for him.

'Caught the wrong bus.' Clare took out his programme.

'800 metres. Third heat,' Stewart prompted him. 'Last lap.' Down on the track the runners were lengthening their stride as they hit the home stretch, eight time keepers for eight athletes rising up out of their stepped seats, clicking their stop watches: One Germany. Two Great Britain. Three Portugal. And four? A toss up between a Spaniard and a Frenchman. Clare took out a pen and marked off the first three qualifiers on his programme; his thoughts still with Montse – black, self recriminatory and frustrated.

'Time for a piss.' The voice of *The Daily Herald* got to his feet and stretched. 'Care for a coffee?'

Clare nodded.

'You might want to take a look at this while I'm gone.' Stewart handed him a scrap of paper.

'What is it?'

'The team for tonight's game. Cleaver got it from the coach.'

Clare had forgotten about the football match. He ran a quick eye over the British team selected to face Sweden: *King, Dowdall, Jenne, Hadaway, Tucker, Hastings, Griffin, Thomas, Hunt, Waddington, Maddox*. The names meant nothing to him. He thanked Stewart nevertheless.

'It's Cleaver you've got to thank.' Stewart stifled a belch. 'How do you take your coffee?'

'Milk. No sugar. *Cortado* rather than *con leche* – assuming there's a choice.'

'I'll do my best.' As Stewart departed, a loud cheer greeted an announcement that the judges had awarded fourth place to the Spaniard.

Clare yawned. It was going to be a long day.

* * * * *

August 14th 1937. The military prison, Burgos. 7.00am. A harsh awakening as the bolts on Clare's cell door were drawn back. 'No breakfast this morning,' a guard shouted at him to get to his feet, 'You're going for a ride.'

Not a great sky to die under, Clare remembered thinking as they were led out across the courtyard to a waiting truck. Too grey. Too many clouds. He might just as well have been in England.

There were thirty others crammed into the truck. All Republican prisoners – a mixture of foreigners and Spaniards. Andreu, his cell mate of three months, tried to be philosophical, 'If I were in their shoes, I'd do the same.'

Clare tried not to shit himself. Every time the truck slowed or braked, he told himself this was it. But to his surprise, they kept on going, jerked and jarred by the worsening road, their progress marked by the clang of bells; goat bells and church bells. A patter of rain began to fall on the canvas roof of the truck. Clare felt hungry; they'd still been given nothing to eat. Then – 'Out!' Suddenly they'd stopped.

No-one moved.

'Out!' A guard drove his rifle butt against the tail gate. Slowly they disembarked, shambolically falling into something resembling two lines.

An officer approached. 'My name is Captain Carton,' he told them. 'It is my duty to inform you that you are to be released as part of a prisoner exchange programme.'

'I couldn't believe that cunt was for real,' Andreu remarked afterwards as they stood on the far side of the river, embracing and laughing, shivering still, but safe behind Republican lines.

Neither could he.

It took them almost a week to get back to Barcelona. Clare remembered feeling curiously detached during the journey, like a train in a siding, watching the war rolling by. The main road from Madrid was now a constant stream of traffic. Reinforcements heading west, the wounded heading east; that the Fascists were on the back foot was obvious, Clare could see it in the skies, on the road, in the faces of the soldiers moving up to the front, taste it even in the meals they were given. Franco, Quiepo de Llana and General Mola were all dead, a truck driver told him. Assassinated. Boom! He mimed a huge explosion.

A commissar confirmed the story. The Fascists had disintegrated into warring factions. The Republicans had launched their own offensive, striking deep into Extremadura, capturing Caceres and Badajoz and cutting the Nationalist forces in two, threatening their supply line to Madrid. An American journalist filled him in some more; they got chatting while waiting for the remains of a bomb charred truck to be cleared from the road. Franco's assassin was an Englishman, an NKVD agent working undercover as a journalist. 'Perhaps you knew him?' the American suggested. 'His name was Kim Philby.'

Clare shook his head. 'No.'

Finally they reached Barcelona, the train drawing to a halt at Sants station early one Sunday morning. Clare had been told to report to the International Brigade hostal on Carrer Mallorca but

Andreu insisted that he instead stay with his family at their hotel. 'We won't even have to share a room, Ricardo,' he joked.

And so Clare had accompanied him home.

The hotel was exactly as he'd imagined it, as Andreu had always described it. Geranium pots on the balconies. To the left of the front door, an arch through which the stables had once been accessed, and where there now lay a dark alleyway. On the façade, there were twin friezes. Two Maenads seductively draped in thin veils, one with a double flute, the other with a tambourine. Why Maenads? Andreu couldn't tell him.

Being a Sunday, the street was quiet and the shutters on the hotel windows all drawn. Andreu rang the bell. They waited, Andreu with his head pressed against the door. 'My sister,' he announced, on hearing the trip of feet on the marble steps, 'Montse.'

The door swung open. 'Andreu!' Montse stared at her brother in disbelief, flinging her arms round him in a wild embrace. 'Mama! Papa! It's Andreu. He's back!'

She too was just as Clare had imagined, as Andreu had always described her. A fireball of energy. Corkscrew dark hair. Eyes the colour of olives. A small mole on the corner of her lip. 'This is my cell mate, Ricardo,' Andreu introduced him. And she'd kissed him too. Thanked him for looking after her brother. And later, much later, after Clare had been embraced and fussed over and made to feel at home by her parents, and after they'd finished eating, she'd sat down beside him in the lounge and asked him what it had really been like. She had been to the front herself. She had fought. She knew the horrors involved and she wanted to know the truth. Always with Montse, this was what mattered. The truth.

And the truth of it was he'd let her down.

* * * * *

8.00pm. As the street lights flickered on and evening once again laid claim to the city, the bird dealers at the top of the Ramblas packed away their cages, the intrusive blast of the tannoys drowning out the excited squawking and chirruping. Around the tourist information booths, crowds stood gathered, hands outstretched for a free copy of the day's results. Already the first Golds of the Games had been decided. The 10,000 metres another clean sweep for the Finns. Luise Kruger leading a German one-two-three in the women's javelin. The high jump retained by Cornelius Johnson of the United States.

'This will do fine,' Clare said, letting the taxi driver know it was okay to drop them off outside the Café Royal. 'We can walk from here.' Wilson settled the fare as Wignall and Stewart piled out of the car, the rest of the British press pack not far behind, looking forward to a few drinks in the hotel bar – the cause of the celebration, Great Britain's one-nil victory over Sweden in the football.

The lobby of the Oriente was as busy as a station concourse at rush hour. 'Too many people who've no right to be here' in Wignall's overloud opinion. It took Clare five minutes to beat a path to the front desk. 'You have one message, Sir,' the hotel clerk informed him as he handed over the keys to his room. For a brief moment, Clare allowed himself to hope that it might be from Montse but it was just a note from his editor requesting a piece on the British modern pentathlete, Captain Markham, currently lying in fifth place after the cross country riding.

'See you at the bar in ten minutes.' Wignall adjusted his watch to the lobby clock.

Clare made his way up to his room on the second floor; the door falling open as he inserted his key into the lock, the sudden rush of air drawing cigarette smoke from within.

There was someone inside.

Clare switched on the light to see a man standing on the balcony with a cigarette between his lips.

A Primeros.

Clare pushed the door shut. There was only one person in the world he knew who smoked that brand.

'Sorry if I surprised you.' Jordan's cigarette glowed red as he inhaled a lungful of smoke. 'I thought we might have a drink. Only the lobby was a little crowded.'

There was a bottle of whisky on the side table. Clare sensed this was as much of an explanation as he was going to receive. He poured them both a glass – 'If you want ice, you'll have to call room service' – then laid his jacket over the back of the chair, noting that the Orquesta Demon's Jazz record he'd bought yesterday was still lying on the desk seemingly untouched beside a copy of his brother's book. A collection of poems about the Spanish war that he'd helped to edit.

'So – you're a journalist now?' Jordan eyed him as he might a suspect brought in for interrogation. '*Special correspondent*?'

Clare caught the scepticism in Jordan's voice. 'I got lucky. They thought my time here might prove useful.'

'And has it?'

'So far – no ...'

Jordan stubbed out his cigarette and lit another with the battered lighter he'd kept with him since leaving Argentina. A deathbed gift from his father. 'You know I met your brother once,' he said. 'At the Playa de Madrid.' A former country club used by front line troops to grab a few days' relaxation.

It was news to Clare.

'I believe there's a reference to our moment in here.' Jordan picked up Gerald's book from the desk.

'You've read it?' Clare was surprised.

'A little. My English is not that good.'

'Nor was Gerald's Spanish. I can't imagine you had much of a conversation.'

Jordan smiled. 'We didn't. We just played chess. Here it is. "The Respite".' He handed Clare the book. But Clare didn't need to look – he knew the lines by heart.

'I'm sorry I never got to know him.' Jordan's eyes flickered with a lizard-like intensity. Across the street, an organ grinder and his dog were turning a tune for the tourists. A barely recognisable version of *I'm in the Mood*. 'How are you finding Barcelona? Had time to look up any old friends?'

'No.' Clare regretted the lie even as it passed his lips.

'But you went to see Esteban Llull?' Jordan was quick to correct him.

'Yes …'

'Why?'

Clare hesitated. Unsure how to answer. Unsure just how much Jordan knew. Then – *Tat, Tat, Tat*. A sudden knock on the door. A moment's reprieve as Jordan swiftly snuffed out his cigarette and slipped his right hand into his jacket pocket, like some New York gangster.

Whoever it was knocked again. This time louder.

'Richard – are you there?' It was Wilson, a clean jacket draped over his shoulder.

Clare opened the door.

Wilson took a step inside, saw Jordan and hesitated. 'I'm sorry. I didn't know you had visitors.'

'It's just an old friend.' Clare attempted an introduction but Wilson didn't have to look twice to know that he was intruding. 'I'll see you downstairs,' he muttered.

'I'll be right down,' Clare called after him – more in bravado than certainty.

The door fell shut. Jordan relit his cigarette – an old habit from the war – and picked up where they'd left off. 'Why go see Llull?' The question still stood.

Clare reached for his whisky. 'I wanted an interview with Picasso. I hoped he might help fix me up with a meeting…'

'And Capdevila? What did you want from him?'

'The same thing.' Clare dug himself still deeper into whatever hole Jordan had opened up for him. 'He wasn't in – so I left a message. I'm still waiting to hear back.'

Jordan met Clare's gaze, held it for a moment, then surprised him by once more changing the subject. 'After you went back to London. Did anyone ever talk to you about your experiences in Spain?'

'What do you mean?'

'MI5? Scotland Yard?'

'There was a man from the Home Office ...' Clare admitted.

'What did he want?'

'He asked me about the war. What it was like living in Barcelona.'

'Did he ask you to go back?'

'Yes.'

'As a spy?'

'He never actually used the word "spy".'

'But the implication was clear?'

'Yes.'

'What did you say?'

'I told him I wasn't interested.'

'Did he try to press you?'

'No.'

'When did this happen?'

'About May of last year.'

'What was the man's name?'

'He said he was called Smith. I've no idea what his real name was.' Clare neglected to mention that Smith had also introduced himself as a friend of Shaw's.

'Did you ever see him again?'

'No.' *The truth.*

Jordan flicked the ash from his cigarette and stepped back out onto the balcony. 'You know – I always hoped you would come back from Paris. You did a good job for us there after the war.'

Clare almost smiled.

* * * * *

October 1938. A crisp sunny day. Clare remembered stepping off the train onto the platform at Gare d'Austerlitz, the cold air a relief after the heat and humidity of Barcelona, the long, suffocating nights stuck inside an airless flat with Montse and Pep.

Jordan had sorted him out with money. A weekly allowance to be drawn from a Romanian bank close to the Cimetière du Père Lachaise. And accommodation. A small hotel on the left bank, near to Picasso's studio in Rue des Grand Augustins.

A year previously when he had travelled to Paris to pick up *Guernica*, Clare had been made to feel welcome by Picasso. But the second time round, he found the artist irritable, at his most childishly awkward, agreeing to see him one moment, then denying all knowledge of the arrangement the next.

On the one occasion he did manage to pin him down to a meeting, a drink at Les Deux Magots, Picasso brought along his lover of two years, Dora Maar. Intense, strong minded and temperamental, Dora seemed to inspire and infuriate Picasso in equal measures. At Les Deux Magots, Clare found himself ignored, Picasso choosing instead to pick an argument with Dora over a gold plated cigarette lighter he claimed to have given her and wanted back. She refused point blank, lighting cigarette after cigarette with the disputed lighter, encouraging Clare to smoke so that she could light him one too, suggesting the two of them go on to the cinema together and leave Picasso to go fuck himself. Picasso seemed genuinely amused by Dora's crude efforts to make him jealous. He told Clare to take Dora, and told Dora he'd even allow her to keep the lighter if she went.

Clare couldn't remember what they'd gone to see, only that it had starred Imperio Argentina. Afterwards, Dora had asked him back to her apartment on Rue de Savoie. There was no suggestion she wanted sex, rather Clare assumed she wished him there should Picasso drop by; his studio in Rue des Grand Augustins was only a block away.

The following weeks saw several such evenings; Clare more often than not ending up with Dora, accompanying her to a party, a gallery opening or the pictures. He soon came to realise that Picasso had no intention of returning to Spain nor even visiting it. He was far too wary of the Communists, frightened that once back in Spain they might never let him leave again.

All of which Clare duly reported back to Jordan.

Christmas came and went. Clare's letters to Montse became more and more apologetic. He'd be back soon, he promised. Meanwhile, life in Paris was good. A few friends came over from London, and in quieter moments, Clare even did a little work; he'd decided to gather together Gerald's poems into a book.

Then at the beginning of January, he had a visitor – Jordan.

Picasso's lifestyle. His routine. His friends. His women. Jordan wanted to know everything there was to know. Clare told him all he could over a sumptuous platter of langoustines at the Brasserie Heininger. 'You must make one last effort to persuade him home,' Jordan ordered him. 'Warn him Paris is about to turn nasty, that there'll soon be open warfare between the Communists and Fascists.'

Clare remembered thinking – *so that's why you're here.*

It started before he had a chance to relay the warning. A swastika daubed on the streetside wall of the courtyard outside Picasso's studio. A crude message in black paint denouncing him as a Communist. Death threats followed. Then more graffiti; on Picasso's front door, on the window of his favourite restaurant, and most chilling of all, on a canvas in his studio. There was no sign of a break-in. Ines, a pretty raven haired girl who lived on the floor below, swore she'd heard nothing during the night. Picasso refused to return to his studio. He checked himself into the Ritz and made preparations to move down to Mougins, the hill top village above Cannes where he liked to spend his summers. But before Picasso could leave, they got to him. Coming back from a gallery opening one night, a van drew up alongside him, a man casually leaning out of the window, pistol in hand.

Clare recalled being woken at five in the morning by Dora. 'They've shot him,' she said.

The bullet had passed through Picasso's left thigh, Clare later learned. A few inches above the knee. A last warning – for it was clear they could have killed him had they wished. Clare read about Picasso's triumphant homecoming in the papers. He heard about it from Dora. How Picasso had decided it was unsafe to remain in France. How he wanted her to come with him but that she'd been refused a visa by the Spanish authorities. How she was still waiting for one and most upsetting of all, still waiting to hear word from Picasso; Dora was neurotically obsessed that their last bust up – not the shooting – was the real reason he'd left for Spain, that he didn't want to speak to her, that it was his intention to sever all contact with her forever.

That evening Dora had been quite hysterical. Clare couldn't get away from her quickly enough. But on returning to his hotel, he'd found a letter waiting for him from the Romanian bank informing him that his account had been closed.

Jordan was pulling the plug on him. Clare's time in Paris was at an end.

* * * * *

'I thought you'd come back for the girl.' Jordan was standing on the balcony staring down at the Ramblas, the air pungent with the scent of cigars and expensive perfume. 'Wasn't there a child involved?'

'Not mine,' Clare was quick to answer. 'Her sister's.'

'What was her name?'

'Montse. Montserrat Rafols.'

'Are you still seeing her?'

'No.' There was a casualness about the question that unsettled Clare. *Had they been following him this morning?*

Jordan took a sip of whisky – his first since being handed the glass. 'If the journalism doesn't work out,' he smiled, 'you should know there's always a job for you here. We could do with men of your calibre. Your experience.'

Clare laughed. 'I'm not a Communist.'

'No-one said you had to be. In fact it helps that you're not.' Jordan drained his glass, placed it on the table, then asked Clare to please surrender his passport. 'It's just routine,' he insisted, but Clare wasn't fooled; without a passport he would be confined to the city. Jordan wanted to keep an eye on him, that much was clear.

'Should you change your mind – you know where to find me.' Jordan gathered up his coat, then as he stepped back out into the corridor, added, 'A last word of advice. Stay away from old friends. It'll make life easier for us both.' There followed a soft, imperceptible click of the latch as the door fell shut.

Clare stood for a moment in the middle of the room, dripping sweat, hardly daring to hope that Jordan's visit had been just that.

A play to recruit him. A gentle warning.

He poured himself another glass of whisky, then walked over to the desk where his gramophone record lay.

Tentatively, he slipped his fingers into the sleeve, feeling for Picasso's sketch. To his relief, finding it still there. Exactly as he'd left it.

A mon ami, RC. His secret still safe.

CHAPTER 6

Monday 29th July, 1940

Programme of the XIIth Olympiad
Athletics, Wrestling, Modern Pentathlon (fencing), Fencing, Polo, Hockey, Football, Weightlifting.

At the Reial Club de Tennis, the fencing strips were laid out on the courts; four to a court, sixteen courts in all. Clare had fenced a couple of times before at school so there was a familiarity to the ring of clashing swords, but what struck him as strange was the outdoor setting, the lack of echo, the sudden flashes of sunlight, the birds flitting from tree to tree.

Last night in the bar when Clare had told Wilson and the others he had to go and interview Markham, their reaction had been unanimous. He was wasting his time. Day one of the modern pentathlon – the horse riding – was by far Markham's best discipline, thereafter he was sure to fade. Best wait until day four, they told him, if he's still in with a chance then you've got yourself a story.

Clare had just shrugged – it wasn't his call.

He found Markham engaged in his second bout of the morning. His opponent – an Austrian cavalry officer. To Clare's untrained eye, the contest seemed evenly balanced. A balletic dance of thrust and counter thrust, but then with a sudden unravelling of blades it was all over, the dance unjoined, the Austrian stopped, an electric light confirming Markham's hit forty-seven seconds into the minute. Markham peeled off his mask and wiped the sweat from his eyes. He was about the same age as Clare, yet contrived to look older. Reddish sandy hair, pale blue eyes and a clipped moustache that said Gentleman Captain of the King's army. Clifton, Oxford and Sandhurst – even without his press notes, Clare might have guessed. 'They told me you'd be here at eleven,' Markham muttered, swapping his épée for a towel.

Clare apologised. No-one had told him.

'Bloody typical. *Evening News*, isn't it? You'll have to come back later. Break time's not 'til eleven.'

Clare wasn't bothered. It was a chance for him to go and find Montse. 'I can use the time to pick up some photographs,' he said. 'Grab a cup of coffee.'

'Do what you bloody like.' Markham wasn't interested. 'Just make sure you're here at eleven.'

'Right ...' Clare sloped off before he could say anything he might regret. He'd come across men like Markham before. At school. At university. On the cocktail circuit in London. Arrogant, narrow minded and talentless, they'd never failed to get his back up.

The press office was located on the top floor of the club house. Wilson hadn't been exaggerating when he'd described the fencing events as the preserve of the central Europeans. German, Czech, Hungarian – Clare supposed these were the languages he could now hear as he passed by the ground floor bar; even the cigarette smoke smelt exotically unfamiliar.

He saw her the moment he walked through the door, standing with her back half turned to him, chatting light heartedly to a colleague, laughing as they sorted their way through a pile of photographs. A third girl called him to their attention. 'Montse! Maria Jose! Visitor!'

'What are you doing here? I told you to stay away.' Montse moved fast to block his entrance.

'I didn't come to see you.' Clare stood his ground.

'Then what do you want?'

'Are you alright, honey?' Montse's colleague called to her. Montse nodded. She had the situation under control.

'I'm doing an article on the modern pentathlon,' Clare told her. 'There's an athlete my office want me to interview. I'm going to need a photograph.'

'What athlete?' She didn't believe him.

'Captain Robert Markham.' Clare pointed out Markham's name on the previous day's results sheet. 'If you'd rather I deal with your colleague?'

'Photographs are printed up over night.' Montse grudgingly handed him a form.

Clare filled in the details. 'What time do I pick it up?'

'You don't.' Montse added his request to a pile on her desk. 'I'll have it delivered to the Casa de Prensa.'

'Montse – can't we please talk about this? Over a drink? Just half an hour.' It wasn't what Clare had meant to say. The words just came tumbling out.

'There's nothing to talk about. I told you. It's finished.'

'You've got it wrong,' Clare protested. 'I tried to come back from Paris. I-'

'It's over.' Montse held the door open for him to leave. 'Now, please go.'

'Don't you even want to know what happened?' Clare made a last ditch appeal. But her expression made it clear there was nothing more to discuss. 'Goodbye, Richard,' she said. *Go home.*

Maybe it's for the best, Clare tried to convince himself as he beat a retreat back down to the bar. If Jordan's men were keeping tabs on him, then far better Montse have nothing to do with him.

11.00am. Half an hour and two cups of coffee later – Clare went back to work. He imagined Markham might want to do the interview somewhere close to the courts but instead he suggested they decamp to one of the many refreshment bars scattered around the grounds.

They found a table in the shade of a jacaranda tree and ordered a jug of freshly squeezed lemon juice. 'So – what have you got for me?' Markham asked, stretching his legs out into the sun.

'I'm sorry?' Clare's thoughts were still with Montse.

'Shaw said you'd have something for me.'

'Shaw?'

'Beat it!' Markham waved away the attentions of a shoe shine boy zeroing in on Clare's scuffed footwear. 'You did say the *Evening News*, didn't you?'

For a moment Clare looked blank. Then the penny dropped. The interview was a set up. Markham was Shaw's contact. A British agent.

Markham laughed. 'You thought you were here to do an interview! I'm flattered you thought me worth it. No – keep it open.' Clare had flipped shut his notebook. 'Keep writing. You never know who's watching.'

Clare reopened his pad, made a note of the day's date at the top of the page and underlined it twice, trying not to let his embarrassment show.

'So what is it you want to tell me?' Markham began again.

Clare instinctively lowered his voice. 'It's about Picasso. He wants to defect.'

Markham looked sceptical. 'He told you this?'

'Not to my face. Through an intermediary.'

'Who?'

'An art dealer. Rafael Capdevila. Someone I know from Paris.'

'A friend?'

'No. More an acquaintance.'

'Can we trust him?'

A fair question, Clare had to admit. The Spanish government had trusted Capdevila during the war to buy arms for them – aircraft, rifles, machine guns. His idea, their money. Set up an art gallery in Paris; the perfect front for buying weapons. An ideal way of circumnavigating the embargo imposed on Spain by the Non Intervention Pact. His idea, their money, and by the end of the war, he'd made lots of it. All accounted for of course, and handed back to the government. Only there'd been rumours of accounts in Switzerland. A small fortune in siphoned off funds. 'Picasso obviously trusts him,' Clare said non-commitedly.

'What's their history?' Markham didn't look convinced.

Clare told him. An edited version of all that had happened up to the moment last Friday when Capdevila had presented him with Picasso's sketch.

'Do you still have it with you?' Markham asked.

'No. It's in my room.'

'Where?'

'Hidden.'

'Get rid of it.'

'Why?'

'Because I said so.' Markham didn't like having his authority questioned. 'Destroy the picture as soon we're finished here. Put it in your basin and burn it. Do I make myself clear?'

A bell rang to signal the end of the rest period.

Markham swiftly finished off his lemonade and told Clare he'd be in touch again before next Friday. 'Until then – do nothing,' he said. 'Stick to your job. Don't give them any reason to suspect you. And stay away from old friends.'

'What about the article?' Clare ventured.

Markham gave a loud laugh. 'Come back at the end of day four. Then if I'm still in with a chance – the story's yours.'

Arsehole. It was all Clare could think as he picked up his notebook and looked for an exit.

Already, he'd had enough of Markham to last a lifetime.

* * * * *

Kathleen Booth sat at her desk idly flicking through the pages of an out of date travel brochure, *Mallorca, La Isla de Oro*. The illustrations were in black & white. Photographs of fishing villages, sea caves and old stone windmills, interspersed with glossy advertisements for hotels, boutiques and various competing steamship lines; she especially fancied the idea of the *Infanta Beatriz*.

The office was hot, the fan having long since ceased to work, while the rear window – jammed open with a sardine can – drew only the faintest whisper of air into the room.

The premises had been left empty since the beginning of the war. The smell of dust still lingered and the date on a wall calendar read *21st July 1936*; the day time stopped still for Señor Jose Sauledo, late owner of the Viajes Sauledo travel agency, executed, according to the man from the delicatessen next door, by Anarchist militiamen during the first days of the war. Kathleen had found a photograph of Sauledo in one of the drawers. A rakishly handsome man in his early forties, she'd pinned the photograph to the wall above her desk, if only to have someone to talk to, as the phone hardly rang and her boss was forever out and about on missions unspecified.

Ordinarily, Kathleen worked as an SIS operative in Madrid – code number 23500 – her duties split between assisting the chief on intelligence matters and maintaining the station's cover as a Passport Control Office. Three weeks ago she'd been sent to Barcelona to set up a temporary office for the duration of the Games. The station chief, retired Naval Captain Philip Holdsworth, had decided he needed a legitimate base in the city, something functional and cheap, cover for the end phase of a three month operation to turn a high ranking Spanish Naval Officer.

Kathleen had stumbled on the travel agency whilst walking past it one day, a block north of the Passeig de Gracia train station. Through the front window, she'd seen the furniture covered in sheets and a thick layer of dust on the floor. The landlady lived upstairs – so the man from the delicatessen next door had also told her – an old girl in her eighties with a heart problem. 'Turns out she's Sauledo's aunt,' Kathleen informed her fifty-eight year old boss in a phone call later that evening. 'The old bird's kept the place just the way it was the day they took him away. Even the phone still works.'

'And she doesn't mind us using it?' Holdsworth thought it sounded too good to be true.

'Seems not,' Kathleen told him. 'So long as we don't mind moving out if Sauledo happens to come back.' They'd both laughed at that; Holdsworth chuckling like a badly tuned motor spluttering into life, short on breath, long in the throat.

The operation to land the Spanish Naval Officer was codenamed "SPRING" – the details known only to Holdsworth and his irritable, Scottish born deputy, Lieutenant Alan Hicknall. It was Hicknall's show, Kathleen knew that much, otherwise Holdsworth wouldn't have given him charge of the Barcelona office. She was sorry about that. Working with Holdsworth was fun. He trusted her enough to perform small tasks, didn't ask her to leave the room when certain calls came through, whereas Hicknall withdrew into himself when she was around, leaving her in little doubt that he regarded her as strictly front of house, unsuited to overhear even the slightest backstage whisper.

Today, like yesterday and the whole of last week, Kathleen sat alone in the office with the ghosts of a dead man's business for company. It was 11.42am, almost time for her second coffee of the morning – she always went to the bar across the road – when the phone rang. She let it ring five times and then once more for Sauledo, her spirits rising with each "tring". At last, after a week, she had something to do. A call to answer. 'British Passport Office,' she said, picking up the phone. 'How can I help?'

There was a code for agents calling in from the field. A simple way for SIS operatives to distinguish themselves from the general public and the caller now gave it. 'I'd like to speak to the chief passport officer,' he told her. 'Extension 23100.' *23000 was the SIS code for Madrid. 23100 the personal ident for the station chief.*

Kathleen reached for a pen and note pad. 'I'm sorry, he's not here at the moment. But I can take a message.'

'I'd like to report my passport lost,' the caller told her. By which he meant he wanted a meeting.

'Your name, please.' Kathleen didn't recognise his voice.

'Captain Robert Markham.'

'Address in Barcelona?'

'Hotel Continental. San Feliu de Llobregat. I'm with the British Olympic team.'

Kathleen scribbled down the details. 'Will you be able to come into the office? You'll need to fill in a form.'

'Not until Friday,' Markham said. 'I've got events all day, every day, until then.'

'Then I'll have someone come see you.'

'Thank you.' Markham told her he'd be at the Reial Club de Tennis until early evening and hung up.

Kathleen logged the call in the duty book, then being thorough, checked Markham's name against the British Olympic team (everything he'd told her seemed to tally). She then locked up the office and went across the road for her late morning coffee.

At last, she thought, some excitement.

Alan Hicknall had been at war with the world ever since he could remember; through childhood, at school, his whole working life. His was a face that had never quite fitted. He was too prickly, too sure of himself, too inclined to speak his mind, all of which explained why, at the age of thirty-eight, Hicknall had failed to rise beyond the rank of station deputy, and why, at 2.50pm on a hot Monday afternoon, life found him sitting in the back seat of a taxi on his way up Diagonal, cursing an unwanted extra errand in what had already been a stressful day.

First – this morning, a "SPRING" meeting in Sitges, a pretty seaside town twenty-six miles south of Barcelona. Urbano – Hicknall's high ranking contact in the Spanish Navy – had insisted they meet there in a small house in the old town at the bottom of a nameless, steep narrow lane overhung with tiled balconies.

During their recent meetings, Hicknall had sensed Urbano to be getting cold feet but today he had seemed decided, ready to take the plunge, declaring himself satisfied with the house in Norfolk and the pension SIS had arranged for him. Urbano had no immediate family to complicate arrangements. Hicknall strongly suspected that he was a homosexual. He was also beginning to suspect that Urbano was an NKVD stooge. Hicknall had crossed swords with the NKVD several times before. First in Prague. Then in Budapest. He had a sense for the way they worked, and this sense was now telling him that "SPRING" was their operation, not his. All this, and much more, Hicknall needed to report to Holdsworth, but first he had to deal with the unasked for irritant that was Markham; Kathleen had briefed him about the call on his return from Sitges.

The taxi drew up outside the Reial Club de Tennis. Hicknall paid off the driver and entered the grounds, buying a ticket for ten pesetas. He found Markham without difficulty, sitting in the shade, resting between bouts. Clifton, Teddy Hall, Coldstream guards, he guessed, 'I'm the passport control officer,' he said.

Markham rose to his feet. 'Haven't we met before?'

'Rome perhaps?' Hicknall suggested. *The station code for Rome was 1800.*

'Or Paris?' Markham countered. *The station code for Paris was 1900. The next in the sequence.*

The two men shook hands. 'Alan Hicknall, deputy head, Spanish station.'

'Robert Markham. "D" section.'

Hicknall nodded curtly. 'What can I do for you?'

* * * * *

Barajas airport, Madrid. 7.30pm. Philip Holdsworth stood on the terminal roof watching the last flight from Barcelona coming into land; a gnat against the vast sky and endless plains reaching out from the city.

The Iberia De Havilland Dragon Rapide touched down on the tarmac and slowly taxied across to the terminal. Holdsworth – no nonsense eyes, nose a little crooked, dark hair greying at the edges – waited for all six passengers to disembark, then went downstairs into the arrival hall to greet Hicknall. Twenty minutes later, they were heading back into the city in Holdsworth's old Citroën.

In the privacy of the car, Hicknall told him about his meeting with Markham. 'London should have let us handle it from the start,' Holdsworth complained. Instinctively, he disapproved of "D" section; a specialised unit set up two years previously to examine alternative forms of warfare. Sabotage in other words. Holdsworth felt it got in the way of the nuts and bolts of intelligence gathering, something he'd given the last twenty years of his life to.

The Citroën pulled up outside a small unassuming building not far from the British Embassy. Behind the peeling façade lay the Passport Control Office, a warren of pokey rooms spread over the bottom two floors; on the top floor lay Holdsworth's own apartment. The premises were – in Holdsworth's opinion – little better than a chicken coop, but then London were notorious penny pinchers; he'd had enough problems persuading them to let him hire Kathleen to help deal with the genuine passport work he had to supervise on top of his intelligence work.

Holdsworth double locked the front door behind them, walked through to the kitchen, a dark, neglected room at the back of the house, and switched on the light, eliciting a feeble glow from a bulb that dangled precariously over the kitchen table. Underneath the stained sink hung a dirty curtain. Holdsworth pulled it back and fished out a bottle of Scotch, supplied at discount by a friend in the Embassy.

Holdsworth rinsed out a couple of glasses, half filled them with Scotch, then adding water from a saucepan he'd boiled earlier that morning, picked up a packet of biscuits and carried the drinks back out into the hall to the broom cupboard under the stairs, where Hicknall sat hunched on an old crate, setting the dials on a short wave radio transmitter. 'Cheers!' Holdsworth pulled up another crate and sat down beside him, ready to start encoding the message.

* * * * *

Hanslope Park, England. 9.05pm. Betty Eade logged an incoming transmission from station 23000. Duration twenty seconds. Confirmed two minutes later on the back up frequency.

She copied down the message in triplicate. One for the house files. And two for London. To be despatched via the hourly motorcycle service.

By 11.00pm, Picasso's request to defect was lying on the desks of the Section I and Section V officers responsible for the Iberian region.

* * * * *

Barcelona. 11.15pm. A still, shaded plaça not far from the cathedral. A child leaned over the edge of a fountain and rippled the water with her hands, pushing a feather further and further out of reach until it stuck fast against the base of the centre stone. From the far corner of the square, the child's mother called at her to quit dawdling, 'Maria! *Ven!*' The girl scooped a last handful of water into the air and scampered off, leaving Clare once more with the space to himself; at this late hour, few people had cause to use the square as a cut through and even fewer cause to be there. The church door was locked, the school room empty since the start of the holidays, and the lights in the houses all turned off.

Clare sat in the dappled moonlight on the edge of the fountain, his trousers specked with droplets of water from where the girl had inadvertently splashed him. Whenever he thought of Barcelona, it was always this square which first came to mind, this quiet, almost forgotten corner of the city where he liked to come when he wanted to be on his own.

Stay away from old friends. First Jordan. Then Markham. It was laughable. The one person Clare wanted to see would have nothing to do with him. Maybe the girl's mother was right. Maybe it was time to go home.

Clare stretched his arms above his head, feeling a click in the base of his neck, then noticed something glinting at him from the water; what looked like moonlight striking the tiled basin of the fountain. Then he saw it again. This time more clearly. A flash of gold. Something hidden beneath a scrap of rotting paper. He reached into the water and pulled away the paper, groping for whatever lay below. Now feeling it. Something metallic. A gold medallion and chain, its lustre long lost in the murk of the fountain.

He gave the medallion a rub with his shirt and held it up to the light. It was a Saint Christopher. The same engraving on the face and obverse. Nothing very valuable. Just a simple, commonplace charm. Without thinking, he slipped it into his pocket and set off back to his hotel, resisting the urge to take the short cut past Montse's flat.

Their flat as it had once been.

CHAPTER 7

Tuesday 30th July, 1940

Programme of the XIIth Olympiad
Athletics, Modern Pentathlon (shooting), Fencing, Wrestling, Yachting, Polo, Football.

At his stall in the Boqueria market, Osvaldo Gomez called for more eggs. His wife, Elena, stood bent over the sink washing the dirty plates. 'I heard you the first time,' she said, drying her hands on her apron before stooping to pick out a dozen eggs from a basket on the floor. These, she carefully placed in a chipped enamel bowl and handed to Osvaldo.

Osvaldo cracked two of the eggs into a heavy metal frying pan, at least as ancient as himself, and letting the whites bleed into the bright orange juices of a chorizo, scraped in the burnt bits and added a dash of salt.

Jordan called Gomez *tio* – uncle. There was no family connection although they both hailed from the same town in Argentina. Simply, Jordan had one day been lured to Osvaldo's stall, not by the smell of chorizo but by the aroma of Argentine cigarettes: Primeros – Jordan's favourite smoke and impossible to buy in Spain. Osvaldo had admitted to having a deal with the skipper of a boat, a deal he was happy to cut Jordan in on, in return for, Jordan had just told him to name his price, Osvaldo had, and so a friendship had begun. Now, every Tuesday morning, before his weekly meeting with Comrade Gavrilov, Jordan made a habit of dropping by the stall for breakfast to pick up his cigarettes and provide Osvaldo with an ear for his reminiscences. 'When an old man starts dreaming of the tastes and smells of his childhood,' Osvaldo liked to say before asking Jordan whether some ice cream parlour or cake shop from his childhood still existed, 'that's when he knows death is close by,' at which point the long suffering Elena would let out a loud "I've heard it all before" sigh before asking him to pass the dirty plates.

The safe house where Jordan and Gavrilov met lay above a launderette close to the Boqueria. The rent – paid weekly in cash – came from Moscow, from the budget of the Iberian section of the NKVD. Nobody in SIM knew of its existence, nor were they aware that since 1938 Jordan had been one of Moscow's top men in Barcelona. A trusted source on the inner machinations of the Spanish Secret Police. An insurance policy against the Spanish developing ideas of their own.

The madam of the launderette, Maria Sol, greeted Jordan with her customary grin, relieved him of his laundry bag and rent money, then for the benefit of the two Chinamen whose washing she was taking in, said in her best voice, 'Your clean clothes are inside. Please come with me.'

Jordan followed her through a doorway hung with glass beads into the engine room of the launderette, low ceilinged, stiflingly hot and reeking of starch. In a large alcove, behind a faded curtain, lay racks of freshly laundered clothes. Neat bundles wrapped in newspaper and tied with string. Beyond this was the back door and a staircase leading up to an apartment, which until recently had been occupied by a pair of identical twins, Maria Sol's daughters, Maria Carmen and Maria Jesus, better known to the neighbourhood by their *noms de boudoir*, Paloma and Freda. The two girls now practised their trade round the corner. Jordan saw to it there was no trouble with the police and in return Maria Sol guaranteed him complete discretion.

Jordan slowly climbed the staircase to the apartment, letting his eyes adjust to the lack of light, careful to step over the two booby trapped steps rigged to act as an alarm. He knocked on the door, spelling out his initials – AJ – in morse, then entered.

'Good morning, Comrade Major,' Gavrilov was waiting for him, gun in hand, a standard precaution, standing by the rear window, slight, dark haired, neat and sharp like a rat, his breathing pinched as though he were frightened of opening up his lungs to the air; a legacy, Jordan supposed, of his childhood in the slums of Kiev.

'Good morning.' Jordan closed the door behind him.

Gavrilov returned the gun to his jacket. Jordan was meant to know him only by his codename "MISHA"; that Gavrilov was a Colonel in the NKVD, a close friend of Marshal Voroshilov and answerable directly to Beria himself, was classified information. But Jordan had made it his business to find out. He liked to know who was handling his material.

The two men moved to the back of the room where the light was strongest. Jordan handed Gavrilov the two documents given to him by Kreiger; Himmler's proposal for an exchange of political opponents.

At the top of the Nazi's wish list, Gavrilov read the name – *Werner Bloch*.

* * * * *

Outside the Casa de Prensa, a shoe shine boy was busy trying to solicit work from the flow of journalists to-ing and fro-ing. '*No gracias*.' Clare skipped past him into the fan-cooled hall; there was something about his footwear that seemed to have the shoe shine boys buzzing all over him. Like flies to shit.

There was too large a crowd congregated in the bar for Clare to bother with coffee, so he passed straight on upstairs to check his mail. There was just the one envelope with his name on it. From Montse. He could tell by the handwriting. He tore it open. Inside were a half dozen photographs of Markham, also a slip of paper on which she had written just two words – *As requested*.

The bitch. Clare threw the paper into the bin and marched on down the corridor to the Press Office to see if Lucia had managed to get Werner his ticket.

She had. And not just one but two.

'You're a darling,' he told her, then – on a sudden whim, still furious at Montse – asked, 'What are you doing this evening?'

Lucia wasn't stupid. There was a tension to Clare's voice that made her suspect that this was more about the girl he'd asked after the first time they'd met, but in a week or so the games would be over and Clare back in England so that was just fine by her. 'Nothing,' she smiled.

'Then let me buy you a drink,' he said.

'Okay.' Lucia got off at eight. They arranged to meet at a quarter past, at the Font del Gat, any further conversation put paid to by a half dozen journalists spilling into the room.

'See you later,' Lucia signed off cheerily.

Clare nodded. *See you later*. His only regret that Montse wouldn't be there too. To see him with Lucia. To see him doing just fine without her.

* * * * *

Back at the launderette, the two Chinamen were gone. Maria Sol was sitting on her comfortable chair in the street, sentinel-like by the doorway, a cigarillo jammed between her lips. The Argentinian and his pallid rat-like friend were taking their time today, she mused. Usually, they were only ten minutes but – she looked up at the market clock – they'd now been together almost an hour. She tried to imagine what was going on upstairs. Big time crooks? Fugitive followers of Franco? Or just a couple of well heeled pansies? Not that she minded a jot one way or the other. Paying her the money they did, they could steal/scheme/fornicate until hell froze over for all she cared.

* * * * *

The rest of the day, Clare spent at the Olympic stadium. 100, 200, 400, 800, 5,000; the length of metres run blurred into one great endless lap as the sun beat down and he stretched and fidgeted and shifted in order to ward off the numbness of eight hours of block S, row AD, seat 194. There was little to mitigate the boredom and too much British involvement to risk leaving his seat for more than a glass of water and a piss. All day long, the incessant clatter of portable typewriters drove him mad, as did the long queues for the press phones and telegraph desks.

The Font del Gat, when at last the time came for Clare to meet Lucia, was a blessed relief; cold beer, a plate of patatas bravas and the shade of a jacaranda tree. His headache eased. An hour passed most pleasantly. Lucia was late but he didn't mind, supposing she'd been held back at work.

From the terrace, through a screen of trees, he could make out the church spires and myriad rooftops of the city bathed in the warm glow of early evening. Where bells had once rung and boys sung evensong, there now swelled the twenty thousand plus voices of the crowd at Les Corts, echoed across the city by countless radio sets and loud speakers as the football match between Egypt and Switzerland (still 0-0) entered the last five minutes of extra time, then – 'Hello, my friend' – Clare looked round to see Balasc, the journalist he'd met on the bus, crossing the terrace towards him, cocktail in hand, smelling of eau de cologne. '*Palare?*'

'What?' Clare presumed him to be speaking Hungarian.

'*Palare?*' Balasc repeated himself, this time louder, drawing up a chair, looking Clare purposefully in the eyes, his manner that of a man who's already had too much to drink. Clare looked blank. Balasc sighed wistfully. 'A beautiful evening.'

Clare nodded, glancing at his watch. Lucia was now forty minutes late.

'You're waiting for someone?' Balasc said.

'Yes.'

'Me too.' Balasc drained the last of his martini. 'So we are in the same boat.' He waved his arm at a passing waiter. '*Garçon*. Another martini! And one for my friend.'

Clare declined the offer.

'You will feel a lot better after a martini,' Balasc pressed him.

'Really. I'm okay.'

'Another beer, then. To keep me company.'

'No, thank you.'

'Just one.' Balasc gave Clare's thigh a sharp squeeze, as though he were trying to pin him to his chair.

Clare pushed him away. 'I said no.'

'Scared you off, have I?' Balasc sounded aggrieved. He turned to the waiter. 'Just the one martini then. Since this fucker won't drink with me.' The waiter took Balasc's empty glass and moved off across the terrace. '*Bona dish*,' Balasc muttered. '*Bona dish*.' This time he said it to Clare, looking him in the eye, drunkenly defiant. 'You don't understand me, do you?' Balasc laughed, lighting a cigarette. '*No palare*. Bugger it! Not my night.' He laughed again.

Clare got to his feet. Balasc had had enough. And so had he.

At the Casa de Prensa, the early evening crush was past its worst but still there were a large number of journalists milling around the bar – Americans mostly, the time difference between the United States and Europe giving them a few more hours to hit their deadline. The door to the Press Room upstairs lay open. A light on inside. Clare gave a little knock and entered. A woman looked up from her work, not Lucia but one of her colleagues whom Clare recognised from before. 'She left ten minutes ago,' the woman said.

Clare hurried back up the hill to the Font del Gat only to find Lucia had already been and gone, last seen heading for the funicular according to one of the waiters who knew her.

At the funicular – a train stood ready.

There was no time to buy a ticket. Vaulting the turnstile, dodging the attempts of a guard to restrain him, Clare raced for the nearest door, only for it to shut in his face.

Too late by a matter of seconds.

'Stand back,' the guard shouted, pulling him away from the carriage, as the cable drum started to turn and the train fell away down the hillside, his date for the evening disappearing along with the tail lights into the gloom.

It was getting dark now. On Paral·lel, groups of men were hovering outside the music halls eyeing up the girls strutting the pavements.

Clare loitered for a moment outside the Ba-ta-clan, then crossed over to the other side of the road and headed off into the Raval, into the stinking narrow streets of the old city. Before returning to his hotel, there was at least one thing he could usefully do.

It took him longer to find the bar than he'd imagined. A small shop opposite St Carmen's church – selling *Valdepeñas* by the glass – confused him into a false turn so that he soon found himself straying into the Barri Xino with its squalid brothels, sordid cafés, deformed beggars and pavement girls dressed in pink celanese petticoats; transparent gauze stretched over their breasts, behind each, a huge man in a vest lurking sinister in the doorway, arms crossed.

Eventually Clare found what he was looking for, recognising first the letter writer's kiosk, then a tailor's shop, then the sound of the radio, tonight playing *Ara Ve Nadal*, a lively one-step by Orquesta Demon's Jazz.

On seeing him, the barman leaned down and pulled a bottle of Scotch from the shelf. Brand new. Seal unbroken. 'Just the one glass,' Clare told him as he discreetly slid an envelope from his jacket onto the counter. 'It's for Werner.' The barman eyed the envelope as if it were a contamination. Clare explained that it was just a ticket; something Werner had asked him for the other night. Reluctantly the barman took it, slipping the envelope between the pages of his newspaper, his expression leaving Clare under no illusion that this was strictly a one-off arrangement.

Clare carried his drink across to a secluded table on the far side of the room.

On the radio, a public announcement reminded listeners not to pester or otherwise beg from those attending the Games.

Clare took out his programme of events and turned to the timetable in the middle, conscious that he was still short of a plan for tomorrow. But as he opened the cover, a card that had become stuck between its pages fell to the floor, the postcard that he'd bought from the kiosk outside the Palau Nacional. The picture of *Guernica*.

Clare could recall at least four times when Picasso's masterpiece had almost been destroyed while in his and Montse's care. Once, when their truck span off the road in the Picos de Europa. Once near Salamanca, when they had been strafed by a Nationalist plane. Another time in Leon, when they'd hit a land mine. And the closest shave of all, at a village fiesta in Extremadura, when a stray firework had landed in the middle of a munitions dump and all hell had let loose, he and Montse driving off down the main street, shells exploding, bullets pinging all around them, miraculously making it out of the town, driving on and on until they ran out of petrol, then making love on the floor of the truck until dawn, high on adrenalin and cheap wine.

Clare had bought the card to give to Montse. He should still send it to her, he decided. A final goodbye – if that's what she wanted. Something more dignified than six photographs of Markham and a comp slip. But what to write? How to know which words to choose? If only his brother, the poet, were alive to help him.

Clare took a sip of whisky, then remembered the letter writer whose kiosk he'd just walked past.

He found the old man playing cards. A youth mending his bicycle in the street outside showed him the way, past the church and up a dark staircase to a cramped room above a bakery. The letter writer's name was Joan. Even in the yellow gloom of the gas light, Clare could see that he was old, his skin like well used blotting paper, his limbs stiff and tired, yet in his eyes there still shone a spark that said life was worth living, that looked forward to the next hand dealt him.

Clare apologised for barging in on the game. All he needed was ten minutes of Joan's time. 'I'll pay whatever you want,' he said. 'I have a pen and a postcard. All I need are the words.'

'What's her name?' Joan asked.

Clare told him – Montse. And yes – he still loved her. Yes – he could have treated her better. No – he hadn't hit her. No – she didn't want to see him again. And no – he didn't altogether blame her. All he wished for was a chance to say goodbye so that the last words to pass between them shouldn't read *As requested*. 'I don't care what you write. What words you use,' he said. 'I don't want to even read them.'

Joan smiled warmly. 'I understand. She'll get it tomorrow.'

CHAPTER 8

Wednesday 31st July, 1940

Programme of the XIIth Olympiad
Athletics, Fencing, Modern Pentathlon (swimming), Yachting, Polo, Hockey, Football, Weightlifting.

Nuria Roca stifled a yawn as the telephone rang. At ten past six, it was the first call of the day. 'Taxis David,' she sleepily intoned.

Manolo, the fourteen year old office boy, sat on the opposite side of the room, heel jigging against the chair leg, the beat of a tune he couldn't get out of his head. Early morning was the time of day he loved best, before the office got busy, when he and Nuria had the place to themselves. Every morning, he'd fetch her coffee, watch her put on her make-up and listen to her tales of the night before, the dances danced, the men who'd danced them with her; he'd imagine himself in their shoes, squeezed against her weighty bosom, high on her scent.

'Yes,' Nuria replied in response to something being said on the other end of the line, with her free hand stirring a spoonful of sugar into her coffee, then 'Yes, Sir,' all of a sudden she sat up straight, slopping the drink over her skirt. Manolo reached for a towel but Nuria frantically waved him away. 'Yes, Sir. I'll do it right now. I'll tell him.'

Outside the office, a fleet of taxis – standard, luxury and commercial – stood parked by the kerb. Nuria anxiously rapped her knuckles against the window of cab number 512. Werner lowered his newspaper and glowered at her, 'What do you want?' In little less than twenty minutes he was going to drive out to Sabadell to look for a fare. He'd heard rumour of complaints from the American team about the laid-on bus service and now here was Nuria no doubt about to give him some half arsed job in town.

'You're to go to Passeig de Gracia. Number sixty-seven,' she told him. 'A Major Jordan wants to see you.'

Werner blanched. 67, Passeig de Gracia was the most notorious of the SIM's fifteen city stations. A death sentence.

'I'm sorry.' Nuria looked close to tears. 'Is there anyone you want me to call?'

Werner shook his head. 'No. Thank you. I'll be fine.'

But in truth, all those who might have cared were already gone. He had no-one left to call.

* * * * *

High over the plains of Aragon – on the first flight of the morning from Madrid to Barcelona – a stewardess took Holdsworth's empty cup and filled it with coffee. '*Gracias*.' Holdsworth felt a wave of exhaustion roll over him as he heaped a spoonful of sugar into his cup, but what he really craved was a cigarette, and for that – he glanced at the engaged sign on the smoking cabin – he'd still have to wait.

The stewardess moved on up the aisle. Holdsworth glanced at his watch. Just sixteen hours had elapsed since London had signalled him their reply. Go to Barcelona. Check out Picasso. If he's kosher, bring him out. Those were his orders. Hicknall had complained bitterly about being left in Madrid. Of all the agents attached to the Spanish station, he knew Barcelona the best. He was the most qualified to plan Picasso's escape route. But Holdsworth needed someone reliable to maintain communications with London and so he'd ordered Hicknall to stay put, even giving him the keys to his flat so he wouldn't have to move from the building until the operation was over.

The door to the smoking cabin slid open. Holdsworth sprang to his feet. The woman vacating the cabin smiled as they passed each other in the aisle. She smelt of menthol.

On most aircraft the smoking cabin was spacious enough to hold four people but somewhere along the line the JU 90 had been modified, leaving the smoking area little larger than a toilet. No matter – it was at last his turn. Holdsworth closed the door, lit a cigarette and inhaled deeply. Away from the distraction of the other passengers, he ran a brief mental check over the list of things he had to do on arrival in Barcelona. Over dinner the previous night, he and Hicknall had devised a simple code so they could communicate by telephone. Holdsworth hoped it would cover most eventualities.

The plane touched down on time. The airport felt busier than Holdsworth had ever known it, aircraft from all over Europe sitting on the tarmac, a swarm of militiamen, police and airport workers making themselves busy. An official scrutinised his passport, made him fill in a form and then he was through – *Welcome to Barcelona. Enjoy the Games*.

Holdsworth idly wondered if he was being watched. If the SIM were alert to his arrival.

Kathleen was waiting for him at Café Zurich on Plaça Catalunya. They greeted each other Spanish style – a kiss on each cheek. 'Do you want the good news first. Or the bad?' Kathleen asked as Holdsworth ordered a jug of hot chocolate and a plate of churros.

'The good.'

'I've got you a room at the Falcon.'

'And the bad news is I have to share it with Vivien Leigh?' Not the greatest of jokes but it made Kathleen smile anyway.

'The bad news is – it's hot, small, and it doesn't have a view. But it's the best I could do,' she hastily added. 'And for the price, nothing short of a bloody miracle.'

Holdsworth laughed. He liked Kathleen. He enjoyed having her around. He'd never married and he doubted he ever would. But if things had turned out otherwise then Kathleen was definitely the type of girl he would have gone for. Pretty in an unflashy sort of way. Bright. Resourceful. Unafraid to speak her mind. He often wondered what she did with her time – whether she had a lover – but he'd always been too shy to ask. He knew from her file she'd once been engaged to a young man, Peter, at the Foreign Office and that he'd died in an air crash. But that had been a few years ago – before she'd joined the service.

Holdsworth checked his watch. He was due to meet Markham at twelve. Say he was finished by one, he could be back in town by half past. 'Free to join me for lunch?' he said.

Kathleen smiled. 'Yes. Thank you. That would be lovely.' And what's more, she meant it. No doubt about it, she found Holdsworth attractive. Not in the same way she had Peter. That would be asking too much. But she enjoyed his company. Already she was looking forward to seeing him later this evening, to hearing more about his meeting with Markham. She appreciated the way he told her things, involved her in what was going on, even sought out her opinion. She was proud to have his trust on such an important case, delighted it was Hicknall rather than herself who'd been left in Madrid. As she finished off her chocolate, Kathleen dreamily wondered whether she'd be mad to embark on an affair with him.

* * * * *

At the other end of the Ramblas, Clare had made a decision. He knew it would be safer to destroy the sketch that Picasso had given him, but he couldn't bring himself to do it. Not yet. Assuming that the drawing was worth at least £400, then that was £800 more than he now had in his bank account. Chances were Markham was just being paranoid. Chances were ... Clare buried the record sleeve in which the sketch was hidden under a pile of press handouts, throwing yesterday's newspaper on top of it for good measure. Chances were his "Picasso" would be safe from any routine security check.

Clare took a last long look at the room, made a mental note of where his possessions lay, then went downstairs to deposit his room key and collect his messages. There were two. One from the BBC commentator and former sprint Gold medallist, Harold Abrahams, agreeing to his request for an interview. And the other unsigned – just two words long. *Habas. Manana.*

It was from Montse. *A change of heart.* She wanted to see him, or rather she was proposing they meet.

Tomorrow. For lunch.

Whatever Joan had written must have worked. Clare put to the back of his mind any thoughts he had of reviving his date with Lucia and strolled out into the street, quietly humming.

"In the mood for all his kissin'

In the mood his crazy lovin'

In the mood what I was missin'

It didn't take me long to say I'm in the mood now."

* * * * *

Outside the gates of Passeig de Gracia, 67, Werner lit a last cigarette, threw the packet to an old man rummaging the rubbish bin at the side of the road, and walked through into the inner courtyard, his eyes instinctively drawn to the legend on the wall – *Servicio de Investigacion Militar.*

'Werner Bloch.' He gave his name to the policeman on the front desk.

'Bloch?' The policeman had no record of his appointment. For one glorious moment Werner thought he might actually be turned away, but then a quick call to Jordan's office clarified the confusion. 'You're German,' the policeman said in an accusatory tone, 'Why didn't you say so?'

He picked up the phone again.

At his office in the German Consulate, Obersturmbannführer Kreiger took the call. *Bloch, W.* Kreiger drew a line through Werner's name, then reached for his file. Colour code amended from red to black.

In neat handwriting, he made a note on the cover. *31.7.40 – Subject Apprehended. Barcelona, Spain.*

CHAPTER 9

Thursday 1st August, 1940

Programme of the XIIth Olympiad
Athletics, Fencing, Shooting, Modern Pentathlon (cross country running), Yachting, Wrestling, Cycling, Polo, Hockey, Football, Weightlifting.

Neither the street nor Fernando's had changed since Clare's last visit. The faded brown paintwork, the crack in the bottom corner of the front window, it was all exactly as he remembered it, even down to the shard of sunlight cutting a line across the front of the restaurant. Like a sun dial, you could tell the time from the angle it hit Fernando's.

Clare pushed open the door. The restaurant was full except for a small table close to the window lying in the one bit of sunlight to penetrate the dark interior; Montse must have told Fernando they were coming.

Clare greeted him warmly. A large, jovial man with a sweet smile and lively eyes, he wanted to know why they hadn't seen Clare for so long. Clare muttered something about having been in England. Fernando called to his son, Felipe. 'Bring Ricardo a drink!' A thick, sweet wine arrived; Fernando's favoured aperitif from his brother's vineyards in Andalucia. Clare drank to Fernando's health, Fernando drank to his, and they both drank to Clare being back in Spain, to Fernando's brother's vineyards and to Andalucia until a sharp voice from the kitchen reminded Fernando of his duty to the other diners. 'Later,' Fernando told him, 'I'll come finish the bottle with you.'

The clock struck two. Montse arrived at five past, wearing a simple dark skirt and a patterned blouse. Clare watched her kiss Fernando on both cheeks, Felipe too, then cross over to him, looking a little frayed, he thought, on edge. 'You look good,' he said, kissing her on the side of the face, somewhere between her lips and cheek.

'I'm sorry I'm late, I went home to change.'

'You got my postcard.' Clare poured her a glass of water. 'I couldn't think what to say so I had a letter writer say it for me.'

'I know.'

'It was that obvious?' Clare felt a little let down. 'What did he write?'

'Nothing. He said he had to see me first. Before he could put pen to paper.'

'You mean – you met Joan?'

'I had a long drink with him – yes. He said you wouldn't pay him unless I agreed to have lunch with you.'

'And you believed him?'

'Of course not.'

'So why did you come?'

For the first time since she'd sat down, Montse looked him full in the eye. 'To let you say goodbye,' she said. 'The way you want. Isn't that why we're here?'

Clare nodded. Of course. He'd been a fool to hope otherwise.

Over her shoulder, he caught sight of old father Fernando shuffling their way in a pair of worn slippers, clasping a carafe of wine and a basket of bread like some doddery old priest; the one job left to him after a lifetime working in the restaurant. '*Bon profit,*' the old man mumbled, placing bottle and basket firmly before them. Clare smiled. Old father Fernando smiled back. Here too nothing had changed. He still had no idea who Clare was.

'So why fencing?' Clare was emboldened to ask a little later, after Montse had relaxed into her second glass of wine. 'If you wanted to avoid me, wouldn't it have been easier to leave town rather than move to your parents' hotel, or wherever else you're staying?'

'It's not that simple,' Montse said dryly. 'Things have changed since you've been away. To leave the city you now need a permit.'

'Since when?'

'A month ago. And besides – all essential personnel have been conscripted into helping with the Games. I speak English. They need me here.'

Clare understood. She didn't have to say anything more. And she didn't.

The next move was his. 'You know I was all set to come back from France. I wanted to–'

'So why didn't you?' Montse cut him short.

'You remember a guy called Russell?'

Montse shook her head.

'Thin. Brown curly hair. Forever trying to grow a beard. You met him a couple of times when I was working at the radio station. He was one of the "comic stars".' Their nickname for the political commissars who'd been attached to the Brigade, for the most part hard line communists responsible for developing the political understanding of the volunteers.

Montse still didn't remember.

'It doesn't matter,' Clare continued. 'The point is – I saw him in Paris just before I was due to leave. We had a drink. He warned me not to come back. He said my life would be in danger if I did.'

'From whom?'

'The SIM.'

'Why would they want to kill you?'

'Russell told me about the purges in the Soviet Union. He told me how the Russians were recalling their military advisors to Moscow. How they were being shot or sent to a labour camp simply because they'd been working abroad. Because there was a chance they might have been corrupted.' Clare could see that he had her attention now. 'Russell warned me the same logic was now being applied to Spain. He told me that no-one was safe anymore. Especially those who'd travelled or who'd had dealings with foreign governments. I mean – what was I to do? I'd been in Paris for three months. Russell told me there was a strong chance that I would be on a wanted list.'

'So – you went back home?'

'Yes.'

'You could have written,' Montse said quietly.

'I did.' *It was the truth. He had.* 'I sent scores of letters. From London. From Paris. I tried every way I could think to contact you.'

'I imagined that if you had written,' Montse was speaking more to herself than in acknowledgement of anything Clare had said, 'then the SIM would have wanted to see me. But they never did. So I thought ...'

'Maybe that's what they wanted you to think. You know what they're like.'

'Maybe ...'

On the far wall, Clare noticed Fernando had hung a poster promoting the Games. A heroic portrait of a crowd marching behind an Olympic banner and red flag below the slogan *Todos Juntos!* All Together! 'I know you're still angry ...' he said.

'That you left – yes. That you came back – no. Not any more.'

'So what now?'

'We finish lunch. Then you go your way and I go mine.'

'We don't have to.'

'Have you got a better idea?'

'Marry me. Come back to England.'

Montse laughed.

'What's so funny?' *He was serious.*

'They wouldn't let me. Anymore than they'll let you stay after the Games are over. And what about Pep? My parents? I can't just leave them.'

Clare didn't have an answer to that.

They ordered habas. Broad beans stewed with chunks of ham and sausage. Something of a tradition when at Fernando's, as well as being the dish that forever reminded Clare of his first few weeks in Spain, training with the International Brigade at Albacete, being invited into the homes of the local villagers, unable to speak Spanish yet always being made to feel welcome, his hosts sharing what little food they had in the name of the common cause. *All Together!* In those heady days, it had really meant something.

They talked about anything but themselves. Barcelona. The post-war deprivations. Montse's job at the Press Office. The Olympic Games – what they meant to Spain. 'Everyone knows it's the Party who are in charge here but they still need the world to believe it isn't so. That's why the Games are so important,' she said, lowering her voice to a level where he could hardly hear her, 'so that the rest of the world can appease Stalin with a clear conscience.' Despite herself, Montse couldn't hold back on the subject and Clare loved her for it, envying her passion, her inability to remain silent about the things that really mattered.

After lunch, they stood on the pavement outside the restaurant. 'I'm going this way,' she said, pointing towards Plaça Catalunya. 'I've got to pick up Pep from my mother's. I promised I'd take him to the beach.'

Clare took it as an invitation. 'I'll come with you, it's on my way.'

'Okay,' she shrugged, 'why not?'

They walked in silence. A route they'd taken a hundred times before up through the Barri Gotic; the streets empty, the shutters drawn for lunch, the occasional clatter of a pan echoing from an open window. On the Ramblas, Clare stopped to buy Pep a present. A model aeroplane with a red star on each wing and retractable wheels. 'You give it to him,' he told Montse. 'You don't even have to say it's from me if you think it'll upset him.'

Montse just laughed. 'There's no harm in him seeing you. He won't even remember you.'

Clare was sorry he'd even mentioned it.

A few minutes later, they reached the Hotel Comercio. Here too, it was just as Clare remembered it: a cat on the doorstep, the balconies adorned with pots of geraniums, a large palm tree throwing a diffuse shadow across the crumbling plasterwork. Montse unlocked the front door and Clare followed her up the marble staircase, clutching the wrapped aeroplane to his chest.

'What are *you* doing here?' Montse's father glared at Clare as they entered the lobby.

'Ignore him,' Montse commanded as she led Clare on through a door marked "Private". Away from her father's angry stare.

In the kitchen, Montse's mother was reading to Pep; Clare guessed she must have known he and Montse were having lunch together for she didn't seem the slightest bit surprised to see him. *'Hola! Guapo!'* she exclaimed, planting a large kiss on both his cheeks, telling him didn't he think Pep had grown, wasn't he a real little boy now? Absolutely, Clare agreed, somewhat bemused to find the screaming toddler that had driven a wedge between himself and Montse, now a walking, talking four year old.

'Granny – read me the story,' Pep demanded, sensing his grandmother's distraction, redirecting her attention back to the last few paragraphs.

Montse's mother – Violeta – was born and bred Barcelona. Her father had run a fruit stall up in Sants, close to the station. She was a small, energetic woman with a strong streak of the young girl about her, a charming naivety that saw only the bright side, that thought why not, why shouldn't I, who got her ideas from the newspapers, from advertisements, from talking to the guests that passed through the hotel, from her children, and now from her grandson, Clare supposed.

The story came to an end. Clare presented Pep with the model aeroplane. *Wow!* His eyes shone like saucers. 'Say thank you,' Montse prompted him.

'Xavi!' Violeta called to her husband. 'Come see what Pep's been given.'

But Montse's father had already made himself scarce; it would take a lot more than a model aeroplane for him to forgive Clare for the way he'd walked out on his daughter.

Clare glanced at the clock. He had thirty minutes to file his report for the last edition. 'I ought to be getting back to the hotel,' he said.

'We'll come with you.' Montse scooped Pep into her arms. 'It's on our way.'

Clare could only guess that there was still something she wanted to tell him.

It was a ten minute walk to the Oriente but it took almost twenty, as Pep insisted on playing with his aeroplane whilst refusing to be carried. But for once, Clare's luck held, there were no queues for the phone. 'Cabin Two,' the receptionist told him, pointing to the bank of empty cabins in the hotel lobby.

Clare left Montse and Pep playing peek-a-boo with the cushions on the sofa and went to make his call, re-emerging ten minutes later dripping with sweat and thanking God for Reuters; he'd managed to pick up a print out of the latest results from the lobby and the rest he'd ad-libbed.

'Pep has something to ask you,' Montse smiled.

The boy buried his head behind a cushion, suddenly shy. 'You ask, Mama.'

'No, you.'

Clare dropped to Pep's level. 'Whisper in my ear.'

Pep shook his head. 'He wants you to come to the beach with us,' Montse interpreted.

Clare thought of the 110 metres hurdle final, the 1,500 metres final and Britain's quarter final football match against Finland. 'Okay,' he said. 'Let's go.'

They took a bus to Barceloneta. A ten minute drive to the far end of the harbour, to the long strip of sand that lay beyond the tightly packed houses and shanty dwellings of the fishermen, dockers and migrant workers.

The beach was as crowded as Clare had ever seen it. Every inch of shade taken. Families camped out on deck chairs. Men stripped to their shirt sleeves and braces, women with their dresses pulled up over their knees. They changed in the open air swimming baths beside the beach, then found a patch of sand in front of the casino where Pep could play safely.

'So what did you tell me in all those letters I never received?' Montse finally asked as they watched Pep skipping in and out of the surf.

Clare thought back to the months of frustration cooped up in his Bayswater apartment, wracked with guilt at the way he'd left Spain, unable to get word in or out. 'I wrote a book,' he said.

'A book?'

'About Spain. The war. My experiences of it.'

'You're joking?'

'No. I'm not.'

'So where is it – this book? Do I get a mention?'

Before Montse could press him any further, an aeroplane flew overhead, a swastika clearly visible on its tail. 'Look, Mama! Look!' Pep pointed excitedly into the sky. 'It's just like mine.'

'Not quite, darling. Your's has a red star on its wing.'

'Oh, yes.' Pep sounded almost disappointed.

'It's much better to have a star,' Montse assured him but Pep didn't look convinced.

'How about a dip?' Clare suggested by way of consolation, as the plane flew on towards the airport at Prat de Llobregat.

'I want to dip,' Pep announced loudly, as if it were his idea.

That settled it. They waded out into the sea, Clare and Montse swinging the boy between them, passing him from one to the other, encouraging him to swim. 'I can do it on my own,' Pep wished them to know, hurling himself into Clare's arms. Montse laughed, and Clare would have done too if he hadn't suddenly been struck by the madness of it all. What the hell did he think he was doing? He was here to cover the Olympic Games, not go swimming with his one time lover and her four year old adopted son.

'Look Richard! I can do it on my own. Like a boat.'

Clare smiled. 'That's good, Pep. That's really good.'

They stayed in the water until Pep had had enough, then bought churros and hot chocolate, and took the tram back into town.

It was the hour of the *paseo*. Pep was exhausted now, asleep in Clare's arms, oblivious to the smell of frying meat and the cry of a girl selling horse chestnuts.

Below Montse's flat, there was a watch shop. Clare could see the owner – Señor Gusi – bent over the window display packing up for the night. As Montse took out her keys to open the front door, Gusi looked up and caught his eye, giving him an embarrassed little wave.

They went inside, the door swinging shut as Montse hit a button on the wall, lighting a feeble bulb at the top of the stairwell. *Tick. Tick. Tick.* They had twenty seconds before the light switched itself off, if Clare's memory served him correctly.

The apartment was on the second floor. Montse had the door unlocked by the time Clare reached the landing, holding it open for him, pointing him towards Pep's bedroom, which had been their's.

While Montse took off Pep's shoes and tucked him into bed, Clare wandered through to the sitting room where he guessed Montse now slept. The room had been repainted, the decoration changed, but there were still a few mementoes of their life together. A photograph of them unpacking *Guernica* into a village church, their old gramophone player, an art deco table lamp that he'd bought for her in Paris, and for these he felt a relief, not to have been altogether airbrushed out of her life. 'You can stay for a drink if you like,' she called from the bedroom. 'There's some whisky in the kitchen. You can pour me one too.'

Clare found a bottle in the cupboard. A cheap Spanish brand that he remembered with little affection. He poured them both a glass, then walked back into the sitting room. 'Thanks for coming to the beach.' Montse emerged from the bedroom wearing a clean shirt. 'It really made his day.'

'Mine too.' Clare felt a sudden, mad urge to kiss her, an impulse swiftly dispelled by a sharp knock on the door.

Montse stiffened. 'Who is it?'

'Me,' a voice called from the landing. It was Pilar – the old snoop from downstairs; for certain she'd clocked two sets of footsteps on the staircase and come up to investigate.

Clare stepped back into the kitchen as Montse opened the door. 'What do you want?' she said.

Standing four foot nine, Pilar was dressed in black from head to toe, her grey hair dyed black, her shoes (one with a three inch raised heel to compensate a shortened leg) polished black, and so too her heart, Clare didn't mind betting.

'There was a man come to see you.' Pilar's hushed voice carried all the way through to where Clare stood hidden behind the door.

'What man? When?'

'Yesterday morning. He didn't say so but I could see he was from the SIM.' Pilar reached up and hit the switch. *Clunk. Tick.* More light to ensure she caught Montse's reaction. 'I thought you should know.' *Let me in and I'll tell you more.*

'I'm sure it's nothing,' Montse said unconvincingly, which was when it dawned on Clare that she might be in trouble, that this was the unspoken agenda of the lunch, not the past but the present. That she needed his help.

'If there's anything I can do for you?' Pilar wasn't going to give up lightly.

'I can manage. Thank you.' Montse forced the door shut. 'Good night.'

Tick. Tick. Tick. Clare stayed where he was. They both did. Until at last, they heard a slow shuffling – Pilar starting off down the stairs – and a *clunk* as the light finally switched itself off.

Montse put a record on the gramophone and retrieved her cigarette from the ashtray. Clare didn't recognise the music. It wasn't anything they used to listen to. 'Is this something to do with that Russo you were involved with?' he said quietly.

Montse's eyes flashed furious. 'Who told you about him?'

'Werner.'

'What else did Werner say?'

'Nothing. Look – I'm not trying to pry. Whatever happened with the Russo, that's your business ...'

'You're damned right it is.' Montse pushed open the shutters and stepped out onto the balcony, but Clare could see that she was shaken – it wasn't every day a SIM agent came knocking. 'I can get you out of Spain,' he said, his voice dropping to a whisper. 'If that's what you want. You and Pep.'

Montse stared at him. Clare gave her a little nod. *No, she hadn't misheard him. He could do it.*

She slapped him. Hard on the cheek. 'Christ!' The pain brought tears to his eyes. 'What the hell was that for?'

'For being an idiot. Now go home. Before you get us all killed.'

'I'll be gone in ten days,' he snapped. 'Isn't that soon enough?'

'Get out! Now!' Montse took a last drag of her cigarette and threw it over the edge of the balcony, then, 'Richard – please. Go home,' her voice softened, 'Don't you understand? The SIM are everywhere.'

'I'll call tomorrow,' he said.

'Not here. It's not safe.'

'Then where?'

'Better you don't. Now, please – go. I can look after myself.' She kissed him twice on the cheek, opened the door and hit the light switch. *Clunk. Tick.* Twenty seconds to reach the front door. 'For God's sake – go!' she implored him. 'Before that bitch downstairs reports us.'

Clare had often heard it said that Barcelona was everything Paris should be, and tonight so it seemed. Walking home, there was a sense of gaiety about the streets, bars and cafés; even the window displays in Carrer Ferran appeared Parisian sophisticated in a way Clare might have presumed was beyond them. On another evening, he'd have wanted a part of it. He'd have joined Stewart, Wilson and the rest of the British press pack in the bar Canaletes – he'd spied them drinking at the counter as he walked past – but this evening all he wanted was to get back to his hotel and the sanctuary of his room.

He ran a tepid bath and lay in the water for half an hour with the lights off, thinking maybe he'd burnt his shoulders at the beach. Thinking about Montse and what had scared her. Wondering if it had anything to do with him?

He washed his hair and got out of the bath, poured himself a Scotch, then noticed his passport lying on the desk. It had been returned.

Clare's eyes leapt towards his Orquesta Demon's Jazz record, which thank God was still lying where he'd left it, seemingly untouched. Curiously, he picked up his passport and flicked through the pages to see that his visa had been restamped.

Montse was right. The SIM were everywhere.

CHAPTER 10

Friday 2nd August, 1940

> Programme of the XIIth Olympiad
> *Athletics, Fencing, Shooting, Wrestling, Yachting, Polo, Hockey, Canoeing, Cycling.*

The pain of Werner's first interrogation was beginning to fade. Of the two of them – Obersturmbannführer Kreiger and himself – Werner felt that it was he who had learnt most from the encounter. Kreiger's questions had been as random as the blows inflicted on his body, there'd been no real agenda that Werner could discern, merely the interrogation seemed designed to soften him up before he was shipped back to Germany and executed; Kreiger's way of reminding him that after two decades his luck had finally run out.

Of course, it was not the first time that Werner had been in jail. In Berlin, he'd served six months for his part in a street battle against Hitler's brown shirts. In Hamburg, he'd been held briefly by the Nazis before being released thanks to an administrative blunder; not that there was much chance of that this time. Whichever way Werner viewed it, his prospects looked bleak; the scratch marks on his cell wall reading as a roll call for the damned.

The bells of a nearby church struck eight. Above the din, Werner heard the sound of approaching footsteps, three men nearing his cell, stopping outside the door, drawing back the bolt. 'Name?' the guard barked at him in Spanish.

'Werner Bloch,' he answered wearily. *Always, they seemed to ask his name.*

The guard stood back to let the other two men into the cell. One – the more senior – dressed in a suit. The other a uniform. Both SIM. There were no introductions. No small talk. Just a single command from the suit. 'Tell me about Richard Clare.'

Werner shrugged. 'I haven't seen him for years.'

The uniform hit him hard in the stomach. 'You were seen together last Friday,' he said. 'In a bar off the Ramblas.'

How the hell do you know? Werner lay on the floor, gasping for breath.

'Now perhaps you'd like to tell me what you were talking about?' The suit lit a cigarette. An Argentinian brand – Werner recognised the smell of the tobacco. A Primeros.

* * * * *

Along the length of the Ramblas, people were sitting out in the sun drinking coffee and digesting the morning news as a seagull wheeled overhead, its screeching lost in the concert of guitarists, violinists, squeeze box players and street pianists serenading the pavement cafés, feverishly trying to earn a peseta or two before – at nine o'clock – the public address system kicked into life, drowning them out and driving them on.

Clare dropped a coin into the boater of an old man playing outside the Café Opera. It had been his patch for years, he remembered, remembering also that the man had always had a dog with him. A little terrier. Although not any more, it seemed.

Then – 'Where the hell have you been?' – Clare felt a tug on his arm from behind. 'Where were you yesterday? I've been looking for you all over.' It was Markham, dressed in a pair of freshly pressed white trousers and a blue blazer, a cut under his eye that hadn't been there the last time they'd met. 'We need to talk,' he said; Clare had temporarily forgotten that he was due to meet Capdevila at six that evening.

'This way,' Markham commanded.

They went for a walk, or rather, Markham took him for one, around Plaça Catalunya, out of earshot of any passers-by, a single circuit of the square sufficient for Markham to brief him on this evening's arrangements. Put simply – all Clare had to do was to meet Capdevila at the Colom, then walk him the short distance to the church of Santa Maria del Mar where Markham would take over. Clare had only one question. 'What do I tell him about Picasso?'

'Nothing,' Markham answered him sharply. 'Just keep quiet. Let me do the talking.'

* * * * *

2.10pm. *Good fresh food at a good price* – a faded notice in the window of bar Antoni informed. On the pavement outside, close to the Mercat de Sant Antoni, a crowd of diners were cheerily waiting in line, drinking beer and *rosado*. Clare pushed his way inside. Despite the open windows and the tortured efforts of an old ceiling fan, it felt hot and fuggy. A heady mix of cooking oil and tobacco.

Clare was looking for Montse's brother, Andreu. On the wall, to the left of the door, there was a large framed photograph. A group of cyclists lined up in front of a banner that read *AC Montjuic, 1939*. On one side of the picture, Clare recognised Andreu with a pair of racing goggles round his neck, his hair divided in a centre parting, lips drawn in a faint, supercilious smile.

The bar belonged to Andreu's father-in-law. Clare had never met Andreu's wife but he guessed her to be the diminutive brunette hovering in the kitchen doorway with a spatula in her hand, talking to Andreu – Clare could see him now at the counter serving beer.

'Andreu! *Hombre!*' Clare greeted his former cell mate as if they'd last met only a few days ago.

'Get out,' Andreu snarled.

What?

'You heard me, you cunt. Get out!'

It took Clare a moment to find his voice. 'I'm sorry you feel this way,' he muttered, somewhat distracted by the flow of beer angrily frothing up over the lip of the glass Andreu was pouring.

'Get out of my bar!'

'All I want is a couple of minutes. A quick word. Then I'll go.'

Half the room were staring at them now. 'Okay. Out the back,' Andreu reluctantly relented, ushering Clare through to the kitchen. 'What do you want?'

Clare coughed. The kitchen was thick with smoke, the floor covered in grease spit. Andreu's wife stood over the cooker, slapping meat in and out of a large frying pan, every few seconds the oil catching fire, sending flames leaping towards the ceiling; a rogue oil field in miniature. 'It's about Montse,' he said.

'What about her?'

'I think she's in trouble.'

'What do you care?' Andreu sneered, the flames' reflection dancing in his eyes.

'We spent the day together. Yesterday.' Clare hoped the revelation might somehow mollify Andreu's anger.

'Then more fool her.'

Clare battled on. 'If she's in trouble. If she needs help. I can–' He never got to finish. Andreu grabbed him by the collar. Spinning him round. Smashing him against the dresser. 'Fuck you!' he said, nose pressed to Clare's chin, knuckles ground against his cheek. 'Stay away from her. Understand. If I catch you within a fucking mile of her – I'll have your balls for dog food.'

Andreu pushed him away. Clare felt a sharp pain in his ribs as he caught the edge of the sink. 'Now fuck off!'

Andreu flung open the back door. Outside a chained dog started barking, clattering the bins. Clare hesitated, damned if he was going to give the beast a free run at his balls.

Andreu picked up a knife. 'Get out!'

'Andreu!' His wife called him to heel. *Enough!*

Reluctantly, Andreu laid the knife down and stood back from the door. Clare was free to leave – the way he came in.

He did so. Hurriedly. Before Andreu could change his mind.

* * * * *

6.29pm. The Colom. The usual Friday evening crowd stood gathered around the base of the monument; families come to watch the boats in the harbour, couples out for a stroll, a busker squeezing out tunes on a battered accordion.

For the tenth time in as many minutes, Clare checked his watch. Capdevila was now half an hour late. *Relax* – he told himself. He could hear the whirr of the cable motor, his heart beat quickening as the doors parted once more. *Surely this time.*

A woman stepped out.

Bugger. There was nobody else inside the lift. No sign of Capdevila.

'I'm sorry I'm late,' the woman said.

It took Clare a moment to recognise her. Not until she caught his eye with that same intense stare he'd been struck by twice before, did he clock her as Capdevila's assistant from the gallery. Margarita Mirabel. Looking totally different. Stylish even. To the casual eye, a tourist from Paris or Berlin. 'Where's Rafael?' Clare asked.

'I'll take you to him,' Margarita answered matter-of-factly. There was no-one else on the observation platform to overhear them.

'Why isn't he here?'

'There's been a change of plan. You'll see him soon enough.'

'Where?'

'Please – be patient.' She hit him again with her eyes. *No more questions.*

They descended the column in silence. Not until they were safely on the ground, crossing over to the Ramblas, did Margarita see fit to speak again. 'Always – we must assume we are being watched,' she said, as they dodged a pair of traversing trams. 'Should they stop us, you're to say you've been sent by my son. He lives in France. He asked you to deliver me a letter.'

'What letter?'

'I have it here.' Margarita patted her handbag.

'But I don't even know your son's name.'

'Yes – you do.' Margarita almost smiled. 'His name is Jesus Mirabel. Rafael said you once met him in Paris.'

Now it was Clare's turn to smile. *Jesus Mirabel.* So that was the connection. Small wonder Margarita was prepared to risk her life running errands for Capdevila.

Jesus owed him his life.

Clare knew the story well. How at the beginning of the war, a mob had battered down the doors of the seminary where Jesus was training to be a priest. How the seminarists had been dragged from their beds, doused with oil and set fire to. Only Jesus had survived, leaping from a second floor dormitory window into the street below. Several of the mob had given chase but somehow Jesus had managed to elude them, breaking into a nearby art gallery, hiding himself behind a canvas in the basement.

The gallery – although Jesus didn't know it at the time – belonged to Capdevila, the canvas to Mariano Fortuny. Capdevila discovered Jesus curled up beside it the following morning with a broken leg, two fractured wrists and a cracked rib. Capdevila took pity on him, found him a doctor and somewhere safe to shelter, and then, when Jesus was finally recovered, he organised his escape to France, fixing papers for him to travel to Paris as his assistant.

'Rafael risked his life to save me. For no more reward than my thanks' – Clare remembered Jesus telling him on more than one occasion. Clare had never thought it his place to mention the hefty price Capdevila had received for the sale of various reliquaries salvaged from the seminary, treasures which Jesus had pointed him towards for safekeeping.

'Did you know my son well?' Margarita asked as they headed up the Ramblas, wrapped into the drift of the evening *paseo*.

'Reasonably. We saw each other a few times.'

'It's curious. He never mentioned you.'

'We didn't exactly inhabit the same circles.' Clare remembered Jesus as a nervous, bookish young man, ill at ease with the Paris sophisticates. 'He was thinking of moving to Lourdes.'

Margarita nodded. 'He lives there now.'

They stopped to buy a drink from a soda fountain as two tourists might, Margarita insistent they shouldn't be seen to be in a hurry, the quiet streets affording her the opportunity to further flesh out the details of Clare's cover story. 'You and Jesus have remained friends since Paris,' she told him. 'Knowing you were coming to Barcelona, he sent you a letter to give to me. On Wednesday you telephoned my apartment.'

'How did I get the number?'

'You looked it up in the book. Plaça Osca, 4, 5a. You offered to come round but I suggested we meet at the Colom.'

'And now?' Clare wanted to know where the evening was heading.

'Now we're talking about my son. I'm asking you how he is. If he's happy. If he's eating well. The things a mother asks.' For a moment her voice cracked.

'And how is he doing?'

'He's doing fine. Thank –' There was a jerk in her voice as she suddenly stumbled, spilling the contents of her handbag over the pavement.

'Sorry, Señora.' The man who'd bumped into her spoke in a rough Valencian accent; his hands, Clare noticed, were covered in engine grease.

Margarita appeared more shocked than hurt.

'I didn't see you,' the Valenciano protested, dropping to his knees to help gather up Margarita's scattered possessions.

Margarita snatched back her bag. 'Here – give me that.'

'Sorry, Señora.' The Valenciano got back to his feet.

Clare stooped to pick up a fountain pen that had rolled into the gutter, then – 'My purse! My purse!' – he looked up to see the Valenciano haring off into the back streets, Margarita screaming after him, 'My purse! Thief! Stop!'

Instinctively Clare gave chase. It wasn't an area of Barcelona he knew well, an alien maze of dingy, dark streets and covered alleyways. But even so, for a brief moment, he thought he might catch the bastard. Bursting out into a small square, shouting to a ten year old kid – 'Which way?' – the boy pointed him down a street hung with drying sheets but there the trail ran dry, petering out by a boarded up church at the confluence of four dark alleyways, each no more than an arm's span in width. *Shit.* Clare took a few sips of water from a drinking fountain while he recovered his breath. *If only he'd been a little quicker off the mark.*

'Did you catch him?' Clare looked up to see Margarita emerge from the near side of the church, from the darkest of the four alleys.

'No.' Clare was confused as to how she'd known where to find him.

Margarita opened the side door to the church. 'In here! Quick! Before anyone sees you.'

Clare understood only the urgency in her voice. Dutifully, he did as bid.

Inside, the church stank of ruin. Four years ago, Anarchist gunmen had massacred the priest and half his congregation, Margarita explained. The pockmarked walls still bore the graffiti from that night. Everything that could be carried off had been stripped from the interior – wood, metal, stone; hacked up as firewood, melted in the foundries of the munitions factories, sunk into the harbour wall. Someone had even had a go at one of the pillars.

'This way.' Margarita led him across the dank, crater strewn floor, pausing only to cross herself where the altar had once stood. Clare shivered. The place unnerved him.

Margarita pointed to a doorway leading into the vestry. 'In here.'

Clare followed her inside.

'Miguel?' Margarita called out in a hushed voice, and before Clare could ask, he had his answer, as a man stepped from the shadows.

The Valenciano.

Clare instinctively recoiled, hit by that same sharp nausea he'd first encountered during the war. A sentiment of approaching death. This was it. Where it was all going to end. In a trap that made no sense. But the Valenciano just smiled and reached out his hand – *pleased to meet you.* It still made no sense, but Clare grasped the man's hand tightly – never mind the engine grease – trying not to laugh as Margarita made the introductions, from not wanting to show his fear, from not understanding, from sheer bloody relief.

'We had to make sure you weren't being followed,' Margarita explained. 'Miguel and the handbag, it was just an excuse. To break into a run without arousing suspicion. To flush out anyone who might have been trailing us.' At this point, they were joined by the third member of the "team", the ten year old boy who'd pointed Clare in the "right direction" out of the square. 'Miguelito?' Margarita asked him. 'Are we safe?'

The boy grinned. Yes. They were safe. No-one had followed them to the church.

Thank God. Margarita instinctively touched the crucifix which Clare now noticed hanging round her neck.

They left by way of a narrow passage connecting the vestry to the house next door, where the Priest had once lived, Margarita told him, as they emerged into a small, simply furnished room that had miraculously survived the desecration unscathed.

Slipping out of the front door, Clare found himself back on the street. There were no road signs, no shops, not even a shaft of sunlight to help lift the uniform gloom of this densely packed barrio, just a series of sullen faces set in dark doorways under a canopy of drying sheets. He had no idea where he was or which direction they were heading until they emerged from the maze onto the corner of Comercio and Fusina, opposite the magnificent wrought iron structure of the Mercat del Born. Clare had often made a detour through the market on his way to Ciutadella park – it was one of those landmarks that connected him to the city – but never had he imagined how miraculous it must seem to those who lived in its shadow, the inhabitants of those fetid, crumbling streets he'd just passed through.

Clare followed Margarita along the north side of the market, the evening sun throwing his long shadow towards hers so that it almost clipped her heels. Outside number 35, Margarita slipped her handbag from her left to right shoulder, her signal to him that this was the building, then walked on. Her job done.

There was only one apartment on the top floor. Clare rang the bell. Three times in quick succession.

Almost immediately the door clicked open.

Inside, the foyer smelt of polish. On the wall to the left of the door, there was a collection of smartly engraved brass plates; a lawyer on the first floor, an accountant on the second, and on the third, a doctor specialising in venereal diseases.

Clare took the lift to the sixth floor.

Capdevila was waiting for him on the landing. Hurriedly, he ushered him inside, closing the door before deeming it safe to speak. 'Thank you for coming,' he said somewhat melodramatically; a radio was playing Tchaikovsky's 2nd Symphony, loud enough to drown out their voices.

'Did I have a choice?' Clare took in the Spartan décor of the flat. Margarita had told him it had once belonged to a friend of hers, a lawyer assassinated by an Anarchist death squad in the first days of the war. The shutters were all drawn. The temperature inside the main room uncomfortably high. The overhead fan rotating with a strange hiccup.

Capdevila poured him a soda water. 'These damned Olympics,' he said by way of an explanation for the preceding charade. 'Do you know how many they've rounded up since the Games started? Three hundred.'

Clare wasn't interested in figures. 'You didn't tell me Margarita was Jesus's mother,' he said sharply.

'You think she shouldn't risk her life for me?' Capdevila caught the implied censure in his voice.

'I didn't say that.'

'I'm her family now,' Capdevila said in all earnestness. 'I'm all she has.'

'You still might have told me.'

Capdevila ignored him. 'Did you speak to your friends?'

'Yes.'

'What did they say?'

'They want to meet you.'

'Where?'

'There's a guy called Markham waiting for you outside Santa Maria del Mar. I'm supposed to take you to him.'

'You'll have to bring him here.' Capdevila lit a cheroot, adding a dash of Nicaraguan rum to his soda.

'What if he refuses?'

Capdevila's eyes twinkled. 'If he's serious, he'll come.'

'He said that?' Markham bristled with indignation, barely able to conceal his irritation at Capdevila's sudden change of plan. For the past two hours, he'd been standing outside Santa Maria del Mar distractedly making sketches of the façade in his note book – his cover story should anyone ask – wondering what could have gone wrong, whether or not to abort the mission, cursing himself for failing to arrange a fall back position.

'Yes.' It was everything Clare could do not to smile.

'The little shit. Who does he think he is?'

The journey back to Carrer Fusina took less than five minutes. As they exited the lift, Tchaikovsky's 2nd symphony was entering its fourth and final movement.

Capdevila ushered them inside with a welcoming smile. 'You're Richard's contact?' he said, as usual speaking in Spanish, shaking Markham's hand as if about to try and sell him a painting.

Markham stared at him uncomprehending, then turned awkwardly to Clare. 'What did he say?'

On his way over to the safe house, Markham had told Clare that his part in the drama was now over – 'just introduce us then piss off' – but within seconds of entering the flat, it became clear that there could be no communication without him. Markham spoke no Spanish, and Capdevila no English. 'You'll have to translate for us, Richard,' Capdevila entreated him. 'Unless your friend can speak French.'

Markham shook his head. He had no French either.

'Then we have no choice,' Capdevila concluded.

Unable to conceal his embarrassment, Markham pulled Clare to one side and warned him that what he was about to say was covered by the Official Secrets Act. 'Breathe a word of this to anyone and you'll go to jail. Understand?'

Clare understood.

Turning back to Capdevila, Markham pulled a sheet of paper from his pocket and laid it on the kitchen table. It was a diagram of the modern pentathlon team bus. A detailed sketch showing how he intended to modify the interior to secretly accommodate one 170 pound, five foot eight, sixty year old man. The team was planning to leave for Italy on Sunday to participate in a further tournament, Markham explained. His idea was to take Picasso out with them. But to do that he needed some help from Capdevila – specifically a mechanic.

Capdevila pondered the matter a moment. 'I have a friend in Poblenou,' he said. 'He could do the job.'

A quarter of an hour later, the finer points of Picasso's escape settled, Clare and Markham were back on the street – Clare's brief foray into the world of espionage now officially at an end. The sun had vanished into the horizon and the market traders were locking up, throwing out their rubbish for the beggars and dogs to scrap over. 'It's time you went back to your games and left us to ours,' Markham said gracelessly, as he hailed a taxi.

Clare waited for him to drive away, then set off back towards Carrer Avinyó. All day – ever since his brush with Andreu – he'd been thinking of little else but Montse and how he could persuade her to open up to him.

At the bar Cervantes, where Clare had too often retreated during those last tense days when they'd still been together, the cards were out and the men settled in for the evening with their bottles and hopes of a few pesetas won. It was half past nine.

The lights in Montse's apartment were off. Perhaps she was still at work? Or picking up Pep from her parents? Clare considered giving the hotel a call then thought again. What if Andreu were there too?

Reluctantly, Clare continued on towards the Ramblas. *Better he try tomorrow.*

Outside the Teatro Principal, he stopped for a few moments to listen to a violinist serenading the queue for the evening performance of *The Night Watchman*. A story of romance and adventure featuring two of Spain's hottest new screen stars, Domingo Herrera and Alicia Sol. Then – 'Good evening, my friend' – Clare felt a tap on the shoulder. He didn't have to look round to know that it was Balasc.

'Good evening, Janos.' Clare smiled civilly.

Balasc was dressed in a cream suit and tie, and smelt of the same eau de cologne he'd been wearing the other night at the Font del Gat. Beside him stood a slender man with dark brown hair and a thin moustache. 'May I introduce my friend,' Balasc said. 'Mr Morris Temple. A compatriot of yours. He's here on holiday. For a fortnight. I couldn't get him into the Victoria so he's staying at the Nouvel.'

'How do you do?' Temple spoke in a nasal Thames Valley accent.

'Hi.' Clare felt the slight embarrassment of two compatriots being thrown together for no better reason than that they spoke the same language.

'I met Morris when I was in England,' Balasc elaborated. 'Working on the Abdication story. I told you about that, didn't I?'

'Yes.'

'Morris works at the Palace. One of His Majesty's footmen. If you ever wish to know the Royal gossip, all you have to do is ask Morris.'

'For a couple of quid I'm yours,' Temple grinned.

Balasc laughed. 'Very true.'

And then the penny dropped. *Palare*. Clare understood now. Once before in a pub in Soho, some man had sat down beside him, an actor or so he'd claimed, although evidently not engaged that night. He and Clare had got talking, even bought each other a beer, then suddenly the actor had slipped into this strange slang; familiar sounding words that made no sense. Clare had presumed they were lines from some new play and when he asked which play, the actor had just laughed and made his excuses. Only later, when Clare had described the episode to a friend did he understand that the man was a queen, on the sniff, looking for something more than a drink in the pub, speaking an undercover homosexual argot, as had been Balasc the other night at the Font del Gat.

'So what rag do you write for?' Temple asked.

Clare told him – *The Evening News*.

'Got one right here.' Temple pulled a crumpled copy from his jacket pocket. 'Do you know Arthur Jenkins?'

'No.'

'I've given him a fair few stories.' Jenkins was court correspondent on *The Evening News*. 'Not that he's dared print any of them!'

'Do you mind if I take a look?' Clare was curious to see what his work looked like in print.

'Take it.' Temple handed him the paper. 'I only kept it for the crossword.'

It was yesterday's edition. Clare found what he was looking for on page eleven under the byline – *By our Special Correspondent*. A gossipy, well written piece about the precautions taken to ensure the "moral welfare" of the women athletes. 'That you then?' Temple asked. 'Special correspondent?'

Clare nodded. 'Yes.' The only problem being that the article wasn't his. Wednesday night he'd filed a totally different piece about a lost four year old who'd been led into the centre of the stadium in order to be reunited with his mother. Somebody else had written this.

'Nice one.' Temple seemed impressed.

Clare made his excuses and walked on back to the hotel, stopping only to throw the paper into a bin, too angry to give any thought as to why the office might reasonably wish to employ someone to ghostwrite his byline. It was a question he would only think to ask himself later – when his life was on the line.

CHAPTER 11

Saturday 3rd August, 1940

Programme of the XIIth Olympiad
Athletics, Fencing, Shooting, Wrestling, Yachting, Swimming, Hockey, Football, Canoeing, Basketball, Cycling.

This morning, Inspector Marin was in a good mood. Yesterday it had been a very different story. On Friday evenings Marin played cards with his friends, a tradition stretching back almost twenty years. The rule was nothing, and nobody, interrupted him on pain of a punishment he had yet to devise, on account of the fact that it had never happened. Then last night, just as his luck at the table was beginning to turn, he'd been rung by the duty officer requesting his presence at the station on the trifling matter of a stolen coach. When at last Marin understood that the coach in question was no ordinary coach but one belonging to the British Pentathlon Team, he'd calmed somewhat, even assuring the duty officer that he'd done the right thing; all police and civic authorities were under the strictest instructions to help their guests in any way they could. Even Marin understood that this did not mean playing cards.

The facts of the case were, it seemed, very simple. The British team, having completed their part in the competition, had attended an official dinner at the Hotel Majestic Inglaterra. It was while the team had been in the hotel that their coach had been stolen, some time between ten and eleven o'clock, when the driver had taken an hour off to eat. Immediately Marin had put six men on the case and within two hours they'd found the vehicle abandoned by a derelict tile factory in Poblenou. The thieves – joy riders obviously – had thrashed the coach about a bit but it was nothing a good mechanic couldn't fix given a few hours. Marin had put a guard on the vehicle and returned to the station feeling good about the way the affair had turned out, although by then it was regrettably too late to go back to his game of cards.

The Hotel Continental, San Feliu de Llobregat. 8.05am. The phone in Markham's room rang. Already showered and dressed, he let it ring a couple of times more, then picked it up. 'Yes?' he drawled in an exaggeratedly weary voice, not wishing to come across too alert.

It was Marin. As expected.

Ten minutes later, Markham was in a taxi heading back into town.

At the police station, a policeman stood waiting on the doorstep, ready to take Markham straight up to Marin's office. On the table, there was a pot of coffee and a plate of freshly baked doughnuts. 'Breakfast?' Marin asked, putting on his best early morning smile.

Markham sank into the worn leather armchair that had been specially brought out for him and thanked Marin for finding their coach so promptly. The press officer translated. Marin smiled. It was all no problem. No problem at all.

'Did you catch whoever did it?' Markham asked out of politeness, adding a spoonful of sugar to his coffee.

Marin shook his head. He doubted they ever would. 'But the important thing,' he hastened to say, 'is that you have your coach back.'

Markham concurred. It had been Capdevila's idea to steal and crash the coach. A way of getting the vehicle to Poblenou without arousing police suspicion.

Marin read out a list of the damage sustained. Dented steering column, punctured radiator, smashed head lights. No more than a day's work for a decent mechanic. Markham handed him a scrap of paper that had also been given to him by Capdevila. 'I have the name of a mechanic,' he said. 'The brother-in-law of our hotel receptionist. She says his garage is somewhere in Poblenou.'

Marin took the paper and read – *Moreno Garcia. Carrer Castanys, 21. Tel: 95776*. 'I'll give him a call,' he said, picking up the phone, grateful not to have to search out a mechanic himself, entreating Markham to please take a doughnut. 'They're from the bakery next door,' he added. 'An experience not to be missed.'

* * * * *

For the third time in seven days Clare made his way up to the tennis club, and for the first time in as many, Montse seemed almost pleased to see him. 'I did something stupid,' he confessed straight up as they sat down to a coffee at the club house.

'How stupid?' Montse had clearly heard nothing about his little *contretemps* with her brother.

'Yesterday morning I went to see Andreu.'

Montse shot a look to the heavens. 'What did he say?'

'That if I tried to see you again he'd kill me.'

Montse laughed. 'He's my brother. What did you expect?'

Clare winced. 'I'm sorry. I had no idea I'd caused you so much hurt. I–'

'Richard,' Montse cut him dead. 'What I said about it being over between us. I meant it.'

'It doesn't have to be.'

'Yes. It does.'

'Why?'

'Not now. Not here.'

Then when? Where? 'Lets talk about it over dinner,' he said. 'Tomorrow night? At the Hotel Gastronomic Number One.' A private joke. During the war, the Ritz had been renamed and turned into a soup kitchen by the revolutionary authorities. 'I won't leave until you say yes.'

'Just dinner?' She wasn't in the mood for a fight.

'Yes.'

'Okay,' she smiled wanly.

'Tomorrow – at nine.'

'I said yes. By the way,' she added, 'that man who dropped by while we were on the beach. He wasn't SIM. Just an old friend from the Generalitat.'

'Anyone I know?' Clare didn't believe her.

'No.'

'That's good,' he said. 'That he wasn't SIM, I mean.' *She was lying.*

'I just thought you'd like to know.'

No doubt about it – she was lying. And tomorrow night he'd get to the bottom of it. However much she didn't want to tell him, somehow he'd force it out of her.

Make her tell him what was on her mind.

* * * * *

At the beginning of the evening news bulletin, and then again at the end, the BBC broadcast an urgent appeal to a Mr Harold Whitman, known to be holidaying somewhere on the Continent. 'Should you hear this message you are to immediately contact your wife, Fleur,' the news reader advised. Across Europe, listeners no doubt imagined a husband going about his holiday ignorant of some terrible family tragedy. Only a select few knew the truth, that the message had been penned by an SIS officer. A signal to Picasso that the defection plan was for real. A green light for tomorrow.

Holdsworth switched off the radio. 'I don't think we need listen to any more of that,' he said, filling up an enamel tooth mug with warm cava. 'Cheers!' He took a sip and handed the mug to Kathleen, who was sitting beside him on the edge of the bed.

'Cheers!' They drank to a successful day.

And it had all gone perfectly. Like clockwork. The police even driving Markham to the mechanic's; Moreno Garcia proving as efficient and reliable as Capdevila had promised he would be. Holdsworth hadn't seen the work himself but Markham had reported it as first class. A false compartment under the floor of the coach discreet enough to survive even the most rigorous of searches.

Kathleen handed Holdsworth back the mug. The cava, bought from a delicatessen on the Ramblas, tasted fine for the price, although granted it might have been better chilled. Holdsworth offered it back to Kathleen. He'd been pleasantly surprised by her insistence on coming back to the hotel with him to listen to the news. 'You might need an extra pair of hands,' she'd told him, 'should something go wrong. And besides, it's not as if I've anything else planned.' Holdsworth wondered whether she might also accept an invitation to dinner.

Kathleen took another sip. The alcohol was beginning to take effect. It had been a long, tense day and she'd had little to eat.

'Why don't we go out? Grab ourselves a bite of something?' Holdsworth plucked up the courage to ask.

'I was rather hoping we might stay in and finish the bottle,' Kathleen smiled suggestively, 'if that's agreeable to you.'

'Yes …' Holdsworth tried not to sound too surprised. 'It would be … most agreeable.'

Kathleen tucked the mug under the bed so that neither of them could kick it over, then slid her hand under his shirt, where his third button would have been had he not ripped it off that morning getting out of a taxi. It had been over three years since Holdsworth had made love. The thought of a woman in his arms – of Kathleen naked and wanting – made him feel more nervous than he'd been at any other point in the day.

They kissed, awkwardly to begin with, then forgetting themselves. Falling back onto the bed.

Becoming bolder.

Realising the moment they'd both long dreamed of.

Making love.

CHAPTER 12

Sunday 4th August, 1940

Programme of the XIIth Olympiad
Fencing, Wrestling, Yachting, Swimming, Basketball, Athletics, Hockey.

Today was his twenty-sixth birthday. Clare remembered as he turned on the shower. *Feliz cumple años.* He wished himself happy birthday and stepped into the uneven fall of lukewarm water (for some reason the hot tap only worked properly if he ran a bath). He thought of himself and Montse two years ago, the day after they'd collected Pep from the orphanage in Sevilla; waiting at the train station, Montse running off to buy him a birthday cake, returning half an hour later with a bag of chocolate churros, a bottle of wine and a street musician, an old man with a violin who'd serenaded him with *I'm in the mood for love.*

Clare washed his hair with the last of the shampoo he'd brought with him from London. At twenty-six, his father had already passed through Westcott House and was working as a curate in Great Yarmouth, a few months away from his first parish. The year was 1904. The Empire stood strong. For God, King and Country – then a young man knew where he stood and where he was going.

At twenty-six, Gerald lay dead.

Clare rinsed his hair and reached for the soap. Once, twice, there was a knock on the door but the splash of water inside the shower was too loud for him to notice. Only when he turned off the tap and stepped from the tub, did he hear an agitated rap. 'Just a moment!' He grabbed a towel and wrapped it round his waist, hurriedly wiping his feet on the bath mat. 'Who is it?'

There was no answer. A quick glance at his watch told Clare it was still only a quarter past eight. Tentatively, he opened the door, at first unable to see who it was, then recognising Capdevila – a finger raised to his lips, *Sshh!*

Clare let him in without question.

Capdevila walked over to the bathroom and turned the shower back on. 'There's been a change of plan,' he calmly announced.

'What do you mean?' Clare switched on the radio to further drown out their conversation.

'Our *friend* has got scared. He wants me to do a trial run. He needs to know that it's safe.'

'What's that got to do with me?'

'I need you to tell Markham.'

'You tell him.'

'I don't speak English. And besides – he won't believe me. He'll think I'm making it up.'

Clare didn't have to say it.

'Come on, Richard – you know me better than that.' Capdevila reached a hand into his jacket. Clare knew what was coming next and Capdevila didn't disappoint. A rolled canvas, eight inches square. A *Madonna and Child*, painted in the early twenties, worth £5,000, more perhaps, God knew he was no expert. 'It's yours,' Capdevila told him.

'So long as I do as you ask?'

'No,' Capdevila insisted. 'It's yours. I can't take it with me. And I haven't the time to go back.'

Clare sat down on the edge of the bath. Capdevila placed the Picasso canvas on the chair in front of him. In the bedroom, the radio struck up an old dance tune – *Flor de Pomer.* In the bathroom, the hot water pipe shuddered.

Clare took a deep breath. 'What time do you have to be where?'

They took a taxi to Poble Espanyol, a model village built on the slopes of Montjuic for the 1929 Exhibition. 'You're a little early,' the taxi driver told them; the attraction didn't open until ten. 'I can give you a tour of the Poble Olimpic. Special rate.'

'No, thank you,' Capdevila said firmly. 'Here's just fine.'

The driver shrugged – *suit yourselves* – and turned back down the hill.

They let him drive off, then continued on up the road to a small sun-bleached kiosk set back from the kerb, where Capdevila ordered coffee and sandwiches. They stood for a moment in silence, gazing out over the Parque de Atracciones and the domed roofs of the pavilions, Capdevila fixing a last image of the city in his mind, Clare wondering what it must be like to do so, thinking of London, if he ever had to leave and not come back, where would he go for that one last moment? Down by the river at Hammersmith Bridge, Hyde Park on a frosty morning, or the *alfresco* restaurants of Percy Street on a warm Saturday night.

They finished their coffee, then took a right hand fork away from the main road, behind the old Oriental Pavilion. To their right lay open countryside, scrub, rock and pine trees, sloping down to the belching chimneys of Hospitalet.

The road itself had seen better days. Chunks of tarmac prised away by flash floods, weeds pushing up through the cracks. As they walked, Capdevila reminisced about his childhood visits to Montjuic. His father, a book seller, had painted as a hobby. As a young boy, Capdevila would often accompany him, helping to carry his brushes and paints, in time graduating to helping mix the colours. His father liked to paint landscapes. On a Sunday his favoured vantage points would be up here on Montjuic or on the slopes of Collserola.

Occasionally he would venture onto the beach but only in winter when there was no-one there. It was from his father that Capdevila had derived his love of art, and from his father also, working summers as a part time assistant in the book shop, that he'd inherited a knack for buying and selling. Put the two together and it was obvious where his future lay – thus his first gallery at the age of twenty-four, in the very same building he still occupied. Or so he told Clare.

They soon came to another fork. A stone track peeling off across the hillside. Here they left the road, Capdevila leading the way, the sun now behind them, not yet too hot, the wild flowers, the throb of cicadas and the scent of pine giving Montjuic the impression of being an island within the city. A patchwork sea of buildings lapping at its shore.

Capdevila asked Clare about London. When this was all over he was thinking of setting up a business there, in Cork Street. Wasn't that where all the galleries were to be found? Perhaps, Capdevila mused, Clare might consider coming to work with him?

Perhaps.

Now the track split again. 'Here,' Capdevila announced. 'This is it. This is where we meet your friend Markham.'

At a glance, Clare could see that the spot had been well chosen, shielded by a clump of pines and a sharp outcrop of rock. Out of sight, yet affording a good view of anyone approaching by vehicle or on foot.

They sat down on the rock to wait. Capdevila lit a cheroot. Overhead, a buzzard hovered. In the distance, Clare could hear the vague tinkling of a goat bell.

The bus was on time. From their vantage point they watched it approach, slowly snaking up the hill, trailing a cloud of dust. The plan was for Markham to pull in on the bend. No longer than sixty seconds. Time enough to secrete a body into the concealed compartment, then back to San Feliu de Llobregat to pick up the rest of the Pentathlon team. A four/five hour drive up the N1, and with a bit of luck, by late afternoon they'd be across the border, safely in France.

Markham swung the bus off the track, crunching to a halt beneath the rock.

Clare and Capdevila climbed down to meet him, Capdevila stubbing out his cheroot. 'Where's Picasso – and what the hell are you doing here?' Markham glared at him.

Clare tried to explain the change of plan. Markham hit the roof. It wasn't Capdevila's plan to change. 'But it's the only way Picasso will come,' Capdevila argued back through Clare. 'If he gets a signal from me that it's safe.'

Markham shook his head. *No*.

Capdevila proffered an envelope. From Picasso. 'It's a letter. He wrote it yesterday. Richard can translate. If you don't believe I'm telling the truth.' Again Markham shook his head. A letter meant nothing. It was too easy to fake. 'Tell him about the sketch,' Capdevila urged Clare. 'Pablo said you'd know it was from him.' Clare tried. But Markham cut him dead. Already they'd wasted three minutes. His every instinct told him to walk. But to come away empty handed? That too went against the grain. Time was ticking by. Stay any longer and he ran the risk of attracting unwanted attention. But there was another possibility. Take Capdevila now. Then contact London. Have them make the final decision. That way he could keep all options open. 'Okay.' Markham relented. 'Get in. Quick.'

Thank you. Capdevila embraced Clare, his relief evident. 'We shall see each other in London, my friend.'

Clare gave him a thumbs up. 'Good luck.'

'Cork Street!' Capdevila grinned.

Fifty-two seconds later the bus pulled away – Markham at the wheel, Capdevila squeezed into a six by two and a half foot space under the floor, being bumped and bounced along the track, at Markham's mercy and being made to suffer for it.

Clare relieved himself on a rock. It was now 10.35am. He could just about make it to the swimming pool by eleven (this morning he'd decided to report on the men's 100m free style). High to his right, he noticed the buzzard again, hovering over the scrub, locked onto a rabbit or a small rodent.

Then – the sharp crack of a rifle shot.

Clare's first instinct was that it had been aimed at the bird. But an immediate and thunderous volley instantly dispelled this thought. Moments later, the bus slewed off the track. From nowhere the hillside was suddenly alive with soldiers and Clare was running for his life.

Just before the first shot – had he heard a voice calling on the bus to stop? As Clare ran he tried to put the pieces together. The flash of a pair of binoculars catching the sun, the sudden eruption of gunfire – two distinct sounds, the smack of rifles from higher up the hill, the thump of a machine gun from the direction of the Poble Olimpic, falling silent as the bus started to roll down the hill – which meant they hadn't yet seen him.

If he could only reach the tree line ahead.

A bullet slammed into the ground behind him. Another whistled overhead. Clare instinctively ducked, jinking as he ran, praying he wouldn't stumble.

They had his range. Any moment now.

A bullet took the air from in front of his eyes. Clare leapt forward, hurling himself into the shadow of a low escarpment as a few hundred yards down the mountain side the bus blew.

He could smell gasoline now. Hear the machine gun opening up again; he thought he'd seen Markham jump clear.

Clare picked himself up and ran on, hugging the rock face. Until the soldiers moved their position he was safe, for ten, maybe twenty seconds. He might yet reach the trees without breaking cover.

For a second time the machine gun fell silent. Did that mean Markham too was now dead? Then – a large crack in the ground. Clare stumbled as he tried to clear it, catching his foot in the exposed root of a thorn bush, striking his elbow as he fell, his momentum carrying him on down the hill, over the lip of a rock, fifteen feet into a gully.

Clare stifled a cry as he hit the ground, reaching out a hand to grasp hold of a shrub to stop himself from sliding further down the hillside.

As the dust settled and the trickle of loosed stones stilled, Clare lifted his head and wiped the dirt from his eyes. *If they hadn't seen him fall, they might conceivably assume he'd made it to the trees.* Gingerly, he got to his feet. Nothing broken. Just a few cuts and bruises and a badly grazed elbow.

Keeping tight to the rock face, Clare limped towards the head of the gully, where the thin lip and overhanging vegetation offered most protection. Pressing on into a thicket of gorse, the sharp thorns ripped at his skin, yet Clare also felt a certain comfort, knowing that no-one would readily search for him through this.

At the head of the gully, there was a narrow fissure in the rock. Dark, hidden, just large enough for a man to squeeze through, it seemed to carve a path right through the mountain.

Hardly daring to hope, Clare groped his way along the rock bed, shuffling his feet across the boulders, terrified of twisting an ankle. Once he'd read an account of an attempt to climb the Matterhorn. Three men had died. But only one of the bodies had been found – a year later. The mountaineer, Clare couldn't recall his name, had miraculously survived the fall only to crawl into a cave to die.

Pushing the thought from his mind, Clare battled on to the end of the cave as quickly as he dared, feeling his way up onto a narrow shelf, tugging loose a thick screen of brambles to see that he'd come out on the far side of the hill. A few hundred yards above the Cementerio del Sur-

Oeste. The two square kilometres of terraced tombs that occupied the southwest side of Montjuic.

Clare hurriedly pulled himself free of the thicket and scrabbled down the hillside, across a scrubby, litter strewn meadow towards the high stone wall that described the outer reaches of the necropolis. Two gypsy women camped by the cemetery gate curiously watched him approach, drawing him in with their eyes, priming themselves to flog him a bunch of lavender or a soft drink.

Sorry. Not today. Clare strode past them with an apologetic shrug.

Only once he was safely inside the cemetery walls did he stop to examine the damage he'd sustained. His face – from what he could see of it reflected in the glass front of a tomb – didn't look too bad. Both arms were badly scratched, as were his ankles, and his right elbow was beginning to throb. All this he could live with. It was his filthy, badly ripped clothes that were the problem, the arrow pointed at him that said misfit, man on the run. These, he needed to be rid of – fast.

A quick glance to check no-one was watching, a sharp thrust of the elbow, and the glass door to tomb number 2285 broke away neatly in three pieces. Carefully, Clare prised loose the largest shard. A little primitive perhaps but wrapped into the arm of his jacket, it would have to make do.

Juan Jose Oller, a fifty-five year old tram conductor from Poble-sec, lay on his wife's grave, his eyes closed and a cigarette between his lips, alone with his thoughts.

The plot had been bought by his father in 1921 at the cheap end of the cemetery, at the highest, furthest point from the main entrance. But Juan Jose Oller had never minded the climb, in fact he'd grown to appreciate the seclusion, the partial view afforded of the port and that there was no-one there to frown at him when he unpacked his picnic and lay down on his wife's grave for a quiet smoke, which was why he initially didn't see Clare, not until he felt a prick in the side of his neck and heard him say, 'I need your clothes,' only then did Juan Jose Oller open his eyes.

'Do as I say,' Clare told him. 'And I won't hurt you.'

Ten minutes later, Juan Jose Oller lay stripped to his underwear, bound and gagged on the floor of a domed mausoleum at the end of the terrace, his ankles and wrists secured with his shoelaces. Clare knew the knots wouldn't hold for long, but then they didn't need to.

In a quarter of an hour the place would be crawling with soldiers.

On a Sunday morning, the cemetery was at its busiest. A steady stream of visitors doing their duty by the departed before a long, lazy lunch back in the city. Clare slipped into the crowd drifting back down the hill towards the main gates, hands in his pockets and eyes to the ground. Just another visitor in his appropriated, cheap, slightly ill fitting suit.

Outside the main entrance, there was the usual Sunday bustle more akin to a flea market than a cemetery, flower girls, shoe shine boys, fortune tellers; roadside peddlers hawking refreshments, parasols and religious artefacts. Gypsies and immigrants all. The put upon *murcianos* from the shanty town that had grown up along the base of the hill beyond the cemetery walls, tolerated so long as they stayed without.

A bus drew up. A family alighted. Clare got on, paid his fare and took a seat. *Go! Go! Go!* His palms were wet with sweat. The driver seemed to be taking an eternity, waiting first for one couple then another. *Go! Damn you!*

At last, the bus pulled away. *Thank Christ!* Clare felt the tension in his fists subside and the adrenaline drain from his body; where he'd dug his finger nails into his palms, there were four white curves.

Capdevila was dead. Most likely Markham too. The SIM had been waiting for them – that much was clear. Somehow they'd known. Looking back up the hill, Clare could see them now, clambering down from the woods to the cemetery.

A fair assumption – they knew about him too.

For a while the road ran parallel to the railway, squeezed between the cliff face and the waterfront. Beyond the tracks lay the first traces of the docks, the wharves and warehouses of the Muelle Morrot, a cluster of cranes bent over a half constructed boat, a goods train standing idle by a rank of unharnessed carts. Across the water, Clare glimpsed the elegant brick tower of the lighthouse. It seemed an age since he'd been sitting in its shadow, quaffing beer with Wilson and the others.

Traversing the tram lines, the bus progressed along the Passeig de Colom, its route staked out by an avenue of palm trees stretching all the way to Ciutadella. Here, the bus steered back towards the sea, passing along the bottom of the park towards the Cementerio del Este, the end of the line and another graveyard. As Clare stepped from the bus, the driver smiled. *You have relatives here too?*

Clare nodded. *Yes. God bless their souls.*

Clare had to assume that the SIM were watching his hotel, his friends, all public places and points of exit. As he stood outside the cemetery gates pondering his next move, he recalled the name of Capdevila's contact, Moreno Garcia, the mechanic whose garage was just a few blocks away, if he could only remember the address on the piece of paper which Capdevila had passed to Markham – Carrer Castanets, Castanyts, Casta … something, somewhere in Poblenou.

Across the road from the cemetery was a newspaper stand. Clare bought a copy of *La Vanguardia* and casually asked for directions. 'Castanys.' the news vendor told him. 'You want Castanys. Off Plaça Unio.'

'That sounds right,' Clare agreed.

'I'm telling you. That's what you want.' The old man pointed him down Carrer Taulat. 'One. Two. Three. Four. Fifth left. It's on your right. Ask for the market if you get lost.'

Clare thanked him.

'Where are you from?' the news vendor was intrigued to know. 'Russia?'

Clare nodded. *Yes*. It was easier that way.

'Stalin!' The old man grinned, baring his few remaining teeth, nicotine stained and set like broken tombstones.

Clare grinned back. *Stalin*.

The old man raised his right fist. '*No pasaran*.'

Clare held his grin. *No pasaran*.

Moreno Garcia's garage lay in a block of jumbled buildings adjacent to a ceramics factory, shielded from the road by a high brick wall. Clare approached cautiously. The main gate into the yard was secured by a heavy chain but as he passed by the wall, Clare thought he could hear the sound of children playing on the other side, the thump of a football being kicked. Encouraged, he pursued the line of the wall away from the street, turning first into a dirt alleyway, then into a scrap of wasteland until he found what he was looking for, the way the kids had got into the yard, an old car left abandoned by the wall – the rusting wreck of a 1928 Hotchkiss Sedan.

Clare pulled himself up onto the roof of the Hotchkiss and over the wall, almost turning his ankle as he dropped down onto a pile of tyres, blowing a whistle on the football game. A six year old urchin with wide eyes and a lop sided grin stared at him suspiciously. The eldest child picked up the ball. 'I'm looking for Moreno Garcia,' Clare announced.

Like rabbits to the smack of a shotgun, the children scarpered.

'Hey! Come back!' Clare shouted after them. 'If it's about you being here, I won't say anything!' But they were already gone, up and over the wall. Even the six year old.

Bloody kids.

Clare refocused his attention on the yard. Two work shops, a petrol pump, air and water gauges and an outside lavatory.

He tried the smaller of the two workshops first. Peering in through the window, he could make out a black Citroën van on a ramp, half its engine laid out on a white sheet.

The door was locked.

The larger workshop – two storeys high and spacious enough to house a bus – seemed to hold greater promise, but try as he might Clare could find no obvious way to force an entrance. The main doors were too heavy, both bolted and padlocked, the downstairs windows barred, and the one upstairs window too far from the gutter for him to get at.

Frustrated and thirsty, he tried the door to the washhouse only to find that too was locked; Moreno Garcia clearly had his problems with break-ins and vandals. Then a sudden thought took Clare back to the smaller of the two workshops, the one window that wasn't barred. Picking up a length of piping, he smashed the glass. Seconds later he was inside. Somewhere, he reasoned, there had to be a key to the lavatory; he couldn't imagine Moreno Garcia going to the trouble of giving each of his workers their own.

Clare found what he was looking for on a hook behind the door, partially hidden by a blue overall. A set of keys with a label attached – "DO NOT REMOVE". One opened the workshop door, Clare let himself out through it. A second – sure enough – unlocked the washhouse; he took a long drink from the tap and cleaned his face and arms. And the third – *click!* – Clare allowed himself a smile as the lock turned in the back door of the main workshop.

He was in.

The garage felt cool and cavernous, like he was entering a church; the altar, a wrecked taxi parked on the ramp, its parts collected like the relics of a Saint, an incense of grease and oil hanging heavy in the air.

At the top of a flight of stairs lay Moreno Garcia's office. A gloomy, pokey room into which had been squeezed a writing desk and two heavy filing cabinets, the only decoration a calendar hanging to one side of the window, a gift from the Ford Motor Company, still open on July. A pile of unopened bills and invoices littered the desk. Otherwise there was little to excite Clare's interest. No money, no car key, nothing that might help him flee the city, only a dusty postcard propped against the window. A picture of the Eiffel Tower, a scrawled note in a woman's handwriting addressed to E.J. Garcia.

Clare contemplated the postcard, idly wondering if he should try calling Garcia at his home address, only subconsciously registering the metallic clank of a chain being unthreaded, the rattle of the garage gates being opened, then hearing it more fully, a car driving into the yard, a black T48 Hispano-Suizo, two suited men walking point on the vehicle confirming his suspicion – it was the SIM.

Clare sprang back from the window and ran downstairs to the rear exit, reaching for the door handle just as the car pulled up outside. 'Get out!' He heard one of the agents say. Clare looked around for somewhere to hide. 'Move it!' A short, fat man spilled out of the back seat of the car, still dressed in his pyjamas, barefoot and bruised about the face. 'Open it!' A third agent, carrying a jerry can in one hand and a pistol in the other, indicated the garage door.

For a split second Clare was ten years old again, playing hide and seek, gripped by a last minute attack of indecision as the seeker neared the end of his count – *thirteen, fourteen, fifteen* – underneath the work bench he spied a stack of cardboard boxes – *sixteen, seventeen, eighteen* – frantically he dived behind them just as the garage door lifted open – *nineteen, twenty! Coming ready or not!*

'On your knees!' The agent with the pistol – the one the others called Captain Caraben – pushed the man in the pyjamas to the ground.

Clare guessed him to be Moreno Garcia.

'I swear – I don't know where he is. I swear it.' Clare watched Caraben half drag Moreno Garcia across the floor to the lip of the service pit. 'He's not here! I swear to God, I don't know where he is!'

Clare smelt petrol. They were going to torch the building. The jerry can that Caraben had been carrying was now being held over a stack of tyres by one of the other policemen. Clare watched him douse the taxi, then pour what was left of the petrol into the bottom of the service pit.

'Where's Clare?' Caraben jabbed his gun into Moreno Garcia's temple.

'I don't know. I swear to you,' Moreno Garcia whimpered.

'For the last time – where is he?'

'I don't know.'

Clare instinctively looked away. There was nothing he could do. He'd seen a man executed before. At Algeciras. A German brigadista, a fifth columnist or so they'd been informed. He remembered all too vividly the firing squad raising their rifles, the look in the German's eyes, a terrified appeal to those around him, *I'm no different to you, no less alive than you, breathing the same air as you, put yourself in my shoes, if I could only put myself in yours. TAKE AIM! FIRE!*

Moreno Garcia fell into the service pit. A bullet through the back of his head.

'Let's go.' Caraben holstered his pistol. One of the policemen lit a cigarette – took a drag – then tossed it into the service pit.

BOOM! Clare felt the rush of heat from where he lay crouched under the work bench. *'Coño!'* Heard the startled cry of the agent who'd sparked the fire, 'Let's get the hell out of here!'

Already the taxi was consumed by flames. Clare counted four seconds, then broke cover as a series of explosions rocked the building. He ran for the back door. The heat intense. A black noxious smoke billowing from the storeroom. One step forward, two steps back – the effort only taking him further away from the door.

It was a chain that saved him, of the variety used to anchor fishing boats in the port; thick, heavy, well greased links threaded through a pulley, capable of hoisting a bus or a tram car. He almost missed it, if the fire hadn't driven him deep into the repair bay he would have done. In the dark, half obscured by smoke, he first mistook it for a pillar, only recognising his mistake as he stumbled over its tail lying neatly coiled on the ground beside the winching handle.

The grease was already beginning to run, the metal hot to touch. Wrapping his hands in rags, and wedging his feet into the links, Clare somehow found himself a grip. Slowly, torturously, he began to pull himself up. *On the pages of The Captain, the magazine he'd once worked for … he was in the seat of a fighter plane spiralling towards the ground, struggling to pull back the jammed roof of his cockpit, flames licking the soles of his feet.*

Clare reached out an arm, searching for a hold on the iron girder from which the chain hung, his other hand slipping as he shifted his weight, his ankle twisting – *now!* – fingers outstretched, he pushed into the dark, clawing at the lip of the girder – *not going to let go, not now, now that he had a hold* – his body stayed, Clare swung his legs up onto the girder.

Not going to let go now.

Half blinded, choking from the smoke, Clare shuffled his way along the metal beam towards the wall. A window. A blue patch of sky.

He was going to make it. He was going to put his fist through the glass pane, feel the cold rush of air on his face. He was going to slide down the roof to the ground below.

He was going to live.

As the garage burned and the neighbourhood watched and passed judgement as to the cause of the fire, Clare quietly slipped away from the scene, back over the wall, the same way he'd got in, by the wreck of the rusting car.

Close by, a church bell rang. Across the city, restaurants were opening their doors for Sunday lunch, reminding Clare that he hadn't eaten since breakfast. A lifetime ago. Somewhere he must be able to find something to eat for – he counted the loose change in his pocket – twenty-six pesetas.

That somewhere turned out to be Can Jordi. A no-nonsense family run kitchen on Plaça Glòries, famed for its *Rabo de toro,* a rich stew made from the tails of the bulls slain in the nearby bullring. The walls were covered with mementos of the Corrida, signed photographs of the great matadors, donated keepsakes, *muletas, espadas, capas* and *agujas*.

Clare found himself a table in the corner – away from the window – and ordered the stew. No-one commented on his singed appearance and he didn't try to explain it. Around Plaça Glòries they got all types.

The meal arrived with a carafe of wine. Clare poured himself a glass, drank it, then poured himself another. Only now was the shock of the morning sinking in – how lucky he was to be still alive – but with it also the realisation that he couldn't keep running. Not for long at any rate. He needed shelter. Help. Money. Someone he could trust.

Clare finished his meal, drank a strong black coffee, then walked across to the public telephone box outside the entrance to the bullring.

A near empty tram clattered by. Otherwise, all was quiet. Tomorrow, of course, it would be a different story, 40,000 people converging on the stadium for the opening day of the boxing competition; Clare had intended coming himself as there was strong interest back home in a young fighter from Shepherds Bush. But that was all in the past now.

45963 – it took Clare two attempts to remember the number.

'Taxis David ...' On the other side of the city, Nuria Roca sleepily answered the phone, her mouth full of chocolate.

Speaking in broken Spanish, Clare told her that he wanted a taxi. A driver who could speak German. 'One of your guys gave me his card the other day,' he said. 'Werner Bloch. Is he free?'

'He's just finishing his lunch, dear,' Nuria tried to keep a straight voice. 'Tell me where you want him to be and he'll be there.'

'Café de Toros,' Clare read out the name of a bar on the opposite side of the street. 'Across the road from the Monumental. On the south side of Gran Via.'

'He'll be with you in twenty minutes,' Nuria assured him. 'What name should he ask for?'

'Stani.' Clare gave the name of Werner's old friend. 'He'll remember me.'

'I'm sure he will, love.' Nuria Roca broke the line with her finger, finished the chocolate she was half way through, then dialled the number Major Jordan had told her to call should anybody try to contact Werner. Momentarily, she wondered where Werner was, whether he was still alive even, then she pushed the thought from her mind and selected another chocolate from the box presented to her by one of last night's admirers. A peppermint crème.

Clare checked his watch. It was now ten to three. A few minutes previously, he'd noticed a truck pulling up outside the bullring, the driver leaving his two colleagues in the cab as he entered the gate house. He could see the driver now walking back to the vehicle, giving the others the thumb's up – they had permission to enter.

The truck started up.

Clare casually fell in behind it, the janitor holding the gate open for him. 'You the last?' he asked, impatient to return to his radio and glass of manzanilla.

Clare nodded. 'Yes.'

Inside the arena, workmen were applying the finishing touches to the two boxing rings. A technician was testing the PA system, while volunteers hung Olympic banners on the *barrera* and royal box.

A sign by the entrance pointed the way up to the *tabloncillo*, the highest row of open seats that lay just below the covered galleries. Directly behind these benches, a windowed arcade circumscribed the stadium, drawing in the breeze, and giving a view out over the street.

A direct eye line to the Café de Toros.

For half an hour, Clare monitored the movement in and out of the café. Noting one departure – an elderly couple and their dog. And three arrivals – a young man in a homburg, and two men in late middle age, one clasping a large book, the other a wrapped parcel. Then at 3.22pm, a taxi pulled up, a yellow lozenge inscribed on its side, Taxis David. Even from across the road, Clare could tell it was Werner from his brilliantined hair and the limp in his left leg.

Clare cautiously scanned the street, looking for a parked car, a motorbike, a passer-by moving too slowly, or a face that didn't fit, but he could see nothing to excite his suspicion, just a woman hanging her washing out to dry on the fourth floor of the house next door.

Werner entered the café. Three minutes later, he reappeared with a cup of coffee. He stood for a moment in the sun, idly stirring it with a pencil taken from his dashboard. Then, placing the cup on the roof of his taxi, he took a handkerchief from his pocket and fastidiously began to wipe clean his windscreen.

Thank you Werner. Clare couldn't see them but he knew they were there. Werner couldn't drink coffee. Not since the war and his wound. Even the smell of it now made him feel sick. Only a friend would know that.

A friend about to walk into a trap.

Of all the ideas Clare considered in the immediate aftermath of his escape from the bullring, the idea of impersonating Balasc's boyfriend was perhaps the most desperate, yet the more he thought about it, and the more he considered the consequences of being picked up by the SIM, the less insane it became, so that by the time he reached the Hotel Nouvel, where he remembered Balasc telling him Temple was staying, it seemed almost sensible. 'I have a room here,' he confidently announced at the check-in desk. 'In the name of Temple. Morris Temple.'

Clare's confidence – such as it was – was based on three assumptions: One – that Balasc and Temple were sleeping together at Balasc's hotel. Two – that Temple hadn't been back to his hotel since checking in on Friday morning. And three – that the desk clerk who had checked Temple in had the weekend off.

'*Buenas dias, Señor*.' The desk clerk in question – Berenguer Obiols – smiled politely. 'We were beginning to think you didn't exist.'

Clare was in luck.

Obiols, a short, conscientious, thirty-six year old widower from Gracia, had witnessed many strange occurrences in his twenty years at the hotel, far stranger than the sight of Clare in his singed, ill fitting suit, the "mysterious Mr Temple" whom he had yet to clap eyes on. 'You've been in an accident, Sir,' he tactfully remarked.

'I met a lady,' Clare confessed. 'Her name was Montserrat. At least that's what she told me.'

'There are many Montserrats in Barcelona,' Obiols sympathised. 'It's a common name.'

'Not one I'll forget in a hurry,' Clare told him. 'This afternoon we went to the beach–'

'You went swimming. And when you came out, she was gone,' Obiols smiled knowingly. 'Your clothes and wallet too. It sometimes happens.' As Clare knew it did. Two or three times during the war, he'd heard similar tales of brigadistas on leave, enjoying the weekend of their lives only to wake up on a Monday morning to an empty bed, a dose of the clap and no wallet. 'Do you want me to call the police?' Obiols politely enquired.

Clare shook his head. 'No, thank you. I'd rather Mrs Temple didn't know.'

Obiols understood. 'Will there be anything else, Sir?'

'Yes.' Clare gestured his ragged attire. 'A gentleman kindly lent me these old clothes. I'd like to return them laundered. And I'll need a taxi please. For five o'clock.'

'I'll call one now.' Obiols handed Clare the key to Room 336. 'Your key, Mr Temple.'

Room 336 lay at the back of the hotel with a view onto a brick wall and the kitchen bins. Clare locked the door, drew the curtains, then laid his watch on the bedside table – he'd given himself twenty minutes.

His first priority was a change of clothing. Neatly arranged in the wardrobe, he found a variety of suits. Anderson & Sheppard, Benson & Clegg, Henry Poole & Co – Morris Temple clearly had expensive tastes – and a range of shoes to match, two tone, sporting spectators, Oxford brogues, enough to dress a small delegation, it seemed. Clare finally plumped for a cotton seersucker "Palm beach" style suit with a single breasted jacket and a pair of brown brogues; fortuitously they took the same size.

Before dressing, Clare allowed himself the luxury of a shower. Nothing could wipe away the trauma of Montjuic and Moreno Garcia's garage, but for a few blissful minutes he lost himself in the hot water and perfumed soap, cleansed the stench of smoke from his pores, and gathered his strength for whatever the next few hours might have to throw at him.

Clare needed money. Searching Temple's bedside table, he found an envelope full of cash; Spanish Pesetas, French Francs and Pounds Sterling, each currency neatly bound with a rubber band, the sum noted on a carefully torn piece of paper tucked into the fold. Clare also found a couple of packets of Wrigley's chewing gum, a spare pair of cuff links, a return train ticket to London, and two books, a Ray Cummings fantasy adventure, *Brigands of the Moon,* and an anthology of horror stories, *You'll need a night light – 15 creepy tales.* He took the money and the chewing gum and left the rest, then returned to the lobby.

The taxi was waiting outside. Clare handed Obiols a generous tip along with a handsome gratuity for "the kind man who'd lent him his clothes" and a false address in Barceloneta to which they could be returned, then he climbed into the cab, one of the crowd again. Simply, a man in a sharp suit such as Jimmy Stewart or Clark Gable might wear.

'*Americano?*' the taxi driver asked hopefully. Clare regretted not. Speaking in English, with a smattering of guide book Spanish, he explained that he was from London and that he wished to visit the celebrated monastery of Montserrat. '*Muy bueno!*' The taxi driver swallowed his disappointment. A thirty-six mile fare more than made up for Clare not being American. '*Bienvenido a Barcelona,*' he grinned.

Clare unwrapped a stick of Temple's chewing gum and settled back into his seat. Montserrat – the hilltop shrine to the Saint that bore Montse's name – seemed as good a place as any to head for. There were at least two hotels that he could remember where he might conceivably pick up a lift, and also a train station, and buses heading inland. His one aim now was to head south. Towards Gibraltar and the Portuguese border. Stick to the byways, keep moving, and put his trust in Our Virgin Lady of Montserrat.

The taxi turned up Diagonal. Soon they would be beyond the city boundaries. Already the metropolis was tapering to a strip of recently constructed buildings soldered to the side of the road. Twenty years ago, the taxi driver assured him, it had all been fields.

A faded sign post read "Esplugues 2 kms". Here the road converged with the N2, the main highway connecting Barcelona to Zaragoza and Madrid. Clare remembered it from the war as one long jam, a conveyor belt of trucks shuttling supplies to the front and returning with the wounded. As if in silent salute to this past, a lone truck lumbered westward, dogged by its shadow, picked at by a thin finger of dust. 'One hour.' The taxi driver tapped his watch. 'Montserrat – one hour!'

Clare nodded – *good* – and sank back into his seat, trying to piece together the fragments spinning loose in his mind. The SIM had been waiting for them on Montjuic. How had they known to be there? Had they been tailing him all along? Or was it Capdevila who had given them away? Markham even? And what had happened to Picasso? Had they been watching him too? Had they known the details of the rendezvous beforehand? But how? Who? What now?

Clare soon gave up trying to make sense of it all. Too tired to think.

Approaching Esplugues, the taxi slowed to let a quartet of old men across the road, one with a battered old dominoes box clutched to his chest, all walking with the stoop of a lifetime spent in the fields and an afternoon in the bar.

The taxi turned right onto the main road. A short distance ahead of them, Clare could see the truck now stopped in the middle of the road, the driver leaning out of his cab, showing his papers to a militiaman. 'What's going on?' he asked, trying not to sound too concerned.

'Most likely looking for Fascists,' the taxi driver said as he drew to a halt at the road block and lit a cigarette.

A minute passed as the militiamen searched the back of the truck, Clare anxiously chewing gum, the taxi driver annoyingly singing the refrain to *Sweet Leilani*. Overhead an Iberia De Havilland DH89 made a last wide turn on its final approach to El Prat airport, then with a slap of the tailgate, the truck was cleared and the taxi waved forward. 'Papers!'

The driver had his at the ready. Clare affected a look of quiet boredom.

'Papers!' This time there was nothing general in the request, the militiaman was looking straight at him. Clare shrugged and shook his head. 'No papers. Stolen.'

'Papers! Passport!' the militiaman insisted.

'Stolen,' Clare breezily regretted, miming someone pick-pocketing his jacket.

At last the militiaman understood. *'Robado?'*

'That's right,' Clare smiled. *'Robado!'*

The militiaman made it clear that this was a serious business. Clare agreed. It was. And tomorrow, when the Consulate opened, he fully intended to report it, but already the militiaman had turned to quiz the taxi driver on where he'd picked Clare up, while his colleague was strolling over to the bar to use the phone. 'He's going to Montserrat,' Clare heard the taxi driver explaining.

Not any more he's not, Clare thought to himself. *Not any more.*

When the call came, Inspector Marin was asleep. It was that time in the late afternoon when he liked to search out a vacant cell, stretch out on the cot and enjoy an interruption free, post prandial snooze.

The timing was unfortunate. For the second time in two days it fell to the duty officer, Chici Parraguez, to bust in on the "DO NOT DISTURB" sign that Marin had hung on his life's door. Marin's initial reaction was as if he'd been stung by a bee, yelling at Parraguez to take himself back to his whore of a mother in Peru before he returned him there himself in a box, producing his pistol as proof of intent, terrifying Parraguez into a full scale retreat back up the stairs. But after a five minute stand off and the accidental discharge of a bullet into the roof of the cells, Marin finally calmed sufficiently to understand Parraguez had his best interests at heart, that if he didn't immediately respond to the militia's request for a car to pick up the Englishman they'd apprehended travelling without papers, his arse would be in deep and very hot water, at which point Parraguez was prevailed upon to accept his apology, Marin assuring him that he had meant nothing by calling his mother a whore, nor his sister and grandmother for that matter, and as for wishing him back in Peru, Parraguez was to consider himself commended, taken for a drink and properly thanked just as soon as these cursed Games were over and life allowed to return to normal.

All the way back into town, Clare indignantly stuck to his fiction. His name was Temple. His passport had been stolen. He was just a tourist trying to see the sights.

A militiaman told him to shut up.

On arrival at the police station, he was shown into an airless interrogation room, and then when the interpreter arrived, taken upstairs to Marin's office. There were five of them gathered in the room: Clare, the interpreter, who introduced himself as Dr

Gispert, Marin, Parraguez, whom Marin had deputed to take notes, and a nameless policeman, who stood guard at the door.

Marin opened proceedings by reminding Clare that visitors to the city had been repeatedly advised to carry their papers with them at all times. Clare – careful not to let on he spoke Spanish – protested that he had done so but regretted that his passport had been stolen this afternoon in an embarrassing episode at the beach. Marin wanted to know if he'd informed the Consulate. 'It's Sunday,' Clare pointed out. 'The Consulate's closed. There's nothing I can do until tomorrow morning.'

'Did you call the police?' Marin pressed him.

'No.'

'Why not?'

Clare reiterated a point already made to the desk clerk at the Nouvel – he didn't want his wife to know about his weekend with the lady from the bar.

Marin looked unimpressed. 'Have you any identification? Is there anyone who might vouch for you?'

Clare shook his head. He was travelling alone.

'Mr Temple – I need proof of your identity.' Marin didn't think Clare quite understood the severity of the situation. 'You will not be allowed to leave here until this matter is resolved.'

'You could always call my hotel,' Clare ventured. 'Speak to the desk clerk.'

'He knows you?'

'Yes.'

Marin gruffly turned to Parraguez. 'Get me the Hotel Nouvel.'

As Parraguez tried for a line, Dr Gispert casually probed Clare about his stay in the city. How long had he been in Barcelona? How much of the Games had he seen? What other sites had he taken in?

Clare confessed to having seen very little of the sport on account of being waylaid by the woman he'd met on Friday night in a bar somewhere near the top of the Ramblas, he couldn't remember its exact name but yes, it was the same woman who'd today fleeced him of his passport and wallet on the beach at Barceloneta, the worst of which was not the loss of his wallet and passport, both of which were replaceable, but his brand new bespoke linen suit, which was not, having been ordered especially for the trip and cut for him by the Duke of Windsor's tailor, Mr Halsey himself, no less –

'I have Señor Obiols for you, Sir,' Parraguez interrupted them. 'The desk clerk from the Nouvel.'

Marin left the matter of Clare's new suit hanging in the air as he took hold of the phone. 'Señor Obiols – I need you to confirm the identity of one of your guests. A Mr Morris Temple.' As Marin began to question Obiols, Clare nervously searched his face for some sign of a reaction, some indication as to whether his story would hold water, but the bear-like police chief had long ago learned to absorb information without the faintest flicker of emotion, a trait that had stood him well during his Friday evening poker sessions. '... He says you called him a taxi? ... At what time would that have been? ... After he returned to the beach? ... From Barceloneta? ... How long has he been staying with you? ... Until? ... Yes ... One moment, please ...' Marin turned to Gispert. 'Please – ask Mr Temple how he entered the country?'

'By train. From France,' Clare replied without hesitation. 'My return ticket's in my bedside table if you want to see it.'

'When did you check in?' Marin asked.

'Two days ago.'

'And when are you leaving?'

'Excuse me?'

'How long are you staying in Barcelona, Mr Temple? It's a simple question.'

Clare had no idea. 'I'm here for two weeks.' He hazarded a guess, vaguely recalling that Balasc had mentioned something about his friend being in town for a fortnight's holiday.

Marin had heard all he needed to.

The taxi dropped Clare off at the Sagrada Familia. It was Marin's suggestion he go there. The desk clerk at the Nouvel had vouchsafed for him and he was now free to leave. But not to Montserrat, Marin regretted, at least not until he'd been reissued a passport. Clare promised – first thing Monday morning, he'd sort it out. 'Until then stay within the city boundaries,' Marin warned him, 'and if you want to visit a monument, try Gaudi's new cathedral.' Dr Gispert seconded the suggestion. The Sagrada Familia might only be a fraction built but in his opinion it afforded a far greater insight into Gaudi's genius than did the Palau Güell or either of his other mansions on Passeig de Gracia. Clare was suitably grateful. His guide book hardly touched on Gaudi. He would – he declared – pay the site a visit on his way back to the hotel to make up for the disappointment of not making it to Montserrat.

At 7.45pm, the Sagrada Familia was deserted. Even the beggars camped all day outside the façade had gone home.

In Excelsis. Gloria. Alone, at last, Clare gazed up at the mosaic inscriptions that decorated the four vertiginous towers. In a church in west London, his father would now be celebrating Evensong. In Lourdes, he imagined Jesus Mirabel at Mass.

Clare stepped through the cathedral door, into the realm of Gaudi's imagination, the interior for now boasting only a few locked workmen's huts, a roped off pile of half carved stone and a view up to the heavens. Progress on the cathedral had stopped with the war. Clare doubted it would ever restart, doubted the door would ever lead anywhere beyond the other side of a wall. Gaudi had cut the face of the city with his extraordinary façade. Over time it would merely heal into a scar. Become a memory in stone.

Clare took a tram back into the centre of town. Slumped against the banquette, his mind drifted once again towards thoughts of Montse. How he'd promised to take her out to dinner tonight at the Ritz. Would she be waiting for him to call? Would she turn up expecting him to be there? What if he never got to speak to her again? What if he just disappeared? Would she merely assume he'd gone back home again, this time afraid to even say goodbye?

Just north of Gran Via, a policeman waved the tram to a halt. A spot check? Clare sat bolt upright in panic. Then to his relief, realised that the driver was merely being asked to wait. Of course – *Thank God* – they were still running the marathon. The road had been roped off to allow the runners past.

The athletes came by in dribs and drabs, the crowd politely applauding their effort, one dehydrated French runner grabbing a carafe of water from a café table and pouring it over his head, to the amusement of those seated at the table, who urged him on, *'Allez! Allez!'*

Slowly the runners passed, followed by the official race car, an ambulance, and a truck rigged with a large hoarding advertising tomorrow's free events. An exhibition rugby match between a Catalan and Scottish XV, a 100 kilometre cycle rally, and an open air concert in the Ciutadella park, a programme of Beethoven, Shostakovich and Sibelius.

On the back of the truck, a volunteer sat waving a green flag, signalling the all clear. The traffic was now free to move.

Leaving the tram at Plaça Catalunya, Clare made his way down to Paral·lel. He needed somewhere to lose himself for a few hours. Somewhere to gather his thoughts. Here, amongst the bars, cafés and music joints, he would be just another suit out for a good time, casing the entertainment – no thank you to the whore beckoning him from her doorway – no thank you to the shoe shine boy rapping his brush against his shins – no thank you to the man with a cardboard suitcase stashed full of cigarettes, chewing gum and aphrodisiac tonic.

Clare joined the queue outside the Pompeya music hall – top of tonight's bill, *La Perlita*. Admission was free but the drinks were expensive, every punter obliged to buy at least one – *the consumacion obligatorio* – a cup of coffee laced with a shot of cheap rum.

Clare paid his dues and settled himself on a bench near the back of the hall. A rain of peanut shells hit the stage as the curtains drew back, and into the spotlight stepped *La Conchita*, a fat lady in a blonde wig, squeezed into black trunks and chemise, a faux diamond cross sparkling between her large breasts. Up struck the music. Playfully saucy. *Oompah!* Conchita rotated her belly, shivering her bosoms and shoulders, provocatively thrusting her hips at the front row, reacting with feigned modesty to the young man who leaned forward to rap her on the arse with his newspaper.

During the entre'acte, Clare bought himself another "coffee" and tried again to make some sense of the previous ten hours. But the harder he tried, the more he went round in circles. Werner, Jordan, Capdevila, Markham, Picasso – there had to be a connection, but Clare was damned if he could find it. The only thing he knew for certain was that he needed somewhere to sleep. Already he imagined the SIM would be making a sweep of the hotels, boarding houses and brothels; soon they would begin trawling the city's dead spots, putting the word out in the bars and clubs, whispering a reward for information leading to his capture; he didn't imagine they would need to offer much.

In the lull before the final act, Clare made his move. Slipping into the wake of a party of inebriated office workers, he made his way up Ronda Sant Pau to the Raval and Montse's parents' hotel.

According to Ancient Greek legend, the Maenads were the Nymphs who'd nurtured Dionysus. Inspired by the God into a mystical frenzy, they'd roamed the countryside wild and naked, inciting Bacchanalian revelry with their frenetic music. Why there were two such spirits depicted in relief on the façade of the Hotel Comercio, Clare had never found out beyond that they predated Montse's father taking control of the business. Bathed in a milky moonlight, they sang to Clare of past frolics with Montse in Room 9 – when her parents were out – and up on the roof when they were not.

Up on the roof. Their old haunt. Clare slipped through a narrow passageway into the dark alley that had once housed the stables behind the hotel, now decayed into a festering, congealed maze of dank rooms that hadn't seen the light of day for decades, where the transient underbelly of the city's workforce slept on sweat stained mattresses rented out by the day or the night, never both.

At the end of the alley, there was an open doorway. Inside, an unlit stairwell. Clare tentatively felt his way up the uneven steps, taking short, shallow breaths, trying not to open up his lungs to the stale air.

During the summer months before the war, people had slept on the roof too, but the neighbours had complained, eventually browbeating the city authorities into declaring it illegal. Now, a rusted padlock on the door said "KEEP OUT", although Clare could see that people still came up here, from the shredded wood around the bolt clamp.

He prised free the lock and pushed open the door. Two steps down, he remembered, both encrusted with pigeon shit.

The rooftop air felt refreshingly cool, a slight breeze blowing in from the sea. A laundered sheet lay draped over a wire line, a seagull perched on top of it, wary of Clare's intrusion into its domain. But it was Clare's world too. Always when life had become too heated below, he'd sought refuge up here, when things were good with Montse, and when things weren't so good, when he'd just wanted to be on his own.

To his right, the patchwork mosaic of church towers, dovecotes, water tanks and drying laundry spread all the way to Montjuic; he could see the beacon beams of the magic fountains cutting a feeble line into the sky. To his left lay the compressed dark roofs of the Gothic quarter, beyond them the lights of a ship at anchor.

Clare clambered over the half dozen parapets separating the staircase from the Hotel Comercio. From the lip of the roof, he could almost see into the family rooms at the back of the hotel. There was a light on in the kitchen. The same old flower pots on the sill. He remembered once lobbing pebbles at the window to signal to Montse he was back waiting for her after being delayed in an air raid.

Clare moved on, using the last rungs of the fire escape to ascend to the top of the hotel. Dwelling on memories wasn't going to help him now.

The dovecote looked untouched since he and Montse had last been there together. An empty bottle of wine lay on the floor. Still inscribed on the wall were their initials and the date on which he'd returned from his first visit to Paris – *2/4/38*.

Clare wiped the cobwebs from the stone slab where they used to lie and stretched himself out. Then, folding his jacket into a pillow, he fell asleep dreaming of his ninth birthday.

Sitting at the breakfast table being handed a present by his father, feverishly tearing off the wrapping paper to reveal a carton of Primeros cigarettes.

CHAPTER 13

Monday 5th August, 1940

Programme of the XIIth Olympiad
Fencing, Gymnastics, Cycling, Yachting, Swimming, Basketball, Boxing, Hockey, Football.

The idea came to Clare in the small hours of the morning. Clear. Simple. It was a wonder he hadn't thought of it before. Too excited to sleep, he lay on the roof of the dovecote running over the details in his mind until they felt like the loop of an old movie. It had its risks – yes – but nothing on the scale of those which he'd endured yesterday.

As soon as it was light enough to see, he was up and ready to go. First off, he needed a new set of clothes. That was the easy part. He had only to lift an arm to take what he wanted from one of the many washing lines criss-crossing the roof. He chose carefully. An innocuous pair of sand brown trousers, a white shirt and tan cardigan, the sort of clothes he imagined an amateur cyclist might wear.

He changed in the dovecote, tearing off the tailor's label in Temple's suit before folding it into a pillow case and stashing it in one of the pigeon holes, another thing he'd have to apologise for should he ever see Temple again. For Montse, he scratched a last farewell message on the wall. Yesterday's date – *4/8/40* – to tell her he'd been there, and a single word – *Siempre*. Forever – so that she would know. Then with a last glance towards the darkened windows of the Hotel Comercio, he made his way back down onto the street to look for a bicycle.

Clare's first thought was to try the Boqueria, behind the market where the trucks unloaded their produce and the barrow boys and stall holders parked their bicycles, but there were too many people loitering, what looked like a system of street kids paid to watch over them, so after a fruitless half hour he moved off to try his luck in the side streets, subconsciously drifting back towards Paral·lel.

Chucho Torranzos couldn't remember the last time he'd ridden his bike to work; that he'd done so this morning was only because he had tickets to this afternoon's football match, Spain's semi-final clash with Austria.

Torranzos worked at the Ferran i Prat bakery on Carrer de Carretes. A cramped sweatbox made just about bearable by a faint current of warm air drawn into the room through an open door held in place by an old petrol can. His bike stood propped against the wall, a sack of flour resting against each wheel.

The radio was playing. An American song, Clare had never heard before, the music loud enough to mask any sudden noise he might make. Coolly, he stepped in through the open door, lifted the sacks of flour to one side and wheeled the bicycle out into the street.

Torranzos heard nothing, and not until he finished feeding a batch of freshly kneaded dough into the ancient brick oven did he look round to see that his bike was no longer there, by which time Clare was already half way to Plaça Catalunya and the start of the People's 100 kilometre Cycle Rally, the open-to-all free event he'd seen advertised yesterday afternoon while waiting for the marathon to pass.

The organisers had promised a large field and Clare wasn't disappointed. At first glance, there seemed to be upward of 4,000 cyclists gathered in the square, enough he hoped to screen his flight from the city. To shield him from the scrutiny of even the most attentive SIM agent.

The public address system was playing *La Rambla*. A rousing march to get everyone in the mood, people of all ages readying themselves for the start, packs of riders waiting restlessly under bright banners – AC Santboiana, PC Rubi, Sport Ciclista Catala, and in their green and white shirts, AC Montjuic.

Andreu. Shit! Clare cursed himself for not having thought of it before, for forgetting that of course Andreu would be riding. No more than ten yards away – Clare could see him now, dressed in a beige cap and goggles, taking a swig from his water bottle while chatting to a colleague; Andreu only had to turn round and he'd be staring straight at him. Clare instinctively dropped to the ground, making as if to tie up his shoe laces, concentrating his gaze on a spot on the road. One, two, three, he counted to ten, then tentatively looked up, relieved to see that Andreu had failed to notice him.

Clare turned his eyes back to the ground, making a mental note to stay well clear of anyone wearing green and white.

'Three, two, one!' Alicia Sol, popular leading actress of *The Night Watchman,* sounded a loud klaxon. 'See you later. Good luck,' she purred as the cyclists moved off, cheerfully honking their horns, bumping and scraping their way up Ronda Universitat.

Standing on the kerb outside the Llorens i Callico radio store, Violeta Rafols nudged her daughter. 'Look,' she said. 'Over there. It's Ricardo!' *She'd been looking for Andreu.*

Montse followed the line of her mother's finger. 'Where?

'Over there. See?'

'No.'

'I see him!' Montse's father broke in. 'Behind that guy in the yellow shirt.'

'Where?' There were hundreds of yellow shirts.

'There. No. He's gone now.'

'Are you sure it was him?' Montse asked anxiously.

Xavi Rafols nodded. 'Yes. Absolutely. It was him alright. The son of a bitch.'

The rally took a northeasterly route out of the city, picking up the main N4 highway on the Meridiana. There were two check points. The first at the intersection with Passeig de la Eulalia and the second on the city boundary. At both, the militia stood back and clapped the cyclists through. Clare kept his head down, pedalling hard, hardly daring to look back until he sensed the Rio Besòs at his side, the steep slopes of the Serra de Matas looming over him, and the haze of the city well behind.

It was not yet half past nine but already the sun had imposed itself on the day. Hot. Not a cloud in sight. No trace of a breeze.

Clare found his pace with a group from the Hispano-Suizo plant in Sant Andreu de Palomar. Together they rode through the outlying villages, then as the road forked inland towards Sabadell and the terrain became more rugged, he dropped back.

By Ripollet, the field had become even further strung out, the road now twisting through alluvium scarred hills cleaved with sharp ravines, pine trees, rosemary and thick gorse. Clare pulled up on a bend in the woods, threw his bike into the long grass and sauntered over to a pine to relieve himself. A group of cyclists rode past. Clare watched them go, then shot into the trees, diving behind a screen of ferns.

Breathlessly, he waited for the rest of the field to pass.

Toc, toc, toc, the staccato rap of a nearby woodpecker measured the passing minutes like a metronome. Head tilted back, eyes closed, Clare lay on the ground trying to recall the map in the back of his *1930 Cook's Traveller's guide to Spain and Portugal*. In the early days of the war it had been his only companion, a well-thumbed window into a new world. His plan was simple: keep northeast and eventually he'd hit the N4 again, somewhere south of Granollers. From there, he could shadow the road up to Vic, Ripoll, Ribes de Freser and the border. He remembered it as the route by which many of the brigadistas had been forced to enter the country; it was only the early volunteers like himself and Gerald who'd travelled to Spain without the adventure of a moonlit scramble across the mountains.

The last of the cyclists strove by. Behind them – the support vehicles: a three ton truck and a field ambulance. Clare gave it another ten minutes, then rose from his hide, wheeled his bike into the heart of the wood, buried it under a bed of branches and fern, and set off down the hill.

It took him almost half an hour to break free of the forest, the trees finally thinning out close to the banks of a fast flowing river, its course peppered with rocks and boulders. Clare filled his water bottle, drank, filled it again, then crossed over to the far side where the ground was good for walking; gentle, sloping hills, laced with wild flowers.

By the ruins of an old chapel, he picked up the course of a dried stream, impenetrable thickets of hazel, hawthorn and alder yielding to woods of beech and ash, walnut groves and fields of silver-leafed olive trees. The shrivelled corpse of a mule gave warning that the locals used the watercourse as an occasional path but all day Clare saw no one, only a dog that attached itself to his heels sometime in the afternoon. Where it came from, he had no idea. There was no sign of an owner. He tried to shoo it away but the animal resolutely refused to leave, so in the end he gave up and let it walk with him; they seemed to be going in the same direction and the dog certainly knew the way better than he did.

Clare christened the dog Paco after a guide who'd been seconded to his brigade before Jarama. They walked all afternoon, stopping only to drink, Clare from his water bottle, Paco from Clare's cupped hands, four mouthfuls every half hour. It made no sense to share his precious water with a stray dog, but Clare reasoned that so long as they were together, they were a team.

With darkness drawing in, they came upon a small strip of cultivated land cut back from the river bed. A mule stood hobbled under an acacia tree, smoke issuing from the chimney of an old stone house. Before Clare could think to backtrack, Paco darted into the building, emerging a few moments later with a man in tow, a dark skinned, grey haired peasant, clad in a dusty suit and blue beret. 'You've found him,' the man said, pointing at Paco.

'He found me.' It was the first time Clare had ever been introduced to anyone by a dog.

'Where are you from?' The man spoke in a thick rural accent.

'England.'

'*Russo?*' England clearly meant nothing to him.

'Yes. *Russo.*'

The man nodded. Russo, he understood. The occasion called for a drink. A bottle of membrillo was rustled up from inside the house, a brown honey coloured liquor distilled *en casa* from his own quinces. 'My name is Joan,' he said, pouring Clare a large glass, passing no further judgement on his presence beyond remarking that it was easy country to lose one's way in. Clare hadn't eaten since breakfast. The first sip went straight to his head and the second to his stomach, inducing a deliciously giddy sensation.

His host – matching him glass for sip – took him on a tour of his orchards, launching into a rambling discourse that embraced the finer points of how to make membrillo, his one trip to Barcelona as a twelve year old to visit the 1888 exhibition, and his beloved dog Bobo, whom he'd found abandoned on a rubbish heap as a puppy. Clare felt glad now that he'd chosen to share his water with the animal.

Darkness fell and the night air began to bite. Joan suggested they retire inside, telling Clare to pick himself something warm to wear from a bedroom to the left of the stairs. Clare understood the room to have belonged to his son. A photograph of a dark haired, serious looking young man stood on the dresser, a silver crucifix draped over the corner of the frame. A second photograph showed the same man with a group of soldiers perched on the body of a stopped tank. A film of dust lay on the bed. Clare guessed the boy had been killed during the war.

He helped himself to a sweater and a pair of trousers, then returned to the kitchen to find a meal waiting for him on the table, a reheated stew and a loaf of bread.

Joan pulled the cork from a bottle of thick red wine and poured them each a cup. Only now did he think to ask where Clare was heading. 'Vic,' Clare answered him, explaining that he was on a walking tour of the region. Joan confessed to never having visited the place but he knew a man who had. Tomorrow he would take Clare to meet him.

After supper, Joan drained his glass and rose unsteadily to his feet. 'You can sleep in the back room,' he said; for a second Clare feared the old man was about to break into tears. It was clear the room had remained untouched since his son's death. A little embarrassed, Joan added, 'Bobo will be fine in here. And don't mind if he starts barking. It's only the martens in the roof. They drive him crazy.'

Joan lit himself a candle and shuffled off upstairs. For a while, Clare sat up with Bobo, sipping the last of his wine, idly listening out for martens but hearing only the call of an owl.

Then Bobo too drifted off to sleep.

It was time to move on. Clare reckoned fifty pesetas more than sufficient to cover the clothes he was taking. He left the money on the table and quietly let himself out, stuffing the remains of the bread into his pocket.

It was a starry night. The road to Vic – Joan had begun to tell him earlier – went through Bigas, and to get to Bigas all he had to do was follow a track northeast from the house to the village of Santa Eulalia de Ronsana, a half hour's brisk walk at the most. Joan was correct to the minute. Even in the dark, Clare had no problem finding the way. The world was asleep and he had the road to himself.

For several hours he walked through a shifting grey landscape, dull to his eyes, a countryside he could picture only through the scent of wild garlic and rosemary, the hiss of a hawk swooping over a nearby field, the touch of a leaf against his cheek. Once a truck passed by. Clare noted the sulphurous glow of its headlights long before it drew close. Dropping into a ditch, he watched it drive by, the glow of a dozen cigarettes hanging over the tailgate.

Soldiers.

Clare caught himself tensing inside, felt the cold terror of his escape from Montjuic as the truck melted back into the night.

A frog croaked. Somewhere close by, a rodent scuttled across the road; Clare wasn't the only one abroad with concerns for his life.

Soon it would be getting light. Clare looked at his watch. It was 3.30am. Time he found himself somewhere to hide. Somewhere to rest up for the day.

CHAPTER 14

Tuesday 6th August, 1940

Programme of the XIIth Olympiad
Fencing, Gymnastics, Yachting, Swimming, Rowing, Basketball, Boxing, Hockey, Football.

It was the dogs that disturbed him; a distant baying from the other side of the hill.

Clare woke with a start, rising from the hollow where he'd fallen asleep, and scrambled up the hill. *Pray God, it was just a party of hunters out for some early morning sport.* Shuffling forward over the thorns and sharp stones, he peered out through the sun bleached grass to see a line of soldiers strung out across the field below, slowly beating their way towards him.

Somehow they knew.

Clare doubled back to the road, his one urgent thought now to put some distance between himself and the dogs.

The hum of an engine warned him of an approaching vehicle. Clare flung himself into a ditch that dropped away from the kerb and burrowed under the dried weeds, pressing his face into the dirt. The earth shuddered as the vehicle sped by; Clare could feel the wind on the back of his neck, see the tail boards of an army truck flashing past, full of soldiers, just like the truck that had passed by last night.

A few hundred yards to his left, Clare found a dried river bed, a narrow gully hewn from red rock that lent a cover of sorts. He ran without a care now, fighting a growing stitch in his side, the dust dry in his throat, stinging his eyes.

A second line of soldiers was sweeping up the valley towards him. Because of the lie of the riverbed, Clare failed to see them until they were almost upon him. Behind him, the men with their dogs were already cresting the hill. He was caught in a noose, with no direction left to turn, no option but to surrender.

The soldier that took him in could have been no more than seventeen years old. A timid, slightly built youth, he approached Clare cautiously, an ancient rifle in his hand, a second soldier covering him with his pistol. This man was older. In his early thirties. More sure of himself, not afraid to shoot or set loose his dog. Slowly and clearly, Clare lifted his hands above his head so that they could see he was unarmed. That he was going to come quietly. Without a struggle.

The return journey into Barcelona was swift. Marched to the road at gun point, prodded, poked, and gawped at like some prize exhibit, Clare was bound hand and foot, then lifted into the back of a truck. They stopped only once. To pick up an SIM agent: a thickset man with a broken nose and farmer's hands, who asked him in a broad Catalan accent to confirm his name, then sat silent for the duration of the journey, chain smoking ducados and drumming his fingers on the wooden slats of the bench.

They took him straight to the SIM offices on Via Laietana. To an interrogation room on the fifth floor, its white walls stained from years of neglect. A chipped basin in the corner. A desk and two wooden chairs for furniture.

There were two men waiting. Both in uniform. Clare recognised one as the SIM agent who'd put a bullet through the back of Moreno Garcia's head – Captain Caraben. The other – Colonel Boix – was in his mid forties, hair cut close, on the cusp of turning grey, a sharp but not unkind edge to his face that reminded Clare of his old science teacher.

'Richard Clare?' It was Boix who spoke.

'Yes.'

Boix reached for a thin manila file on the desk. 'You should know that your accomplices – Capdevila and Markham – are both dead.'

'They're not my accomplices,' Clare protested.

Boix looked unimpressed. 'Richard Markham is a member of the British Intelligence Services. Rafael Capdevila is a Nationalist spy. You were with them on Montjuic.'

'I'd like to speak to Major Jordan.' Clare had already decided that this was his best course of action. *His only course.*

'Major Jordan has no part in this interrogation. You will say what you have to say to me.'

'But–'

'Speak when spoken to,' Caraben added menacingly.

Clare fell silent. Boix unscrewed the lid from his pen, laid a pad of paper on his desk, made a note of the date and time, then declared himself ready to hear Clare's confession.

'I was no more than a go-between.' Clare tried to impress just how peripheral his role in the whole affair had been, how one thing had led to another, had led to him waking up in a ditch this morning. 'All I did was pass on the message.'

'Bullshit!' Without warning, Caraben clamped his arm around Clare's throat, jerking him up out of his seat, the movement so sudden Clare had no time to draw breath. 'Fucking bullshit!' Caraben hauled him across the room, ramming his head into the corner basin, holding him down as he turned on the tap. 'Fascist!'

Slowly the water level rose. Clare could feel his arm about to break, his neck twisted against the bottom of the sink, his sense of focus strangely narrowed to the refracted line of an electric wire that ran from the ceiling to a light bulb suspended overhead. The water closed over his scalp. Warm. Soothing in its suffocation.

Clare supposed he was dying, then – 'Arsehole!' – Caraben ground his knee into his groin and Clare's lungs imploded; the vacuum filled by a rush of water.

Clare dropped to the floor, whooping like a rusted pump, caught between the urge to vomit and the instinct to force some air into his chest.

Caraben lit a cigarette.

Boix pulled a photograph from the file on his desk. Slowly – painfully – Clare returned to them, clambering to his feet, wiping the blood from his mouth, from where he'd bitten his tongue.

Boix waited for him to settle, then handed him the photograph, a black and white print; it took Clare a while to focus on the grainy image. A stolen shot of himself, Capdevila and the Duke of Alba in a Parisian nightclub – the Duke smiling at something he had just said, Capdevila pointing to the neck of a champagne bottle resting in an ice bucket, signalling the waitress, just visible on the left hand side of the picture, that they wanted another bottle.

'8th December 1938,' Boix read the date from his file. 'You and Capdevila met the Duke of Alba in Paris.' The Duke of Alba had been Franco's ambassador to France. 'What was the purpose of this meeting?'

Clare nodded. He remembered the occasion well enough. He could see now where Boix was coming from and he wanted to explain, to dispel any misunderstanding. 'Capdevila was trying to sell the Duke a Goya,' he said. 'A portrait of the Marchioness of Villafranca. He asked me to come along. To impress him. He told the Duke I was his London agent.'

Boix took back the photograph. 'When did you first meet Capdevila?'

Clare tried to remember. 'Sometime in March, I think.'

'1938?'

'Yes.'

'Who introduced you?'

'No-one. Capdevila was Picasso's agent. He helped organise the paperwork for *Guernica*.'

'Then you met him in Paris?'

'Yes.'

Boix again consulted his file. 'You were sent to Paris to bring Picasso's painting back to Spain?'

'That's right.'

'Your orders were to introduce yourself to Capdevila?'

'Yes.'

'Then somebody must have given you Capdevila's name.'

'I suppose so,' Clare conceded. 'Yes.'

'Who?'

'I can't remember.'

'Esteban Llull?'

'I really can't remember.'

'Was it Llull's idea that you go to Paris?'

'No.' Clare could now see the connection Boix was trying to make. 'Llull just put me in touch with the Ministry of Culture. But only because I asked him to. I was looking for a way to stay in the country.'

'Then you admit that you wanted to stay?'

'Yes ...'

'Why?'

Clare faltered. 'There was a girl. I didn't want to leave her.'

Again Boix checked his file. 'The sister of your cell mate from Burgos. Montserrat Rafols?'

'Yes.'

Boix made a note of Clare's answer in the margin, then drew a typed document from the file. A complete itinerary of Clare and Montse's tour of Spain. A list of every frontline town and village they'd visited with *Guernica*, starting 8th April 1938, ending 24th July. Clare didn't dispute the facts. More or less, they were as he remembered them. 'What was the procedure for passing back information?' Boix asked.

'I'm sorry?'

'Did you send the information yourself or did you have a contact?' Boix handed him a second photograph. A Colonel in Nationalist uniform. 'Do you know this man?'

'Yes.' Clare's hand trembled as he took the picture.

'His name, please?'

'Colonel Boet. He's the man who interrogated me. After I was captured.'

'In Burgos?'

'Yes.'

Boix returned the photograph to his file. 'How many times did he interrogate you?'

'Just the once.'

'Bullshit,' Caraben snarled from somewhere over Clare's left shoulder.

Boix left the threat hanging in the air. 'What did Boet want to know?'

Clare couldn't remember. 'Mostly – stuff about the Brigade. Its strength. What kind of weapons we had.'

'Bullshit!' Caraben again. This time louder.

'What did you tell him?'

'Nothing. That I'd been cut off from my company. That –'

'Did he offer you money? Or did he just promise not to kill you?' Clare could smell the garlic on Caraben's breath as he span him round – 'Neither' – to slam a fist into his right kidney – 'I …' – and then his left, a vicious blow that dropped him to the floor.

'April 1937 – you were captured by Nationalist forces and taken to Burgos military prison.' Through the pain, Clare could hear Boix reading from his file in a flat monotone. 'There you were interrogated by Colonel Boet who recruited you as a Nationalist agent. In August you were released as part of a prisoner exchange programme and you returned to Barcelona. On Boet's instructions you made contact with Esteban Llull.

Llull introduced you to Capdevila – another of Boet's agents – and together you came up with the idea of taking Picasso's painting of *Guernica* on a tour of the frontline.' Clare tried to focus on the window, a tiny patch of blue sky visible over Boix's shoulder. 'For four months you travelled the country, noting down everything you saw, sending the information back to Llull and Capdevila. Information, they then passed on to the Duke of Alba.' Boix wasn't looking for answers. He was stating facts. *Guernica, Burgos, Paris* – he had already made the connections. Clare's guilt was beyond question. His confession prepared. He could sign now or later; it made no difference to Boix.

'Water …' Clare felt as if he was going to be sick.

Boix pressed a button under the rim of his desk. The door opened and two guards entered. 'Take him downstairs,' he said.

Clare turned and vomited.

They hauled him along the corridor into an elevator large enough to fit a gurney, its walls stained with blood and scuffed from years of use. They were going down to the basement – how many levels Clare couldn't tell and he no longer cared.

One of the guards lit a cigarette. The other cleaned the dirt from under his thumbnail.

"You must have been a beautiful baby,
You must have been a beautiful child."

From nowhere, the words of the popular song played in Clare's mind. Loud and insistent, so trite it made him want to laugh.

"When you were only starting to go to kindergarten
I bet you drove the little boys wild.
And when it came to winning blue ribbons
You must have shown the other kids how."

From the elevator, they half dragged, half threw him into a bare, windowless chamber. A metal hook hung from the ceiling and the air stank of cheap detergent. First they handcuffed him, then they took off his shoes and socks and blindfolded him.

"You must have been a beautiful baby
You must have been a beautiful child."

Beyond the chamber lay another room. There was no lock, just a bolt that he now heard being slid back. One of the guards held the door open, the other took a rough hold of his arm and threw him inside. As Clare fell forward, he heard the guards laughing and the door slam shut, then only the echo of his scream as he felt a slice ripped from his toes, his thigh stabbed, his forearm lacerated, a cut across his ribs and shoulder.

For five minutes – longer even – Clare lay motionless as the shock subsided and the pain grew, then tentatively, he reached out a hand, feeling with his fingers and the chains of his handcuffs, sharp stakes embedded into the floor all around him.

Broken glass set in concrete – it took him a while to realise.

The bastards. Move. Sit. Feel for a wall to rest against and he'd cut himself to shreds. Whatever nonsense it was that Boix wanted him to confess to, he was prepared to put his name to it.

Better a bullet in the back of the head than this death by a thousand cuts.

* * * * *

The news of Markham's death had left Holdsworth feeling more unsettled than he cared to admit. The first sign that something was amiss had come soon after midday on Sunday, when Kathleen reported seeing Picasso at a cultural function he'd long been scheduled to attend. Why was he not at Montjuic? Had he not heard the previous night's message on the BBC? No sooner had Holdsworth set about trying to find out what had gone wrong, he'd received the first reports of an accident on the hillside behind the Olympic stadium. A large explosion, and according to some witnesses, the sound of gunfire.

A few hours later, the authorities released a short statement to the press announcing a tragic accident involving the British Modern Pentathlon team coach. One man was dead – the athlete Captain Robert Markham. The body had been badly charred in the fire and would be released to his next of kin, just as soon as the pathologist had concluded his report. Meanwhile the site of the accident had been closed off and the remains of the bus taken away for forensic investigation.

Holdsworth was under no illusions. The operation had been fatally compromised. But how had the SIM known? Had Markham been tailed? He didn't think so. Two or three times over the previous week he'd personally followed him to check that he was clean and each time there had been no hint of a tail. More likely the leak was down to Capdevila or Clare. But here, to Holdsworth's intense frustration, the trail ran dry. Both men had vanished. Capdevila's gallery was closed; the door to his apartment on the floor above locked and the shutters drawn. And as for Clare, he'd looked for him at his hotel, at the Casa de Prensa, and this morning in the port where the other British journalists were covering the yachting and everywhere he'd been met by the same response, the last anyone had seen of him had been on Saturday night.

Hot and exhausted, Holdsworth had finally retreated back to Kathleen and the Passport Office. They'd made love in the back room, then sat naked against the wall, sharing a cigarette. Kathleen had suggested they have lunch at the station restaurant round the corner. Holdsworth had at first resisted, he had too much to do, but Kathleen had pointed out that whatever he had to do, he would do it far better on a full stomach and of course he'd relented. But still he couldn't relax. There was too much he didn't yet understand. All he had were fragments, scraps amounting to one dead agent, a missing journalist, a disappeared art dealer and a would be defector.

The clock struck two. Kathleen gulped back the rest of her coffee. It was time to return to the office. 'I want you to ring Hicknall,' Holdsworth told her; that was another thing that had been bothering him, that Kathleen might become sucked into the fall out, that her life was in danger. 'I want you to tell him, I'm pulling you back to Madrid.'

He might as well have asked her to take off her clothes and dance naked on the table. 'I'm not going,' she said.

Holdsworth tried to make her understand that it wasn't safe in Barcelona any longer. 'For Christ's sake – be sensible. A man's dead.'

But Kathleen just laughed. 'Send me back and I'll never sleep with you again.'

'You don't mean that!'

'Try me.' She dropped a few coins onto the table – her half of the bill – and got to her feet. 'See you later.' She kissed him on the forehead, on the tidemark of his receding hair.

Holdsworth nodded in feeble surrender, knowing he should be annoyed with himself, and with Kathleen too. But such feelings were beyond him. That Kathleen had accepted him into her bed made him the luckiest man in the world and tonight – God willing – she would do so again.

Holdsworth caught the waiter's eye as the door swung shut behind her. 'Another coffee,' he said, trying hard not to smile.

What a time to fall in love.

* * * * *

'Hello, my friend.' Clare smelt the cigarette first – Primeros – then heard the slide of the door bolt, the crunch of glass under boot. 'I would have come sooner. Only I just learned you were here.'

Clare felt two strong arms lift him onto his feet and carry him out of the chamber. *'Coño* – you look a mess.' The two strong arms – a guard, Clare could tell from the rub of the man's uniform – set him down on the floor, then unlocked his handcuffs and pulled away his blindfold.

Clare looked at his foot. His toe had all but disappeared under a crust of congealed blood.

'I'll have a doctor treat your wounds.' Jordan was standing in the doorway, his face half in shadow, the smoke from his cigarette collected in the harsh glare of a naked bulb suspended in the corridor outside. 'I'll be in my office when you're done.'

They took him back up to the second floor.

The doctor, pale skinned and anaemic, patched him up in silence. Swift and efficient. Too scared even to make eye contact, as if afraid of the infection that was Clare's guilt. *It's enough for them just to see us together* – Clare remembered Werner's warning to him in the bar.

'You were lucky,' Jordan said later, as they sat together in his office. 'I've known prisoners who've bled to death from their injuries.'

Clare could well believe it. The glass had shaved a couple of millimetres from his toe. It hurt like hell, but not so much he couldn't walk.

'Colonel Boix is of the opinion you're a Nationalist spy.' Jordan casually tossed the accusation at Clare, as if he were passing on a piece of gossip. 'One of Boet's agents. Part of the HAWK network.'

'Boet never approached me, I was never his agent.'

Jordan looked almost amused. 'I believe you. I'll admit it's an obsession with Boix. The enemy within.'

Looking around him, Clare could see that they were in the same room in which he and Jordan had first met two years previously. The portrait of Companys had been replaced by that of André Marty but otherwise little had changed except that today there was a plate of tortilla, bread and ham on the table alongside the pot of tea. 'Help yourself.' Jordan lit a cigarette. 'You must be hungry.'

He was. Clare took a hunk of bread and ham.

'Tell me about Capdevila. Where did you first meet?'

'In Paris.' Clare finished his mouthful. 'March 1938.' He remembered now that it was Llull who'd given him Capdevila's name, scrawled on the back of an old envelope. 'We met at his gallery on the left bank.'

'Rue Saint André des Arts?'

'Yes.'

'Go on.'

Clare did so. Jordan listened quietly, without taking notes or making reference to the files on his desk, rather every now and again he lit another cigarette and turned his chair to face the window, as if contemplating his next move in a game of chess. Only when Clare had finished – when Capdevila lay dead on Montjuic and Clare was running for his life through the Cementerio del Sur-Oeste – did Jordan see fit to interrupt and take him back to Paris and the war. Did Clare know that Capdevila had been involved in purchasing weapons for the Republic? Yes. Had Capdevila ever mentioned this side of his life to him? No. Did they ever talk business? Not really – although Clare admitted that on occasion Capdevila had sought his opinion on some painting or other.

'Did Capdevila ever mention any trips he made?' Jordan ventured.

'Trips?'

'Business trips. Abroad?'

'Only when he went to London.' Clare took another sandwich. 'Not that I think he ever went. He just wanted me to think he did.'

'What makes you say that?'

Clare shrugged. 'That's how he was. Capdevila had a bit of a chip on his shoulder. Compared to the crowd he mixed with – he wasn't well travelled.'

'How could you be so sure? That he never went to London – I mean.'

'I don't know. The details just didn't add up. The little things. It's like he got his information from an out of date guide book.'

'So – where did he go?'

'Hard to say.' Clare really couldn't remember. 'He once told me about a trip he'd made to Brussels. He'd seduced a rich widow into selling him some painting.'

'What painting?'

'I don't remember exactly.'

'But you think he went there?'

'Yes.'

Jordan paused. 'Did he ever mention a visit to Switzerland?'

'No.'

'Or anywhere close to Switzerland? Lyon? Mâcon, perhaps?'

'No.'

'You're sure?'

'I would have remembered.'

'Did he ever offer you a job?'

Clare shook his head. 'No. But we did have this running joke that I was going to be his partner in London.'

'But you didn't take him seriously?'

'No.'

'Why not?'

'Again – it didn't seem real.'

'In what way?'

'I always got the sense his mind was elsewhere.'

'So he never asked you to make any trips for him?'

'No.'

Jordan reached into his pocket and brought out a silver key, embossed with the crest of the Credit Syon bank and a four digit number. 'We found this on his body.' He pushed the key across the desk towards Clare. 'Ever seen it before?'

'No.'

'It fits a safe deposit box in Geneva. On its own, it's quite useless. In order to access the deposit – you need a second key.' At that moment, the telephone rang. Jordan answered it impatiently – 'Yes? ... Tell him to wait' – then turned back to Clare. 'Right now – whoever has that second key, they're going to be wondering where it is. Why Capdevila hasn't yet shown. What's gone wrong. Answers only you can give them.'

'Me?'

'Yes. You. You're Capdevila's contact. You helped him escape the country.' The way Jordan said it, it sounded like an accusation.

'All I did was go with him to Montjuic,' Clare demurred.

'Perhaps. But they don't know that.' Jordan stubbed out his cigarette and pulled open the drawer, retrieving Clare's wallet and press card. 'Whatever Capdevila has hidden in Geneva – it belongs to the Republic.'

And then Clare understood. This had nothing to do with money – the thousands Capdevila was reputed to have siphoned off into a Swiss bank account during the war. In Paris, there had been other rumours too, dark whispers that said Capdevila was working both sides simultaneously, passing intelligence from one to the other and back again, every deal, every bribe, every act of extortion noted in a little "black book", protection against the day the world turned on him. And now Jordan wanted that book, Clare could see it in his eyes. It wasn't the money that interested him. But intelligence. Information. Power. These were the currencies Jordan dealt in.

'You will return to your hotel and act as if nothing has happened.' Jordan wrote out a telephone number and handed it to him. 'When Capdevila's associates contact you – you will let me know.'

Clare couldn't believe it – Jordan was letting him free. 'And if they don't?' he asked.

'They will. They want that key.'

Just as you do, Clare told himself.

'You will go about your job as normal,' Jordan continued. 'Assume that Capdevila's people are watching you. You may call your office from your hotel, from the Correos, or the Casa de Prensa. All calls, of course, will be monitored. Any attempt to ask for help or to communicate with British Intelligence and I will hand you back to Boix – or shoot you myself – do I make myself clear?' Clare nodded. *Yes.* 'You will also need to explain where you've been these last few days. It took you forty-eight hours and a trip to Picasso's country house to secure but I think you'll find your editor in a forgiving mood.' Jordan handed him two sheets of typed foolscap. *An interview with Pablo Picasso, Mas Llunes, 6th August 1940.*

Clare had to admire Jordan's gall. Not withstanding a carefully orchestrated statement delivered at the beginning of the Games, Picasso had yet to speak to the press, much to the frustration of the world's leading newspapers.

Jordan picked up the phone and asked the operator to get him an international line – 'London. Central 6000.'

A few minutes later, a woman's voice answered. '*London Evening News.*'

Jordan handed Clare the phone.

'Put me through to the editor.' Clare didn't need to be told what to say.

'Who should I say is calling?' The woman sounded reassuringly English, so much so that Clare felt an overwhelming urge to ask her how the weather was and what was playing tonight at The Adelphi. 'Tell him it's Richard Clare from Barcelona.'

Jordan nodded. *Just stick to the script.*

Ten minutes later, Clare was done. The "interview" was total propaganda from start to finish. Utter bullshit. But no-one at the paper was complaining. By Thursday the article would be syndicated round the world, in the words of his editor – a nice little earner, and one in the eye for *The Standard.*

Jordan handed Clare back his wallet and press card. 'Your passport, I'm afraid I must surrender to Colonel Boix. It's a condition of your release.'

Clare somehow doubted it. But he understood. Jordan wished to keep him on a tight rein.

'I'll have a taxi drive you back to your hotel.' Jordan summoned a guard to escort him from the building. There were no promises on offer. No deal. Just the vague hope that one thing might lead to another, might lead to him being set free. 'Don't let me down, Richard.' Jordan tossed his now empty packet of cigarettes into the bin.

Clare smiled weakly. 'I won't.'

They let him out by an anonymous door at the back of the building into a dark, narrow street rarely penetrated by the sun, still less by passers-by. A faded "To Let" sign decorated the shutters of the only commercial property, the former Bar Chipi, while a stray dog lay in the gutter licking its sores. Clare had walked down such streets before during the war; abandoned through fear. The domain of the lost and the damned.

He could see the taxi waiting for him at the corner. A black Hispano-Suizo sedan. On the rear door, the lozenge shaped logo of Taxis David. At the wheel, a familiar face.

Jordan's way of saying – *I'm watching you.*

To begin with they said nothing. Like an awkward meeting between two old friends, each felt a slight embarrassment, an uncertainty as to where to start.

Werner took a right turn into Via Laietana. Clare glanced back through the rear window to see if he could work out their tail.

'It's the Buick.' Werner already had him marked. 'Three back.'

Tucked behind a bus, Clare noticed a dark green bonnet, a young man in a cap and brown jacket at the wheel, a second man on his shoulder. Werner slowed to let a horse and cart into the traffic. 'Where are we going?' he asked.

Clare had no idea. 'Wherever Jordan told you to take me.'

'He didn't.'

'Then just drive.' Clare needed some space to clear his head. Time to allow a second dose of painkillers to kick in.

'They told me you were working for the Nationalists,' Werner said bluntly.

'I'm not working for anyone.'

'Not even the British?'

'No.'

'A pity. It seems like we could do with some help.'

Clare almost smiled. 'Last Sunday. At the bullring ...' He wanted to thank Werner for trying to save him. 'I would have understood if you'd let them take me ...'

'Maybe I should have.' Werner kept his eyes on the road in front of them. 'How far did you get?'

'Somewhere beyond Ripollet.'

'Further than I thought you would.'

'I was lucky. I owe you one.'

Up ahead the lights changed, bringing the traffic to a halt. An old man shuffled towards them, cap in hand. Werner waved him away. 'I wasn't sure you'd remember,' he said. 'The coffee – I mean.'

'How could I forget?' Two years ago at the Café Zurich, Werner had ordered a double *solo* and promptly vomited over the pavement. The following day he'd come back, had an omelette, another coffee and been sick all over again; it had taken the doctors three months to diagnose a caffeine allergy.

'How did they find you?'

The lights changed again but no-one moved. A truck had stalled. 'They knew where to look. Someone must have tipped them off.'

'That figures.' Werner indicated right towards Colom. 'That night we met in the Raval – Jordan knew all about it. Someone told him about that bottle of whisky we shared.'

Clare thought back to who else had been in the room with them. 'It had to have been those militiamen.'

'It wasn't them.'

'How can you be so sure?'

'Because they never looked at my papers.'

'Then maybe it was the barman?'

'No.' Werner was just as dismissive. 'He never knew your name.'

'Then who?'

'To begin with – I thought it was you.'

'Me?'

'Sure. I figured you had to be working for them. But then after they picked me up. After Jordan started asking me all these questions, I realised I'd got it wrong. They were looking for you. It was why he let me go free. As a means of getting to you.'

Clare shook his head. 'Then I don't understand ...' *But he did. He had told somebody else. Montse. That first morning – when they'd met on the bus. When he'd followed her up to the tennis club.*

Werner caught his eye. 'What is it?'

'Remember – you asked me if I'd seen Montse ...' Clare felt sick. *It had to have been her. No-one else knew.* 'I didn't understand at the time why you wanted to ... why ... I thought it a strange question but afterwards I saw her on the press bus ... we got talking ... I told her we'd met ...'

'What did you say?'

Clare thought of all the things he had said; at Fernando's, on the beach, and afterwards in her flat. None of it meant anything now. She'd betrayed him, just as he'd betrayed her, he supposed that's the way she saw it. Only this time there were lives at stake.

The traffic started up again. 'What did you say?' Werner prompted him again.

'Only that we'd had a drink. That you were driving a taxi. That's all.'

Werner nodded grimly. 'That was enough.'

'I'm sorry. I didn't realise.'

'It's the way they operate.' Werner switched lanes across the tramlines, a quick glance in the mirror to check whether the Buick was still with them.

It was.

'Gol! Gol Gran Bretana!' From the far side of the road – from the radios of the waterfront bars and churros stalls – they heard the roar of the crowd from Les Corts. A city tuned into the drama being played out only a few miles away, the semi-final that Clare had forgotten about. Britain versus Peru. 'How much longer until the final whistle?' he asked suddenly.

'Fourteen minutes.' Werner didn't need to check his watch to know.

'How long will it take us to get there?'

'Where? Les Corts?'

'Yes.'

'You won't get there in time.'

'How long?'

'In this traffic. A quarter of an hour.'

'That's fine.'

'You want me to take you there?'

The bitch. 'Yes.'

'Okay.' Werner glanced up at his rear mirror at the Buick still nestled behind them. 'I hope you know what you're doing.'

Clare forced a weak smile to his lips. *So did he.*

By the time they reached Les Corts, the match was over. Like a flood flushed river, the stadium had burst its banks, propelling a tidal wave of fans into the surrounding streets, engulfing the traffic, and bringing Werner's taxi and the Buick to a standstill.

Clare eased open the car door. He could see the Buick stuck some fifty yards behind them, the taller of Jordan's two agents craning his neck to get a fix on him, his colleague fighting hard to stand still. Head bowed, elbows to the fore, Clare bore into the crowd, then dropping his shoulder, he span himself round against the flow into the slipstream of a man tall and broad enough to screen him against the two men from the Buick.

They'd already lost him. Clare could see them now, flailing, frantically scouring the crowd as the weight of the departing fans swept him back down the road, back past the Buick and Jordan's two agents, back past the churros stand they'd driven by on the way up.

Back towards the city.

Carrer Avinyó. 7.50pm. Clare approached Montse's flat circumspectly, cutting down through Sant Miguel, checking the street twice before daring to knock.

Montse let him in without question, pulling the shutters down over the windows as he climbed the stairs, quickly closing the door behind him.

Clare turned on the radio. 'I don't have long,' he said.

Montse touched her hand to his cheek. 'What are you doing here? What's going on?' The questions came tumbling out. 'They said you'd killed a man.'

'Who did?' Clare still couldn't quite bring himself to look her in the eye.

'The police.'

'When?'

'Two days ago. They came to the hotel.'

Clare glanced towards the bedroom. 'Is Pep here?'

'He's asleep.'

Clare gestured the radio. 'It's not too loud?'

'No. It's fine.' Montse lit a cigarette. 'Richard – I've been so worried.'

Clare laughed.

'What's wrong? Why are you looking at me like that?' *He was looking at her like that*. 'What's going on?'

Outside, Clare could hear raised voices, drunks taunting a dog; against the thump of his heart, a voice on the radio detailing tomorrow's weather. 'You're working for Jordan.'

Montse said nothing.

In the window pane, Clare caught the starry reflection of a firework bursting over the waterfront, heard the distant whine of a rocket spiralling into the sky.

'How did you know?'

'Does it matter?'

'I guess not.' Montse stepped up into the light, the spill of the street lamp catching the side of her face. 'Yes – Jordan asked me to spy on you,' she held his gaze without flinching. 'But no – I didn't tell him anything.'

'You told him about Werner.'

'I had to tell him something. Or they said they'd take Pep away ...'

'Werner's been arrested.'

'Is he …?' She hardly dared ask. 'Did they …?'

'Shoot him? No. Not yet.'

'I'm sorry …' She dropped onto the sofa.

'Tell that to Werner.'

'Go to hell!' She was back on her feet again, moving towards the kitchen – 'I didn't ask for you to come back' – returning with a bottle of cheap wine, 'You've no idea what they're like.'

'What's that supposed to mean?'

She took a swig and thrust the bottle at him. 'A few days after I saw you on the bus, a man came to see me.'

'Jordan?'

'Yes.'

'What did he want?'

'He wanted me to spy on you.' *What do you think?* 'I told him I couldn't help. I told him we weren't talking to each other anymore. That was when he told me about the orphanage. Where they take the children of the people they shoot … the people they put in prison …' Her voice faded to a whisper.

'So you asked me out to lunch?'

'Yes.'

'His idea or yours?'

'Does it matter?'

'Yes. It does.'

'His.'

Clare blanched. 'Then everything that's happened since. It's all been a charade?'

'No … not everything.'

'You could have told me …'

'I tried to …'

'So – why didn't you?'

'You scared me. All that talk of escaping the country. The less you told me, the less I could tell Jordan … I was frightened you might get hurt.'

But he was hurt. And so was she. He could see that now. They were both winged and at Jordan's mercy. 'When did you last speak to him?'

'Who?'

'Jordan.'

'Last Sunday. Two days ago. He came round to the hotel with this other man. A thug.'

'Caraben?'

'Yes. I think so. They said you'd killed a man.'

'They were lying.'

'They said you might try to get in touch with me. That if you did – I was to let them know.' She drew breath. 'We saw you on Sunday. At the cycle rally. We were there to cheer on Andreu. It was Papa who called the police. We tried to stop him but he wouldn't listen. Not even to Mama. You know what he's like. What he ...' She brushed a skein of hair from her eyes. 'Richard, what's going on?'

'You tell me.'

'Why are they looking for you? Why did you come back?'

'Why do you want to know – so you can tell Jordan?' Clare regretted the words even as they passed his lips. From somewhere deep inside the building the water pipes groaned, the radio spat static and the lights flickered. 'I'm sorry,' he said. 'I didn't mean it like that.'

So tell me. Her eyes bore into his.

Clare was too tired to argue. *What did it matter? Jordan knew it all anyway.* So he told her. The whole story. About Picasso. And Capdevila. And Markham. A truncated version of what he'd already told Jordan. Except for one small detail. A small seed planted in the thick of his story that, should it ever come to light, would tell him for sure whether they could ever trust each other again. Capdevila's safe house in Carrer Fusina – the one card of any value he had left in his hand, something he'd kept from both Boix and Jordan, he now told Montse all about it.

When finally he'd finished, she spoke just two words – 'Thank you.' *Now she understood.*

And so did he.

The clock struck half past, the lights settled and the radio refound its voice, an old Ethel Waters number, *Shadows on the Swanee.*

'I'd better go,' Clare said.

Montse nodded.

Clare waited for her to say something, and then when she didn't, he quietly turned and walked from the room.

Back at the Oriente, the desk clerk clocked him in at 8.57pm. The discreet glance at his watch, the poker face as he retrieved Clare's room key – no comment as to why he'd been absent for two days – told Clare everything he needed to know, that as soon as his back was turned the clerk would be on the phone to Jordan. In a matter of minutes the Buick would be sitting outside the hotel.

The desk clerk handed him his messages. There were two, both from Harold Abrahams. One suggesting a breakfast meeting on Monday, one cancelling it – could he make Tuesday lunch instead? There was also an envelope. Clare tore it open. Inside, there was a piece of paper. A typed message. *Café Zurich. 2.00pm. Wednesday.*

So Jordan was right – someone did want to see him.

Clare hurriedly pocketed the message and turned back to the desk clerk. 'I'd like a line to London,' he said. 'Central 6000.'

'Cabin One.' The desk clerk pointed him to the nearmost booth.

The connection took somewhat longer than usual to come through. Clare imagined the line had first to be routed through the SIM headquarters on Passeig de Gracia, not altogether inappropriate as the call was intended for Jordan's benefit,

Clare's way of explaining his disappearance. He'd been up at the stadium talking to the fans, gathering material for the article he was now going to dictate to the sports desk. In short, doing what Jordan had told him to do. His job.

The call completed, his copy filed, Clare walked across the lobby into the bar. Wilson, Wignall, Stewart and Forsyth were at their usual table getting stuck in for the evening, Wilson regaling the others with a story about the time he'd covered the ABA boxing championships for *The Times* from a hospital bed. 'Well, hello stranger!' Forsyth cheerily hailed him as he entered the room. 'Grab a pew.'

Clare pulled up a chair.

'Where have you been?'

'Did you hear about Markham?' Wilson asked before Clare had a chance to answer.

'No.'

'Killed in a road accident.'

'Jesus!' Clare feigned appropriate surprise.

'Rolled the team bus taking a short cut across Montjuic. Silly bugger.'

From the corner of his eye, Clare noticed the two men from the Buick – one smoking a ducados, the other chewing gum – making their way over to the bar and ordering a drink with a "Don't even think about pulling another stunt like whatever it was you just pulled or we'll break every bone in your body" look in their eyes.

'So – come on then, tell us. Where have you been?' Wignall wanted to know. 'A Guinea says there's a girl involved.'

Forsyth grinned. 'We want every last sordid detail.'

'Starting with her name.'

'And how you met?'

'And does she have any sisters?'

CHAPTER 15

Wednesday 7th August, 1940

Programme of the XIIth Olympiad
Fencing, Gymnastics, Yachting, Swimming, Rowing, Equestrian Sports, Basketball, Boxing, Hockey.

The first thing Clare noticed on entering the breakfast room was there'd been a change of shift. The men from the Buick had been replaced. In their shoes, a young couple dressed to look like tourists. They were almost convincing – a French guide book on the table, the room key, a copy of *Le Monde* – until a passing guest wished them good morning and Clare caught the Catalan accent in the man's mumbled reply and the slightly embarrassed look in his "girlfriend's" eyes.

'Bon jour!' He walked on past.

To his surprise, Clare found Wilson and the others also up early, a taxi ordered to take them down to the port; this morning British eyes were focused on the final of the double sculls – Jack Beresford's attempt to win a sixth Olympic medal. Clare declined the offer of a lift. 'I'll catch up with you later,' he said. 'There's a few things I need to do first.'

He ate alone, a plate of scrambled eggs and coffee, checked the front desk for messages – there were none – then wandered out onto the Ramblas. 'For the love of God. Please help an old soldier.' An emaciated beggar bore down on him with an out-thrust beret. The doorman roughly pushed the man aside. 'Get lost. Or I'll call the police.' 'Just one peseta, Señor. Please.' The beggar stank of cheap brandy.

Clare hurried on up the street. 'Arsehole!' the beggar called after him.

At the Boqueria market, Clare stopped to buy a packet of cigarettes, a cheap imitation zippo and a refill bottle of lighter fluid. An idea he'd been mulling over since before breakfast was beginning to bite. Not a very subtle idea, he had to admit (indeed, it better belonged to the pages of *The Captain*) but one that had its merits.

He stepped out into the road and hailed a taxi. 'Maricel parc,' he told the driver. Maricel parc was the venue for the gymnastics. 'Montjuic.'

* * * * *

67, Passeig de Gracia. Jordan stubbed out his cigarette and reached for another, trying not to appear too impatient as he waited for his boss, André Marty, to finish reading the report he'd just handed him. *Top Secret*. Three typed sheets of foolscap outlining the events leading to the shootout on Montjuic; Jordan's conclusion that Picasso's "defection" was nothing more than a deception dreamed up by Capdevila to hoodwink British Intelligence into arranging his escape from the country.

'How can you be so certain Picasso wasn't involved?' Marty's first question held no surprises. Predictable. Unimaginative. That of a mind inclined to see conspiracies where there were none.

Picasso was under twenty-four hour surveillance. He could do nothing, see no-one, speak to no-one without Jordan being made aware of it. There was – as Jordan had pointed out in his report – no evidence to suggest that Picasso and Capdevila had ever communicated, still less tried to plan an escape. 'Of course, our operational assumption is that Picasso is complicit,' Jordan was quick to reassure Marty, only too aware that "lack of evidence" had never prevented the Butcher of Albacete from pursuing his suspicions in the past. 'We've increased the surveillance team. Placed extra listening devices at his home. Restricted his engagements.'

Marty couldn't help but sense a slight scorn in Jordan's voice. 'What about Capdevila?' he frowned. 'Shouldn't he have been arrested months ago?'

'He had protection, Sir.'

'What kind of protection?'

Jordan lit his cigarette. 'The personal backing of the chairman of the Communist Party.'

'But the man's dying ...' *It was an open secret that José Diaz was suffering from stomach cancer.*

'Perhaps that's why Capdevila chose this moment to run,' Jordan tried not to sound too patronising in pointing out the obvious. 'Given Diaz's fading health, Capdevila knew it would only be a matter of time before we picked him up.'

'Why the hell would Diaz want to protect a piece of scum like Capdevila?' Marty fumed.

'The word is that Capdevila had insurance.' Jordan calmly drew on his cigarette. 'A "little black book". A record of certain indiscretions committed during the war.'

'What indiscretions?'

Jordan shrugged. 'We don't know. It's only a rumour. There's no certainty the book even exists.'

'Of course it exists,' Marty snapped, 'if you're telling me that Diaz was protecting Capdevila. What further evidence do you need?'

'It may have been a bluff.'

'A bluff?'

'Capdevila may have encouraged the rumours in order to protect himself.'

Marty stood his jaw aggressively on his fist. 'Are you trying to tell me this book doesn't exist?'

'Not at all. It's just a possibility we should consider.' Straight away, Jordan knew he'd made a bad call, placed too much emphasis on a point of logic. It was right there in Marty's eyes; the suspicion that his head of counter intelligence was plotting against him, casting doubt on the book's existence in order that he might later use it for his own advancement, and – Jordan cursed himself for pushing his luck – the irony was, for once Marty's instincts were spot on, it was exactly what he had in mind. 'We've got leads,' he added hastily, a none too subtle retreat. 'The moment we have something,' – he now came clean about the safe deposit key and Clare's links to Picasso – 'you'll be the first to know.'

The Butcher of Albacete didn't need to say anything; he just smiled. The cold smile of a man responsible for murdering over 500 members of the International Brigade.

* * * * *

Maricel parc. 9.35am. Already the temperature was pushing eighty; the sky an electric blue, clear except for three clouds strangely stacked one above the other, sitting right over Tibidabo.

Clare passed through the turnstiles and headed over to the makeshift stands erected on the southwest side of the park. Through a screen of trees, and against the glint of sunlight, Barcelona lay peacefully below, the clink of coffee cups, the clatter of loose change and the swish spit of the shoe shine boys sounding the death knell on breakfast, as the city lazily turned its mind to the coming day.

In the outdoor arena, it was the turn of the women; the first event of the morning, the side horse. Clare sat with the press corps, one eye on the gymnastics, the other on his tail; he'd lost sight of the couple after getting into the taxi but he now had them marked again, two seats in on the eighth row of the main stand, the woman wearing a long, dark wig, the man with a pair of binoculars, both sporting a change of clothes, looking for all the world like typical Barceloneses.

He gave the gymnasts until ten thirty, then slipped out of the arena and made his way down to the Casa de Prensa. Now that the athletics were over, the press office wore the feel of a quiet country railway station waiting for the one train of the day to pass through. The bar was deserted, a bucket and mop propped against the wall; no sign of the cleaner nor the security guard, who usually hung around in the background.

Clare walked through to the exchange and booked a call to England. *Richard Clare. Hotel Oriente.* The telephonist made a note of his request and handed it to an office boy. It was common knowledge that the SIM kept a record of every call made from the Casa and Clare presumed it was the office boy's job to run each request to a room located somewhere behind the exchange.

Once again the connection took longer than usual to come through, and once again Clare was unbothered by the delay. This call too was for Jordan's benefit. Clare's excuse for being in the building; no-one back home was going to be the slightest bit interested in what he had to say about the women's gymnastic competition. 'Cabin number two.' A green light illuminated the booth. Clare had his line. Three minutes later, he was done. 'Get your arse down to the port' – his editor's parting shot – 'Fuck the gymnastics! I want to know what's happening to Beresford.'

Clare went to the bar and ordered a coffee, then moved on upstairs to collect his mail. In the few days he'd been away, his post had piled up – invitations, press releases and a few concerned notes from Wilson and company – *Where the hell are you? You okay? Call us!*

He loitered for a few minutes in the mailroom, waiting for the corridor outside to clear, then walked on up to the third floor, where the residential part of the building was located; the sanatorium and a half dozen bedrooms rented out by the Ministry to favoured guests.

Clare pushed open the door to the sick room. Inside were two neatly made beds on either side of a simple wooden table and a faded portrait of Stalin on the wall.

He started the blaze in the wardrobe, dousing the bed linen with lighter fluid, feeding the flames with short strips of wood broken from the drawers of the bedside table; the smell of paraffin an uncomfortable reminder of Caraben and his can of petrol, Moreno Garcia's body burning in a sea of flaming gasoline, like the photographs he'd once seen in *Picture Post* of an Indian funeral pyre drifting down the Ganges.

Clare waited for the fire to take hold, then went back downstairs to the bar and ordered a beer. Five minutes later, the alarm bell rang. Another minute passed. Then a faint whiff of smoke. A cry from upstairs and a rush of feet. 'Fire! Fire! Everybody out of the building!'

One, two, three – Clare counted the bodies evacuating the exchange – ten in all, five journalists, the telephonist, the office boy, and three men he'd never seen before, one in uniform. SIM. 'Everybody outside.' The security guard tapped him on the shoulder. Clare nodded, waited for the guard to go check the toilets, then darted across the lobby into the exchange, pulling the door shut behind him, quickly, quietly making his way past the desk into an area marked – "No Entry. Staff Only". Here, he found a small utility space: basin, toilet, a couple of lockers and, set back behind a row of coat hooks, a reinforced steel door that in the haste to evacuate the area had been left unlocked.

Clare cautiously pushed the door open and stepped into a brightly lit, windowless room – the dark heart of the Casa de Prensa – crammed full of sophisticated listening equipment:

microphones, yards of dirty black cables and along the back wall, a mass of filing cabinets. Standard issue, metallic grey, organised in the same way as the mailroom upstairs.

Clare wanted to know which of his colleagues had been ghostwriting his column. British journalists A – F. He started with Hylton Cleaver, running his eye over the three index cards contained in his file; each call being listed by date, time, number dialled and duration.

Outside the building, the police were ushering journalists and staff onto the other side of the road. Out of harm's way.

Drawing a blank with both Cleaver and Forsyth, Clare moved on to the next drawer, N-S, where – *Monday, 29th July. 10.00am. London, England* – he found what he was looking for – *Central 6000. Duration: 14.08 mins.* A first call made by Peter Stewart to *The Evening News* the morning after Clare had received the message to go interview Markham. A dozen more in all. At least one a day, almost always in the evening, the last listed yesterday at 19.33 hours.

Clare had his man. As the security guards made a last sweep of the corridors, he quietly slipped out of the building.

'Everyone back!' 'Keep your distance!' the police harangued the on-lookers as the first fire truck arrived, thick, black smoke spewing from the third floor windows. Clare looked for his tail. He couldn't afford to have Jordan think he might be trying to give him the slip. Once he might get away with. But twice? Jordan wasn't the type to believe in coincidence.

'Away from the road!' The police pushed a couple of photographers back onto the pavement. Clare stepped forward so as to make himself more visible, drawing a predictably sharp rebuke. 'I said – get back!' Then he saw them – the couple from Maricel park, hovering at the edge of the crowd, for a brief second their eyes joined to his by an invisible thread. Time enough for their expression to change. For Clare to know that they'd seen him too.

Clare turned his thoughts back to Peter Stewart. What did he know of the man? Not much – if truth be told. The son of a railway man from Swindon. A mild, unassuming fellow who owed his job on *The Herald* to his father's connections in the Union. On their first evening in the hotel bar, Stewart had confessed his one true ambition to Clare, he'd liked to have been a cricketer, he'd even played a couple of games for his local club, but realising he lacked the talent he'd decided to settle for a career reporting it instead. After a couple of beers, Stewart had surprised Clare by owning up to being jealous of him. Hadn't he once seen him play in a Varsity match at Lords? Clare's eighth wicket stand had helped rescue the match for his side. 'You've a good memory!' Clare had made light of his achievement, yet felt flattered his one moment of sporting glory hadn't passed by entirely unnoticed. 'I never forget an innings,' Stewart wistfully remarked.

From the Casa de Prensa, Clare made his way back up the hill to the cable car station; below him, the bare masts of the sail ships, like telegraph poles stacked in the lee of the great cargo vessels, ranks of cranes rigid on the wharves, a large crowd on the Moll de Barcelona come to watch the Olympic regatta.

Clare squeezed through the turnstile into the waiting cable car. As the *transbordador aeri* swung out into the ether, he steadied himself against the outer shell of the cabin, pulling his feet out from under the shoe of the man standing next door to him; but for the sun and the sea below, he might have been on the London Underground in the morning rush hour.

On the Moll de Barcelona, a race had just started. Press card to the fore, Clare pushed his way into the Club de Regattas, unsurprised to find his colleagues in the bar running over the morning's one talking point – although only Cleaver had actually witnessed it – an Italian crew arguing amongst themselves after they'd been unexpectedly disqualified, one of the oarsmen smacking the other in the jaw and knocking him into the water.

Clare bought himself a coffee and pulled up a chair. 'There's been a fire at the Casa de Prensa,' he blandly announced.

Wilson looked at him in disbelief. 'No way. You're bullshitting us!'

Clare shook his head – *No, he wasn't.*

'Jesus – how the hell did that happen?' 'Anyone hurt?' 'How many in the building?' The questions followed thick and fast. 'You were there? Hey, hang on a minute.' Forsyth took out his notebook. 'We want to know exactly what happened. From the beginning – how did it start?'

Clare told them. Or rather he didn't. Leaving the actual cause of the flames to their fevered speculation.

A bell rang to signal the start of the next race.

As the table rose to find a phone, Clare shot Stewart a discreet glance – *I need a word* – and wandered out onto the terrace.

A few moment's later, Stewart joined him.

On the water, the crews were lining up for the next heat. If Jordan's men were watching them, all they'd see were two journalists exchanging notes on the race. 'I need your help,' Clare said without ceremony. 'I need you to put me in touch with SIS.'

Stewart stared awkwardly across the water. 'How did you know?'

'Why else would anyone have you write my column? What did they tell you? That I was working on a matter of national importance?'

'Something like that.'

'What else?'

'Nothing – just to file an article to the *Evening News* every night. In case you didn't have the time.'

'Not to keep an eye on me?'

'No. Nothing like that. It's not my kind of thing.'

'But you can get a message to them?'

'There is an emergency procedure.' Stewart nervously flicked at his cigarette. 'But –'

'Tell them I know about Markham.'

'What about Markham?' Stewart looked genuinely blank.

'Markham was working for SIS.'

'Jesus!'

'He was shot by the Spanish secret police.'

'How do you know?'

'Because I was there.'

On your marks! Get set! Bang! A starter pistol brought them to. They stopped for a moment to watch the race. Oars dipped, backs bent, faces creased with effort – Clare remembered just how much he hated rowing. Those cold, mist laden early mornings on the river – for House and College. *Come on, Clare! Dig deep! You can do it!* And for a while he had.

'I'll do what I can,' Stewart said quietly. 'Anything else you want me to tell them?'

'No. Just get me out of here.'

Plaça Catalunya. 1.50pm. Clare cut a lone figure as he traipsed across the square towards Café Zurich. Hot, still, quiet and empty – even the pigeons had seen fit to sit out the heat on the great stone fountains that defined the concourse, the street vendors long ago having beaten a retreat underground into the shaded cool of the subway.

'Bocadillo de Jamon queso y un Vichy Catalan,' Clare ordered first, then found himself somewhere to sit. An outside table where Jordan's men would have a good view of whomever it was who wanted to meet him.

An hour passed. Clare ate his lunch, read the newspaper, read it again, then ordered a coffee, beginning to wonder if Capdevila's contact had got cold feet. Then – 'Señor Clare.' A waiter tapped him on the shoulder, pointing a thumb at the bar. *'Telefono.'*

Clare followed the man inside, glancing at the surrounding tables, trying to figure out if he was being watched. Behind the bar, a battered radio was broadcasting a message from the Generalitat, the Prime Minister, Juan Negrin, congratulating the country on the success of its athletes.

Clare picked up the receiver. 'Hello?'

'Señor Clare?' It was a woman's voice.

'Yes.' Clare thought she sounded vaguely familiar. 'Who is it?'

'A friend of Rafael Capdevila.'

'What do you want?'

'Is he safe?'

'I'm sorry.'

'Is Rafael safe?'

'Yes. Yes. He's in France –' But before Clare could elaborate, the line cut dead; whoever was on the other end had heard enough.

So Jordan was right; they still thought Capdevila was alive. Clare handed the phone back to the barman. *Now what?*

Three hours later, Clare had his answer. Standing outside the Opera House, looking for a taxi to take him back to the port, a bright blue Packard pulled up by the kerb. 'Get in!' The driver leaned out of the window, the sun's reflection catching him in the eye.

Clare recognised him as the SIM guard from Via Laietana.

They drove due west towards Plaça Espanya, a burst water main forcing them into a detour round the School for Matadors. Through the fence, Clare glimpsed a young boy training on a wooden bull, floating a dusty yellow cape over its battered horns, elegantly stepping to one side as the hand held cart trundled past rocking on its wheels.

The taxi drew up outside the Palau Nacional. 'Room four,' the driver told him. 'Turn left through the entrance and keep walking.'

Clare did so.

Jordan was waiting for him inside the gallery. Alone. Quietly contemplating an altarpiece by Lluis Dalmau. 'Spain's answer to van Eyck,' he said, without taking his eyes off the painting. 'You can see the similarities.'

'They called,' Clare told him.

'They?'

'A woman. She didn't give her name.'

'What did she want?'

'Just to know that Capdevila was safe.'

'What did you say?'

'I told her he was in France. Then the line went dead.'

'Did she believe you?'

'I think so.'

'Then she'll be back in touch. Or one of her associates will.' Jordan turned his eye once more to the altarpiece. 'You know Dalmau painted this in the same year that Gutenberg invented the printing press. It was commissioned by the city council. In those days, they had taste.' He indicated the Madonna at the centre of the altarpiece. 'Stay a few minutes. She's worth it.'

Clare looked up at the painting. The Madonna was sitting on an ornately carved throne with the baby Jesus on her lap, the city councillors kneeling in adoration, a sea of faces crowding in on her, all wanting a piece of the action. Her expression – given the circumstances – seemed remarkably calm, cognisant of the role demanded of her, yet there was something about her face, about the look in her eyes, that said, 'You've got ten more minutes and then I'll kick the lot of you out of here.'

Clare turned back round to see that Jordan was gone. And then it struck him. The voice on the telephone. The woman.

It was Capdevila's friend – Margarita Mirabel.

CHAPTER 16

Thursday 8th August, 1940

Programme of the XIIth Olympiad
Fencing, Yachting, Swimming, Rowing, Equestrian Sports, Basketball, Boxing, Hockey, Football.

Clare sat alone in the gilt breakfast room of the Oriente Hotel, distractedly flicking through the pages of *La Vanguardia*, an article on a new film being shot in Barcelona loosely catching his interest. *Cinco dias*. Five days. A melodramatic treatment of the events of May '37, the civil war within a civil war that had seen the Communists seize control of the city.

'Mind if I join you?' Clare looked up to see Stewart fresh from the shower, his collar damp from where he'd failed to dry himself.

'Sure.' Clare had been waiting all morning for him to surface.

Stewart pulled up a chair. 'You alone?'

'Ten o'clock.' Clare indicated the one other diner in the room; diminutive, dark haired, a scar above his right eyebrow, already into his fourth cup of coffee.

'Got you.' Stewart reached for the menu. 'What are the eggs like?'

'Go for the poached. Did you speak to SIS?'

'Yes.' Stewart poured himself a cup of coffee. 'You're to go to the airport. Wait for one of our chaps to make contact.'

Which at least explained the message from his editor that Clare had picked up earlier at reception, asking him to cover Goering's arrival at the Games. It was all over today's newspapers.

At eleven o'clock the Prime Minister, Juan Negrin, was going to be at the airport to welcome the Reichsmarschall. 'How will I recognise your man?' Clare asked.

'They didn't tell me,' Stewart admitted. 'Only that you're to go to the airport.'

Clare had hoped for more. Since the early hours of the morning he'd lain in bed, in the bath, on the bed again, restless, running over his options, focusing on the irreducible, inescapable truths of the mess he'd landed himself in. That one – the moment he handed over Capdevila's associates, Jordan would kill him. Two – come Sunday and the end of the Games, whether he'd handed over Capdevila's associates or not, Jordan would kill him. And three – if he tried to make a break for it or to contact Shaw, Jordan would kill him. His only hope lay with Stewart. 'How come you're involved in all this?' he asked.

'I did something stupid,' Stewart confessed, stirring a large spoonful of sugar into his coffee. 'Something I shouldn't have. What about you?'

'Same story.' Clare understood. They had their hooks into him too.

Fear of anti-German sentiment had put the airport on high alert. Not since the war had Clare seen the terminal so overrun with security; militiamen armed with machine guns, SIM agents on every corner, a tank parked outside to intimidate would-be troublemakers.

Inside the Arrivals Hall, a carefully vetted crowd patiently waited. Fresh faced young Communists, dutiful party members, factory workers given the day off and a free meal in return for a few hours of their lives. Standing apart from the others, like an air bubble trapped under ice, a small pocket of German dignitaries self consciously counted the minutes until Goering's arrival. The ambassador, embassy heads of staff and the president of the German Olympic Committee.

Opposite them, the world's press stood waiting under a heady cloud of cigarette smoke; Melachrino Egyptian, Demont, Salome, Tiedermans No. 10 and Westminster Turkish.

Goering's plane was on time. A four engined Junkers G-38. Even from a distance, there was no mistaking the swastika emblazoned across its tail. As the aeroplane taxied over to the terminal, a river of celluloid swept through the gates of the newsreel cameras trained on its cockpit, an excited hush bubbling into frenzied speculation – he's flying it himself. Thumb raised, grinning broadly, Goering swung the aeroplane round to face the crowds.

The Reichsmarschall had landed.

Inside the Arrivals hall, the theatre continued. Flashlights popped. A schoolgirl stepped forward to present a large bouquet of flowers. Goering responded all smiles and warm words, standing two steps behind him the actress, Lotte Haller, according to the gossip columns, his latest squeeze. And then came the handshake. The moment Negrin couldn't avoid. Welcome to Barcelona. Welcome to Spain. Welcome to the Olympic Games. Clare could almost hear the bomb scorched cries of Guernica's dead protesting at this grotesque visitation. *Go home!*

A militiaman held open the door. Goering and his entourage swept through to a waiting limousine. The press stampeded for the taxi line, and the crowd, now excused, dispersed, like Negrin their duty done, a bus ride back into town and a few pesetas their reward. Clare felt a tap on the shoulder. 'Care for a lift?' The voice was English; reassuringly so. 'The name's Philip Holdsworth. You don't know me. But for God's sake, look as though you do.'

Clare turned to take in a face marked by a lifetime of active service; handsome in an unassuming, bashed about way. 'You work for Shaw?' He took hold of Holdsworth's outstretched arm, feeling the firm shake of a man who'd just met an "old friend".

Holdsworth nodded. 'With Shaw. That's correct.' He was dressed in a navy blue blazer embroidered with the badge of the British Olympic team, white trousers and sharply polished shoes. 'The old girl's outside,' he said, pointing to the car park.

It was a short walk from the terminal. Holdsworth filled the silence by explaining that his car belonged to the President of the British Fencing Association, Walter Hayes, as did his blazer and the accreditation papers sitting in his breast pocket. 'Should your friends in the SIM want to know who you've been talking to,' Holdsworth instructed Clare. 'Tell them I'm Hayes. You've been after an interview with me all week.'

The car was a Crossley 2 litre sports saloon; sleek yellow and black aluminium body, mahogany and black leather interior, a top speed of 76 mph. 'Be careful not to get any dirt on the seats,' Holdsworth warned him as he unlocked the door. 'Hayes will murder me if I don't return it spotless.'

Overhead a plane took off, banking away from the sun towards the Serra de la Guardia and Madrid. Holdsworth switched on the ignition. 'If the traffic's anything like it was on the way out, we've got about fifteen minutes. I want you to start with what happened last Sunday. Stewart told me you were there when Markham was killed.'

'That's right.'

'I gather you were somewhat lucky to get out alive. Any idea how they found out about the rendezvous?'

It sounded to Clare as much an accusation as a statement of fact. 'It wasn't me that told them,' he said flatly.

'No. Of course not.' Holdsworth gave him a politician's smile. 'I wasn't insinuating that you had.'

They were seven minutes into the journey when it happened – just past the village of Cornella – Clare reliving the moment he'd been thrown blindfolded into a sea of cut glass in Via Laietana, Holdsworth slowing down to take a right onto the

N9. The motorcycle came up fast behind them. The man riding pillion reaching into his jacket, levelling a gun at the front windscreen.

Clare heard three shots.

The steering wheel span out of Holdsworth's grip as the Crossley slewed across the road, clipping a large metal bin, spewing a sludge of potato peelings over the verge.

A dog barked.

Through the shattered remains of the windscreen, Clare saw an old woman retreat indoors, closing the door firmly behind her; whatever it was that had just happened at the crossroads, it was none of her concern. The village lay deathly quiet. The dog threw one last bark at the Crossley, then turned to address the spilled contents of the bin, the motorcycle having long since roared off in the direction of Barcelona.

Clare lifted a hand to his forehead and touched blood. Not his but Holdsworth's. The station chief of SIS Madrid sat slumped beside him, blood seeping from a hole where his tie knot had been and also from another, smaller spot in his left temple. The third bullet had penetrated the bonnet.

Clare pushed open the door. The Crossley had come to rest in a piece of dirt scrubland twenty feet back from the road, undamaged except for the shattered windscreen. A black Hispano-Suizo sat pulled into the far side of the road, engine idling in the shade of a diseased olive tree. Two men in the car. One behind the wheel, the other in the back seat. *Come to finish off the job?*

Clare dived back into the car. Somewhere Holdsworth had to have a weapon. Something with which he could defend himself. In his blazer or his belt, in the glove compartment, under the seat, even taped to the top side of the sun screen like he'd seen in American gangster movies. Then a miracle. Slowly, deliberately, the Hispano-Suizo moved off, the man in the back seat removing a pair of dark glasses just long enough for Clare to recognise the scar above his right eyebrow. It was the man from the breakfast room this morning. They weren't going to kill him. Not yet. This was just a warning.

A fly settled on Holdsworth's open lip. Clare beat it away. Then threw up over the floor.

A car drove past. Then another. Clare brushed the vomit from his mouth and set about looking for Holdsworth's wallet, eventually finding it tucked under the dashboard. Inside were a hundred pounds worth of pesetas, French francs and American dollars, an identity card describing Holdsworth as the Chief of the British Passport Office, a receipt from the Café Zurich and a ticket stub for the Opera House in Madrid. Clare put the wallet in his pocket and removed the keys from the ignition. A pathetic, futile gesture, he knew, but he imagined the SIM would soon be along to tidy away the evidence and he was damned if he was going to make life easy for the bastards.

It was a seven kilometre walk back into town. Despite the traffic, Clare resisted the temptation to hitch. He needed some time alone, a few hours to free his mind from the violence of Holdsworth's death, to lose himself in the contours of the earth, feel the clouds' shadow, share a few words with the old man hawking melons by the side of the road, remind himself that there were lives beyond his and Holdsworth's.

Beyond Barcelona.

By the time Clare reached the outskirts of the city, the cement works and ceramic factories of La Bodeta, his dreaming was done, his legs ached and he felt thirsty. Now all he wanted was to get back to his room.

Approaching the Oriente, he saw the black Hispano-Suizo parked outside, Scarface leaning against the bonnet reading a comic book, a faint grin on his face. 'Go to Hell,' Clare muttered angrily as he brushed past him into the hotel.

Inside the lobby, a party of French tourists were preparing to go through to lunch. Clare made his way to the front desk and asked for his messages. There was just the one – from his father – with the news that Gerald's book was going into a second print, and a postscript, *Your mother and I enjoyed your piece on Picasso. You'll be pleased to know it made The Times*. Clare pocketed the message and went into the cloakroom to wash; there was nothing he could do now except wait for Stewart to return, and maybe treat himself to a good lunch.

The restaurant was full. Clare declined the maitre D's offer to come back in an hour, telling him he'd look elsewhere, perhaps Merce's he thought, for old time's sake. Then – a voice from across the lobby. 'Clare! Thank God! I've been looking for you all over.' It was Wilson.

Clare caught the anxious look on his face. 'What is it?'

'It's Stewart.' Wilson hardly knew where to start. 'He's been hit by a car. Crossing the street.'

It took Clare a moment to find his voice. 'Is he dead?'

'No, thank Christ. He's in hospital. Selwyn's there with him.'

'Selwyn?'

'He was there when it happened.' Wilson pulled a cigarette from a crumpled packet in his breast pocket. 'But he can't communicate with the doctors. You speak Spanish ...'

'Of course. Which hospital did they take him to?' *Clare would do what he could*.

'Sant Pau. Here, I have the address.' Wilson handed him a scrap of paper. 'It's somewhere up near the Sagrada Familia.'

Clare nodded. He knew the place. He'd been there once during the war, looking for a friend who was rumoured to have been transferred there. As with so many rumours at the time the information had proved inaccurate. His friend had died in transit.

'I've been trying to get through to the British Consul,' Wilson continued. 'But the line seems to be out of order.'

No surprise there. 'When did it happen?' Clare asked.

'About an hour ago.'

'Where?'

Wilson made a vague gesture in the direction of the sea. 'On the Passeig de Colom.'

'And the driver?'

'I don't know. He didn't stop.'

'Did Selwyn notice what kind of car it was?'

'Yes. A black Hispano-Suizo. But they're two-a-penny. Unfortunately he didn't catch the number.'

But it didn't matter. Clare already knew it. AF 529. He'd bet his life that it was the same car now parked outside the hotel. 'Don't worry,' he said quietly. 'I'll go to the hospital. You wait here.'

'Thanks.' Wilson lit his cigarette and inhaled deeply. 'Thank God, you're here. What a bloody 'mare ...'

* * * **

Picasso's studio. Plaça Lesseps. At eleven minutes past two came the moment Picasso had been waiting for, had been dreading all week, the sound of the courtyard gates swinging open to let in the laundry van, three minutes later than yesterday, ten minutes earlier than Tuesday, the 300 bed hostal opposite his studio the last stop-off point on the van's daily rounds.

Picasso took a step back from his work, his hand trembling, the connection to his paint brush broken, the half finished canvas blurred into a jumble of disconnected thoughts and fears. All his life, he'd been obsessed by the "dark arts" as he liked to call them – the world of spies, of subterfuge and intrigue – until today, practised from the safety of a court convened for his own amusement and with himself at its centre. But now – and the thought frightened him far more than he would ever care to confess – the game was for real. He was scared. He didn't want to be caught. He didn't want to die. He wanted to live, to paint and love, and be loved for what he did better than any man alive.

Did he have the balls to go through with it? To step out from behind the canvas? To take off his crown and face life like any other mortal?

Would he ever be able to live with himself if he didn't?

Nervously, almost apologetically, Picasso took the first step – one that didn't yet commit him. He scratched his ear. A signal to his model, Gloria, that she was to ask for a toilet break.

Ten seconds passed. The large chested chorus girl from the Ba-ta-clan appeared not to have noticed. Picasso felt sick. Close to fainting. Furiously now, he gave his ear another scratch. 'Hey Pablo!' Gloria's aggrieved reaction told him the prompt was unnecessary as she breezily stretched out an arm, drained the rest of her glass of water and let out a soft belch, 'I need to take a piss!'

Not so loud. Not so obvious. Picasso shrank back into silence before remembering himself. He looked across to his minder. A chain-smoking SIM agent from Madrid. Twenty-five years old. Shoulder length brown hair. Slim boyish body. Beautiful enough to pass as his lover should the world wonder what she was doing glued to his shoulder, hard enough to put a bullet through his head should he step out of line. 'Lieutenant?' When they were together, it amused Picasso to address her by her rank rather than the name – Adele – she'd asked him to use. 'Could you show Gloria where to go.'

Adele – real name, Ines Ramirez – looked at her watch with ill-disguised irritation. 'We'll break for lunch. She can go in the restaurant.'

'I'm not ready yet.' With a certainty that surprised him, Picasso lifted his brush back to the canvas. *The artist at work – do not disturb.*

'You want me to do it here?' Gloria looked to Ramirez as if it were no skin off her nose. 'Hey, Pablo! You got a jar. A big one mind you – I'm bursting!' She gave a loud, coarse laugh.

'Come with me.' Ramirez stubbed out her cigarette.

'Suit yourself, honey!' Gloria threw a robe over her naked body, and picking her way through the regal disorder of Picasso's cluttered studio, followed Ramirez out of the door.

For a brief second, Picasso was struck by a strange frisson such as he hadn't experienced since he was a schoolboy. The thrill of a practical joke set in motion. Smug. Superior. Blind to the consequences of what he'd just done. Just as quickly, he pushed the feeling aside, disappointed with himself that he should react in such a childish manner, when what he wanted to feel was strong, resolute, calm.

Picasso looked at his watch. He had less than four minutes.

Owner sought for collection of African parrots – the advertisement placed in today's *La Vanguardia* told him that the British secret service were finally ready to spirit him out of the country. If he was ever to escape Barcelona, then he had to do it now. On his own. Putting his trust in the only idea he could come up with.

Downstairs in the courtyard, the van driver was half way through lifting his load of dirty linen into the back of his van.

Two floors above, Ramirez waited for Gloria to relieve herself.

Outside, the four militiamen standing guard at the studio cheerily looked forward to the end of their shift and a three course lunch back at the station canteen, unaware that the next time they'd be offered any food would be two day's hence in the interrogation cells of the SIM building in Via Laietana.

'Son of a bitch!' Lieutenant Ramirez stood in the doorway, staring in disbelief at the empty studio that greeted her return from the toilet. 'You little fuck!' She whipped the butt of her pistol hard across Gloria's face. 'Where is he?'

'How the hell should I know.' Gloria picked herself up from a pile of old canvases she'd fallen against, spitting blood.

'You've ten seconds!' Ramirez put her gun to Gloria's head.

'He gave me twenty pesetas,' Gloria bleated. *Picasso had taken her for a ride the same way he had Ramirez.* 'To get you out of the room – so he could sneak a cigarette. All I had to say was I needed a piss. He told me the doctor had forbidden him to smoke. His lungs. God's truth.' It sounded lame even as she said it. *And all for twenty pesetas, she chided herself.*

Ramirez had heard enough. As surely as if she'd just listened to her own death sentence, she knew now it was no coincidence that the studio toilet had been blocked since Monday. Picasso must have sabotaged the piping, just as he'd made sure he'd been working with a new model today, one who wouldn't know the way to the only toilet still working in the building; up two flights of stairs and at the far end of a confusing corridor.

Ramirez hauled Gloria to her feet and half pushed, half ran her down to the gates at the front of the studio. 'Has anyone been in or out of the building in the last five minutes?' she screamed at the startled militiamen on duty outside.

'No. No-one. Only the laundry van.' the senior of the four men answered her confidently.

'Idiot! Did you think to check inside?' Ramirez guessed the van could only have been gone a few seconds. 'Which way did it go?' Without waiting for an answer, she ran over to Picasso's car, shouting at three of the militiamen to come with her. 'No guns,' she warned them. 'No shooting. We need the bastard alive.'

Back in the studio, Picasso quietly lifted open the lid of the chest into which he'd squeezed himself. A battered old wooden box filled with reams of Holland paper and ancient magazines. The room was quiet. Miraculously empty. Not even a guard left posted on the door.

From a bag of clothes which he sometimes used to dress his models, Picasso pulled out a carefully folded suit, hat and coat, and quickly changed, then checked the windows. At the front of the building, he could see one of the militiamen standing guard over Gloria. At the back – nothing.

He had his way out.

Two minutes later, the world's most famous artist was on the street, his features shaded by the brim of his hat. To the casual observer, a tired old gentleman heading out for lunch.

Waiting for him two blocks away was a parked car. In the glove box, a map with directions to a safe house. There he'd be able to breathe again. Be himself once more. In his mind, rewrite the history of these last dreadful few minutes.

The world would want to know the truth of what had happened in Barcelona and he would have to find them that truth. But without the fear, and without the hesitation, and without the realisation that in his heart he was not, nor ever would be, the man he'd always imagined himself to be.

But such concerns would have to wait.

What he needed to know now from Capdevila were the final details of his escape. Where did the British want him to be? And when?

* * * * *

In the guide books, the hospital de la Santa Creu i Sant Pau was described as a shining example of Barcelona's *modernisme* architecture. A miniature city within a city. A park of formally arranged pavilions located at the far end of the Avinguda Gaudi. Stewart had been taken to the Accident & Emergency department. 'Second building on the left,' the receptionist pointed Clare through the main doors, 'The Pavello de Nuestra Señora del Carme.'

An old man feebly rattled a collection box under his nose; for disabled veterans. Clare dropped a couple of coins into the box and hurried on into the courtyard, past a young man plugged into a drip, his family gathered around him, kicking away a flock of over eager pigeons as they shared out their sandwiches.

'Thank God, you're here!' Selwyn sprang to his feet as Clare entered the pavilion. 'I can't make head nor tail of what's going on.'

'How is he?' Clare asked.

Selwyn coughed on his cigarette. 'I don't know. They won't let me see him.'

Clare turned to the nurse on the front desk. Brittle mouth and humourless eyes. 'I have a friend here. Peter Stewart. I'd like to know how he is.'

'I've told your colleague already,' the nurse answered him. 'You must wait until the doctors have finished.'

'The bitch hasn't smiled since I got here,' Selwyn muttered.

'Forget her.' Clare pulled up a chair. 'Tell me what happened.' Apart from anything, he needed to take the weight off his foot. His wound was beginning to seep again.

'We were on our way back from the port ...' The trauma of the moment was still written on the face of *The Times* sports correspondent. 'On our way to the Correos. About level with the General Motors building. There was this gang of youths. Gypsies. I don't know where they came from. One grabbed my wallet. Another knocked Stewart straight into the path of an oncoming car ...'

'A black Hispano-Suizo?'

'Yes.' Selwyn reached for the ashtray. It was the reason he'd started smoking again. Four years ago, while driving back home in the rain from a football match in Preston, his car had come off the road sending him through the windscreen and into a ditch. It had taken them two hours to find him; the memory of it still haunted him at nights. When the Hispano-Suizo had mown down Stewart, all he could think of was that ditch and the wet grass and the smell of petrol mingling with his cloying blood.

'And then what?' Clare prompted him.

'The bastards ran off.' Selwyn sounded almost indignant.

'Into the Barri Gotic?'

'Yes.'

'What about the Hispano-Suizo?'

'It just drove on.'

'And the driver?'

'I didn't see him ...'

Clare imagined it must have happened shortly after they shot Holdsworth.

'His leg was busted,' Selwyn went on. 'I think his lung may have been punctured too. I tell you – he's lucky to be alive.'

'Where is he now?'

Selwyn indicated a pair of swing doors beyond a sign that read "STAFF ONLY". 'They took him through there.'

'Okay. Wait here.' Clare turned back towards the nurse. '*Los servicios?*'

'Upstairs. First on the left.' The nurse pointed to the ceiling.

'Hang on!' Selwyn said. 'Where are you going?'

Yolanda Tusquets sang softly as she washed the young man's foot. The young man couldn't see her, the accident that had destroyed his leg had also left him blind, but he could feel her, the damp touch of her sponge on his toes, the sweet warmth of her breath, the faint pressure of her bosom against his chest, and it made him smile, a smile that in turn excited Yolanda and made her think of what might have been had they encountered one another on the dance floor at La Paloma, this good looking young boy and –

'– I'm looking for a friend. An Englishman.' A blunt, unfamiliar voice ripped Yolanda from her reverie. 'He was brought in a couple of hours ago.'

The nineteen year old nurse sprang back from the young man's bed to see Clare standing in the doorway. 'You're not supposed to be here …' she said. 'You should ask downstairs.'

Clare gave an apologetic shrug. 'I already have but they won't tell me anything.'

Yolanda picked up the young man's bedpan and emptied it into a bucket, a melancholy about her manner that suggested a life that had already seen too much.

'I have to ring his fiancée,' Clare persisted. 'I don't know what to say.'

'You can tell her, he'll live,' Yolanda said quietly – medical staff were strictly forbidden to converse with the public. 'Now – please go.'

'Then he's conscious?'

'Yes. His right leg's broken. And a couple of ribs. But there's nothing internal. He was fortunate.'

'Can you tell me the name of the doctor treating him?' Clare was pushing his luck now.

'Doctor Llambrich. Now please go …' Yolanda had the same frightened look to her as the doctor who'd patched him up at Via Laietana, as though by just exchanging a few words with him she'd somehow be implicated in his guilt.

'Thank you.' Clare had what he'd come for.

'I don't understand. Wait until my friend comes, damn you!' Downstairs in the lobby, Selwyn was trying to make himself understood to the pavilion administrator, a stocky, grey haired man in a cheap suit and the smell of peanuts on his breath. 'Ah! Here he is!' Selwyn greeted Clare's return with relief. 'It's Stewart. I think they're trying to tell me he's dead.'

'Please, come with me,' the administrator urged.

'Dead?' Clare looked from one to the other – incredulous. 'But that's impossible ...'

The administrator nodded sympathetically. 'I am sorry. There was nothing we could do.'

At the end of the corridor, there was an old operating theatre. The door was open, a pile of defunct surgery lamps lying in the corner gathering dust, long since stripped of any parts that worked. The administrator ushered Clare and Selwyn inside. At some point, Clare could see that the room had been used as an office – a faded poster on the wall trumpeted the benefits of an old vaccination programme – but its function now was clearly that of a storeroom. A space to park the dead before transporting them to the morgue.

Stewart lay on a gurney beneath the window, beside a stack of cardboard boxes donated by the French Red Cross; cleaning fluid and sterilising equipment.

'Is this your friend?' The administrator pulled back the sheet covering Stewart's face.

Selwyn nodded. There was a line of dried blood running from Stewart's temple, otherwise his face and neck were unblemished.

'How did he die?' Clare asked quietly.

'Your friend suffered massive internal haemorrhaging.' The administrator handed him a piece of paper. 'It's all here. On the death certificate.'

Clare looked at the signature on the bottom of the page. 'Who's Dr Reig?'

'The doctor who operated on Mr Stewart.'

Which made Dr Llambrich what? 'I'd like to speak to him,' Clare said.

'I'm sorry. Dr Reig has gone home.'

'Already?'

'He's been on duty since early this morning.'

'Come on, Clare. Let's go.' Selwyn had had enough.

So too had the administrator. 'We will contact your embassy,' he said with the air of a man unused to having his authority questioned. 'Ask them to see that the body is picked up.'

Clare took a last look at Stewart's lifeless face. There was no doubt he'd been murdered.

Run out before his innings took shape.

And all because Clare had asked him to make a phone call.

They caught a taxi from outside the hospital. Pulling into the traffic, Clare glanced Jordan's tail starting up after them. A dark blue Citroën Traction Avant, an automobile club of Catalunya shield mounted on the front fender. Three men inside.

'I can't believe Stewart's dead.' Selwyn lit another cigarette, his hand trembling, shock setting in.

Clare had seen it a hundred times before during the war. 'There's nothing you could have done,' he said, too tired to take issue, too tired even to mention the anomaly of the two doctors. 'Nothing anybody could have done. It was just bad luck.'

Selwyn nodded. 'Poor bastard ... and all for a measly couple of hundred pesetas.'

The taxi turned right onto Aragó. On the sunken track beneath them, a train clattered past heading towards Sants. Clare wound down the window and caught a whiff of the flower market, as with so many of the city's olfactory darts, the scent taking him straight back to Montse. Memories of getting up early on a Saturday morning, rooting out the freshest cuts from the market, taking them back to her mother in the hotel, and receiving a plate of eggs and chorizo, and a cold glass of beer in exchange.

The taxi slowed to take a left into Balmes.

Then – 'Stop!' – Clare leaned forward, tapping the driver on the shoulder. 'Over there. By the shoe shop.'

The driver pulled into the kerb, the Traction Avant braking sharply behind them.

Clare leaped out onto the pavement, gesturing Selwyn he'd catch up with him later. 'There's something I forgot to do,' he said, one eye on Jordan's agents tumbling out of the Citroën after him. 'I'll see you back at the hotel. Got to run.'

The hostal was still as Clare remembered it from the war. Mallorca, 233. A large, six storey building used by the International Brigade as somewhere cheap to stay while on leave, now under the auspices of the Young Communists, Clare noted the change in legend as he darted inside, otherwise the décor looked reassuringly familiar, faded brown walls, a strip light in the hall, Olivier's Alsatian lying on a chewed bit of carpet by the front desk.

'*Hola* Olivier,' Clare called out to the aged caretaker, already half way up the stairs by the time Olivier registered his greeting, the two agents tailing him still yards behind outside on the pavement.

A party of sixteen year olds were coming down the stairs. Clare pushed past them without stopping, vaulting the steps two at a time, knocking against a cage of canaries into which an American volunteer had once famously placed a rat he'd caught riffling through his bedclothes. The American, Glenn Howard, had been fined a month's wages and had his leave cut in half. On his last night, a half dozen of them had sneaked out over the roofs after curfew. There was little Clare could remember about the episode other than that they'd ended up at the Pompeya music hall with *La Cubana* perched on Howard's lap singing *Yankee Doodle Dandy*, Howard protesting his undying love and complaining later that somebody had filched his wallet.

The way out over the roofs was part of brigade lore; from the sixth floor dormitory window, a drop onto the ledge below and a short hop across to the church on the corner of Balmes and Provença. Clare scuttled across the tiles like it was only yesterday, breaking into the bell tower by way of a smashed window.

In the old days, they'd kept a box of candles hidden behind a loose brick at the top of the narrow stone staircase. Clare found it still there. Gratefully, he struck a match, the flame flaring with a damp sizzle to reveal the walls around him to be covered in bird shit; a set of initials carved into the stone – *LCS 1.4.38*.

Clare lit a candle. Carefully shielding the flame with his hand, he made his way down the spiral staircase into the church. During the war, the building had been used as a garage for repairing trucks; the floor was still glazed with engine grease and a faint whiff of petrol pervaded where once an incensory had swung.

To the right of the side chapel, a small door led out onto the street. From where he stood, Clare could see the blue Citroën parked outside the hostal, the driver nervously pacing the pavement as one of the two men who'd been tailing him called down from an upstairs window. 'The little fuck's disappeared!'

Hurriedly, Clare jumped onto the first tram driving past. *Direction – Plaça Catalunya.*

* * * * *

Jordan picked up a half smoked Primeros from his ashtray and inhaled deeply. Recently, he'd found his thoughts all too often being invaded by some memory or other from his childhood in Argentina, and it had begun to bother him. Not because the memories were unpleasant – although some undoubtedly were – but because the part of him that had never left Argentina was beginning to think like Osvaldo, *when a man starts dreaming the tastes and smells of his childhood, that's when he knows death is close by*. A stupid superstition – Jordan was aware – but one that his father had shared, and his father before him, and his father before him too for all he knew.

Jordan stared at the phone in frustration. It had been two hours now since he'd been informed of Picasso's disappearance and as every minute passed, so his anxiety increased.

At the closing ceremony in two days time, the world's press had been told to expect a few words from Picasso, words carefully drafted by André Marty himself, designed to reassure the international community of Spain's commitment to justice and democracy. Coming from the mouth of the world's most celebrated artist, they might just be believed. But now? Jordan could see the whole fiasco lying ahead of them. Picasso all of a sudden popping up in London to denounce the government as a sham, bringing the whole carefully constructed artifice tumbling down. And Jordan with it. Marty would make sure of that. Simply, come five thirty on Sunday afternoon, either Picasso was at the Olympic stadium or Jordan was on the train to Moscow. On a one way ticket.

The phone rang. Jordan had the receiver in his hand before the second trill. 'Yes?'

It was Carreto: the agent in charge of following Clare. 'What is it?' Jordan snapped impatiently.

'Clare's gone.'

A pause, then. 'You mean – you've lost him.'

'No, Sir. He lost us.'

'Where?'

'Carrer Mallorca.'

'Find him.' Jordan didn't have to say it, nor did he have to spell out the consequences to Carreto if he were to fail to do so.

'Yes, Sir.' Carreto understood well enough. His life depended on it.

* * * * *

First Markham, then Holdsworth, then Stewart; Clare knew now if he hadn't already that it would soon be his turn. How it happened no longer mattered. Tonight. Tomorrow. The day after. It was only a question of time. A question of when Jordan decided that he was no longer of any use to him. All that remained to him were these last few hours. A final chance to see Montse again. To say all the things he wanted to say. Before it was too late. Before they put a bullet through his head.

She arrived just after eight, unsurprised to find him waiting on the doorstep. 'Uncle Richard's come to say good night,' she told Pep as she reached into her handbag for the front door key.

The boy beamed at Clare. 'Can we go swimming tomorrow?'

'Not tomorrow,' Clare regretted. 'Maybe some other day.'

'If you're good,' Montse added, pushing open the door, encouraging Clare into the hallway. 'Come on, monkey. Race you up the stairs. Ready. Steady –' but Pep was already half way up the first flight, 'Go!'

Clare picked up the shopping basket and followed them upstairs.

'What are you doing here?' Only when Pep was safely tucked up in bed did Montse finally see fit to pose the question; they were sitting on the sofa with a glass of wine, the gramophone on, the shutters drawn and the lights dimmed.

'I came to say goodbye.' Clare no longer cared that she might have betrayed him. They were beyond that now.

'Why?' Montse took the news calmly. 'What's happened?'

Briefly, Clare explained. All that had passed since they'd last met. How Holdsworth and Stewart had been murdered. How his efforts to escape the city had come to nothing.

The record reached its end.

Clare flipped over the disc. Outside he could hear the lottery vendor calling out the day's winning numbers. Someone shouting at a couple of kids to go play elsewhere. 'There must be something you can do,' Montse said.

Clare gave a rueful shrug. 'Pray?'

'It's not funny.'

'I'm not joking. I–'

'Ssh …' Montse raised her finger to his lips. 'I don't want to hear any more.'

Clare was okay with that. He had nothing more to say. He kissed the tip of her finger.

She smiled. Then kissed him back. Gently. On the lips.

Clare felt the hard curve of her back, her breasts tight against his chest, and for a moment it was as though they were back in her room at her parents' hotel. The first time they'd been together.

Each touch electric.

The spin of the world shrunk into the embrace of their bodies.

As then, as now, tenderly, urgently, they made love.

Afterwards – they lay together on the sofa for what seemed like hours. Her olive skin smooth in the moonlight. His face resting against her breast. Their bodies entwined like a Cubist painting, oblivious to the *click click click* of the gramophone needle at the end of the record.

Montse shivered.

'You're cold.' Clare rose from the sofa and handed her a dressing gown that was hanging on the back of the door. Montse wrapped it round her shoulders and lit a cigarette. The clock struck ten. 'I'd better go,' he said. 'Time to face the music.'

Montse said nothing. She just watched him dress, sucking on her cigarette, holding the image in her mind, knowing that in the days, weeks, months to come, it would be to this moment that she would return. 'I'll try to get word to you,' Clare said. 'But don't come looking for me. Promise.'

She promised.

He gave her a last, long kiss, then picked up his jacket and opened the door. 'Say goodbye to Pep.'

'I will.'

On the wall behind her, Clare noticed a photograph of them unpacking *Guernica*. He tried to recall the name of the village but remembered only that it was somewhere near Jaen. 'Take care,' he said.

Montse nodded. *You too*.

There was nothing more to say. A last smile. A final whispered kiss. Then Clare turned and tramped slowly down the stairwell and out into the street.

Inside the flat, Montse lifted the needle back to the beginning of the record. Orquesta Demon's Jazz. Their tune for evermore.

Outside, it was now almost dark. Clare crossed over to the far side of the road before looking back to see Montse standing at the window in her dressing gown. For a brief moment, they held each other's gaze across the crowded pavement, the smell of roasting peanuts billowing up from a kerb side brazier; Clare uneasily reminded of the ancient Greek legend of Orpheus and Eurydice – Orpheus's journey into the underworld to rescue his dead lover – morbidly recalling the end of the legend, an end conveniently overlooked in the popular books; Orpheus's body torn to pieces by wild dogs, his remains being picked over by scavenging birds.

Clare returned to the Oriente to find Jordan's men waiting for him in the lobby. As he knew they would be. Scarface and one other he hadn't seen before; tall, thin, an ill-fitting suit. They moved quickly. Angry. No attempt at civility. Not even a sardonic grin as they grabbed hold of his arms and hauled him across to the lifts, almost colliding with a French couple emerging dressed for dinner. *'Bon soir.'*

Scarface hit the basement button. *Going down.*

They took him to the laundry room. The airless, deserted underbelly of the hotel where even the cries of the dead would go unheeded. Here, they set about him with their fists. Expertly. Without menace. A job that needed doing. Scarface holding, thin friend punching. And vice versa.

Enough! Clare silently screamed.

They left him gasping on the floor. Spitting blood. The worst of the pain in his kidneys and his foot; they'd taken special care to grind their boots into his wound. Clare crawled over to a spilt laundry basket and curled up in the dirty linen, knees drawn into his stomach, gently rocking like a baby with colic.

It was the cigarette smoke that dragged him back from whatever black hole he'd drifted into. Primeros. 'Where is he?' It took Clare a moment to realise that Jordan was talking to him, then a moment longer to muster the strength to speak. 'Who?' he croaked.

'Picasso.'

'Picasso?'

'Where is he?'

'I don't know –'

Scarface hit him again. Fist to throat. Arm reaching out to haul him to his feet. Dragging him across the room. Head smashed against the wall. Clare fell to the floor in a heap, retching violently. 'Where were you this evening?' Jordan walked over to where he lay. Glacial. Wreathed in cigarette smoke.

Clare coughed, eyes swimming from the hurt; his vision clouded by the green glare of the neon strip reflecting off the tiles. *All that mattered was to keep Montse's name out of it.* Jordan's finely polished brown shoe planted itself by the bridge of his nose. 'Where were you this evening?' he asked again, his voice laced with quiet menace.

'I went back to get Holdsworth's car ...' Clare coughed blood. 'I hoped you hadn't got round to moving it yet. After what happened to Holdsworth and Stewart ... I had to ... I just wanted to get away ...'

'We found these in his pocket.' Scarface handed Jordan the keys to the Crossley, taken from him during the beating. *A corroboration of sorts.*

'Where's Picasso?' Jordan asked again.

Clare felt the metallic rim of a gun barrel being pressed against the back of his head. 'I don't know!' he said. 'I told you – I don't know.'

Jordan was losing patience. 'One last time. Where is he?'

'The voice on the phone,' Clare stuttered. *He had to give Jordan something.* 'The woman who rang me yesterday. It was Margarita Mirabel. Capdevila's assistant at the gallery. He uses her as his courier ...'

A beat. Then Jordan lowered his gun. 'Take him outside.'

The black Hispano-Suizo was waiting for them at the rear of the hotel, the door held open as Clare was roughly bundled onto the back seat, sandwiched between Scarface and his thin looking friend, now accorded the name Jorge, as in 'Jorge, open the window.'

Jordan sat in the front. No-one spoke. They were taking him to La Rabrasada – Clare was sure of it. A quick bullet in the back of the head. A shallow grave in the pine trees.

Outside La Luna, Clare glimpsed the proprietor, trademark toothpick between his lips, taking orders for dinner. In the worst days of the war, the bodies on the La Rabrasada road were so numerous that the authorities had been compelled to dump them in a mass grave.

The Hispano-Suizo slowed as it passed the restaurant, then swung left out of the square, to Clare's relief steering west up the Ronda Universitat.

So maybe they weren't heading for La Rabrasada. Maybe they weren't going to kill him. Not yet.

Jordan lit a cigarette. The way he struck the match – holding it up to his eyes and nudging the end of his cigarette into the flame – reminded Clare of an old comrade from the war. A clerk from Carlisle, Gerry Coney. The first time they were hit by enemy bombers, it was Coney who'd made them all find a piece of wood – six inches long and a quarter of an inch thick – a fine stout twig should do the job he'd told them, something to bite into while the bombs fell, a good way to avoid shell shock. Clare had been as sceptical as the rest of them, but for whatever reason, theirs was the only platoon that day not to suffer shell shock.

Jordan dropped the spent match into the ashtray, the open window sucking the smoke from his cigarette straight back into Clare's face, causing him to vomit again, coughing what remained of his guts onto the floor.

Five minutes later, the car pulled into a quiet side street and killed its lights. At a guess, Clare assumed they were parked somewhere near Sants station; dimly he'd been aware of passing through Plaça Espanya, the laser beams from the Poble Olimpic reflected in the car window.

From an upstairs window, came the sound of a young woman being given a singing lesson, *Un Bel di, vedromo* from Madame Butterfly.

'Vedi? E venuto!

Io non gli scendo incontro ...'

Clare had heard better.

Inside the car they waited in silence. Ten minutes passed. Then a tan T48 Hispano-Suizo pulled in behind them.

'Out!' Scarface held open the door.

They crossed the street, following Jordan through a narrow passageway into a small, paved square – Plaça Osca. At either end of the open space, people were eating and drinking, a gaggle of girls playing hopscotch under an ancient acacia tree, their brothers chasing an old leather football up and down the square, a youthful terrier snapping at their heels.

An eerie silence descended over the square as the SIM agents converged on an innocuous looking, rust coloured door next to the hairdressers. Only an old man on a bench feeding bread crumbs to the birds seemed not to notice.

There was a light on in the first floor. Jordan hammered on the door. Hard and insistent. 'Open up!'

A terrified face appeared in the window. A grey haired man in a white vest. Moments later he was at the door, a grubby jacket pulled over his chest.

'Señora Mirabel?' Jordan asked.

'Second floor.' The man pointed to the ceiling; relief that they hadn't come for him.

The SIM agents drew their guns, Jordan taking the time to light himself another cigarette as he and Clare followed them up the narrow staircase.

'Shit!' The lead SIM agent lashed out in frustration as he hit the landing. 'The fucking bitch!'

Margarita's apartment was locked. The heavy wooden door reinforced with steel.

'If you need a key,' the man from downstairs ventured. 'The guy who runs the paint shop two doors down – she usually leaves a spare set with him.'

Five minutes later, they were inside. Two days too late. Margarita had fled the coop, evidently intent on being away for some time. The windows were sealed, the furniture draped in sheets, and the kitchen cupboards cleared of all perishables.

As the SIM began their search of the apartment, Jordan led Clare into the bedroom, simply furnished with a heavy oak *armoire* and a cheap, mass produced dressing table; the artwork on the wall religious, part popular reproduction, part original painting.

On the bedside table, there were two photographs. One of Margarita on her wedding day; her husband, a stern faced man with a moustache and brilliantined hair, at least twenty years her senior. The other was of a priest, a young man in his twenties, pale skinned and fleshy necked.

Jordan picked up the photograph. 'Recognise him?'

Clare nodded. 'That's her son. Jesus. I met him a couple of times in Paris. He was staying with Capdevila.'

Jordan ripped open the back of the frame and removed the photograph.

'Hey, Major.' One of Jordan's agents poked his head round the corner. 'In the kitchen. We've got something.'

Jordan followed him through to a pokey, airless room at the back of the flat. Taped to the underside of the sink, his men had found a white canvas bag. Inside were a box of bullets, a stack of Nationalist pamphlets and a medal – the Grand Cross of the Order of Isabella the Catholic.

Jordan picked up one of the bullets. '9mm. Most probably a Walther P38. Any sign of the gun?'

The agent shook his head. 'She must have taken it with her.'

Jordan turned to Clare. 'If she calls again. Tell her you want a meeting.'

Clare nodded. Faint with relief. *They weren't going to kill him tonight.*

Jordan stubbed out his cigarette. 'You've got forty-eight hours.'

CHAPTER 17

Friday 9th August, 1940

Programme of the XIIth Olympiad *Fencing, Yachting, Swimming, Equestrian Sports, Rowing, Basketball, Boxing, Hockey.*

Jean Patou. En Provence. Contains pure extracts of lavender, larkspur and malva flowers … Clare poured the whole bottle into the bath, then lay for an hour in the hot water feeling much as he had after that first lull at Jarama, unable to think, dulled by the immediate needs of the body. He'd slept only intermittently. Awake at two, awake when a truck stopped outside the hotel to make an early delivery, and awake at first light when, for the third morning in a row, he'd given up trying to sleep and run himself a bath.

Forty-eight hours. Two days. Slowly, Clare felt his fear returning. A good thing, he tried to tell himself. If nothing else, it meant he was winning back control of his body.

This morning, the brutes were out in force. One in the lobby, one in the breakfast room, a third loitering by the telephones. Clare took a seat at a table by the window and ordered eggs, bacon and coffee. Lots of it. Then picked up the newspaper, noticing a photograph of Picasso and the Interior Minister on the front page, purportedly taken yesterday at about the same time Jordan must have discovered him missing.

The cover up had already begun.

The waiter brought him a pot of coffee. Clare added milk and took a sip, feeling the caffeine course through his veins.

Then it hit him. That he knew where Margarita must be. And Picasso too. Supposing, that is, they were together and still in the city. 'Carrer Fusina, 35,' Clare telephoned Jordan directly after breakfast and gave him the address.

Twenty minutes later, the SIM chief was with him. It was not something Clare felt especially good about. But what choice did he have? His only option now was to survive for as long as he could. Pray for Shaw and the arrival of the 7th Cavalry.

They met in Clare's room, two of the brutes posted guard outside whilst they talked. Jordan stood by the window, chain smoking Primeros, as he detailed exactly what it was he now wanted Clare to do. 'Tell them you've got the green light to get Picasso out of the country. I want you to get close to them. I want names and faces. A list of who's involved.' He made no reference to the events of the previous evening. 'I want to know where they're hiding him.'

And you want that key, Clare reckoned to himself.

Jordan stepped away from the window, signalling to his men that he was ready to leave. 'If you'd only told me about Capdevila's safe house earlier.' He regarded Clare as he might some wayward child. 'It would have saved you a lot of trouble.'

Clare didn't doubt it. But then, nor did he care. For Jordan had just told him something far more important.

The door fell shut. Clare poured himself a glass of water and stood at the window, watching the play of the sun on the trees, the dappled awning of a streetside café, the birds flitting from branch to branch; an unremarkable, sentimental snapshot of life on the Ramblas that left him feeling strangely uplifted. Jordan hadn't known about Capdevila's safe house on Carrer Fusina. So Montse hadn't told him. She hadn't betrayed him. She hadn't been lying when she'd told him he could trust her, when she said she still loved him.

Clare closed the window and placed the glass back on the bedside table. In his book, that was worth a whole world of trouble.

The weather forecast had predicted a cloudy start to the day, but as Clare emerged from the hotel he encountered a blue sky. Bright and clear.

He walked slowly up the Ramblas, easing the stiffness from his limbs, the thread of a thousand stories, maybe even as desperate as his own, entwined in its tangled knot of bars, cafés and pavement rendezvous; reflected in the hardened face of a back street prostitute, the starved eyes of a young boy looking for a dropped coin or a left packet of cigarettes, the lascivious attentions of a sharp suit towards his trophy mistress.

Out of curiosity, he stopped at a news stand and looked for a copy of *The Times*. The most recent edition they had was from Tuesday – too old to include his piece on Picasso – but he bought it anyway, then hailed a taxi.

Up ahead, the traffic was stopped for a passing parade of Young Communists. Clare unfolded the newspaper. Once again, Winston Churchill had stolen the headlines with a thunderous speech against Hitler's designs on the Sudetanland delivered to the Birmingham Conservative Association, the full text of which was reported on page 5. The Prime Minister, Neville Chamberlain, had described the speech as unhelpful given the delicate state of international relations.

The taxi dropped Clare off by the Mercat del Born alongside a horse and cart. The horse – an old grey – was eating from a nose bag, ankle deep in pigeons. On the back of the cart lay a sleeping dog, its head burrowed under a foreleg. On another day, Clare would have stopped to take a photograph; it was the kind of picture the cheap end of the *Weekly Illustrateds* paid good money for.

Clare crossed the corner of the market to Carrer Fusina. The house stood towards the centre of the block, five storeys high, its dark façade stepped with wrought iron balconies, coloured with potted flowers and a tumbling fall of jasmine.

Outside, a pretty young girl was cleaning the steps. Clare rang the bell. Three times in quick succession – as he'd done before – then stepped back into the road so that he could be seen from upstairs, so that Margarita would know it was him.

Almost immediately, the door clicked open. 'Morning, Sir.' The cleaning girl stood back to let him pass.

'Good morning.' Clare hurried inside, a quick glance at his watch telling him it was not quite nine thirty.

'What are you doing here?' Margarita was waiting for him at the top of the stairs, dressed in black, a beige, floral patterned scarf tied somewhat incongruously over her head.

'Rafael sent me. There's been a change of plan.' Clare had rehearsed his story during the short walk from the market. 'You're to let Picasso know we're ready to go. Tonight.'

'Picasso?' Margarita hurried him inside, sliding a heavy bolt across the lock.

Clare caught the surprise in her voice. 'Rafael wants you to get a message to him.'

'To Picasso?'

'That's what he said.'

Margarita eyed him suspiciously. 'You say you've spoken to him?'

'To Rafael? Yes.'

Margarita looked doubtful. 'Where?'

'On the telephone. He called me from France.'

'From Lourdes?'

'I don't know. He didn't say.' Clare hadn't imagined he'd have to elaborate any further.

'What did he say?'

'Just to come here and give you the message. He said you'd know what to do.'

Margarita walked over to the window and looked out across the street. 'Either you're lying or it wasn't Rafael you spoke to.'

'It was definitely him.' Clare stuck to his story.

'How did he sound?'

'Like normal.'

'Not stressed?'

'Not that I could tell.'

'How did he address you?'

'What do you mean?'

'What name did he use?'

'Richard.'

'Was that usual?'

'Yes.'

Margarita drew back from the window. There was no one outside – at least not that she could see – although Clare didn't doubt for a moment that Jordan had the house surrounded. 'Rafael and Pablo don't speak to each other,' she said matter-of-factly. 'They are no longer friends.'

For a moment Clare wasn't sure he'd heard her right.

'They haven't spoken for over a year.'

'But Rafael told me Picasso wanted to defect. Two weeks ago. At the gallery. I handed you an envelope to give to him. Inside was a letter for Picasso ...'

'He never received it,' Margarita cut him short.

'But Rafael said he'd given it to him.'

'Impossible.'

'How can you be so sure?'

'Because Rafael asked me to deliver it to someone else.'

'Who?'

'Alicia Sol.'

The name meant nothing to him. 'Do you have an address?'

Margarita nodded. '21, Avenida de Tibidabo.' She gave the Castilian appellation despite the fact that since the end of the war all street names and road signs had been translated into Catalan.

'But then – what about Picasso?' Clare didn't understand. 'Why would Rafael tell me he wanted to defect?'

'I told you.' Margarita pulled the shutter down over the window. 'Rafael and Pablo are no longer friends.' Somehow she contrived to make it sound as if she were talking about a small child who no longer liked a favourite food. 'After the war – when Rafael came back from France, Pablo accused him of stealing some of his pictures. It was the last time they spoke.'

'Did he?'

'Did he what?'

'Steal the pictures?'

'No. Of course not.'

'The other day at Café Zurich,' Clare was guessing now, 'after we spoke on the phone. Rafael asked you to do something for him, didn't he? Once you knew he was safe.'

Margarita poured herself a glass of water. 'For my digestion,' she said, taking a coloured pill from a tin box and swallowing it.

'Please, Margarita, it's important.'

Margarita hesitated, instinctively touching her hand to the silver crucifix that hung round her neck, then, as if she'd made up her mind, said, 'He asked me to put an advertisement in the paper.'

'A message to someone?' Clare hazarded another guess.

'Possibly.'

'Who?'

'I don't know. He didn't tell me.'

'What did it say?'

Margarita opened a drawer and brought out a copy of yesterday's *La Vanguardia*. 'Here,' she said, pointing to a small notice in the personal ads section – *Owner sought for collection of African parrots. Only serious bird lovers need apply. PO Box 150.*

'That's it?'

'Yes.'

'P.O. Box 150?'

'It doesn't exist.'

The telephone rang. Margarita crossed over to the other side of the room to answer it. Clare picked up the paper. *Alicia Sol. African parrots.* None of it made any sense. But at least he now had an address. A friend of Capdevila's. Someone who could possibly help him if he could only give Jordan the slip.

Margarita stood with her back to him, speaking in a low, guarded voice, so it was only when she replaced the receiver and turned to face him that Clare realised there was something wrong. 'It's the SIM,' Margarita said quietly. 'Outside. They must have followed you here.'

'Where?' Clare moved swiftly towards the window, anything to avoid having to meet her eye. 'I can't see anyone.' *It was true – he couldn't.* 'Are you sure?'

'Yes.'

Clare turned back to face Margarita to see her standing by the *petit bureau*; a panel twisted open to reveal a secret drawer. A gun in her hand.

Clare froze.

'You must leave. Over the roof. There's a way down by the cinema.'

'What cinema?' Clare had assumed she was about to shoot him.

'You'll have to jump.' Margarita seemed not to have heard him. 'There's a spot where the street narrows. By the cinema. You'll see.' She handed him the gun. A Walther P38. On the grip, a small plaque engraved with a dedication – *Ernesto Mirabel. Saludos Emilio Mola Vidal.* A gift to her husband from the Nationalist General.

'What about you?'

Again Margarita ignored him. 'Before you go,' she said. 'I have a favour to ask.'

Clare nodded. *Of course.*

'I want you to shoot me.'

'What?'

'I'm too old to jump. I would never make it and I have no wish to be captured. My son might argue the semantics. But I think even he would consider a mercy killing is not suicide.'

A mercy killing? Clare had as good as pulled the trigger the moment he rang on her doorbell.

Margarita handed him a cushion covered with a Burgundy and cream floral design. 'Place this against my head. It will help muffle the sound.'

I can't shoot you.

Margarita unfastened her silver crucifix and handed it to him. 'When you see my son, please give this to him.' A last request. Calmly delivered.

All Clare could do was nod weakly.

Margarita caught the look in his eyes. 'Please don't worry for me. I have been waiting for this moment a long time.' She dropped to her knees, and pressing her hands together, began to pray, '*Pater noster, qui es in caelis. Sanctificetur nomen tuum. Adveniat regnum tuum. Fiat voluntas tua, sicut in caelo et in terra.*'

Clare held the cushion against her face.

'*Panem nostrum quotidianum da nobis hodie, et dimitte nobis debita nostra sicut et nos dimittimus debitoribus nostris.*'

Slipped the safety catch.

'*Et ne nos inducas in tentationem …*'

And pulled the trigger. *Amen.* As a mess of splintered bone, blood and snow white goose feathers hit the carpet.

Clare had seen men die before. One more made no difference, he coldly told himself as he pocketed Margarita's gun and found his way out onto the terrace and up onto the roof. Later there'd be time enough to reflect on what he'd done. But right now only one thing mattered.

Head for the cinema, Margarita had said. Cupping a hand over his eyes, Clare frantically scanned the skyline. The four spires of the Sagrada Familia. Montjuic. Santa Maria del Mar. The green tiled cupola of the Merce church. And then he saw it, almost directly in front of him, El Cine Royal, distinguishable only by its first two letters – CI – protruding out of a haze of rooftops, framed by the slender lines of an art deco façade.

Outside the greengrocer's shop that had been in her mother's family for generations, five year old Elvira Romeros picked a stone out of the gutter and threw it at a pigeon she'd noticed edging too close to a box of cherries. *Got you!* The pigeon leapt back with an indignant thrashing of wings. *Shoo!* Elvira ran after the bird, waving her arms and stamping loudly. *Go away!*

The pigeon at last got the message and took flight, drawing Elvira's gaze up towards the roof of the cinema, which was when she saw him – a flash across the sky, describing an arc like a falling mortar shell (she'd once witnessed an artillery bombardment over the fields outside the village where she'd spent the first year of the war, before her mother died).

Elvira thought she must have been dreaming it until she saw Clare's back leg strike the top of the parapet, and felt the crumble of masonry dust in her eyes. She wanted to shout out to her grandmother that she'd just seen a man flying across the street but she knew that her grandmother would never believe her and that in any case she was far too ancient and busy to climb the 105 steps up to the roof to go check. So Elvira said nothing. Instead she just picked up another stone from the gutter.

The next pigeon, she would hit right in the face. That would teach it a lesson.

At the end of the last century, when Barcelona's great industrialists and bankers had built their villas, many had bought plots on the tree-lined hill that later became known as Avinguda del Tibidabo, in a matter of decades transforming this cool slope into a fairy tale parade of mansions that wouldn't have looked out of place in Los Angeles.

Number 21 – the address given to Clare by Margarita – stood towards the lower end of the avenue. A Gothic weave of colonnades and towers painted pale yellow, replete with a heptagonal spire and monstrous gargoyles; between the street and the house, an emerald lawn cut with exotic shrubs and flowering cacti, shielded by high black railings and a sentry box, where two militiamen stood guard with machine guns.

Clare stood outside the gates in quiet disbelief. Parked in the driveway, he could see five chauffeur driven black T-48's. Government vehicles.

Had Margarita remembered the wrong address? Or was this her idea of a joke? A last laugh at him from beyond the grave. Revenge for the bullet he'd put through her skull?

The front door opened. A dozen suits spilled out of the house, whatever meeting they'd been attending obviously now over. But it was the man climbing into the lead limo that caught Clare's attention. Even out of uniform, there was no mistaking him. André Marty – the Butcher of Albacete.

Clare hurriedly walked on by.

In the grounds of the house next door, a gardener was raking the grass. A dark skinned, elderly man, wearing what looked like an old postman's uniform and a navy beret. 'What's all that about?' Clare gestured a thumb towards the departing convoy of Hispano-Suizos.

'Can I help you?' the gardener enquired, looking up from the lawn.

'I was just wondering who lived next door?' Clare said loudly; the man was evidently half deaf.

'Ah!' The gardener nodded, as if the same question had often occurred to him. 'It's that new minister. What's his name? I read about him in the paper yesterday.'

'Luis Cornet?' Clare ventured. He'd seen Cornet's photograph on the cover of the *La Vanguardia* in Capdevila's apartment. A rising star of the PSOE. Recently appointed Catalan Minister for Industry. Young. Good looking. Tipped to go far.

'That's the guy. Moved in a couple of months ago.' The gardener stood his rake against a palm tree and took out a packet of cigarettes, biting off the filter as a tram trundled past packed full of school children on their way up to the amusement park. 'Can't say I've ever met him. But the housekeeper – she says he's alright. For a politician.'

Clare mumbled his thanks and continued on up towards the *funicular*.

Alicia Sol. Another blank drawn. Another door shut on him.

* * * * *

'The slug was a 9mm.' The SIM forensics officer showed Jordan the bullet he'd extracted from Margarita's skull. 'A Walther P38 – I would guess.'

'Okay, Gabi. She's all yours.' Jordan gestured to the police photographer to start taking his pictures; on the far side of the room, his agents were still meticulously combing the crime scene for evidence.

Caraben energetically worked a piece of chewing gum from one side of his mouth to the other. 'You think she was done with her own gun?' He contemplated Margarita's lifeless body as he might some curiosity in a shop window.

'The way I see it …' Angel Carreto was keen to make amends for his earlier fuck up, 'the old girl rumbles Clare. She pulls a gun on him. Then gets too close. Or maybe she doesn't have the guts to do him, I don't know which, but before she knows it …' he clicked his fingers, 'Clare's got the gun and she's on the floor with a pillow to her head.'

Jordan quietly pointed out the fault in Carreto's reasoning – no sign of a struggle.

'What struggle?' Carreto made as if it were obvious. 'She's as old as my mother! Some guy does for my mother – I don't see her putting up much of a fight.'

'Smells to me like an execution.' Caraben sounded almost sorry not to have pulled the trigger himself. 'Bullet through the back of the head. It's the way I would have done it.'

'But why?' Jordan was beginning to feel like events were overtaking him and he didn't care for it.

Caraben shrugged. 'Guess that's something you should ask that bastard Englishman. Want me to put out an alert?'

'And tell people we've fucked up again?' Jordan countered dryly.

Caraben just smiled. 'Don't worry, Boss. He won't get far.'

* * * * *

A café by the funicular station. The end of the road. Shaded by jacaranda and bougainvillea, Clare sat on the terrace, looking out across the pine trees and scrub that covered the lower slopes of Tibidabo.

In the distance, the sea lay calm and hazy.

Clare finished his coffee and ordered another, clinging to the moment. The serenity of the almost empty café. The faint sound of music from the kitchen. The pregnant cat sleeping in the sun at his feet. He imagined Gerald sitting there with him, penning a farewell poem, certain that his brother would have known how to draw the right emotion from this last moment of peace. To find the words that would serve as his epitaph.

Death. It took Clare a third coffee before he was reminded of Stewart lying cold on a slab in the hospital morgue. 'We will contact your embassy. Ask them to see that the body is picked up.' The words of the hospital administrator hit him like a freight train. *'Ask them to see that the body is picked up.'* Clare glanced at his watch. It was eleven o'clock. Perhaps, he was already too late.

Hurriedly, he summoned the waiter and asked him to call a taxi. 'Hospital de Sant Pau,' he instructed the driver when it finally arrived. 'Quick.'

The pavilion that housed the morgue lay in the northeast section of the hospital gardens. Clare had the taxi drop him off half way along the street and entered by a side gate in order to avoid the main lobby. Inside the gardens, a half dozen patients were sitting in the sun, reading and smoking; Clare recognised the young man he'd seen yesterday attached to a drip, now alone with a chess board.

In the morgue, a bored young woman – dyed blond hair, painted lips and dull eyes – sat slumped at the front desk, filing her nails, a half written letter stuck in her ancient typewriter. Presenting his press card, Clare announced himself as an attaché from the British Embassy, come to deal with the body of a Mr Peter Stewart, deceased yesterday, Thursday 7th August, in a car accident. The receptionist stifled a yawn. 'Your colleague arrived twenty minutes ago,' she said, pointing to a well used set of swing doors through which he'd just passed. 'First floor. Second on the right.'

So he wasn't too late after all. 'Thank you,' he smiled.

'You're welcome.' The receptionist returned to her unfinished letter – *clack, clack, clack* – her head sinking wearily, even as her fingers groped for the keys.

Clare went back outside and found himself a bench in the sun. For a few blissful minutes, he allowed his thoughts to drift, as ever towards Montse. The memory of her touch. The playful inflection of her voice. The smile in her eyes watching him, watching her, coloured now by the certainty that she hadn't betrayed him.

Clare was expecting a man – which is why he almost missed her – initially mistaking the well dressed woman being courteously escorted from the building to be just another visitor. She was wearing a navy, mid-calf length skirt with a well cut jacket and beret to match. Dark hair. Just a dab of make-up. In her left hand, a scuffed leather document case. In her right, a recently lit cigarette. 'Thank you, Miss Booth,' he heard the director say, 'Have a safe trip,' then, 'I won't be accompanying the coffin,' Clare caught the English accent in her reply and jumped to his feet.

'But you'll be at the airport?' the director wanted to know.

'Of course.'

'Your name's on the paperwork,' the director explained. 'Without your signature, they won't release the body.'

'I'll be there,' Kathleen assured him as they shook hands and parted.

Keeping his distance, Clare discreetly followed her across the hospital gardens and out onto the street.

'Miss Booth?' Clare waited for Kathleen to hail a taxi before making his move.

'Yes?' The sun caught the high line of Kathleen's cheek bone as she swung round to face him.

'My name is Richard Clare. I need to speak to you. I need your help.'

If Kathleen was surprised, she didn't show it. 'Get in,' she said, as the taxi drew up alongside them.

'The SIM want me dead. I have to get out of the country. There's a man named Shaw…'

'Now!' Kathleen held the door open for him.

Clare did as he was told.

'Valencia y Passeig de Gracia,' Kathleen instructed the driver as she climbed in beside him.

Clare threw Kathleen a discreet glance as if to say 'what now?' Wondering who she was. How much she knew. Noticing the embossed letters on her document case – *KB*.

'The K stands for Kathleen,' she said matter-of-factly, taking a powder box from her handbag, angling the mirror so as to be able to see out of the back window. 'Are you alone?'

'There's no-one following me if that's what you mean.'

Kathleen snapped the powder box shut. Satisfied, it seemed.

The journey passed in silence. *Not in front of the driver*, the unspoken instruction. Not until they reached Viajes Sauledo – temporary home to the British Passport Office, Kathleen explained as she unlocked the door and ushered him inside – did she seem to relax. 'I'm sorry if I seemed rude back there.' She draped her jacket over the back of a chair. 'But you can't be too careful. Care for a drink?' She vanished into the back room to fetch him one. 'There's beer or lemonade. Or water if you'd prefer?'

'Beer will do fine, thanks.' Clare sneezed. There was a vague smell of dust about the place. A hint of sour milk despite the open window held in place by a can of sardines.

Kathleen returned with a gun. A pistol trained right at his midriff. 'Put your hands on the table,' she said – it took Clare a moment to register that she was talking to him – 'Spread your legs. Slowly. So I can see you.'

Clare could tell she was frightened. But also that she knew how to fire a gun. The safety catch was off. Her grip straight out of training school. 'Whatever you're thinking, you've got it wrong,' he said in as unemotional and calm a voice as he could muster. 'I'm British. I need to get back home. We're on the same side.'

'Quiet. Do as I say.' Kathleen kept her eyes firmly on his. 'Empty your pockets. Everything. On the table.'

Slowly – starting with his breast pocket – Clare obliged, taking out his press card, pen and notebook, Holdsworth's wallet …

Kathleen stopped. Stared. Hardly able to speak. 'Where did you get that?' she gasped.

'It belonged to a man called Holdsworth …'

'Belonged?' Kathleen steadied herself against the table, jabbing her gun up hard against Clare's face. 'What are you saying? Is he dead? He went to meet you! You killed him! Didn't you?'

'No. I didn't.' For a moment, it seemed to Clare that she was going to pull the trigger.

'Then who did?'

'The SIM.'

'You're lying.'

'No, I'm not. I was there. In his car. He was shot by two men on a motorcycle. They must have followed us from the airport.'

'And they let you walk free?'

'Yes …'

'I don't believe you …' She wanted to kill him. Make him suffer. This man who had Philip's wallet. Protruding from the fold was the receipt from their last meal together at the Café Opera. She'd had sole meunier, he'd had steak, and an isle flottante for dessert which they'd shared.

'There's a man called Shaw.' Clare discreetly slipped his hand into his pocket, feeling for Margarita's gun. 'In London … He works for SIS. Ask him.'

'You killed him.' Kathleen wasn't listening.

Clare eased off the safety catch.

'Did you look him in the eye before you shot him? Or did you kill him from behind? He said it might be a trap.' She was sobbing now. Hysterical. 'I didn't want him to go. I told him to–'

Clare pulled the trigger. *Before she did.*

At the top of the building, too deaf to hear the shot, Sauledo's aunt turned the page of her book. A translation of William Faulkner's *As I lay dying*. Downstairs, Kathleen lay sprawled across the floor. Her gun spun from her hand. A bullet sized hole in her right shoulder. 'I'm not going to hurt you,' Clare heard himself say, as he lifted his hand from his pocket and laid Margarita's gun on the table.

Kathleen groaned. Clare knelt down to inspect the wound, gently tearing away the cloth from her shoulder. The bullet had passed clean through the muscle. He told her she was lucky. That he was sorry he'd shot her. And that hers wasn't the first wound he'd dressed.

She told him to go fuck himself.

Clare found a first aid kit in the cupboard and did what he could, then fetched a glass of water from the sink. 'It'll do you good,' he said, adding a shot of whisky from a bottle on the side.

This time, she accepted without protest.

'Where do you keep the passports?' Clare knew it was only a matter of time before Kathleen's colleagues began to question where she was. 'I need to know.'

'In the safe. But you're wasting your time. Holdsworth has the key.'

'You're a bad liar.' Clare discovered what he was looking for in her handbag, along with Kathleen's identity card and a room receipt from the Hotel Falcon.

Inside the safe, he found a cardboard box full of unissued passports.

'Without photographs – they're useless,' Kathleen said sourly. Even as a small child, she'd never been a good loser.

'Get up.'

'Why? What are you going to do to me?' Now she was frightened.

'In there.' Clare pointed to the store cupboard.

'No!'

Clare offered her his hand. 'I won't hurt you. I promise.'

'Go to hell!' she sneered.

Clare took the rear exit out of the building, back onto the street by way of an interior yard littered with cast-off junk, abandoned chairs and rusted filing cabinets. A shoe shine boy pitched outside the Credit Lyonnais hailed him with a grin and the opening lines to a well practised patter. 'Not now,' Clare cut him short. He'd left Kathleen locked inside the store cupboard with a glass of water, a three week old copy of *Picture Post*, and the radio switched on to drown out any cries for help. 'Two minutes,' the boy hit back. 'You don't like. You don't pay.'

Clare crossed over to the other side of the street. *Not now*.

On the corner of Pau Claris and Corsega, he found a café in which to rest up for a few minutes, full of well heeled tourists and men in blazers; the grey haired cogs of the Olympic movement. He ordered a *carajillo* – a black coffee laced with brandy – and bagged himself a table at the back of the room, luxuriating in the cool breeze of the overhead fans as waiters busied themselves between the tables, serving cups of steaming, thick hot chocolate, long glasses of ice tea and exotic aperitifs. A world apart from the post war ruin so evident on the streets outside.

Montjuic. Not for the first time today, Clare dragged his mind back to the events of last Sunday morning. The mountainside full of soldiers lying in wait with their machine guns. In light of this morning's interview – Jordan's genuine surprise at being told about the safe house on Carrer Fusina – Clare reasoned he could now safely draw two conclusions.

One: neither himself, Capdevila, or Markham had been followed by the SIM to Carrer Fusina.

Therefore ...

Two: the leak must have emanated from British Intelligence. Someone in Madrid, London, or Barcelona, had been keeping Jordan informed of his every move. Not Markham. Nor Holdsworth. Nor Stewart. Because they were all dead. But someone else. Someone prepared to kill to cover their tracks.

And there, Clare's reasoning ran dry. Too tired to think anymore, he drained his cup of coffee and gathered up his jacket. 'All yours,' he told a couple next door, who were eager to add his chair to their table. '*Bon profit.*'

Wearily, he walked over to the bar and stood in line for the phone behind a businessman from Madrid who was busy sorting out the details of his next meeting, something to do with a consignment of engine parts. A clock above the mirror read one fifty-six. Time was slipping away. The day becoming like a fast ride through a series of dark tunnels. Intense, rapid bursts of light, staccato moments of clarity, followed by long stretches of blind fumbling and confusion, which was where Clare felt himself heading again now as he picked up the receiver – the Madrileno having concluded his business – and dialled the number given to him earlier by Jordan. Seconds later, he was connected. 'I'm in a bar. I can't talk long,' he said, for once his anxiety playing in his favour; he needed Jordan to think he was taking a risk in calling. 'I have to be quick.'

'Where are you?' Jordan sounded no less anxious.

'Somewhere up town. I'm not sure where.'

'What happened this morning at the apartment?'

'Tomorrow. At 8.00pm.' Clare ignored him. 'I'm meeting a man at Café Zurich. He'll take me to Picasso.'

'I have to talk to you,' Jordan interrupted. 'Face to face.'

'Impossible.' Clare was looking to buy himself some time; to get Jordan off his back until he could escape the country on Kathleen's passports. 'I'm with them now.'

'With who?'

'His name's Enrique. He was with Margarita this morning. When he saw you guys outside the house he shot her. To stop her talking,' Clare added, pausing for effect. 'I've got to go now. He's coming back. Tomorrow. Eight o'clock. Café Zurich.' Clare cut the line and replaced the receiver, leaving Jordan's protestations hanging mid-sentence.

The clock struck two. He had thirty hours to make it across the border.

* * * * *

Passeig de Gracia, 67. A little less than a quarter of a mile away, Jordan turned to his assistant. 'Does the name Enrique mean anything to you?'

The man shook his head.

'I want you to go through the files. Capdevila's known contacts. Picasso's too.'

'What am I looking for?' The assistant didn't like the sound of Jordan's voice.

'A name.'

'Real or *nom de guerre*?'

'I don't know.' And that was the problem. He really didn't. But he needed an answer and fast. Friends in the NKVD were already warning him that André Marty was agitating for his dismissal. A certain death sentence. Unless he could somehow find a way to turn the tables on his boss.

* * * * *

At Radio Barcelona, Miguel de Silva's morning programme was coming to an end, his last tune a favourite old foxtrot, *Flor de Pomer*. Miguel slid the record from its sleeve, wiped his cuff over the vinyl and placed it on the turntable. A signature exit – played every week – reminding him and his audience of the good times before the war. Carefree nights at La Paloma. Chocolate and churros on the way home. Making love far into the morning and beyond.

Above the studio door, a red light spelt out the words "ON AIR". Clare stood outside waiting for the programme to finish, a mental image of Miguel on the other side of the door surrounded by his precious discs, heels on the table, tapping out a step he'd danced a hundred times before; he and Beatriz, the waitress at Café Luna, one eye busted by a sailor's fist, one arm skewed from an argument with a car. Beatriz – his muse, his lover and his ruin.

The red light switched to green. Programme over. Clare turned the door handle and entered the studio. 'Richard!' Miguel looked up in surprise from his "throne", a tatty, coffee stained old swivel chair he'd liberated from the pavement one night on his way home from the bar. 'Werner said you were in town.' They embraced. Warmly. There'd never been any complications between the two of them, not like it had sometimes been with Werner. Miguel was always welcoming, nicotine stained teeth bared in a broad smile, an agreeable twinkle that made a mockery of the greying hair and deep lines that described his face. 'How's Montse?' he grinned. 'You two together again?'

Clare smiled. 'We're working on it.'

'That's good. You were always made for each other.' Miguel carefully returned his beloved foxtrot to its well worn sleeve. 'You look well,' he said.

'You too,' Clare told him. They were both lying. Like so many in the city, Miguel looked tired, gaunt and undernourished. And Clare, well, he looked like shit and he knew it.

'I'm on my way to La Luna,' Miguel said. 'Why don't you join me?'

'Another time,' Clare regretted. 'I have to be somewhere by three.'

'Too bad. Beatriz would have liked to have seen you.'

Clare was sorry too. He'd have liked to have seen Beatriz; her and Miguel's story was part of station lore. How every day Miguel had gone for lunch at Café Luna, and how every day Beatriz had made him wait, way longer than she made anybody else wait; the worst service in town Miguel used to describe it, so bad that one day he was moved to confront her. 'Why so slow? Why always me?' 'Because I like the look of your face, angel,' she'd told him. 'I like having you around.' And since then, he had been. Sort of. 'Tell her next time,' Clare said. 'You know how it is.'

Miguel did. 'So amigo – if not lunch, what is it you want from me?'

'A favour,' Clare confessed.

Miguel lit a cigarette. 'You being watched?'

'No.'

'That's good.' He opened his locker and took out his jacket. 'What kind of favour?'

'A few minutes in Personnel. There are some old files I need to check out.'

Miguel's smile faded. Clare took out 200 pesetas from his wallet and placed it on the table. 'Ten minutes. That's all.' Miguel hesitated. There was a half of him that was curious to know what was going on, and a half that wasn't. 'You want more?' Clare reached for his wallet again.

'No, no. The pasta's fine.' Miguel swept the money into his pocket. 'You remember Irina?'

Clare recalled a pretty, plump-faced eighteen year old in Personnel. 'Sure.'

'She and I – we see each other sometimes, when Beatriz is in one of her moods.' Clare wondered if there was a woman under thirty at the station who hadn't shared Miguel's bed. 'I'll take her to lunch for you. You're in luck. That shit boss of hers is away on holiday.'

'Ignacio?'

Miguel nodded. 'But just ten minutes – okay?'

'You have my word.'

'And mind no-one clocks you.'

'They won't. Send my love to Beatriz.'

'I will.' Miguel gave him a friendly pat on the shoulder. 'Stay well, amigo.'

Clare found Personnel empty, just as Miguel had promised. On the wall, by a notice advising what to do in the event of a fire, someone had pinned up a picture of Dolores Del Rio. Scrawled in lipstick, a note left on one of the desks read – *Back soon.*

Unfamiliar with the layout of the office, it took Clare a few minutes to find what he was looking for, to work out that employees who'd worked at the station post 1936 enjoyed a different system to those who'd been hired before.

Clare, Richard. The file was so slim he almost missed it. Inside – just a half dozen sheets of papers. His personal details. A contract signed in October 1937, terminated the following February. The station manager's assessment – *A bright beginning. Initial promise failed to materialise. Heart elsewhere.*

A fair appraisal, Clare reckoned as he dug out a pair of scissors from the drawer and carefully cut out the black and white photograph affixed to the top right hand corner of the file, 3.5cms X 4.5cms, as specified by His Majesty's Passport Office.

The second file proved more problematic. *Bloch, Werner.* In the space where Werner's records should have been, there was just a slip of paper. A memo noting that the file had been requested by the SIM. *Department of Internal Security – 8th July 1940. In accordance with directive 31C.*

Clare sneezed. His ten minutes were now almost up.

Outside, he could hear the station breaking for lunch. Voices shouting at one another down the corridor – 'Hold up!' 'Just a minute!' 'I'll be with you!'

He'd done what he could for Werner.

But as he made a move for the door, Clare noticed a half dozen unopened letters lying on the table – one franked with the official stamp of the Servicio de Investigacion Militar. On an impulse, he opened it. Inside was a brief, typed letter from the Department of Internal Security explaining that they were returning Werner's records – *Particulars noted. Thank you.*

It seemed the Gods were with Werner, after all.

Hastily, Clare cut out Werner's photograph and placed it in his wallet, then buried the file deep in a folder entitled *Employees' allowances, 1935*. By the time anyone thought to question its whereabouts, Werner would be toasting his escape with a glass of French wine, safely across the border on one of Kathleen's passports, or just another SIM statistic. A nameless body on the side of the road to La Rabrasada.

The whole business had taken Clare less than half an hour, from the moment he first entered the radio station to the moment he walked back out onto Plaça Catalunya.

Outside Café Luna, a street musician was packing up his violin, a ritual being mirrored the length and breadth of the Ramblas as minds turned away from the travails of the morning and towards thoughts of food and rest. Already Miguel and Irina would be back in Miguel's apartment, stripped naked and making love, a thought which prompted Clare to remember how in the early days he'd used to rush home to Montse too.

Heart elsewhere. The station manager hadn't been wrong.

* * * * *

Passeig de Gracia, 67. 2.15pm. Alone in his office, Jordan poured himself a glass of Vichy Catalan. Generally, he drank only after eating in order to aid his digestion, but today he was in no mood for food. The dead body in Carrer Fusina. Clare's garbled phone call. The rendezvous at Café Zurich. It wasn't how he'd envisaged the end game unfolding.

And still, there was no sign of Picasso.

Jordan took a sip of mineral water and picked up the phone. It was time to bring his Queen into play.

* * * * *

Viajes Sauledo. 3.30pm. Clare returned to find the passport office exactly as he'd left it; the radio tuned to Radio Barcelona, Kathleen slumped against the wall of the cupboard, her bandage encrusted with blood. 'I didn't think you'd come back,' she glowered.

Clare ignored her. 'How's the shoulder?'

'It hurts.'

'Try a couple of these.' He gave her a bottle of aspirin, then went into the kitchen to fetch some water. 'How long do you intend keeping me here?' Kathleen's voice followed him from the office.

'As soon as I'm over the border, I'll phone the authorities.' Clare returned with a glass, waited for her to swallow the pills, then when she was ready, said, 'I need you to issue me with three passports.'

'Do you have photographs?' Kathleen was still angry at herself for not having searched him properly when she'd had the chance, for allowing herself to become distracted by Holdsworth's wallet.

'Right here.' Clare had arranged everything she might need on the desk. A stamp, bottle of glue, fountain pen, blotting paper and ink. 'This is the first one.' He took a passport sized photograph of Montse from his wallet. A picture he'd had for years.

'Your girlfriend?'

Clare ignored the jibe. 'Her name is Lena Wickham. Wickham with an "h". Née Cruz. Born April 14th 1915. Havana, Cuba.' On the way back from the radio station, he'd sketched out a rudimentary cover story that had Montse travelling as his Cuban born wife, and Werner as her elder brother.

Kathleen took up her pen. Then – a click. The faint rattle of glass as someone tried the front door.

Clare looked to Kathleen. 'Are you expecting anyone?'

Kathleen shook her head. *No. She wasn't.*

Clare put a finger to his lips and drew his gun. Kathleen could read the fear in his face, certain it was reflected in her own.

Cautiously, Clare eased open the door that led back into the main shop to see two men standing on the pavement outside, a third emerging from a parked black Hispano-Suizo, his face half obscured by the brim of an olive brown fedora. Captain Caraben.

Clare shrank back into the office. 'SIM. Quick. Out the back!' But Kathleen was already ahead of him, half way across the yard. 'Stop!' Clare raised his gun, aiming at the small of her back, the sound of breaking glass from the front of the shop telling him he had only seconds to get out.

Kathleen ran on.

Clare hesitated, then lowered his gun. *What was the point? She was already gone.*

Head hunched, hands thrust into his pockets, he hurriedly followed her out onto the street, melting away into the crowd before anyone could think to challenge him.

'Coño!' Inside the travel agency, in the time it takes for an eye to blink, Caraben took in the scene. The blood on the floor. The spilt cartridge case. First aid kit. Newly opened bottle of aspirin. Three passports. And the photograph of Montse left lying on the desk.

Caraben picked up the photograph and turned it over in his hand. The face didn't register. But Caraben knew it wouldn't take them long to find her.

It never did.

It was sheer panic that took Clare back to the tennis club. The security men on the door, the journalists, the girls in the press office, any one of them might recognise him but he was no longer thinking straight. He was running scared now. Trying to get to Montse before they did. There was nothing he could do for her, of course, nothing she could do for herself, but he needed to be the one to tell her, to warn her, Montse, I've screwed up, I'm sorry.

'Off sick, honey.' A face he didn't recognise told him she'd gone home. He rang her flat – no answer. Then her parents' hotel – no answer there either. Then took a taxi to the Miramar. A nice, long, slow ride up Montjuic past the Palau National and the Olympic stadium, the dappled shadows of the roadside trees stroking the windows of the taxi, at the edge of his consciousness the fuzzy memory of a bullet-ridden bus bouncing down the hillside, his feet skipping over rocks, tripping, falling into a chasm, fingers clutching at a rain of skree.

Why the Miramar? Was it sheer instinct that had driven him here? To the edge of the cliff. To this window over the city. Clare wasn't sure. As he tumbled out of the taxi and onto the terrace, he was aware only of the city lying still before him, a pebble at the edge of the sea, cracked by the heat and awaiting night's relief. The balm of a clean, cool breeze.

In one of Clare's best stories for *The Captain*, he'd saved his hero from certain death by having him stow away on a ship under the cover of darkness. Clare fed a coin into the telescope mounted at the end of the terrace and trained it on the ships lying at anchor in the docks, no more than a few hundred yards away as the crow flew. Most were Russian; he had no intention of ending up in Sebastopol or Leningrad. But one vessel, a Turkish cargo ship, *The Tarsus*, excited his attention, the quayside crane swinging dock to deck, the ship's heavy water line and the steady flow of men traipsing up and down her gangplank, all pointing to the likelihood that she was making ready to sail.

The ship lay on the east side of the Muelle Poniente, the only point of access through a well guarded gate. But further along the waterfront, where the tourist boats offered sightseeing trips around the harbour, Clare noted a gaggle of small dinghies and row boats. *Will our hero escape the clutches of the evil police chief? Find out in next week's exciting episode!* The thought that he might steal unnoticed aboard *The Tarsus* and live to fight another day seemed insane, more preposterous even than the most far-fetched pages of *The Captain*, but from where Clare stood now, it seemed the only straw left in his grasp, then – 'Clare?' – a familiar voice hooked him out of his desperate fantasy.

'Henry!' It was Forsyth from *The Mail* – on his own, thank God – clutching a portable typewriter, flushed from his usual long lunch.

'You look terrible,' Forsyth said. 'Where have you been?'

For a brief moment, Clare toyed with the idea of telling him, but the thought of Stewart lying naked in the morgue, Holdsworth slumped against the steering wheel of his Crossley, and Margarita's brains splattered all over Capdevila's apartment, stayed him. 'It's a long story,' he muttered; those he involved in it had a habit of ending up dead.

'Let me buy you a coffee. You can tell me all about it,' Forsyth insisted. 'You look like you could do with one.'

'I'm fine. Really.'

'No. You're not.'

No. He wasn't. Forsyth was right. His mind was a muddle and he needed to sleep. 'I'm sorry. I can't involve you,' he tried to explain.

'Try me.'

'It's for your own good, Henry.'

'For Christ's sake, Clare! I'm not a child.'

Clare was too tired to argue. 'It's government business ...' he mumbled.

'You mean Official Secrets. That sort of thing?'

'Yes.'

Forsyth let out a low whistle. 'Well, I'll be damned!'

So now Forsyth knew. So now there could be no harm in asking. 'There is one thing you could do,' Clare said hesitantly. 'I need somewhere to rest. A few hours sleep. I can't go back to my room.'

'You mean – you want to use mine?'

'Just for a couple of hours.'

'Of course.' Forsyth laid a sympathetic hand on his shoulder. '*Mi casa es su casa*. As they say in these parts.'

'Thanks, Henry.' Clare felt close to collapse.

Forsyth grinned. 'Lucky you bumped into me.'

They took a taxi back into town. A few blocks short of the Oriente, Clare directed the driver to drop him off. Jordan was certain to be watching the front of the hotel but at the rear of the building, close to where the staircase came down to the breakfast room, there was a fire door. All it needed was for someone on the inside – Forsyth – to open it. 'Okay. I'll do it', Forsyth somewhat reluctantly agreed. Lending out his room was one thing, playing shadow cops and robbers with the SIM quite another. He was, after all, just a scribe. A sports hack with an average salary and too tight an expense account.

Clare waited for the taxi to drive off before continuing on towards the hotel. Mid-afternoon, there were few people around; a vagrant picking cigarette stubs from the gutter, a few children kicking a ball against the wall, a young couple kissing in the shadows, a half consumed bottle of *Valdepeñas* precariously balanced on a window ledge beside them. Nothing to excite his suspicion.

Forsyth was waiting for him by the fire door. 'You were right about the goons in the lobby,' he said uneasily. 'I counted three of the buggers.'

They took the back staircase up to the third floor. Forsyth's room was at the front of the building, the last place Jordan would think of looking for him, but even so, as they entered the room Clare switched on the radio and pulled the shutters to.

'Here – give me that.' Forsyth took Clare's jacket and hung it on the back of the door, as he did so feeling the weight of Margarita's pistol in the pocket. Clare shot him a look – *don't ask* – and wandered through to the bathroom, a quick glance at the mirror telling him nothing he didn't already know. Forsyth was right – he did look awful. Blotchy skin, bloodshot eyes, head spinning from exhaustion. The morning after a night that hadn't happened.

It was four o'clock. Clare set the alarm for eight. 'I'll be gone by nine,' he said.

Forsyth nodded. Nine was fine. Although eight would have been better. Guns unnerved him.

An awkward silence fell over the room, neither man quite knowing what to say; in two weeks all they'd really learnt of each other were the name, rank and number of civilian life. Henry Forsyth. Educated Eton (until his father's ruin in '29) and Marylebone Grammar School. Damaged by both. A loner to Clare's reckoning with a point to prove. A romantic without the temperament. Better born a Czech or a Pole, Clare's comment to Wilson a few days earlier.

Forsyth tore a fresh packet of cigarettes from the carton in his top drawer. 'I ought to get going.'

Clare took off his shoes. The wound in his left foot was beginning to seep blood again. Forsyth had already seen enough. 'Good luck,' he said, opening the door to leave, before adding somewhat hesitantly, 'See you in London.'

Clare took off his watch and laid it on the bedside table, wryly noting Forsyth's choice of reading material – *Appointment With Death* and *The Big Sleep*. Personally, he'd never got on with Agatha Christie, and as for Chandler he had yet to give him a try, although several of his friends had been badgering him to do so. Clare flicked a glance at the opening lines. *I was neat, clean, shaved and sober, and I didn't care who knew it. I was everything the well-dressed private detective ought to be*. Not bad, he thought. If I ever get out of this mess, perhaps I'll give it a go.

Clare returned the book to the bedside table and switched off the radio, already asleep by the time his head hit the pillow.

6.11pm. Two hours later. He woke to the sound of Edith Piaf. *Je n'en connais pas la fin.*

'Ha ha ha ha,
A mon amour,
Ha ha ha ha,
A toi toujours ...'

Someone had entered the room and switched on the radio. Someone was shaking his shoulder. A man. 'Wake up.' An Englishman. Not Forsyth. Nor any of the others. Yet the man's voice sounded vaguely familiar. 'Wake up, damn you.'

Clare let out a low groan and rolled over onto his other side.

'Si l'amant fut méchant pour elle,
Je veux en ignorer la fin ...'

'Sorry old man, there's no other way.' Clare came to as if he'd been shot, his face wet with water, explained by the upturned glass in the man's hand. Clare blinked. It was Shaw – 'Where the hell have you been?' – sounding exactly as he had four years ago when they'd met in the Fitzroy Tavern; that same blend of calm authority and paternal concern – 'We've been looking for you all over.' He was dressed in a light suit and white shirt, faintly mottled with patches of dried sweat. His thick, black hair was cut short and parted to the right. In the gloom, his eyes seemed as dark as dirt.

Clare drowsily groped for the sheet and wiped himself dry. 'Where's Forsyth?'

Shaw didn't answer.

Clare staggered out of bed and into the bathroom. 'I need to know what's going on,' Shaw's voice clawed at him from the bedroom.

'Holdsworth's dead.' Clare poured himself a glass of water.

'We know.'

'Stewart too.' He lifted the toilet seat.

'An unfortunate business. Our fault, I'm afraid. We should have used a professional. Someone with training.'

'Holdsworth had training. So did Markham.' All Clare could manage were a few drops.

'Two good men,' Shaw conceded. 'I don't mind telling you – it's a right hornet's nest you've stirred up here.'

Clare flushed the toilet anyway. 'How did you find me?'

'Forsyth told me you were here.' Shaw drew the blinds on the balcony, letting in a flood of sunlight.

'Forsyth! Working for SIS?'

'Good God, no!' Shaw waited for him to re-enter the bedroom before continuing. 'When we couldn't find you, we put the word about. Discreetly. If you happen to see him, leave well alone. Give us a call. That sort of thing.' He took out a packet of cigarettes. 'Mind if I smoke?'

Clare shrugged. 'It's not my room.'

'Sit down.' Shaw lit his cigarette. 'There's a few questions I need to ask.' There was no courtesy in the request, it was more an order. Shaw handed him a photograph. 'Ever seen this woman?'

Yes. 'No.'

Shaw caught the hesitation in his voice. 'You seem uncertain?'

Clare stared at the photograph in disbelief. 'No. I've never seen it before …' It was Montse's photograph. The photograph that had been in his wallet just a few hours ago. The photograph he'd left at Viajes Sauledo. 'Who is she?' Clare could barely extract the words from his throat.

'We think she had something to do with Stewart's death.'

For a brief moment Clare was tempted to pull Margarita's gun from his pocket and put a bullet through Shaw's head there and then.

'No matter.' Shaw took back the photograph. 'We'll find her soon enough. There's other more important matters we need to discuss. Top of the agenda – how to get Picasso out of the country. I need you to set up a meeting.'

Shaw – an agent for the SIM. Clare bent down to put on his shoes. Anything to avoid having to look him in the eye.

Shaw said it again. 'We need to set up a meeting.'

Shaw had known all along. Everything. Even before it had happened.

'Think you can do it?'

'What?'

Shaw looked at Clare askance. 'Is something troubling you?'

'I already have …' Clare re-engaged.

'Have what?'

'Set up a meeting.'

'With Picasso?'

'With his people – yes.'

'Excellent. What time?'

'Tomorrow evening.' Clare knew that his life depended on Shaw believing him. On him buying the same bullshit he'd sold Jordan.

'Where?'

'At Café Zurich.'

'On Plaça Catalunya?'

'Yes.'

'What time?'

'Eight o'clock.'

'What happened there?' Shaw affected to notice Clare's bloody foot.

'The SIM threw me into a cell full of broken glass.' *As you well know, you bastard.*

'They tortured you?' Shaw looked suitably shocked.

'Yes.'

'Then let you go?'

'They needed me to lead them to Picasso.'

'When was this?'

'Last Tuesday.'

'Where did they take you? Passeig de Gracia? Here – let me help you with that.' He noticed Clare's shoe lace unravelling.

'No. Via Laietana.' Clare scooped the loose end into a bow, with an effort pulling it tight. 'It's okay. I've got it.'

'Who interrogated you?'

'First, there was a Colonel. His name was Boix. Then a Major – Jordan.'

'Antoni Jordan ...' Shaw let slip a smile. 'Well – that certainly makes life a little more complicated.'

'Why?'

'If Jordan's involved, then so too are the NKVD. Jordan works for the Russians. But don't worry. We'll think of a way round it. The important thing is not to give them any reason to suspect we've spoken. You've told him about Picasso, I take it? About your meeting at Café Zurich?'

'Yes.'

'Does he know where you are now?'

'No.'

'That's good.' Shaw drew thoughtfully on his cigarette. 'Last Tuesday – you say?'

'Yes.'

'Jordan tortured you. Then let you go?'

'Yes.'

'Hoping you'd lead him to Picasso?'

'Yes.'

'But my information ...' Shaw assumed a look of slight bemusement '... is that Picasso didn't go missing until Thursday.'

'Yes. That's right ...' So much had happened since Tuesday that Clare had completely forgotten Jordan's initial concern. 'To begin with ... before Picasso became the issue ... Jordan wanted me to help him find a key.'

'A key?'

'Yes.' Clare understood now where Shaw was leading him.

'What key?'

Whatever it was that was in that box, Jordan still wanted it. Badly enough to put Shaw up to the job. 'There's a safe deposit box in Switzerland,' Clare elaborated. 'When Capdevila died he was carrying one of the keys needed to open it. Jordan wanted me to help him find the other one.'

'Did he mention the name of a bank?'

'Yes. Credit Syon.'

'Go on.'

'Jordan was certain Capdevila would have entrusted the second key to one of his associates.'

'That makes sense. Did he mention any names?'

'No. But soon after he let me go – Capdevila's assistant, Margarita Mirabel, made contact with me.'

'What did she want?'

'She wanted to know if Capdevila had made it out of the country okay.'

'What did you tell her?'

'I said he was in France.'

'What else did she ask?'

'Nothing.'

'That was it?'

'Yes.'

'Then what?'

'Nothing. Until Picasso went missing. Then Jordan … well, he seemed to forget about the key. His priority shifted to finding Picasso. Before Sunday …'

'Well, quite.' Shaw let out a little chuckle. 'I wouldn't like to be in his shoes right now. So – what about this Margarita woman? Where can we find her?'

'We can't. She's dead.'

'Dead?'

'This morning …' Clare paused, gathering his thoughts, wondering how much Jordan had managed to piece together. 'I worked out where she was staying. Jordan wanted me to go meet her. Find out what she knew.'

'And did you?'

'Yes.'

'Where?'

'At a safe house used by Capdevila. On Carrer Fusina.'

'This morning?'

'Yes. But there was this other guy there. Enrique …'

'Second name?'

'He didn't say.'

'Describe him to me.'

Clare tried to remain vague. 'My height. Average weight. About thirty years old. Catalan.'

Shaw said nothing.

'Soon after I arrived ... There was this phone call. A warning. That the SIM were outside.'

'They didn't suspect you?'

'No ... Margarita knew me as a friend of Capdevila.'

'And Enrique?'

Clare ignored the question. 'Margarita told us there was a way out over the roof. But it involved a jump. She was too old to make it. So Enrique ...' For a moment Clare faltered. At the memory of it all. 'He shot her ... rather than let her fall into Jordan's hands.'

'What about the key?' Shaw persisted.

'The key?'

'Margarita didn't have it?'

'Not that I could see.'

'Nor Enrique?'

'I wouldn't know.'

'But you were with them all the time? If she had given it to him, you would have known?'

'Yes.'

'Then you've no idea where it is?'

'No.'

'Are you sure?'

'Yes.'

'A pity.' Shaw let the matter slide, although there was something about the way he said it that told Clare he didn't altogether believe him. 'Anyway, what's important now,' Shaw idly reached across to the bedside table and picked up Forsyth's paperback. 'Our number one priority is to bring Picasso back home.' He flicked open the book – *Appointment with Death* – his eye drawn to the name of one of the characters. 'Lennox Boynton ... I wonder ... I once knew a Jeremy Boynton ... but I don't suppose there's a connection ...'

'What about me? When do I go home?' Clare felt obliged to ask, although he was under no illusion as to his ultimate fate.

'You don't. Not yet. I'm afraid, you'll have to stay in town until the job's done.' Shaw closed the book and returned it to the bedside table. 'Now the genie's out of the bottle, we're going to need you to help us pop him back in.'

And so the debrief went on – for almost an hour.

And for another hour after that, after Shaw had left, Clare sat on the bed in the dark, in a cold sweat. At Jarama, on the second day of the battle, a bullet had passed within half an inch of his ear. Clare had felt the wind of it; the bullet had even left a faint scorch mark on his beret. The soldier behind him – Harold Collins, the boy he'd met on the ferry from England – had caught the round full in the throat. For days afterwards, Clare had replayed the moment again and again in his head, every angle, every fraction of a second, trying to get a fix on the stumble, the faint nudge, the drop in wind that had saved his life. And every time he'd let his mind loose on the conundrum, it had churned his stomach and left him shaking, hot and clammy – just as he felt now.

Shaw had told him to play along with Jordan. Together they would turn the tables on the SIM. Spring Picasso from his Iberian prison and return home in triumph. Pats on the back all round. An extra bonus if they could locate Capdevila's key. Clare could picture Shaw now sitting in Jordan's office, laughing at him over a cup of tea. The ultimate stitch up. An agent with two masters. One and the same. It was little wonder Jordan had cut him so much slack, always knowing he'd run to Shaw.

But Clare was still one step ahead of them and with a trump card in his hand; taken from Kathleen's bag. A letter of confirmation from the Hotel Falcon made out in the name of Mr Philip Holdsworth.

Room 801 – he knew where to find her.

Clare took the discreet way out of the hotel – Jordan's way – through the laundry room. "Staff Only" a sign on the door advised, but no one seemed to pay him any mind. Wash. Dry. Iron. Go home. Every face wore the same dull expression except for two girls folding sheets who asked him if he was lost, who when he didn't answer just giggled and returned to their folds.

Outside the hotel, Clare caught a whiff of the Raval. A pungent blend of garlic, tobacco and drains. On the wall opposite, someone had pasted a notice advertising a cure for VD. An address in Carrer Carme where the remedy could be obtained – evenings only.

There was no sign of Jordan's goons.

Clare cut across the Ramblas, following his nose up through Plaça del Pi to the cinema on Portal de l'Angel. The show had already started. 'Come back in an hour,' the girl in the kiosk told him.

Clare insisted he didn't mind. 'Give me a ticket, the cheapest you have.'

The girl took his money – front three rows only – and went back to her book. A cheap romance. *What did she care?*

Clare walked on through into the foyer, what little curiosity he had as to which film was showing answered by a large poster on the wall. A picture of a lone dockside bar. A man and a woman standing outside it, their faces caught in the moody spill of a street lamp. Above them, the legend: *The Night Watchman. Starring Domingo Herrera and Alicia Sol.*

Clare took a moment to register the name. *Alicia Sol. The address in Tibidabo. The African parrots.*

It was her.

He took a seat in the front row, undisturbed by the few bodies dotted around the auditorium, framed by the flickering light of the ancient projector. On the screen, two cars were involved in a chase. The scene – a deserted dockside road. Street lamps reflected in puddles of oily water. An old man stooped over a brazier. A woman drawing her curtains. The hero throwing his vehicle this way and that, trying to shake off his pursuers, one of them leaning out of the window emptying a pistol in the general direction of the disappearing tail lights. Then a cut to the interior of a bar. A couple of sailors drinking whisky. A couple more playing cards. Alicia Sol (it had to be her) distractedly cleaning a glass. Contemplating the clock.

Clare now remembered reading an article in the paper about her most recent film currently shooting somewhere in Barcelona. A melodrama set around the Communist coup of May '37. Looking at the screen, he could see what all the fuss was about. Spain's answer to Hedy Lamarr. Thick dark hair swept back over naked shoulders, soulful eyes fixed on some far away point, the shadow of a fan playing across her cleavage, her dress simple, low cut and patterned with roses.

Alicia Sol. Pablo Picasso. Rafael Capdevila. Margarita Mirabel. Luis Cornet. There had to be a connection somewhere but Clare was damned if he could figure it out.

He watched the film for a few minutes more, then slipped out through the fire door; under foot the crunch of empty pipas shells and discarded paper cones. A dry, dusty corridor – paint peeling off the walls – led him to the back of the cinema, where a rusted door – pushed open at the second time of asking – brought him out into daylight, into a shaded alley that cut back down onto Santa Anna. He waited for a couple of minutes on the corner, long enough to flush out any possible tail, then set off back towards the Ramblas, as confident as he could be that Jordan had called off his men and left the field to Shaw.

The Hotel Falcon. 6.15pm. In the lobby, a pianist was playing a forgettable tune from *Anything Goes.* A faux blonde in a black cocktail dress and mink stole stood close by, chatting to a middle-aged man in a suit, something she said causing him to laugh. A prostitute. French. Very beautiful.

Clare remembered Forsyth mentioning there'd been an influx of such girls from the top Parisian brothels.

The receipt in Kathleen's bag was for a room on the eighth floor. The lift only went as far as the seventh. The last part of the climb was by staircase, bare, wooden steps leading up to the maids' rooms. Clare drew Margarita's gun from his pocket and knocked on the door. 'Who is it?' He heard Kathleen call out.

'Telegram.'

'Just a minute.' Kathleen unlocked the door. 'Oh ...' He'd caught her totally by surprise. *You.* She was wearing a light blue bathrobe, a pair of slippers and a change of dressing; Clare could see the bandage where her robe hung loose over her shoulder. 'Close the door,' he said, stepping inside.

Calmly, she did so.

'Turn on the radio.'

'Any particular channel?' If Kathleen was frightened, she seemed determined not to show it.

'That'll do fine.' Clare stopped her on a light classical channel. Tchaikovsky. 'How's the shoulder?'

'Stiff.'

Clare took in the room. Not much of one if truth be told. Cramped, hot and poorly decorated. He pushed open the door to the bathroom, a tiny space hewn out from under the eaves. 'How did you find me?' Kathleen's voice pulled him back.

'You left a receipt in your bag.'

She nodded weakly. 'How stupid of me.'

'I'm not going to hurt you,' he said. 'I'm on your side.'

'You've a funny way of showing it.'

Clare returned Margarita's gun to his pocket. A goodwill gesture. To show he meant her no harm. 'Look – the reason Holdsworth died. The reason the SIM got to Markham and Stewart is because they have an agent working in British Intelligence.'

Kathleen's mouth curled in disbelief.

'I have evidence.' Clare laid his cards on the table. 'A name. Shaw.'

'Don't move. Hands in the air. Where I can see them' – a voice from behind cut him short – 'Nice and slow. Take his gun.' A man's voice, soft, authorative, with a hint of a Scottish burr. 'This the guy who shot you?' Kathleen nodded. 'Sit down. Legs apart.' A voice with a face now. A quiet arrogance, an impatience about the way he spoke, consistent with his bearing, compact, upright, shorter than Clare by a couple of inches, he seemed to want to compensate by pushing himself upwards, neck straight, shoulders square. 'The name's Hicknall,' he said. 'I work with Miss Booth.'

'Richard Clare. *London Evening News*.' It sounded funny even as Clare said it.

'I know who you are.' Hicknall unclipped the magazine from Margarita's gun and stowed it in his brief case.

Clare cursed himself for not checking behind the bathroom door – Kathleen's anxiety, her change of dressing, he should have guessed that she wasn't alone.

'Who sent you here?' Hicknall motioned Clare to sit down, hands under his thighs, palms against the seat of the chair.

'No-one.' On the radio, the Tchaikovsky had come to an end cueing a switch in tone. A programme of dance music. A Viennese waltz introduced by a German émigré, the former leader of a Munich orchestra. 'I'm not a spy – if that's what you mean.'

'Then what are you doing here?'

'Trying to get back home.'

Hicknall gave a dry smile. 'Is that why you shot Miss Booth?'

'That was self defence.' Clare stole a glance towards Kathleen, who stood by the door subconsciously scratching her dressing. 'She had a gun. I thought she was about to shoot me.'

'Why would she want to do that?'

'He killed Philip,' Kathleen interrupted.

'I was with him when he died,' Clare took issue. 'But I didn't kill him.'

Hicknall looked to Clare. 'Then who did?'

'The SIM.'

'He's lying.'

'Why would I lie?'

'You tell me.'

'Holdsworth was betrayed by a man named Shaw.'

'Impossible.'

'Shaw's a double agent. A Communist. He's here in Barcelona. I saw him an hour ago.'

Hicknall laughed. 'Shaw's in London. I spoke with him only yesterday.'

'No, he's not. He's staying at the Colon.'

'Crap!'

'God's truth.' This time, Clare started his story at the end. A few hours ago, waking in Forsyth's hotel bedroom, Shaw showing him Montse's photograph, the one he'd left behind at the travel agency. Clare looked to Kathleen for support. *A woman in her twenties. Dark corkscrew hair. Olive eyes. A small mole on the corner of her lip?*

Kathleen gave a reluctant nod. Yes – she remembered the photograph. And yes – she conceded it could have been left behind in the rush to escape the SIM. 'There was only one way Shaw could have got hold of that photograph,' Clare put the point as forcefully as he could. 'From the SIM.'

'Assuming Shaw has the photograph.' Hicknall wasn't about to concede the point. 'Assuming he's here at all.'

Clare ignored him. 'Exhibit B,' he continued. The apartment on Carrer Fusina. Jordan hadn't known of its existence, therefore he couldn't have been following them, therefore the SIM must have learned about the rendezvous on Montjuic from some other source. A tip-off from British Intelligence. Shaw.

'Go on.'

Whatever Hicknall was thinking, Clare could tell he had his attention now. He told him about his interrogation by Jordan. About the key to Capdevila's safe deposit box. He told him everything that had happened since last Sunday, about Montse and Werner, how he'd hoped to help them escape the country too.

Hicknall listened in silence, interrupting only to clarify a couple of minor points. Where had Clare and Stewart been when Clare had asked him to call London? What time had he met Holdsworth at the airport? How long had they been together in the car before Holdsworth was shot?

Kathleen opened the window to let in some air, drawing in the sound of music and laughter from the Ramblas, prompting a twinge of regret from Clare that he and Montse would never again walk its length hand in hand, never again join in the evening *paseo* as they'd once used to. He told Hicknall about Holdsworth's death. Twice. Hicknall extracting every last detail from him, then making him go over it again to check the two versions tallied, as a detective might investigating a murder, or in this case a triple murder.

Clare asked for a glass of water. The heat, the incessant questioning and relentless crackle of the radio, was beginning to give him a headache. Hicknall lit a cigarette. Kathleen raised the issue of food. Did they want some? Should she call down to room service to have someone bring up a tray?

Then the phone rang.

Hicknall looked at Kathleen. 'Expecting anyone?'

'No.'

Nor me. Clare threw his own look of alarm into the ring.

Tentatively, Kathleen picked up the phone. It was the front desk. 'Yes … this is Miss Booth …' She cupped her hand over the speaker. 'There's someone at reception asking to see me.' Whoever it was now took hold of the other end of the line – Clare caught the look of surprise on Kathleen's face. '… Yes …

yes, Sir … Alan's with me now … just the two of us … yes, Sir … of course. First door on the left. Room 801.' She hurriedly replaced the receiver. 'It's Shaw,' she said. 'He's on his way up.'

Hicknall was the first to react. 'You.' He pulled Clare sharply to his feet. 'In there.' *The bathroom*. 'Not a sound.'

Clare didn't need any further encouragement. His only concern – what would happen if Shaw decided he wanted to use the toilet. 'Put the chair back – Quick!' He heard Hicknall telling Kathleen, then a knock on the door, 'Good Evening, Sir … Good flight?'

The bathroom was dark and airless. There was no window, just a line of light rigid along the bottom of the door sufficient once Clare's eyes had adjusted to the gloom for him to distinguish the sheen of the enamel bathtub from the glaze of the tiles, the ridge of the floor boards scuffed and warped.

Clare sat on the edge of the bath and listened as Hicknall and Kathleen traded small talk with Shaw, pouring him a whisky, then filling him in on what little they knew; Shaw in turn telling them how he'd just got in from the airport, sent by London to clear up the mess. 'Holdsworth's dead,' he coldly announced. 'Our chaps at the embassy received a message to say he's been involved in a car accident.'

'We know,' Kathleen said quietly.

'Any idea how it happened?' Hicknall asked.

'I can only assume Clare shot him, that he's been working for the SIM all along.'

You bastard. I hope you hang for this. From behind the bathroom door, Clare could hear every word.

'You and Miss Booth should return to Madrid as soon as possible,' Shaw continued. 'First flight tomorrow morning.'

'What about the office?' Hicknall again.

'Leave that to me.'

'You should know, Sir,' Kathleen ventured. 'This morning –

after I got back from the hospital. From dealing with Stewart's body. There was someone there.'

'Where?' This was news to Shaw.

'In the office.'

'Who?'

'I don't know. A woman. She got away.' Kathleen peeled back her bathrobe so that Shaw could see her wound. 'She shot me in the shoulder.'

'My God!' Shaw looked genuinely shocked.

'It was my fault, Sir. I shouldn't have let it happen. I didn't think she'd be armed.'

Shaw took Clare's photograph of Montse from his pocket. 'Is this the woman?'

'Yes. Who is she?'

'We don't know.' Shaw handed the picture to Hicknall. 'Ring any bells?'

'No. Where did you find it?'

'In a file. In London.' Shaw took back possession of the photograph. 'What we need now is a name.'

'I can check our records in Madrid,' Hicknall said.

'Do that.' Shaw stepped over to the window and took in the view. The back wall of a school. A dirty patchwork of tiles and terraces fading into a fuggy haze. A strong smell of drains and cooking oil. 'Not much of a place to spend your last night, is it?' he remarked casually.

'No, Sir,' Kathleen quietly agreed, resisting the urge to tell him how Holdsworth had spent his last night in her arms in this very bed, twenty years young again, that's how good he'd told her she'd made him feel as they'd made love one last time before he'd left to meet Clare, *before you killed him, you bastard*.

'Was this the best you could do?' Shaw asked her. He meant the room.

'At such short notice, Sir – yes. Everything was booked up.'

'At five pounds a night?'

Kathleen bridled. 'To begin with they asked for ten.'

Shaw didn't take issue. He'd made his point. London liked to keep a tight rein on its purse strings. 'A fine man – Holdsworth,' he said blandly. 'We'll miss him.' He looked at his watch. 'Christ – is that the time? No need to worry about Clare,' he told Hicknall. 'I'll put D-section onto it.'

Clare felt his heartbeat quicken. Shaw had it all thought out. Down to the last detail. His death.

'I'm staying at the Colon,' Shaw said. 'Room 411 – should you need to contact me.' He picked up his jacket and opened the door. 'You'll hear from London in a couple of days. Until then, I'd advise you both to lie low. Assume your cover's blown.'

'Yes, Sir.'

'Oh! And Kathleen – make sure you see a doctor.'

'I will, Sir. As soon as I get home.'

'Good girl.'

* * * * *

67, Passeig de Gracia. 8.20pm. Jordan opened a second bottle of Vichy Catalan and allowed himself a moment's indulgence. An image of André Marty being lined up against a wall in Dzerzhinsky Square, the glare of the naked light bulb overhead extinguished by the blindfold pulled down over his face, the executioner's pistol pressed against the back of his head, then a single shot and a thud as Marty's body hit the floor.

Jordan let slip a smile. The net was drawing in on Picasso. Shaw would deliver him the key to Capdevila's safe deposit box – Jordan was convinced Clare knew more of its whereabouts than he was letting on – and then maybe, just maybe, he could see a way to silence Marty for good.

* * * * *

Carrer Avinyó. 9.00pm. Montse was running late. The traffic. Pep. Her mother. Everything was conspiring against her. And now the road was blocked; up ahead, a wheel had come off a cart and a large crowd had gathered round the stricken vehicle to discuss how best to move it. 'I can walk from here,' she said, paying off the taxi driver and hauling Pep out onto the pavement.

'But I want to stay at Grandma's,' Pep protested.

'Grandma doesn't want us. Not tonight.' Montse reached into her bag for her house keys.

'Why not?'

'Because she doesn't.' Then – 'What the hell?!' – as Montse moved to unlock the door, a figure shot out of the shadows, a hand clasping her arm, pulling her back from the doorstep. 'Jesus – you scared me!' It was Clare. 'What the hell are you doing here?'

'You can't go home,' he said, guiding her away from the building. 'It's not safe.'

'Why? What's happened?'

'Keep walking. Not too fast. And don't look back.' Clare steered her in the direction of a dingy, dark alleyway that ran behind the Correos.

'Why? What's going on, Richard?'

'Is there anywhere you can stay? Somewhere the police won't think of looking?'

'I don't understand.'

'Montse – it's important.'

'What's important?' Pep demanded to know.

'Think. Damn it!' Clare instinctively changed direction to avoid two militiamen patrolling the street ahead.

'There is someone,' Montse said hesitantly. 'His name's Reynaldo. He has an apartment on Castillejos.'

'Will he be in?'

'I have a key.'

'He's your boyfriend?' Clare felt a tug of jealousy.

'We see each other from time to time – yes.'

'Won't he mind us just turning up?'

'He's away.'

'Where?'

'Moscow – if you must know.'

'He's a Communist! For God's sake – how long have you been seeing him?'

'We can take the bus.' Montse had had enough of his questions. 'A 24 will take us right there.'

Pep picked up a stick from the pavement and started banging it against a lamp post. 'Stop it,' Montse snapped at him. 'How many times do I have to tell you not to pick things up from the street?' She tore the stick from his hand and threw it into the gutter. 'So aren't you going to tell me?' She turned back to Clare. 'What the hell's going on?'

'There's been a fuck up.'

'What kind of fuck up?'

As they waited for the bus, Clare tentatively filled her in on the debacle at the travel agency. How he'd tried to procure her a passport, how events hadn't quite worked out as he'd planned, how her photograph was now in the hands of the SIM, how it would only be a matter of time before Jordan joined up the dots and the police came knocking; her only comment when he'd finished, 'I never asked for any of this.'

To which Clare had no answer.

The bus dropped them off outside Reynaldo's apartment block. 'Where are we going?' Pep asked as Montse hurriedly unlocked the door.

Clare hid a smile. *So she obviously didn't know him that well.*

Reynaldo's apartment was on the second floor of the building. Clearly he'd been gone a while as the hall reeked of must and a layer of dust covered the floor.

Pep sneezed as Montse walked through to the sitting room and opened the window.

On the sideboard, Clare caught sight of a framed photograph. A picture of Montse standing on a hillside, the sea behind her, and what he took to be a slightly awkward smile on her lips, although that was probably just wishful thinking.

Montse found a bottle of Moscatel, brushed off the dust, and poured them each a glass – Pep curled up on the bed, tired now.

As Montse soothed him to sleep, Clare sat by the open window listening to her telling Pep a story he'd heard her tell before. A fairy story. About a wood cutter, his chickens and a pack of wolves. Clare tried to conjure up similar memories from his own childhood. Scenes he knew almost by heart. A winter in Wales with the hillsides around covered in snow, his mother reading him *The Adventures of Doctor Doolittle.* A camping trip to Devon, where it had rained so hard they'd dug a trench around their tent in which he and Gerald had re-enacted the Battle of the Somme. But somehow Clare couldn't quite force the images into focus. It was as though they belonged to someone else. To another life.

Pep fell asleep before the end of the story.

Montse walked back through to the sitting room, kicked off her shoes and tucked herself on the end of the sofa, knees drawn into her chest. 'You know we can't stay here forever,' she said.

Clare poured her another glass of Moscatel. 'I can get you out of the country. The three of you. You, Werner and Pep.'

'How?'

'I've made a deal with Hicknall. London wants Picasso. I'm the only one who knows where he is. It's a straight swap.

Three passports and safe passage out of the country. In return, I tell them how to find Picasso.'

'They agreed to that?'

'I can't say they liked it.' Clare didn't care to repeat Hicknall's exact words. 'But they don't have a choice.' Nor did he care to tell her it was all a bluff. He had no idea where Picasso was holed up.

'What about you?' she asked. 'Aren't you coming with us?'

'I'll be along later,' he said, gently brushing aside a strand of hair that had fallen loose over her eyes. 'Don't worry. It'll all be alright.'

Hollow words that meant nothing.

All he had was one last throw of the dice – Alicia Sol.

CHAPTER 18

Saturday 10th August, 1940

Programme of the XII Olympiad
Fencing, Swimming, Equestrian Sports, Boxing, Football.

Clare woke early to find Montse and Pep curled up on the bed still asleep. Quietly, he rose from the sofa, dressed, and let himself out of the flat, returning fifteen minutes later with a bag of pastries and a bottle of Vichy Catalan.

The previous evening, he and Montse had talked into the small hours. About what to do if Hicknall reneged on the deal – no decision reached. About themselves – where it had all gone wrong, whether they could put the pieces back together again – no decision reached. About the fragile state of the world – if war broke out, might they not find themselves fighting on opposite sides? Again no decision reached, at which point they'd given up and gone to bed. Too tired to make love. Too tense and on edge.

The bottle of Moscatel stood empty on the sideboard, witness to their indecision. Beside it, a small pair of scales, a box of weights used for weighing letters and the photograph of Montse. It had been taken near Begur, she'd told him; Reynaldo's family had a house in the town to which he'd invited her last Easter.

In the top drawer, Clare found a pair of scissors. Carefully, he traced a 4.5 X 3.5 centimetre frame about her face and cut it out; the end result not exactly to the standard of a studio photograph but at least the lines were straight and the sea offered some kind of unity to the background.

Not wishing to wake Montse, Clare left the pastries and water on the table, together with a note telling her to stay put until he returned. Since Picasso had gone missing, he'd noticed an increase in militia on the streets, heightened security checks on the buses and trams. She'd told him she wasn't afraid – at least not for herself – and he believed her. He knew enough about her time on the Aragon front during the war to know that she wasn't bullshitting him, but he also knew that she wasn't yet ready to leave. Neither her family nor Spain. Half joking, Montse had wondered if she wouldn't be better off turning him in. Clare hadn't liked to say it but the same thought had occurred to him too.

Anonymous in the pull of the early morning shift, Clare tramped towards the Barri Gotic, part of a tired flow that had him thinking back to his first days on *The Captain*. The commute from his flat in Bayswater to Knightsbridge. That sinking feeling every time he headed into the tube.

He reached the bar del Pi twenty minutes early. The outside tables were all taken. But in the far corner of the main salon, he found Hicknall and Kathleen impatiently waiting for him, already into their second coffee. 'We'll talk outside.' Hicknall didn't even bother to ask where he'd spent the night. 'I have a car parked by the Urquijo Catalan.'

The car was a dark red Traction Avant with Madrid plates. Hicknall drove, every now and again checking the rear mirror to ensure they hadn't picked up a tail. He'd spoken to London, he told Clare. Twice. Shaw – it was agreed they could deal with later. But right now the priority was to extract Picasso.

Clare handed him the photographs he'd been asked to provide. The picture of Montse from Reynaldo's flat and the two passport photographs he'd cut from the files at the radio station, which he still had in his wallet.

'Tell your friends – no luggage,' Hicknall said. 'It's just themselves and the clothes they're wearing. The passports will be ready by lunch time. We'll meet again at one. At Casa Alfonso. By Urquinaona.'

Clare knew it well.

Hicknall pulled into the kerb, alongside the entrance to the Diagonal metro station. There was nothing more to discuss.

'Suppose he tries to double cross us?' Kathleen asked, as Clare disappeared into the metro, the steps strewn with the loose pages of an old newspaper that had been used to wrap meat.

Hicknall just grunted. 'Then he's more of an idiot than he looks.'

Security on the gates of the La Bordeta studios was tight; two militiamen checking visitors in and out of the premises. 'Richard Clare. *London Evening News.* Here to interview Alicia Sol.' Clare handed one of the men his press pass. It had taken a phone call to Miguel at the radio station to establish that the actress was at the studio, two weeks into shooting *Cinco Dias*.

The militiaman checked his list. 'There's nothing here,' he said blankly.

'It was arranged this morning,' Clare impatiently explained. 'Miss Sol is expecting me now.'

The militiaman hesitated, then waved Clare through – a thick ear for keeping the star waiting not on his agenda for today. 'They're on B Stage,' he said, pointing Clare to a large aircraft hanger of a building. 'If there's a red light on, it means they're filming. You'll have to wait.'

Clare found the actress on set. A mock up of the roof of the Hotel Colon. The rest of the cast – a half dozen actors dressed as Communist gunmen – and the crew patiently waiting for the make-up girl to finish dabbing a drop of sweat from her brow. The heat from the lights was intense. Huge great brutes, each chucking out 10,000 kilowatts.

'Stand by!' A fresh faced young man called the crew to attention as the make-up girl retreated from the set and Alicia Sol took up her start position, marked out for her on the floor by a strip of white tape.

'Roll camera!'

'Camera rolling!'

'And Action!'

Alicia stepped forward towards the camera, a large earthenware pitcher in her hands. *Lemonade for the troops.* The script called for her to pour the gunmen a drink during a lull in hostilities. The director, a small, balding man in late middle age, made her run through it eight times; Alicia bearing his carping instructions with a cheerful equanimity that belied her status as a star.

'Print one, three and eight.' The director finally pronounced himself happy and the set relaxed, the lights killed, and the doors thrown open to allow in a rush of air.

Alicia Sol disappeared off to her dressing room, accompanied by a plethora of personal assistants, wardrobe and make-up. Clare made a move to follow her but found his way barred by a surly man posted on the door to keep people like himself at bay. 'Tell Miss Sol I have a message for her,' he said. 'From Galeria Capdevila. She'll understand.'

If she didn't, he was stymied. His last lead come to nothing.

A few minutes passed. Clare anxiously watched the technicians setting up for the next take, hungry, realising that he hadn't eaten since breakfast. Then a tap on the shoulder; it was the third assistant. 'Miss Sol will see you now.'

He was in.

Second door on the left. Clare knocked and entered to find Alicia alone at her dressing table, a light cotton robe draped over the clothes she'd been wearing on set, a freshly lit cigarette in the ashtray, a hint of anxiety where before she'd been all smiles. *His doing?*

'Shut the door,' she said.

He'd done so. But he shut it again anyway. 'My name is Richard Clare. I'm a friend of Capdevila.'

'I know who you are.' She leaned into the light to get a better look at him, a curl of cigarette smoke wrapped around her eyelash, the fall of her hair making her seem, if anything, more beautiful in the flesh. 'You're Pablo's friend from Paris.' There was a hint of Andaluz in her accent; Clare remembered the newspaper article describing her birth place as some two bit town on the road from Sevilla to Cadiz. 'He told me about you. You were in love with Dora.'

'We were friends,' Clare corrected her.

'He said lovers.'

Clare caught a hint of tease in her voice. 'It amused him to think so. But there was nothing between us, I promise.'

Alicia didn't believe him. Nor did she care. What concerned her was why it had taken him so long to make contact. Picasso was getting jumpy. So too was she.

It was all Clare could do not to smile. The African parrots. The ad in *La Vanguardia*. He'd guessed correctly. Alicia Sol was Capdevila's conduit to Picasso. Play his cards right now and just maybe he could still save himself. 'I had the wrong address ...' he tried not to let his relief show. 'I went to this house on Avenida de Tibidabo. It turned out it belonged to Luis Cornet.'

Alicia gave a nervous laugh. 'Luis is my lover. He lives with me.'

'But then Pablo –'

'– is also my lover. Didn't Rafael tell you?'

'No.'

'What's the matter?' Alicia misread his reaction. 'Don't you English take lovers too?' She proffered a pack of cigarettes. Lucky Strike.

'I don't smoke.'

'Neither do I. It's the waiting ...' She tossed the packet to one side. 'Rafael thought it would be safer if I acted as a go-between. He knew they would be watching Pablo.' She took a last drag from a cigarette she'd hardly begun to smoke and stubbed it out. 'We were beginning to fear something had gone wrong. Where is Rafael?'

'He's in France. Safe. You can tell Pablo he has no cause to worry. It all went like clockwork.'

'Rafael's in France?' Alicia's gypsy eyes flashed brilliant.

'Yes.'

'Then who placed the advertisement in the paper?'

'I did. On Rafael's instructions ...' Clare hastily added.

'The bastard!' Alicia let fly at the wall. 'After all Pablo's done for him. I'll kill him.' *Capdevila had deceived them all. Used Picasso to effect his own escape.* 'Where in France?'

'I have no idea ...'

But already her anger had passed. 'What does it matter? Pablo will never talk to him again.'

Outside – a bell rang.

'We've got five minutes. Tell me what we have to do.' Capdevila's deceit was no longer of interest to Alicia. 'When do we go?'

We? Clare couldn't help but show his surprise.

Alicia faltered. 'Rafael did tell you?'

'Yes ...' Clare wondered what else Capdevila had neglected to tell him.

'So when do we go?'

'Tomorrow.' *What the hell? Alicia was SIS's problem not his.*

'What time?'

'Ten o'clock. There's a British agent – a man named Hicknall. He'll brief you on the details.'

'How will we know this man?'

'I'll introduce you.'

'Where shall we meet?'

'There's a village – just south of Girona. Sant Mateu de Montnegre. Can you be there by tomorrow morning?'

Alicia nodded.

'On the road into town. You'll find the fourteen stations of the cross. We'll meet at the ninth.'

Alicia smiled. 'Then you are a religious man, Mr Clare?'

'No.'

'So why the ninth? Why not the seventh? Or the third?'

'Nine's my lucky number.'

She laughed. 'So you are superstitious then?'

'No. Just precise.' *But he had his reasons.*

'Where do you think they'll take us?' Alicia mused. 'London? New York? Not Paris,' she added.

'Why not?'

'Because Dora's there. America,' she said. 'Perhaps we will live in Hollywood. Have you ever been to Los Angeles, Mr Clare?'

'No.'

'Me neither.'

There was a knock on the door. It was the third assistant again. The crew were waiting. Alicia gathered up her script.

Clare extended her his hand. 'Goodbye, Miss Sol.'

Alicia laughed and kissed him on both cheeks. 'Don't be so English,' she smiled.

* * * * *

For Señor Gusi, the morning's drama had started just before nine as he was opening up his shop. Two police cars and a black Hispano-Suizo. A half dozen policemen and as many SIM agents forcing their way into the building. Disappearing up the staircase. A raid on the second floor apartment, he learned later from a gleeful Pilar.

'I always knew that girl was no good.' How many times had Pilar told him so? But now it seemed she was right. The officer in charge – Captain Caraben – had even interviewed him as to Montse's whereabouts. The last time he'd seen her, the last time they'd spoken. 'Think carefully,' he'd said. 'It's important.' And Señor Gusi had, but all he'd been able to do was corroborate the evidence of a half dozen others. At about half past nine yesterday evening, Montse had returned home with her son. She'd been met by a man on the doorstep. From where he was standing, Señor Gusi couldn't say who the man was, only that she'd left with him in the direction of Passeig de Colom, since when the lights in her apartment had remained switched off and the shutters closed.

It was now eleven o'clock. Caraben and his men were still upstairs searching Montse's flat, stripping the place to pieces by the sound of it. Gusi wondered if he shouldn't shut up shop and call it a day, settle for a long lunch at Can Culleretes, or maybe a stroll across town to Plaça Monumental to see if he couldn't pick up a ticket to the boxing. It was a shame about Montse, he thought, she'd always seemed a decent enough young woman – good with the kid – although he'd never understood her attraction for that Englishman who used to hang around her flat, who on the evidence of a few nights ago was back on the scene, which was when it struck Gusi that's whom Montse had met last night. The man on the doorstep, it was the Englishman.

Gusi cursed himself for not realising earlier. Caraben ought to be told. Montse had disappeared with the Englishman. He was sure of it now.

* * * * *

11.20am. Clare returned to Reynaldo's apartment and rang the buzzer. Two short bursts. One long. As he and Montse had agreed.

No answer.

Both windows were open. Clare tried again. Still no answer.

Thirty minutes later, he found her eating tortilla in a café on the other side of the street. 'For Christ's sake, I told you to stay put.' He couldn't believe she'd been so stupid.

'Pep was hungry,' she answered him sulkily. 'And so was I.'

Pep grinned. A dark stain around his mouth from where he'd covered himself in hot chocolate. *That's exactly how it was.*

'What about the pastries I bought?' Clare said.

'He didn't like them.'

'So you risked your life to get him something he did like?'

'You said you'd be back soon. It's now almost twelve.'

'I met Hicknall.' Clare didn't want to tell her about Alicia, and it wasn't the time for a fight. 'Tomorrow morning, you should be across the border. Free.'

'From what?' she asked tartly.

'You can't stay here.'

'I want to go home.'

'Home?'

'To the flat.'

'Why?'

'To get my things.'

'You can't. No luggage. Hicknall was firm about that. It's too dangerous.'

'But I told Pep we'd collect his teddy.'

'Then you'll have to tell him we can't.'

'You tell him.'

'Tell me what?' Pep wanted to know, his mouth full of chocolate.

'That Teddy's not going to be coming with us,' Clare said sharply.

'Why not?'

'Because someone needs to look after your home when you're gone. To make sure the wicked witch from downstairs doesn't break in and steal everything. Don't you think Teddy could do that?'

Pep looked doubtful. 'He's not very brave.'

'You mean he might need help?' Clare said. 'I have a teddy back in England. We could ask him. What do you think?'

'What's his name?'

'Perry.'

Pep shrugged. *It might work.*

Montse stubbed out her cigarette on the side of her plate. 'I'm sorry. I don't mean to sound unreasonable. I am grateful.'

'Mean what, Mummy?'

'Drink up, darling. It's time to go back.'

'Why?'

'Because it is.'

Back in Reynaldo's flat, there were a million and one things Clare wanted to say but Pep stood between them, obstinately clinging to the hem of Montse's dress, insisting that whatever was said, was said to him and him alone.

Perhaps, it was for the best, Clare mused afterwards, on his way to meet Hicknall, this way it didn't really count as a goodbye, this way it allowed him to believe they really would meet again, that it was all going to work out for the good.

'Suppose they try to double cross us?' Montse asked. A last question as he left the flat.

'We'll work something out,' Clare promised her. 'It'll be okay.'

Hicknall and Kathleen were waiting for him at Casa Alfonso. Over a lunch of *jamon y queso* served with a mountain of *pan con tomate* – toasted bread smeared with garlic, olive oil and tomato – Hicknall brusquely spelled out the arrangements.

Clare's friends were to meet Kathleen outside the Museu Arqueologia. At 19.00 hours on the dot. 'If they're not there by five past,' he said, 'then they've missed the boat. We'll meet an hour later. Outside the main post office on Urquinaona.'

Clare nodded. He understood. It was all quite clear.

The Olympic stadium. 5.30pm. The final of the football competition. Spain v Great Britain. Clare ducked a row of upraised arms as he made his way towards his seat, the one vacant space in the whole tier. 'I didn't think you were going to come.' Werner greeted him with a handshake, returning the programme he'd been reading to his jacket pocket.

Clare discreetly took in the fans to either side of them. A father and son to his left. A group of four middle-aged men to his right. 'Are we alone?' he whispered.

'Twelve o'clock. Four rows back.'

'How many?'

'Two. Brown suits. One with a moustache. Behind the woman dressed in blue.'

Clare cast a surreptitious glance over his shoulder. 'Got you.' On the pitch, the teams were lining up for the national anthems. 'Think you can get rid of them?'

'Sure. Why?'

'Because I can get you out of the country.'

Werner looked almost amused. 'Why would you want to do that?'

To pay you back for the other day. To make up for the fact I got you arrested. 'I want you to look after Montse,' Clare told him.

Werner waited for the national anthems to finish and the stadium to once more become engulfed by the noise of the crowd, before answering, 'You owe me nothing.'

'I know.'

A silence, then, 'You know I once played for SC Olympia ...' some memory, some incident from the past brought a wan smile to Werner's lips. 'I was a goalkeeper. If it hadn't been for the Nazis ...' But there, the thread quietly vanished as the referee blew for the start of the game, the British team posting their intent with an immediate assault on the Spanish goal, a speculative shot from the edge of the penalty area that dipped just over the cross bar. 'When do we go?' he said.

'Now. Half time. They'll be waiting for you at the Museu Arqueologia.'

'They?'

'Her name's Kathleen Booth.'

'How will I recognise her?'

'She'll have her arm in a sling.'

'That should be easy enough.'

'I shot her,' Clare confessed. 'A mistake.'

The first half finished with Spain one up. Five minutes before the break, Werner slipped off. No emotion in his departure, just a faint squeeze of Clare's arm, a tap on the shoulder, thank you and goodbye, see you in London or on the road to La Rabrasada, and don't worry about your girlfriend, I'll look after her as best I can.

* * * * *

Las Ramblas. 6.15pm. The city was already taking on the air of a celebratory fiesta. Crowds spilling out of the cafés onto the streets. Champagne corks popping. Trees festooned with streamers. That Spain might lose the match was unthinkable. Even the side roads were clogged, like on the big holidays; Sant Joan, Los Reyes and La Merce.

Three quarters of an hour. There was just enough time, Montse told herself. The thought had been brewing all day but it was Pep – suddenly remembering that he'd left his teddy bear with her parents – who'd decided her to act. Simply, she couldn't leave town without saying goodbye, without telling her mother and father what she was up to. She knew what Clare would say – that she was mad to take the risk – and she knew that he was right. But she also knew it was something she had to do.

The hotel door – when Montse finally made it through to Carrer Tallers – was open. In retrospect, a warning that something was amiss. But at the time she was in too much of a hurry to think about it, thankful not to have to waste another minute searching her bag for the key.

The light on the staircase was switched off. Pep ran on ahead of her, the tap of his shoes echoing through the hallway. 'Grand Papa! Grand Mama!' he called out in his shrill voice.

'Pep! Wait!' Montse shouted after him, as Pep disappeared through the door at the top of the landing.

The front desk was deserted. Not unusual in itself but given the open door downstairs, it should have been enough to make Montse stop and think.

Seconds later it was too late.

'Montse Rafols?' A man's voice. Matter of fact. A hint of an out of town accent. Zaragoza. Or maybe even further afield. Early thirties. Neatly dressed. Nothing too expensive but recognisably SIM. In his right hand, a revolver aimed at her chest. 'You are under arrest.'

Through the glass door dividing the reception area from the family living space, Montse could see Pep hugging her mother's leg, looking more confused than frightened.

'For what? She's done nothing wrong.' Montse's father stepped forward into the lobby.

'Hands. Legs. Against the wall.' The SIM agent ignored him.

'Get your hands off her,' Xavi Rafols remonstrated.

Montse had never seen him so agitated. 'Papa, please.'

'Xavi!' Violeta took hold of her husband's arm. 'Not in front of the child.'

Her father backed off.

'Okay, lets go.' The SIM agent had Montse cuffed before she knew it. As she caught the pained look in her parents' eyes, all she could think of was the hurt she'd caused them during her short life. Her boyfriends. Going to war. Bringing up Pep on her own. They'd bourne her wilfulness stoically. Too late now, she wished she'd done better by them. 'I love you,' she whispered.

'It'll be alright,' her mother tried to reassure her. But they both knew it wouldn't be.

'Be good.' Montse threw Pep a kiss. 'Do what Grandma says.'

'Come on. Let's go.' The SIM agent roughly grabbed her by the wrist.

Xavi reached a hand into his pocket.

If the SIM agent had thought to look back over his shoulder, it would have been the last thing he saw – Montse's father standing in the doorway, Andreu's old service revolver in his hand, pointed at his head. Three steps forward and Xavi Rafols pulled the trigger. Point blank. The explosion loud enough to rattle the glass of his tropical fish tank, the impact half removing the SIM agent's head.

Xavi calmly laid the gun on the front desk.

The agent's body lay twisted on the floor, blood pumping from his neck, from where the base of his skull had once been joined to his spinal cord.

'You did the right thing.' Violeta gently took hold of her husband's hand and kissed him on the cheek.

Pep stared at the remains of the agent – wide eyed.

'I killed him. He didn't frisk me. He didn't cuff me.' Montse was the first to react, hurriedly digging into the agent's pockets for the keys to the handcuffs, talking all the while. 'Have you got that, Papa? I had the gun on me the whole time.' She picked up Andreu's revolver and put it in her coat, returning the handcuffs to the agent's pocket, wiping them clean of her prints. 'Papa!' Her father was still in shock. 'It's important. They won't suspect you – if you stick to the story. It's me they want.'

'What have you done?' Her mother hardly dared ask.

'Nothing … Mama, I haven't time to explain now.'

'Where will you go?' Violeta didn't profess to understand what was happening.

'France. That's what I came to tell you. I have a passport. Richard fixed it for me.'

'But you'll be alright? He'll look after you.'

'Yes, Mama. He will.'

'And you'll let us know you've arrived safely.' It was as if Montse were fifteen years old again, going up to the mountains to spend a fortnight with her cousins.

'I'll send a postcard.' The clock struck seven. Montse hurriedly kissed her parents goodbye.

'Go!' Violeta waved her towards the door. 'Go! Before it's too late.'

Outside the Museu Arqueologia. 7.05pm. Kathleen stood waiting. Ready to leave. Where the hell were they? She checked her watch. Five minutes. They knew the score. Every second she now waited, she endangered the operation, her own life and Werner's too.

On the far pavement, a group of men were setting up a half dozen tables, stretching banners from tree to tree in preparation for a street party. Until ten past – Kathleen decided. She'd give them another five minutes.

Inside the car, Werner's thoughts were with Stani. His only true friend murdered four weeks ago by the secret police. Stani, who'd always loved the Museu Arqueologia, who'd often stopped by the bar opposite for a cup of coffee and a game of chess; his friends there probably didn't even know he was dead, most likely they assumed he was away on holiday, disappeared up the coast for a day or two to escape the Olympics.

Across the street, a stray dog edged too close to the table. PARP! One of the men gave the dog a blast in its ear with his trumpet, sending the animal scurrying off with its tail between its legs.

Then – 'There she is' – Werner saw them, emerging from a side street, half walking, half running.

'A man came to take Mummy away,' Pep announced excitedly as Kathleen bundled them into the car. 'But Grand Papa killed him. With a gun,' he added gleefully. 'Didn't he, Mummy?'

'That's right, darling. He did.'

* * * * *

Across the city in the Olympic stadium, the score stood at 2–1. Eighty-three minutes into the game, the Spanish had just scored again, a fierce shot from outside the penalty area that had somehow squeezed through a throng of white shirts before deflecting into the top left hand corner. Clare had never seen or heard anything like it. The noise. The carnival dance. Grown men throwing their hats into the air, embracing one another, whooping like banshees.

Seven minutes to rescue the game. The British team raced the ball back to the centre circle. Straight from the kick off they poured forward, a powerful shot from the centre forward clipping the cross bar, evoking a torrent of obscenities from the crowd, at the man who would dare stop their dream.

Wave after wave, the British team kept up their assault on the Spanish goal, a desperate finger tip, a stretched boot somehow keeping them at bay, the noise so intense now that even Clare got caught up in the excitement. Then, with thirty seconds left on the clock, a break away, two on two, a slip from the British defender and the ball was in the back of the net. 3–1. Game over. An eruption of noise. Spectators spilling onto the pitch. Ecstatic scenes all around. Somewhere in the melee below, eleven heads hung in despair.

It was time to leave.

Hicknall was waiting for him outside the main post office in Urquinaona. 'Your papers are in the glove compartment,' he said, as Clare climbed into the car. 'Your name's Robert Hardisty. You work for the Foreign Office – Cultural Attaché at the Paris Embassy.' Hicknall started up the engine and slipped out into the traffic, one eye as ever on the rear mirror as he followed the signs to the N1. 'You're on your way back home after a week's holiday. You can gen up on the rest as we drive.'

Clare slit open the envelope. The passport looked well thumbed. Entry stamps for Germany, Turkey and Switzerland, all in the last year. *Robert Michael Hardisty. Born Cairo, 25th December 1914*. Not difficult to remember.

Clare studied the photograph on his French residence permit. His photograph. From the style of his clothes and the cut of his hair, he guessed it to have been taken some time soon after he came down from university, only he had no recollection of the moment. 'How did you get this?' he asked.

Hicknall didn't answer him. 'When you're done reading, burn it,' he said sharply. 'Throw the ashes out the window.'

* * * * *

Plaça Catalunya. 8.15pm. On the terrace of the Hotel Colon, Jordan took a sip of Vichy Catalan and lit a cigarette.

Across the square an old man was feeding the pigeons. Jordan watched impatiently, waiting for him to pick up his bag and shuffle on – the prearranged signal that Clare, or Clare's contact, Enrique, had reached Café Zurich. Up on the roofs, at the corner of every street leading into the square, his team were in place.

All that was missing were the two principle players.

* * * * *

Just beyond the city limits, on the bridge over the Rio Besòs, Hicknall's Peugeot reached the last checkpoint this side of Mataró. *'Bo viatjar.'* The militiaman wearily waved them through. Hicknall took back their passports, Clare trying hard not to smile, not even a second glance – they were through.

Behind them, the dipping sun, the line of the hills and the underside of the clouds catching the glare of the street lamps, suggested Barcelona as a volcano ready to erupt. Clare's last ever view of the city.

He wound up the window as the car gained speed. To his right lay the Mediterranean, a calm blue dotted with the lights of distant ships, as if in reflection of the darkening sky. To his left, the Serra de Sant Mateu, rugged pine clad slopes cut through by fast running streams that tumbled down to the sea's edge.

They stopped for petrol at Vilassar de Mar. 'We're staying the night in Sant Feliu de Guixols,' Hicknall informed him. 'At the Hotel Marina.' Clare nodded; he remembered once meeting a nurse who had been posted there during the war. The hotel had been requisitioned by the army as a convalescence home for wounded soldiers.

Beyond Mataró, the road cleared, just the occasional vehicle now lumbering its way up the coast. 'Your file says you fought in the war,' Hicknall finally broke the silence. 'With the International Brigade.' Clare wondered what else it said. 'Ever know a chap called Ritchie? Pete Ritchie?' Clare shook his head. 'He fought at Jarama. Copped it on Casa Blanca hill. I was in the Navy with him.'

'You were in the Navy?' Clare didn't know why but he was surprised.

'Ten years …' Hicknall paused to overtake a bus, allowing his thoughts to slide into silence. As if he'd already revealed too much.

* * * * *

'He's not coming.' Caraben was stating no more than the obvious. In the middle of Plaça Catalunya, the old man now sat slumped on a bench, mumbling to himself in the manner of some homeless bum; that he hadn't been moved on by the police was beginning to look suspicious to anybody that might be watching.

Even the pigeons had lost interest.

Jordan stood up to leave. *No Clare. No Enrique.* He snapped open his lighter and lit himself another cigarette. *The guy probably never even existed. Clare had been bullshitting them all along.*

'So what now, boss?' Caraben was impatient to get going.

'We go back to the office.' Jordan calmly returned the lighter to his pocket. There was a whole host of questions he urgently needed to put to Shaw – principally who was running this show? Himself or Clare?

* * * * *

Carcassone, France. 10.00pm. A small pension by the Midi Canal. Holiday maker, Kenneth Hill sat in his room listening to the radio. After the BBC news – the personal announcements. Since the Czech crisis, there had been a noticeable change in the nature of these messages. Nonsensical. Sometimes lyrical. Often surreal. 'In five days the sun will rise over Broadway' – another such example. Hill switched off the radio, assuming that someone, somewhere, would know what it meant.

In an isolated farmhouse across the border, Alicia Sol had also heard enough. She got up from her chair and crossed over to where Picasso sat at the table with his sketch pad. 'What are you working on?' she asked.

'A self portrait.'

She contemplated the half dozen or so drawings strewn over the table. 'You look like a cross between a Greek God and a bullfighter,' she teased him.

Picasso affected a look of surprise. 'You think so?'

Alicia nodded. 'I like it.'

Picasso smiled. So did he. *Self portrait facing exile (1940)*. He'd found his truth.

* * * * *

Le Perthus. A few minutes to midnight. The border crossing lay quiet. Inside the guardhouse, Carlos Bonay poured himself a cup of coffee from a pot on the stove.

Outside in the trees, a scops owl hooted. Bonay knew that it was a scops owl because three days ago he'd seen the very bird whilst taking a piss out the back. The owl had been perched on the lower branches of a pine tree, the glare of the arc lights picking up the reflection of its eyes. Bonay had made a note of it in his diary. It was how he helped pass the time while on guard duty, making a record of all the wildlife he saw. So far this evening he'd already spotted an Egyptian vulture, two distant Lammergeiers and a young hooted eagle being harried by a kestrel and two crows.

In two minutes, Bonay's shift began. Draining his coffee, he picked up his rifle and coat and stepped outside. In the distance he saw the headlights of an approaching car. 'All yours,' his colleague told him as they swapped places.

The scops owl took to the air.

The car was a '36 Daimler-Benz. British plates. Four occupants: a man, two women and a child. 'Papers, please,' Bonay asked in a flat voice. The driver – Werner – handed them over. Two Argentinian passports (himself, and Montse and Pep – all in the name of Alberdi) and one British: Kathleen Booth. Her real name.

Bonay flicked them open. They looked genuine enough. Visas valid. Entry stamps all correct. Photographs matching the faces in the car. He checked the boot, flashing his torchlight along the back seat. Nothing untoward there either. 'What's your name?' he asked the boy.

'Carlos,' Pep answered. Exactly as Montse had tutored him.

Bonay smiled. 'So's mine.' He handed Werner back the passports. 'Car documents, please.'

Werner reached into the glove box and retrieved them. Bonay made a brief pretence of scrutinising them, then said, 'Wait here.'

'Anything wrong?' Werner wondered whether they should try to make a break for it.

'Just a routine check.' Bonay's heart was pounding furiously. *It was them*.

Back in the guardhouse, Bonay picked up the phone and demanded to be put through to SIM headquarters in Passeig de Gracia. Moments later he was speaking to Major Jordan himself.

'Describe them to me,' Jordan said.

Bonay did so. 'Shall I arrest them, Sir?'

A hundred miles away, Jordan turned to Shaw. 'Well?'

Shaw gave a little shake of his head. *No.*

Jordan nodded. 'Let them pass. Tell them their papers are in order.'

'Yes, Sir.' Somewhat disappointed, Bonay replaced the receiver.

In the trees behind the guardhouse, the scops owl started hooting again, its call echoed by the sound of a second bird further up the hillside.

Something to record in his diary, Bonay supposed.

CHAPTER 19

Sunday 11th August, 1940

Programme of the XII Olympiad
Equestrian sports, Closing ceremony.

Sant Feliu de Guixols. Half an hour before sunrise, Clare took a short stroll along the beach. The sea lay clear, the fishing boats drawn up on the sand, the nets all laid out to dry. Somewhere far beyond the horizon, he imagined a tramp steamer chugging up the coast with its cargo of Moroccan ore or Asturian coal.

Hijos del pueblo a las barricadas! Daubed across the church doors, a faded call to arms told him there would be no service today; whatever need the town might once have had for a priest, they now had the political commissar to look to for matters spiritual. *No Pasaran!* Belief in the triumph of the collective will, where once a candle lit to St Elmo would have been enough to see a husband or son safely home through the storm.

The attractions of the sea front exhausted, Clare returned to the hotel to find Hicknall waiting for him, sitting out on the terrace with a cup of coffee and a copy of last Thursday's *Diari de Catalunya*. 'Your friends are safely across the border,' he said. 'Kathleen's just called.'

'I want to speak to them,' Clare told him.

Hicknall nodded. 'Come with me.'

They went upstairs. Only the front side of the hotel was in use. The remainder of the building still bore the scars of its wartime use, wooden hand rails nailed to the corridor walls, ramps laid over the stairs, soldiers' names and those of their sweethearts carved into the bed heads and panelling.

'Where are they?' Clare asked.

'Perpignan.' Hicknall unlocked the door to his room. 'With friends.'

They had the floor to themselves. There were only six other guests; Hicknall had discreetly checked them out the previous evening. All were Spanish. All resident from the previous week. Holiday makers from Lleida, so the waiter had informed them over a late dinner.

'Perpignan 1506.' Hicknall placed the call with the front desk. Two minutes later they were connected. He handed Clare the phone. 'Be quick.'

'Richard.' It was Montse who spoke first, repeating herself so that Clare would know that there was no mistake. *Richard.* Their private code. Her way of telling him that she had indeed made it safely across the border. Any other term of endearment – *Cariño, Ricardo, Tigreton* – and he was to assume she had a gun to her head, that they were trying to trick him.

'Is Werner there too?' Clare tried not to sound too relieved.

'He's right here. He wants to know how the match ended.'

Clare laughed. 'Where are you?' In the background, he could hear bird song.

'I don't know. Somewhere close to the sea.'

The same sea that lay before him now. 'Tell him Spain won 3-1.'

Hicknall tapped his watch. *Enough chat.*

'I love you,' Clare said.

'Have a safe trip.' Montse echoed the sentiment with a kiss, then the line cut dead.

'Everything okay?' Hicknall took back the receiver.

'Yes. Thanks.'

'Good. Then lets go.'

They had the road to themselves, the sun brushing the tips of the trees as they drove inland towards Girona. To their right lay the twin peaks of Puig Gros and Puig d'Arques; a thin snaking mist trapped between them.

Only now that they were within striking distance of the rendezvous did Clare finally let on exactly where they were heading. 'From the main road up to Sant Mateu de Montnegre,' he told Hicknall. 'You'll find marked the fourteen stations of the cross. He'll be waiting for us by the ninth.'

Hicknall consulted his map. The main road was little more than a dirt track leading up to the peak itself. 'Been there before?'

Clare shook his head.

'Then you've no idea what the road's like?' Hicknall was thinking of the last time he'd taken the Peugeot down such a track; he'd suffered the ignominy of being hauled out of a rut by a passing horse and cart.

'No.'

'So what on earth possessed you to choose such a place?' Hicknall eased down a gear as the road bent back along the course of the stream they were following.

'I don't know.'

But that was a lie. It was Gerald who had been to Sant Mateu de Montnegre, in the summer of '34, with Paul Eluard and a few friends. A visit he'd never talked about. It was only when Clare had been going through his brother's papers that he'd found a half written poem on a scrap of note paper … *Should I fall, say a prayer for me in Sant Mateu.*

Clare had never been able to fathom the connection. A woman? A perfect day? A shelter? But since finding the line, he'd resolved to one day pay the village a visit. In the absence of a body to bury – to say a prayer. To lay his brother's soul to rest.

'I only hope you know where to find a good mechanic,' Hicknall muttered tartly.

In the event, the road turned out not to be quite as bad as Hicknall feared, yet still it took them a full half hour to negotiate the seven kilometre stretch, Clare every now and again obliged to get out and shift a large rock or keep the car steady on the lip of a deep rut.

Christ condemned to death. The first station of the cross. A metal crucifix inscribed with the Roman numeral I. Clare was the first to spot it. Half covered by the shade of an old olive tree, it marked a fork in the road where the main track continued on up to the peak, leaving a short spur leading off towards the village of Sant Mateu itself, now visible a little further on along the line of the hill, a cluster of stone dwellings clinging to the base of a church, a hazy smoke hanging low over the tiled roofs, shot through by the rays of the rising sun.

Hicknall stopped the car and took out a pair of binoculars. One, two, three, he counted his way along the line of crucifixes staggered like telegraph poles by the side of the road. Seven, eight, nine. Pulled into the kerb, partially obscured by a mound of red earth, he glimpsed the bonnet of a car. A dark red Hispano-Suizo. And a shadow. A woman's leg. A face. Hidden behind a scarf and dark glasses, but instantly recognisable from a hundred film posters. Alicia Sol. And with her – Picasso – wearing a white shirt and light Mackintosh, flicking the hair from his brow and nervously smoking a cigarette.

'It's them.' Hicknall checked his watch. It was 8.50am.

Clare took the binoculars from him. He wasn't quite sure why.

The next thing he knew he had a gun to his head. 'Make a noise. Make a move. And I'll shoot you.' Hicknall launched a kick at each of Clare's ankles forcing his legs apart.

For a brief second, Clare had a fleeting vision of his section at Guadarrama being torn to pieces by an artillery shell. He could smell the burning flesh. Feel the flying clods of earth. See the mess tin full of tea, left miraculously unspilt by the edge of the crater. Then his senses returned. 'I …'

'Not a word.' Hicknall briefly frisked him, relieved him of Margarita's gun, then pushed him onto the back seat of the car. 'Hands spread wide where I can see them.'

In the distance, Clare could hear the faint sound of an approaching jeep.

'Why?' he croaked.

'I said be quiet.'

Five minutes passed.

Clare thought of Gerald. A few days before his death. Resting against an acacia tree, notebook in hand, penning the first lines of a new poem, Sant Mateu de Montnegre, *Should I fall, say a prayer for me …*

Now Clare knew. The unfinished verses were meant for him. It was time to start praying.

The jeep drew to a halt alongside the Peugeot, blowing a cloud of dust in through the open door. Clare coughed, his face pressed into the leather seat.

A click as the jeep door swung open. A crunch of gravel underfoot. Then a familiar voice – 'Where are they?' It was Shaw. 'Who's the woman?'

'Alicia Sol.' Clare half expected Hicknall to answer in Russian. 'The actress.'

'Should I know her?'

'The other man in her life is the Catalan Minister for Industry.'

Shaw let out a chuckle. 'That'll put the cat among the pigeons.' Then, 'Get out of the car.' Shaw was talking to him now; with the sun in his eyes, all Clare could make out was a silhouette. 'Cigarette? No, I forgot. You don't, do you?'

Shaw lit himself one.

By the side of the road, Hicknall was unpacking a field radio.

For a split second, Clare thought about running. But Shaw was already there. A silenced gun in his hand. 'I want you to know that your girlfriend is safe', he said matter-of-factly. 'There's no need to involve her in any of this. Provided, of course, you haven't told her about me.'

'Go to hell!' Clare sneered.

Hicknall looked up from the radio. 'Sir, it's Jordan.'

'Thank you.' Shaw swapped his gun for the headset. 'Jericho. Jericho. This is Damascus. Do you read me? Over.'

All Clare could think of was Montse. What they must have done to her. Most likely put a gun to Pep's head and made her talk. *The bastards*.

Shaw sat crouched over the radio set. 'Affirmative. PP is waiting for us in Sant Mateu de Montnegre. Eight K east of Girona. Over ... No hiccups. Repeat no hiccups. Clare led us straight to him. Over ...' The radio crackled static. 'No. We have him trapped. Clare obliged us there. There's just the one road leading into the village. Over ... fifty minutes. I'll be waiting for you. Out.'

Hicknall relieved him of the headset.

Overhead, a hawk hovered in the breeze, the sky as blue as that day at Jarama when Clare had first been convinced he was going to die, when he'd lain in a fox hole wracked with thirst, watching a dog fight overhead; two planes twisting and turning, the distant rat-a-tat-tat of their machine guns.

Shaw took back his gun from Hicknall and turned towards Clare, aiming the silenced barrel at his chest. 'Any last words?' He sounded almost apologetic. 'Anything you want me to say to the folks back home?'

'What will you tell them?' Clare struggled to extract the words from his throat.

'That you died for King and Country.'

'No. Wait!'

Shaw tightened his finger on the trigger. 'I'm sorry, old man. But needs must.'

'Tell Jordan I know where to find the key!' It was all Clare could think to say. 'The key to Capdevila's deposit box – I know where it is.'

In the distance, a church bell began to ring. The hills echoing its chime. Shaw regarded Clare curiously. 'Give me one good reason why I should believe you.'

'Margarita Mirabel.'

'Capdevila's assistant?'

'Yes.'

Shaw pressed his gun to Clare's temple. 'You'll have to do better than that.'

'The key's in France.' Clare was running on instinct now. 'It was Capdevila's guarantee. If he ever got taken by the SIM, then he'd have something to bargain with. Margarita told me where to find it. Before she died ...' he added hopefully.

'Where in France?'

'I'll take you there.' Clare had nothing more to give.

Shaw glanced at his watch. It was ten past nine. Jordan wouldn't be with them for another three quarters of an hour. 'You're lying.'

'Kill me and you'll never know.'

Behind them – Hicknall stood waiting.

Shaw held Clare's gaze. Inscrutable. A second that felt like ten. Then he nodded – 'Okay' – motioning him to get back into the car. 'On the back seat. Face down. Arms where I can see them. Now!'

Clare did as he was told.

To his right, the hawk swooped.

Shaw walked across to where Hicknall stood waiting by the radio, the crunch of stone under foot, a muffled exchange of words, all Clare could hear, then the crackle of the radio. 'Jericho, Jericho. This is Damascus. Do you read me? Over ...'

Clare offered up a silent prayer. *Dear God. Give me strength …*

'… You were right, Sir … Yes. The bastard knew more than he was letting on …' Shaw sat crouched over the radio. Clare couldn't see him but he could hear his voice, intermittent above the buzz of the static. '… I don't know … France. Over … No, he wouldn't say … Yes, he still trusts me … just nervous … frightened we'll leave him here … Over … No, I'm on my own … Clare? He's with Hicknall. A half mile down the road … No, neither of them suspects a thing … Yes, Sir … I can send Hicknall … it won't be a problem. Over … Understood. Out.' Shaw stood up and brushed the dust from his trousers. 'Okay,' he turned to Hicknall. 'There's been a change of plan. You're to take Clare across the border tonight.'

'Yes, Sir.' If Hicknall was surprised, he didn't let it show.

'As soon as you have the key – call London. They'll let me know.'

'And if he's lying?'

'We revert to plan A.' Shaw drew a finger across his throat, then strolled back over to the Peugeot. 'Get out!'

Clare sat up.

'There's no time for explanations.' Shaw helped him to his feet. 'All you need to know is that I'm a British agent. Working for the Russians – yes. But only to deceive them into thinking I'm one of them.'

'But–'

'Shut up and listen. You've caused enough trouble as it is. If you want to get out of this alive, then do as I say. You've got forty-eight hours to deliver me the key. Once you've handed it over – you can go home. No questions asked. We don't exist. This never happened. Understand?'

No. 'Yes.'

'Alan stays with you at all times. Whatever he says – do it. Step out of line, make a run for it – and he'll put a bullet through your head.'

'We're ready, Sir.' Hicknall had the radio stowed.

'You better get going.' Shaw kicked a loose stone over the edge of the hill, watching it ricochet off the rocks. 'Before Jordan arrives. Before it's too late.'

'I'll call you from Narbonne,' Hicknall said.

'I'll be at the Colon.' Shaw lifted the binoculars back to his eyes. Slowly, he scanned the approaches to the village, satisfying himself that there was nothing he had missed, no hidden track; that Picasso and Alicia Sol were truly alone.

'What about Picasso ...?' Clare ventured.

'Picasso is no longer any of your concern,' Shaw said dryly.

Cap Begur. 6.00pm. Hicknall pulled the Peugeot off the main road into the forest and cut the engine. 'From here, we walk,' he said, tossing the keys into the undergrowth and covering the car with ferns and branches.

Clare knew better than to ask where they were going. On the drive from Sant Mateu, he'd tried pumping Hicknall for information. Markham, Stewart, Holdsworth. Three men dead and for what? Picasso betrayed. His own life dangling on a promise made in desperation. It was hard to know where to begin. But all Clare had so far been able to glean was that until Friday night, Hicknall had been as much in the dark as he had. It was only because Hicknall had taken Clare's suspicions to the very top, to one of the few men in SIS privy to the truth, that he hadn't inadvertently blown Shaw's cover wide open.

From the end of the track, a narrow path dropped down through the trees to the sea; that it was still in use evidenced by the occasional empty cigarette packet and dried up donkey dropping. Where the trees gave out close to the promontory, they found a fisherman's hut, an old man sitting with his back to them looking out to sea, a bottle of wine at his side, a cigarette ground between his lips, an ancient radio tuned to the closing ceremony at the Olympic stadium. Tied to the upper branches of a pine tree, Clare noticed a homemade aerial; a metal wire bent round a broomstick leading all the way back down into the house.

Cautiously, he and Hicknall edged their way along the course of the wall. On the radio, a familiar voice, now audible above the static. Picasso. Broadcasting live from Montjuic. A carefully scripted endorsement of Juan Negrin and his government.

Clare hurried on by, catching himself against a tree as he followed Hicknall down a steep path to the beach below, Picasso's words already fading into the break of the waves.

A mon ami, RC. No more.

They waited on the beach for darkness to fall. Clare drifted off to sleep, curled up on the stones and surrounded by driftwood. Just before eleven, Hicknall woke him. A rough shove on the shoulder. 'They're here.'

The boat was an inflatable dinghy. Two oarsmen pulled her up onto the shore, their faces covered in black grease paint.

Clare got to his feet, strangely aware how everything – Picasso, Jordan, Shaw, this morning at Sant Mateu – it all seemed to have been leading up to this one moment, him standing on a moonlit beach, alive only because he'd said he knew where to find the key to Capdevila's safe deposit box, not even knowing why it should make a difference.

At the entrance to the bay, lying low in the water, he could just make out the silhouette of a submarine.

Hicknall looked at him. 'Ready?'

Clare nodded. 'Yes.'

CHAPTER 20

Tuesday 13th August, 1940

Lourdes, France. 7.45am. 'Hail Mary, full of grace. Blessed art thee among women, and blessed is the fruit of thy womb …' As Jesus Mirabel rose to his feet, his stomach let out a loud and embarrassing rumble; like his mother, Jesus suffered from bad digestion.

One by one, the monks took their leave of morning prayers, shuffling out of the chapel and across the yard to the refectory, where breakfast awaited. Hot coffee. Bread and jam. And today – a boiled egg.

Jesus ate in silence, contemplating the day ahead. First item on his agenda – a meeting with Father Laurent, leader of a group of pilgrims from Luxembourg. It was Jesus's job to shepherd the pilgrims through the bureaucracy of their two day visit to the Sanctuary, to arrange a time for them to attend Mass and take the waters. Jesus had dealt with Father Laurent twice before – last Easter and September – and he looked forward to picking up on the threads of his last visit. Then, they'd found time to talk about Laurent's former life as an accountant in the Belgian Congo, working for *La Compagnie Maritime Belge.* Jesus had always had a fondness for boats, and it was his one great ambition – fuelled by a childhood passion for the novels of Rider Haggard and Edgar Rice Burroughs – to sail to Africa. To experience a little of the dark continent for himself.

'Jesus!' A hand tapped him on the shoulder. It was Father Javier, one of the elder priests, a compatriot from Salamanca. 'You have a visitor.'

'Who?' In the two years that Jesus had been at Lourdes he'd never once had a visitor.

Javier didn't know. All he could say was that the man was waiting outside and that he had an English accent.

* * * * *

Thirty-six hours previously. A slight breeze running east to west – the British T-class submarine, *HMS Tribune*, reached the end of her short journey from the Costa Brava.

'Ten minutes,' a crewman called out. Clare pulled back the curtain that sectioned off his bunk from the rest of the galley and angled his watch into the light. 4.22am.

'Cup of tea?' Hicknall thrust a mug into his hand. It was the first time that Clare had seen him since the journey began, although once or twice he'd overheard him conversing with the crew, and more discreetly with a dark haired, serious looking man dressed in an Aran sweater, whom Clare took to be SIS.

'Stand by to surface!' The submarine rose gently up out of the water, five miles off the French coast, its periscope probing the early morning haze, searching for their rendezvous.

'He'll be here soon,' Clare heard the man in the Aran sweater say. 'He's not let me down yet.'

Clare lay back on his bunk, the tea too hot to drink. He was thinking of Montse, wondering where she was now? Whether she was still asleep? Earlier, he'd asked Hicknall if he might speak to her again but his request had been met by a point blank refusal. 'You go nowhere – speak to nobody – until we get the key.'

A crewman threw open the hatch to the conning tower. *Tic-a-tic-a-tic-a-tic-a.* He heard the engine first, then saw the slim line of a mast, the prow of the French fishing vessel – *Nicolette.* 'Starboard! 200 yards!' he called down to the bridge.

'Right on time ...' the man in the Aran sweater muttered.

Bertrand Romy – captain of the *Nicolette* – manoeuvred

his boat alongside the submarine. *'Allez! Vite!'* he shouted at his crew to throw out a line. Today's forecast predicted clear skies. Even this far out to sea, there was always a risk they might be spotted.

The two hulls kissed in the swell.

'Time to go,' said Hicknall.

An hour later, the *Nicolette* landed its catch.

The man in the Aran sweater had a car waiting on the quayside. An old baker's van. Clare squeezed onto the front seat, sandwiched between the two SIS agents; faded lettering – stencilled onto the wall of the town's one café – telling him they'd been put ashore at Port Leucate.

Three hours later, they were in Narbonne.

An hour after that, on the train to Lourdes, the Canal du Midi running along one side of the track, from the opposite window, a view stretching all the way to the Pyrenees.

On Clare's first trip along this stretch of track – on the "red train" from Austerlitz – the corridors had been full to bursting with volunteers. How many of them were now dead? he wondered. There was Harold Collins, the boy from the ferry, for sure. And three of the four Americans who'd shared a carriage with him on the way down …

By the time the train passed through Carcassone, Clare was asleep.

* * * * *

Jesus Mirabel followed Father Javier into a sparsely decorated office, where his visitor sat waiting for him on a wooden bench below a sentimental print of St Francis of Assisi. Jesus recognised Clare instantly. The last time they'd seen each other had been at a drinks party in Paris. Clare had only spoken to him to ask if he'd seen Dora, but it was during their brief, ensuing chat that Jesus had told Clare he was thinking of moving to Lourdes.

'It's Rafael – isn't it?' Jesus immediately feared the worse.

'Is there anywhere we can talk?' Clare said. 'Somewhere private?'

'Is he dead?' Jesus seemed not to have heard him.

'No.'

'Thank God.' Jesus instinctively crossed himself.

'I need to talk you alone.' Clare threw a discreet glance at Father Javier, a lack of sleep now fast beginning to catch up with him. The previous evening, he and Hicknall had booked into a cheap hotel that, on reflection, they would have done well to avoid. Their fellow guests had all been pilgrims, the room next door occupied by an Italian, a consumptive with a hacking cough. When the poor unfortunate hadn't been spewing up his lungs, Clare had been forced to endure the muttered imprecations of his wife through the paper thin walls, like a stuck gramophone, *'Ave, Maria, piena di grazie ...'*

'Of course,' Jesus re-engaged. 'Come with me – please.'

Clare followed him up to the second floor. As they reached the landing, a nun bustled past with a basket of clean linen. 'Tuesday's laundry day,' Jesus said by way of explanation, as he showed Clare into a room every bit as small as Clare had imagined it might be. A metal bed, bedside table, wardrobe, writing desk and washstand. The only personal touch – a framed photograph on the wall; the same wedding day portrait that Clare had seen in Margarita's apartment.

A pigeon alighted on the window ledge.

'Rafael's in jail,' Clare announced without ceremony.

'I knew it ...' Jesus sank onto the bed as if he'd been shot.

Clare walked over to the window and looked out across the Domain towards the Basilica of the Rosary, where Hicknall stood waiting for him, the bulge of a Walther P.38 in his coat pocket.

One leg lifted, head askew, the pigeon eyed him curiously.

'What happened?' Jesus rasped.

'He was caught trying to leave the country.' Clare wasn't sure how privy Jesus had been to Capdevila's plans.

'And my mother?' Jesus gave the impression of having had the air sucked from out of his lungs.

'She's safe.'

'Where?'

'It's better you don't know.'

From somewhere nearby, there sounded a loud clap like a car backfiring, frightening the pigeon into flight.

'I need the key,' Clare said casually.

'What key?'

'The key that Rafael gave you. Silver. About three inches long. Embossed with the crest of the Credit Syon.'

Jesus paled. 'I don't have it.'

'Yes – you do.' *You're lying*. Clare could see it in his eyes. It was something Margarita had said to him in Carrer Fusina that had helped him fit together the final pieces of the puzzle. A single word – Lourdes. At the time he'd thought nothing of it. Only later, after being interrogated by Shaw, did he think to ask himself why Lourdes? Why had Margarita presumed Capdevila to be there? And then he'd realised. Lourdes was where Jesus lived. Lourdes was where the key must be. Capdevila had intended to retrieve it from the safekeeping of the one man in the world whom he could rely on not to betray him.

'I can't help you,' Jesus said.

Clare reached into his pocket and took out Margarita's crucifix. 'Your mother gave me this,' he said, handing it to Jesus. 'She said you'd need proof.'

'Proof?'

He couldn't be wrong – could he? Clare calmly explained. The SIM were prepared to make a deal. A straight swap. Rafael's life for the key.

Jesus clasped his mother's crucifix in the palm of his hand. He thought of the last time he'd seen Capdevila. Rafael had surprised him by handing him a small silver key. 'Once I saved your life, one day, you'll save mine. Keep it for me,' he'd said. 'Somewhere safe. Somewhere secret. Somewhere they won't find it.' 'They?' Jesus had asked. 'My enemies,' Capdevila had replied in his usual melodramatic manner. 'They're legion. Trust no-one. Not even your own mother,' he'd added only half in jest.

Jesus laid the crucifix on his bedside table, beside a well thumbed Bible. *Father in Heaven. The Light of Jesus has scattered the darkness of hatred and sin. Called to that Light, I ask for Your guidance …*

Clare poured a glass of water from a half filled jug on the table and handed it to him. 'Here – drink this.'

Gratefully, Jesus drank. *Did he trust this Englishman? Did he have a choice?* Wearily, he rose from the bed. 'To tell you the truth,' he said, 'it'll be a relief to be rid of it.' Hand trembling, praying that he was doing the right thing, Jesus picked up a paper knife and lifted his parents' photograph from the wall. 'I never liked having it here,' he admitted. 'Only Rafael said there was no-one else he could trust …'

Clare watched Jesus run the blade along the edge of the frame. *He'd guessed right.*

'You know, he never even once told me what it was for …' Jesus slid a finger under the paper backing and drew out a faded envelope, inside which was a key.

'Me neither.' Clare took it from him. Save for the four numbers inscribed below the bank's crest, it was identical to the key that Jordan had showed him in his office. 'Thank you.' He slipped it into his pocket.

'You should take this too.' Jesus reached for his mother's crucifix.

But Clare stayed him. 'No. She wanted you to keep it.'

'She said that?' Jesus looked surprised.

'Yes.' *Before I shot her. Before I put a gun to her head and blew her brains out. But that's another story …*

'God bless you.' Jesus laid a hand on Clare's shoulder. 'You're a good man, Richard. Know that my thoughts and prayers go with you …'

Indeed. Clare hurriedly took his leave before he said anything he might regret. Before his guilt betrayed him.

Outside, a grey sky threatened from the east but for now both the Domain and the Basilica still lay in sunshine. Twenty degrees and rising. Clare walked with his hand in his pocket, fingers curled tightly around Capdevila's key, as if he somehow feared it might slip through a hole in his trousers, or fall into the hands of a pickpocket.

A group of pilgrims were joyously chanting, *'Ave, Ave, Ave, Maria!'*

'Hester! Come here! You'll dirty your dress!' He heard a mother call her five year old daughter away from a guide dog leading a blind war veteran.

Hicknall was waiting for him on the east side of Rosary Square, casually flicking through a four day old copy of *Paris-Soir* that he'd picked up in the waiting room at Narbonne train station. On seeing Clare, he folded the newspaper into his coat pocket. 'Do you have the key?' he asked.

Clare gave it to him.

2. 7. 1. 0. Hicknall checked the four digit number on the side, then gave a droll smile. 'Shaw was right,' he said. 'You are a dark horse.' He handed Clare back his passport and wallet.

'So what now?' Clare asked.

'You're free to go.'

'You mean – you're just going to let me walk away?'

'Yes …'

'Where's Montse?'

'I don't know.'

'I don't believe you.'

'I don't care what you believe. Go home. Now. Before I change my mind.'

From all directions, pilgrims were converging on the Basilica. The healthy and the sick. A cripple rising from her wheelchair intent on climbing the last few steps on her own. A priest trying to coral his group towards the entrance, explaining himself in three different languages.

Would they dare shoot him here? Before so many witnesses? 'Tell Shaw – I want to see her,' Clare said, then slowly, deliberately, he turned his back on Hicknall and took a first step towards the road leading back into town, like Orpheus ascending from the underworld, too afraid to look over his shoulder.

Half expecting a gun shot. But hearing only the peel of bells – calling the faithful to Mass.

CHAPTER 21

Wednesday 21st August, 1940

Zurich. A perfect summer's morning. The cloudless sky reflected in the waters of the lake, the twin towers of the Grossmünster clear against the Alps. On the streets, a calm procession of men and women making their way to work. Clerks and accountants heading for the great banks and financial houses around Paradeplatz. Well dressed, orderly and uncomplaining.

A clock on the face of the Deutsche Bank struck nine. Jordan stopped for a tram to pass, then took a right turn off Paradeplatz into Talacker, conscious as he did so of the millions of dollars worth of cash and bullion lying hidden in vaults deep under his feet. Enough, he imagined, to finance a small war.

On the corner of Bahnhofstrasse, he took another right turn. Ahead of him – on the other side of the road – lay the stately portals of the Zurich branch of the Credit Syon. 'Good morning, Sir.' The doorman welcomed him as if he were an honoured guest returning to a favourite hotel. 'Good morning.' Jordan returned the greeting with equal warmth, although both he and the doorman knew that neither had ever set eyes on the other before.

'Can I help, Sir?' A clerk, taking in Jordan's well-tailored English suit, expensive cologne and smartly polished shoes, hurried over to greet him.

Jordan politely explained that he wished to make a withdrawal from his safe deposit box. He spoke with a slight Mexican accent, in keeping with his cover – Señor Alfredo Cuaron, President of the American Zinc Company.

'Of course, Sir.' The clerk ushered Jordan across the marble floor into a small office, returning a few minutes later with the manager in tow. An unctuous, slightly overweight Swiss German. 'Señor Cuaron – a pleasure to meet you.' The manager extended Jordan his hand. 'How may I help?'

Jordan gave him the number of Capdevila's account. No further information was offered. None asked for. 'If you'd like to follow me please, Sir.' The manager took him straight down to the vaults. A series of strong rooms on the other side of an eighteen inch steel door.

Capdevila's safe deposit box measured twelve inches by thirty-six. Jordan inserted first one key, then the other. A perfect fit. A click as the lock turned and the lid sprang open. 'Just knock on the door when you're finished,' the manager said, showing him into a private booth where he could conduct his business undisturbed. 'I'll be outside.'

Jordan waited for the door to close before addressing himself to the contents of Capdevila's deposit box. A half dozen diamond necklaces, bracelets, rings, pieces of gold and silver. A horde of treasured heirlooms smuggled out of Germany by Jews fleeing from the Nazis, sold to Capdevila for a fraction of their value. Sheaves of shares and government bonds, made over to the bearer. More difficult to put a value on, but of sufficient worth to understand why Picasso's former agent had been so keen to escape Spain. And, lying at the bottom of the box, not so much a black book as a paper bound, pocket-sized ledger, of the type a small shopkeeper might use to keep a track of the day's transactions.

Jordan ran a quick eye over the first page. A batch of figures and a half dozen names relating to the purchase of 4,000 Berthier rifles in February 1937. A flick through the rest of the pages promised more of the same. Columns of figures interspersed with neatly written paragraphs in red, blue and green ink – a comprehensive record of Capdevila's dealings and double dealings in the international arms market. A treasure trove of intelligence that would never see the light of day.

Jordan delved into his pocket and brought out a wrapped brown parcel. Inside was a scuffed notebook purchased three weeks ago from a tabac in Boulevard St Germain. A fabricated record of Capdevila's double dealings in Paris, his handwriting expertly forged by an old con from Zaragoza, whom Jordan had relied on for such work before. A subtle mix of gossip, raw intelligence and lies.

Jordan now made the switch, slipping Capdevila's notebook into his pocket and leaving the forgery in the deposit box along with Capdevila's other valuables.

His plan was simple. The culmination of an idea that had been gestating since the discovery of Margarita Mirabel's corpse. On Friday morning, he would summon his NKVD contact, Major Gavrilov, to an emergency meeting at the safe house behind the Boqueria market. He'd hand him the two keys to Capdevila's deposit box along with a plausible story as to how they had fallen into his possession, then he'd sit back and watch as events took their course.

By Monday, the NKVD would have an agent at the bank, possibly Gavrilov himself. By Tuesday, Capdevila's diary would be in Moscow, its authenticity unquestioned amidst the excitement engendered by the bait he'd woven into its pages. An oblique trail of intrigue and subterfuge that linked the head of the SIM, André Marty, to dissident Nationalist and Trotskyite elements in Paris.

It was only a matter of time before Marty was arrested and taken to Moscow. Twenty-four hours in an interrogation cell at Dzerzhinsky Square and his execution would come as a blessed relief.

Jordan locked the deposit box and gave the door a knock. He was ready to leave.

'Will we be seeing you again soon, Señor Cuaron?' the manager enquired, as he returned the box to its place in the vault.

Jordan shook his head. No. He was afraid not. Regrettably he had to return to Mexico.

'Very good, Sir.' A final handshake. A last *bon voyage* and Jordan's business at the bank was done.

Back out on the street, he took a packet of Primeros from his pocket and lit a cigarette, his thoughts already turning to the day when he would be rid of the Butcher of Albacete. To the last moves of an endgame that would see him gain control of Spain's security apparatus.

CHAPTER 22

Friday 23rd August, 1940

54, Broadway. 7.30pm. Shaw took the lift to the fourth floor. 'Good evening, Sir.' The janitor acknowledged him with a cursory nod.

'And you, George …' Under his arm, Shaw was carrying a slim, pale green file.

Most of those who worked in the building had already left for the weekend. At the night desk, the duty officer sat engrossed in a cheap paperback. On the first floor corridor, an elderly cleaner was busy emptying the bins, an ex-Naval rating who'd been with SIS for as long as Shaw could remember.

'Sherry?' C lifted an eye from his desk as Shaw entered the room.

'Thank you.'

'Help yourself.'

Shaw did so from a decanter that stood on the sideboard, pausing only to take in the view through the corner window. A lively crowd enjoying the evening sun in St James Park.

'All done?' C pushed his work to one side and reached for his pipe.

'And dusted.' Shaw dropped the file he'd brought with him onto the desk. His report on "Operation Drake". Personally typed and marked *Top Secret*. A brief chronicle of Picasso's failed attempt to defect. The blame for the debacle at Montjuic placed squarely on Markham and Holdsworth. A sanitised version for the official archives, Joint Intelligence Committee and the Prime Minister's Office.

'Are Hicknall and Booth alright with this?' C would read it later.

'They won't talk,' Shaw said. 'If that's what you mean.'

'How much have you told them?'

'Obviously they know about "GABRIEL".' *The codename given to the operation to infiltrate Shaw into the NKVD; the details known only to Shaw himself, C, and his counterpart at Horseferry road, Sir Vernon Kell.*

C lit his pipe and sucked thoughtfully on the mouthpiece. 'Do they understand why we did what we did?'

'Yes.'

'And they have no problem with that?'

'Hicknall's one of us. He understands that the country's interests are sometimes at variance with those of the government.'

'And Miss Booth?'

'She doesn't care. She's still in grief.'

'What about this journalist – Richard Clare?'

'All in hand.' Shaw lit a cigarette, the last of a packet of Primeros that Jordan had given him after he'd handed over the key.

'Good.' Through the open window, they could hear the sound of a military band practising on the parade ground of the Wellington barracks. *Some talk of Alexander.* 'You'd think they might have the decency to give it a rest after six,' C muttered, then recovered his thread. 'You know – it's not only "GABRIEL". It's Winston. He could be ruined if this ever got out.'

'It won't, Sir.'

C inwardly shuddered at the prospect. 'I just hope to God events don't prove us right.'

Shaw agreed but he knew there was little chance they wouldn't. Spain had only been the first battle in what promised to be a long conflict. Hitler's thirst for *lebensraum* would precipitate Europe into another war. If not this year, then the next. Or the year after.

The only uncertainty in Shaw's mind lay on whose side would Britain be fighting. Nazi Germany's or Soviet Russia's?

CHAPTER 23

Thursday 5th September, 1940

The call came just after 10.00am. Clare had been back in England for three weeks, holed up in his flat in Bayswater Road, still waiting for news of Montse. Where was she? Why hadn't she been in contact? He'd given her his telephone number and address but so far the only mail he'd received had been a letter from *The Evening News* regretting that his contract was being terminated along with a cheque to cover his wages for the rest of the month.

Clare had looked everywhere and tried everything. The refugee agencies. The Home Office. The police. He'd hung around SIS headquarters in Victoria hoping to catch a glimpse of Shaw, Hicknall or Kathleen. He'd tried leaving messages for Shaw at the RAC club only to be told that there was no member of that name. He'd even thought about writing to his MP until he learned that the man sat on the committee of Imperial Defence. Then finally this morning – a phone call.

'Mr Richard Clare?' It was a woman. No-one Clare recognised.

'Yes?'

'My name is Miss Smith,' the voice said. 'Mr Shaw's secretary.'

Clare caught his breath. 'What do you want?'

'Mr Shaw would like to have lunch with you.'

'Today?'

'Yes.'

'Where?'

'The Fitzroy Tavern. He said you'd know how to find it.'

'What time?'

'One o'clock.'

'I'll be there.'

It had started to rain, a light, persistent drizzle, but still Clare chose to walk. A long meander through Hyde Park, Mayfair and Soho. A chance to clear his head and shake off the slough of the preceding weeks.

Passing a news stand on Piccadilly, Clare glimpsed a selection of children's magazines. On a whim, he bought a copy of *The Captain* and retired to a Lyons corner house for a cup of coffee. Flicking through the pages, he was pleased to notice that the one character he'd created was still doing battle. An adventure seeking Egyptologist who went by the improbable name of Morten Runnymede. Clare idly wondered if the series wouldn't make a good film and then, thinking of films, was abruptly reminded of Alicia Sol, a few days after his return reading of her death in the paper – a tragic car accident on the very night she'd finished shooting her latest picture.

Clare felt his anger returning. Finishing his coffee, he made a detour down to the Embankment to take a look at the river, then wandered up to Foyle's to see if Gerald's book was still in stock. His own too. The answer was yes and no – leaving him with the depressing thought that Morten Runnymede may yet prove to be his most enduring literary legacy.

On Tottenham Court Road, a queue was forming outside the Dominion for the early performance of *The Great Dictator*, Charlie Chaplin's satire on Nazism and Adolf Hitler. A half dozen blackshirts stood on the opposite pavement, hemmed in by a cordon of policemen, hurling abuse at the cinema goers, undeterred by the hostile reaction of the passers-by.

Clare waited for the traffic lights to change, then crossed over into Percy Street, his collar turned up against the wind, the legs of his trousers damp from the rain, his mind no more settled than it had been before he'd set out.

He reached The Fitzroy Tavern on the stroke of one. Shaw was already there waiting for him, sitting in the same booth where they'd met four years previously. 'Glad you could make it,' he said, putting *The Times* crossword to one side. 'Take a pew.'

'Where's Montse?' Clare sat down without even bothering to take his coat off.

'She's safe.'

'I want to see her.'

'All in good time.'

'Where is she?'

'What are you going to have to eat?'

'I'm not hungry.'

'Don't be so tiresome.'

A waitress stopped by their table. A pretty, vivacious, eighteen year old, her hair swept back Rita Hayworth style, her accent broad Yorkshire. 'The steak and kidney's off,' she said breezily. 'So's the liver.'

They both ordered shepherd's pie.

Clare finally took off his coat. 'What is it you want from me?' he said.

'Nothing,' Shaw smiled. 'We just needed to know that we can trust you. That you can be relied on not to go off half-cock.'

'And?'

'You passed the test.'

'And that's supposed to make me feel good?'

'We want you to work for us.'

'What?'

'We're offering you a job.'

'I don't want it.'

'You want to see your girlfriend, don't you?'

At the bar, a party of accountants suddenly broke into song. A rambling rendition of *Happy Birthday*. 'You wouldn't dare ...' Clare stuttered.

'She's living in Paddington.'

'Where?'

'That's classified information.'

'You bastard.' Clare wondered if this was how they'd recruited Stewart.

'A simple yes – and you can meet her for lunch tomorrow. At that Spanish restaurant you like. Off Tachbrook Street.'

'You've been following me?' The restaurant was just round the corner from the SIS offices; Clare had been practically living there for the past fortnight.

'Keeping an eye on you – yes.'

'Why?'

'Because you know too much.'

Clare could appreciate the logic. Either they silenced him or they made him one of their own. 'Okay,' he said. 'I'll do it.'

'Excellent. You start on Monday morning.'

'And Montse?'

'You can see her tomorrow.'

'How much have you told her?'

'She thinks you're in Scotland. On a training course.'

'You've already told her I'm working for you?' Clare didn't know why he should be so surprised.

'We thought it would be easier. But that's all she needs to know.'

'And what about me? What do I need to know?'

'There you go, love. Two shepherds pie. Salt and pepper's on the table. And I'll just go get you a knife and fork.' Their lunch had arrived. A large helping of potato with a mush of grey meat buried underneath.

'Essentially, it all boils down to the national interest.' Shaw reached for the brown sauce.

'What does?'

'Picasso. What happened in Barcelona. Sauce?'

'No, thank you.'

'You know if I'd been your age in '36 – I'd have done the same thing.'

'I'm sorry?'

'I'd have gone to Spain. Like your brother. Joined the International Brigade. He was right. You all were. Fascism is the great evil of our age and it has to be stopped.' Shaw hesitated for a moment as a young man paused within earshot, looking for somewhere to sit.

'I don't understand ...'

'Had we given Picasso sanctuary,' Shaw chose his words carefully, 'had we offered him a platform from which to denounce the Soviet Union, we would only have been playing into the hands of those who would seek an accommodation with the Nazis.' Shaw was referring to the loose coalition of appeasers, industrialists and far right politicians, who since the end of the Spanish war, had come to regard Hitler as a necessary bulwark against Communism. A powerful lobby with the ear of the Prime Minister, and half of Fleet Street eating out of their hands.

'So you betrayed him?'

'When I first got your note,' Shaw ignored the question, 'when Markham's report landed on my desk – my initial reaction was to put a lid on it. Say we weren't interested. Only the trouble was that mine wasn't the only desk on which it landed. News soon got around. The world's greatest artist wants to defect. Hell of a coup. Chance to show the Soviet Union in its true light. Etcetera, etcetera. All totally misguided of course. But the damage was done. My hand forced. I had to do something.'

'So you betrayed him?' Clare wasn't going to let it rest.

'Yes. We betrayed him. We had no choice. We had to spike the operation somehow.'

'We?'

Shaw smiled. 'Those of us who believe that we should be concentrating our energies on defeating Hitler.' It wasn't the whole story, of course. There was "GABRIEL" too. SIS's plan to convince Jordan that Shaw's loyalty lay with the Russians. One of the difficulties of playing the double game was to know exactly how much to give up to the other side. Too much and the endeavour was worthless. Not enough and they became suspicious. But Picasso's defection had handed Shaw the perfect opportunity to give Jordan something of value while protecting the "national interest". A simple sacrifice. Dreamed up by himself and C over a brandy at the RAC club. A pawn for a queen. Picasso for the chance to secure the trust of one of the rising stars of the NKVD.

'Three men died,' Clare said dryly. 'I hope it was worth it.'

'Markham was regrettable,' Shaw conceded. 'The others unlucky. They were never part of the plan. Any more than you were.'

'Unlucky?'

'Consider them as the first casualties in a long war if it makes you feel any better.'

'Is that how you saw me at Sant Mateu?' Clare bristled. 'A casualty of war?'

'You were in the wrong place at the wrong time,' Shaw said matter-of-factly. 'I couldn't afford to let you fall into Jordan's hands. You would have blown my cover.'

'So you were going to kill me?'

'Jordan wanted the key to Capdevila's deposit box. He was convinced you knew where to find it. At the very least I had to show him a dead body …'

'Here you go, love.' The waitress had returned with their cutlery.

'Thank you, Vera.' Shaw counted out one and fourpence in loose change. 'You couldn't bring us two pints of beer, could you?'

'Pale or bitter, love?'

'Bitter for me.' Shaw looked to Clare.

'Bitter's fine …'

Vera smiled brightly. 'Anything else?'

Shaw shook his head and turned back to Clare. 'If I'd let you go without good reason, then Jordan would have known he couldn't trust me.'

Clare said nothing.

Shaw picked up his knife and fork. 'You know – the tragedy of the Spanish war is that, ironically, we would be in a far better place now had Franco won.'

'Better – how?'

'Well, for one ...' Shaw paused for a moment to make sure he had Clare's full attention, '... there would be no ambiguity over where our best interests lay. Think about it. Spain, Germany, Italy – a Fascist axis. Britain and France stuck in the middle. Desperately playing for time. There would be no doubt that it was Hitler who had to be stopped. But as it is ...'

But Shaw didn't have to explain. Clare had often thought it himself. The irony of the Republican victory. That by winning the war, they'd merely succeeded in frightening the rest of Europe into Hitler's embrace.

'History. Well, unfortunately that's the one thing we can't change,' Shaw extracted a piece of gristle from between his teeth. 'I say – I'm sorry about the food. Usually the grub here's pretty decent. Next time I'll treat you to lunch at my club.'

'The one you don't belong to,' Clare said wryly.

Shaw smiled. But he hadn't yet finished. He needed to be sure that Clare fully understood. Why he would have killed him at Sant Mateu. Why he still would kill him if circumstances demanded it. Why Winston Churchill was right when he called Nazi rearmament the greatest threat to European peace. Why saving Picasso might have shattered that fragile peace. Why, whatever the horrors of Communism, Britain was going to need the support of the Soviet Union in standing up to Hitler's aggression. Why British Foreign policy had to be wrenched from the hands of Neville Chamberlain and the appeasers. Why, ultimately, the country would only be safe with Winston Churchill at the helm.

And when he was finally done, Shaw had only one question, 'Put yourself in my shoes,' he said. 'What would you have done?'

To which Clare had no answer.

CHAPTER 24

Friday 6th September, 1940

The café had first been recommended to him by a market trader on Tachbrook street – 'Isabel's. First left by the pub. Best Spanish food in London' – Clare pushed open the door and stepped into a welcome fug of olive oil, garlic and Spanish tobacco.

'Hola guapo!' Isabel called to him from across the room. She was a slight, energetic woman in her early twenties, who reminded Clare of Montse's mother. *'Hola mona!'* he called back affectionately; since his return to London the café had become his second home.

Clare took a seat by the window and waited, watching the minute hand on his watch slowly edging towards the appointed hour; on the radio, a brief interlude between programmes – confirmation from the BBC news desk that the wet weather was set to persist until well into next week.

Montse arrived five minutes early. She was wearing an ankle-length navy blue dress pulled in at the waist, a matching coat and beret, and her face and neck were damp from the rain. She stood for a moment in the doorway, shaking the water from her hair, looking for Clare through the crowd of diners. Then –

'Richard ...'

'Montse ...'

– she saw him. And in that moment, Clare knew that it would be alright.

'I thought for one dreadful second you weren't here.' She walked over to the table and kissed him. Once on each cheek, and then on the lips.

Where are you living? How are they treating you? Where's Werner? How's Pep? There was so much Clare was dying to ask but the only words that escaped his lips were, 'You found it alright?'

'Yes …' She sat down. 'I took the bus.'

'From Paddington?'

Montse nodded. 'They found me an apartment close to the station.'

'You and Pep?'

'Yes.'

'What about Werner?'

'He's in Edinburgh. Working for the German Refugee Aid Society.'

'And you?'

Montse shrugged. 'Waiting for you.'

'Well – you don't have to wait any longer.' Clare lifted her hand to his lips and kissed her finger.

A waiter dropped a carafe of wine onto their table.

'How was Scotland?' Montse asked.

'I haven't been there yet.'

'But they said–'

'I know …' Clare took a sip of wine, then, *a propos* of nothing, caught himself grinning.

'What? What is it?'

Clare laughed. 'Nothing …'

'It must be something,' Montse insisted.

'No. Not really …' Clare was thinking about what Shaw had said in the pub. About the irony of the Spanish war. Thinking how, if Franco had been victorious, then Montse would have been forced to flee Barcelona at the end of the war. These last two years, they would have been living together in London. The Olympic Games, Picasso, today at Isabel's even, none of it would have happened. 'Maybe in the long run it won't matter,' he said.

'What won't?'

'Anything.'

Above the noise of the radio and the babble of Spanish voices, they heard Isabel calling to the kitchen for more bread. Clare gestured to the chalked up menu on the wall. 'What are you going to eat?' he asked.

'Same as you ...' Montse smiled. She didn't need a menu to know what she was going to have. 'Habas.'

* * * * *

NOTES & ACKNOWLEDGEMENTS

Many of the supporting characters featured in this book actually existed, Picasso obviously, but also Dora Maar, André Marty, Peter Wilson, Trevor Wignall, Hylton Cleaver and David Selwyn to name but a few. The events described are historically accurate up until the end of May 1937, the moment I chose to explode my hypothetical bomb and kill Franco. Not surprisingly perhaps, others too had the same idea. Recently declassified MI5 files revealed that in 1937 Stalin instructed the NKVD to arrange Franco's assassination. The source of this information, General Walter Krivitsky, a Soviet intelligence officer who defected in 1940, recalled that "a young Englishman" was sent to Spain to mastermind the operation. Years later, MI5 officers concluded that this agent was Kim Philby, then working as a journalist for *The Times*, covering the Spanish war from the Nationalist side.

Those familiar with Barcelona will, I hope, recognise many of the bars, streets and buildings described. I have tried to conjure as accurate a picture of the city as I can, wherever possible drawing on contemporary photographs, maps and written accounts. Obviously, there has been the odd occasion when I have felt the need to alter the geography of the city for narrative convenience. There is, for instance, no church that I am aware of that backs on to the old International Brigade hostal on Carrer Mallorca, nor are there any caves that cut through Montjuic.

In 1931, Barcelona submitted a bid to host the 1936 Olympic Games but lost out to Berlin by 43 votes to 16. In 1936, the newly elected left-wing Spanish government decided to boycott Hitler's Olympics and hold an alternative games of their own. This so-called 'People's Olympiad' was scheduled to begin in July but was cancelled after the outbreak of the Spanish Civil War, although some of the athletes stayed on to fight.

Guernica was painted by Picasso in response to the bombing of the Basque town of Guernica by German and Italian aeroplanes in April 1937. The painting was originally displayed at the Spanish pavilion at the Paris International Exposition. When the World Fair ended, it was sent on an international tour to create awareness of the atrocities perpetrated by the Fascists, first to Scandinavia, and then to England. It now hangs in the Reina Sofia museum in Madrid.

My grateful thanks go to Emma Rose, formerly of Random House, for her kind words and encouragement. Also to Simon Trewin, Luigi Bonomi, Fiona Neill, Harry Enfield, Anthony Sattin and Jon Elek. I am especially indebted to Alan Aboud for his brilliant cover design and all-round support and advice, and to all at Aboud Creative, especially Jo Mansfield. Thanks also to Penny Chilvers for the long-term loan of her catalogue of the 1929 Exhibition, and to the man who very kindly sent me a photocopy of an original programme for the 1936 Berlin Olympics. I feel terrible for having forgotten his name. I think it was Kevin, but in any case, whoever you are, thank you. My thanks also go to the team at Matador, Amy Cooke, Amy Chadwick, Sarah Taylor and Aimee Fry. Finally, a large thank you to my family, to my mother for encouraging an early love of history, to my father for steering me all those many years ago towards the thrillers of John Le Carré, Len Deighton *et al*, and to Sophy, Ava, Lara and Romy for their love and support, and for just being there.

www.SavingPicasso.co.uk